Robert Goddard was born in Hampshire and read History at Cambridge. His first novel, *Past Caring*, was an instant bestseller. Since then his books have captivated readers worldwide with their edge-of-the-seat pace and their labyrinthine plotting. His first Harry Barnett novel, *Into the Blue*, was winner of the first WHSmith Thumping Good Read Award and was dramatized for TV, starring John Thaw.

Robert Goddard can be found on the web at **www.robertgoddardbooks.co.uk**

Also by Robert Goddard

In order of publication

PAST CARING

A young graduate starts to investigate the fall from grace
of an Edwardian cabinet minister and sets in train a bizarre
and violent chain of events.

'A hornet's nest of jealousy, blackmail and violence. Engrossing'
DAILY MAIL

IN PALE BATTALIONS

An extraordinary story unfolds as Leonora Galloway strives to solve the
mystery of her father's death, her mother's unhappy childhood and a
First World War murder.

'A novel of numerous twists and turns and surprises'
SUNDAY TELEGRAPH

PAINTING THE DARKNESS

On a mild autumn afternoon in 1882, William Trenchard's life changes
for ever with the arrival of an unexpected stranger.

'Explodes into action'
SUNDAY INDEPENDENT

INTO THE BLUE

When a young woman disappears and Harry Barnett is accused
of her murder he has no option but to try and discover what led
her to vanish into the blue.

'A cracker, twisting, turning and exploding with real skill'
DAILY MIRROR

TAKE NO FAREWELL

September 1923, and architect Geoffrey Staddon must return
to the house called Clouds Frome, his first important commission,
to confront the dark secret that it holds.

'A master storyteller'
INDEPENDENT ON SUNDAY

CAUGHT IN THE LIGHT

A photographer's obsession with a femme fatale
leads him into a web of double jeopardy.

*'A spellbinding foray into the real-life game
of truth and consequences'*
THE TIMES

SET IN STONE

A strange house links past and present, a murder,
a political scandal and an unexplained tragedy.

'A heady blend of mystery and adventure'
OXFORD TIMES

SEA CHANGE

A spell-binding mystery involving a mysterious package, murder and
financial scandal, set in 18th-century London, Amsterdam and Rome.

'Engrossing, storytelling of a very high order'
OBSERVER

DYING TO TELL

A missing document, a forty-year-old murder and the Great Train
Robbery all seem to have connections with a modern-day disappearance.

*'Gripping...woven together with more
twists than a country lane'*
DAILY MAIL

DAYS WITHOUT NUMBER

Once Nick Paleologus has excavated a terrible secret from his
archaeologist father's career, nothing will ever be the same again.

*'Fuses history with crime, guilty consciences and human fallibility...
an intelligent escapist delight'*
THE TIMES

PLAY TO THE END

Actor Toby Flood finds himself a player in a much bigger game when he investigates a man who appears to be a stalker.

'An absorbing display of craftsmanship'
SUNDAY TIMES

SIGHT UNSEEN

An innocent bystander is pulled into a mystery which takes over twenty years to unravel when he witnesses the abduction of a child.

'A typically taut tale of wrecked lives, family tragedy,
historical quirks and moral consequences'
THE TIMES

NEVER GO BACK

The convivial atmosphere of a reunion weekend is shattered by an apparent suicide.

'Meticulous planning, well-drawn characters and an immaculate
sense of place... A satisfying number of twists and shocks'
THE TIMES

NAME TO A FACE

A centuries-old mystery is about to unravel...

'Mysterious, dramatic, intricate,
fascinating and unputdownable'
DAILY MIRROR

FOUND WANTING

Catapulted into a breathless race against time, Richard's life will be changed for ever in ways he could never have imagined...

'The master of the clever twist'
SUNDAY TELEGRAPH

LONG TIME COMING

For thirty-six years they thought he was dead...
They were wrong...

*'When it comes to duplicity and intrigue,
Goddard is second to none'*
DAILY MAIL

BLOOD COUNT

There's no such thing as easy money.
As surgeon Edward Hammond is about to find out.

*'As always, Goddard delivers a
thoughtful and fast-moving tale
with well-drawn characters'*
IRISH INDEPENDENT

DYING TO TELL

Robert Goddard

CORGI BOOKS

TRANSWORLD PUBLISHERS
61–63 Uxbridge Road, London W5 5SA
A Random House Group Company
www.transworldbooks.co.uk

DYING TO TELL
A CORGI BOOK: 9780552164986

First published in Great Britain
in 2001 by Bantam Press
an imprint of Transworld Publishers
Corgi edition published 2002
Corgi edition reissued 2011

Addresses for Random House Group Ltd companies outside the UK
can be found at: www.randomhouse.co.uk
The Random House Group Ltd Reg. No. 954009

The Random House Group Limited supports the Forest Stewardship
Council (FSC®), the leading international forest-certification organisation.
Our books carrying the FSC label are printed on FSC®-certified paper.
FSC is the only forest-certification scheme endorsed by the leading
environmental organizations, including Greenpeace. Our paper-procurement
policy can be found at www.randomhouse.co.uk/environment.

Typeset in 11/14pt Giovanni Book by Falcon Oast Graphic Art Ltd.
Printed and bound by CPI Group (UK) Ltd, Croydon, CR0 4YY

2 4 6 8 10 9 7 5 3 1

ACKNOWLEDGEMENTS

I have been given a great deal of help in the writing of this story generously and cheerfully, by old friends and new acquaintances. Ann Symons shared with me her memories of growing up in Street, Hugh Loftin provided invaluable insights into the shipping business and Toru Sasaki smoothed the path of my researches in his enchanting homeland. I am also indebted, in many different ways, to David Cross of Tilbury Container Services Ltd; Koichi Hirose of NYK; Assistant Inspector Shoichiro Harada of the Kyoto Police; Dr Boyd Stephens, Coroner of San Francisco; Senator John Vasconcellos and his assistant, Sue North; Jack Roberts; and Miyoko Kai. Thank you all.

DYING TO TELL

SOMERSET

CHAPTER ONE

That day started just like any other for me: late and slow.

I didn't draw the curtains full back at first. There looked to be too much sun out for me to face before a shower and half a gallon of strong coffee. It had no business being so bright towards the end of October. In duller weather, the bills lying on the doormat wouldn't have been so obvious. Nor would those shadows under my eyes I found myself studying as I shaved.

With my thirty-seventh birthday only a few weeks away, I wasn't looking bad – for a forty-five-year-old. The fact was that I needed to take myself in hand. Or find someone to do the job for me. Neither eventuality seemed very likely. If the turn of a millennium couldn't magic some improving resolution out of me, what could?

My problem's always been that it doesn't take much to make me feel better. A bacon sandwich and a clean T-shirt were enough to put me in a goodish mood that morning. I left the flat and went round to Magdalene Street to buy a paper. The Abbey car park was already full. Half-term, was it? There were certainly enough kids around. One of them managed to shout to a mate of his so loudly and piercingly as he roller-bladed past me that I jumped from the shock of it – much to his amusement.

The bar of the Wheatsheaf a few minutes before noon was a blessedly child-free zone, though. And dark to boot. I slid onto my usual stool under the photo-montage of the pub's last fancy-dress night, sipped a healing Carlsberg Special and applied my mind to the quick crossword as a tune-up for trying to pick a winner from the afternoon races at Chepstow and Redcar.

Les, the landlord, was gently gearing up for the day with some polishing of pumps and checking of optics. The only other customers were a couple of aged regulars not given to talking much called Reg and Syd. It was quiet and soothing and safe. It was absolutely normal and very far from memorable.

But I do remember it. In every detail. Because that was the last time my life was quiet and soothing and safe. The door of the pub was about to open. And normality was about to slip through the window.

I didn't know that, of course. I had no idea. It happened as it happened. It didn't feel like fate or destiny or anything very significant. But it was. Oh yes. It most assuredly was.

I didn't recognize her at first glance. Winifred Alder had to be pushing sixty and didn't look much better for her age than I looked for mine. She was spare and gaunt, with iron-grey hair cropped jaggedly short – like she'd done it herself with scissors in need of sharpening.

There was no trace of make-up. The red patches on her prominent cheekbones were windburn, not blusher. And make-up would hardly have been in keeping with her clothes – coarse grey sweater, brown shin-length skirt and a mud-stained mac. It was her shoes that gave her away. Clarks seconds, unpopular colour (purple originally, now faded to a murky mauve), circa 1980. They were what joined up the memories. It had to be her.

Or her sister, of course. Mildred was a pea from the same pod. A couple of years younger, though that was unlikely to amount to much of a visible difference at this stage in their lives. But, just as my mind dithered between the two possibilities, Winifred's direct, stern-eyed gaze made it up for me. Mildred had always been more of a flincher.

'Come in out the rain, have you, luv?' asked Les, grinning at her as the sunlight twinkled on his swan-necks.

'Are you looking for me, Win?' I put in. (There didn't seem to be any other way to account for her presence; she wasn't likely to have dropped in for a port and lemon.)

'The waitress in that café you live over reckoned I'd find you here,' Win replied, advancing a couple of cautious steps towards me.

'A lucky guess.'

'One you could have put money on, though,' said Les.

'Would you like something to drink?' I ventured.

'I'd *like* a word with you.'

'Talking's allowed here,' said Les. 'But I don't have a dancing licence. You ought to know that.'

'A private word.'

'Don't worry,' said Les. 'I'm noted for my discretion. And Reg and Syd have got their hearing aids turned off.'

Win's gaze wasn't getting any softer. In fact, it was a deal more eloquent than her tongue. 'We could go into the garden,' I suggested. 'If it's open.'

'Oh, it's open,' said Les. 'Shall I bring the drinks out to you?'

'What drinks?'

'Well, you'll soon be needing another. And for the lady . . . ?'

Win looked round at him, then ran her eye along the bar. Nitrokegs and alcopops were clearly a mystery to her. 'A small cider,' she finally announced. 'Not fizzy.'

The garden was open in the sense that the door to it wasn't locked. It was actually a cramped backyard accommodating two rusty tables divided by a washing-line sagging under the weight of half a dozen drying bar mats.

'It could be worse,' I said. 'At least it's not Les's day for washing his smalls.'

Win looked at me as if I was speaking a foreign language and made no move to sit down. 'Have you heard from Rupert?' she asked abruptly.

'Rupe? No, I . . .' Rupert was her youngest brother. More than twenty years separated them, Rupe being something of an afterthought on his parents' part. He was in fact a few months younger than me. We'd been friends at school and university and while we'd both been working in London. But I hadn't seen much of him in recent years. Contrasting fortunes shouldn't separate the best of friends and in some cases maybe they don't. But they had us. While he'd gone on going up, I'd gone the other way. And, to prove it, there I was, out with the empties in Les's so-called beer garden, while Rupe . . . Well, yes, what *about* Rupe? 'I haven't heard from him in a long time, Win.'

'How long?'

'Could be . . . a couple of years. You know how—'

'Time flies when you're having fun,' said Les, his last orders baritone bouncing back at us from the walls of the yard. He plonked a bottle for me and a cloudy glass of cider for Win down on the table between us.

'Thank you, Les.'

'Want me to pick in these mats?'

'No.'

'It's no trouble.'

'*No.*'

'All right, then. Please yourselves.' He departed with a theatrical flounce.

I sat down and pushed out another chair for Win. She lowered herself slowly onto it, at any rate onto the edge of the seat, where she perched awkwardly, a string-bag I hadn't noticed till then cradled between her knees. 'I'd hoped . . . you might have heard from him,' she said hesitantly.

'Haven't you?'

'No. Not even . . . indirectly.'

What she meant by 'indirectly' wasn't clear. Rupe's family led a withdrawn life, keeping themselves to themselves. His mother had been alive when I'd first known them, his father long dead. Penfrith, their ram-shackle home in Hopper Lane, down at the Ivythorn

Hill end of Street, had once been a farm, before old man Alder's death had forced them to sell their stock – cows, I mean – and most of the fields. It still looked like a farm of sorts, or had the last time I'd seen it. Rupe had flown the coop long since by then. His mother's funeral was his last visit to Street that I knew of, back in '95. Since then, Winifred, Mildred and their other brother, poor simple old Howard, had lived on at Penfrith, unemployed and unattached to anything much except one another, without so much as a telephone to maintain contact with the world. As a matter of simple fact, I had no idea how Rupe stayed in touch with them, as apparently he did. Letters it had to be, from London or wherever his career took him.

'We should have done, you see. Should have heard from him.'

'How long's it been . . . since you did?'

'More than two months.'

'You've written to him?'

'Oh yes. We've written. No reply, though.'

'Telephone?' (There *were* call-boxes, after all.)

'Just the same. No reply. Just his . . . whatever you call it.'

'Answering machine.'

'Yes. That'll be it.' She broke off to drink some cider, gulping down about half a glassful and wiping her mouth with the back of her hand. 'Well, it can't go on, can it?'

'I expect he's abroad. You'll hear from him soon.'

'Something's wrong.'

'I shouldn't think so.'

'Someone's got to go to London and find out.'

Someone. Now Win's journey to Glastonbury began to make sense. Not sense I much liked the sound of, though. I tried to talk it down. 'When are you thinking of going?'

'Me? To London? I've never been there in my life.'

'*Never?*' Stupid question, really. Did I seriously think Winifred Alder had ever visited the Big Smoke? A Sunday-school outing to Weston-super-Mare was probably the limit of her worldly travels. 'Well, it'll be a new experience for you.'

'We want you to go.'

'Oh, come on, Win, I can't just . . .'

'Drop everything and go?'

'He's your brother.'

'He's your friend.'

'Even so . . .'

'You won't go?'

I shrugged. 'Can't see the need. It's not as if—'

'There's need.'

'Look, why don't you just . . . leave it a little longer?'

'We've left it long enough.'

'I don't think there's anything to be worried about.'

'How would you know?'

'How would *you*?'

Win stared at me sullenly. She took another gulp of cider. Then she said, 'He saved your life.'

'Yes. So he did.' It was true. Though in another sense you could say he'd also put it at risk. Still, facts were facts. I wouldn't have been able to make my present contribution to the grand struggle of mankind but for Rupert Alder. '*His* life's not in danger, though.'

'It might be.'

'There's no reason to think so.'

'Lancelot . . .'

It took me aback to hear someone use my full name, I don't mind admitting. Lance was how everyone knew me. And just about everyone thought that's how I'd been christened. I only wished they were right. Winifred Alder, of course, knew better. And she wasn't one for diminutives. She called her sister Mil, it was true. But Mil was a special case. Rupe was always Rupert. And I, apparently, was always Lancelot.

'He sends us money,' she whispered, leaning towards me. 'It's how we live.'

'Don't you get . . . social security?' No, I supposed, reading her faintly contemptuous gaze, they didn't. They'd have called that charity. And they wanted nothing to do with the world, even its charity. But, still, they had to live. 'You don't have to tell me about it, Win.'

'He's stopped.'

'Stopped?'

'There's been nothing since the end of August.'

'I see.'

'He wouldn't do that to us.'

'No. I don't suppose he would.'

'Will you go?' She gave me what I think she intended to be a pleading look. 'I'd take it as a kindness, Lancelot.'

'Have you contacted the people he works for?'

'They say he's left. "Left the company". That's all I could get out of them. And it took me a purseful of coins to get that much. Most times I called they just . . . played music to me.'

I felt sorry for her then. I had a sudden mental

glimpse of her, fumbling with her purse in a call-box while trying to make sense of the computerized telephone system she'd briefly been connected to. 'I'll phone them,' I said. 'See what I can find out.'

'You'll have to go up there. It's the only way.'

'I'll phone, Win. This afternoon. I won't let them fob me off, I promise. If that doesn't work . . .'

'You'll go?'

'Maybe. But I don't suppose it'll be necessary.'

'It will be. There's something wrong. I know it.'

'Let's wait and see.'

'This afternoon, you say?'

'Without fail.'

'Unless you drink too much of that . . . lager . . . and forget all about it.'

'I won't.' I smiled sheepishly at her. 'Forget, I mean.'

'I had to go to your parents for your address.' The remark almost amounted to light conversation. 'They seemed well.'

'Oh, Mum and Dad keep pretty fit.'

'Your father asked me to send you their regards.'

'Did he?'

'Struck me as odd. I mean, you must see a good bit of them, living so close.'

'Just his sense of humour, Win.' I forced a grin. 'That's where I get mine from.'

The day definitely wasn't unfolding as I'd anticipated. And it was about to take another unwelcome twist. I saw Win off on her way to the bus stop, then made a bee-line back to the bar of the Wheatsheaf, where the sly sparkle in Les's eyes forewarned me of mischief.

'Lancelot, is it?'

'What?'

'Lance is short for Lancelot. I'd never have guessed.'

I took a slow breath. 'We went into the garden for a *private* conversation.'

'I was checking the soap in the Ladies'. Just in case your friend wanted to powder her nose. And the windows happened to be open, so . . .'

'How long did it take you to check the soap?'

'I did a thorough job.'

'Naturally.'

'Well, you said your dad has a sense of humour. Lancelot proves it, I'd say.'

'Would you?'

'Who's this Rupe, then?' Les lacked the Falstaffian figure of the classic landlord, but liked to throw himself into the father-confessor part of the role. 'Never heard you mention him.'

'A friend of mine. I do have some, you know.'

'Pity you don't bring them in here. How's he related to raincoat woman?'

'Brother. He and I went to school together in Street.'

'Millfield, was it?'

'We were born and bred in Street, Les. We went to Crispin, like everyone else.'

'How'd he come to save your life?'

'It was a caving accident.'

'*You*, caving?'

'A long time ago.'

'What happened?'

'Does it matter?'

'Background colour on my regulars is always valuable.'

'I can't see how.' But I could see he wasn't going to rest until he'd wheedled the story out of me.

Back in the summer of 1985, Rupe had persuaded me to join him on a caving expedition in the Mendips. He was a member of a caving club, but a reluctant one, preferring to go it alone, which he assured me wasn't as risky as it sounded. Several times *more* risky was how it seemed to me once the two of us were underground. And negotiating a couple of ducks – short stretches of flooded cave where there was precious little air space between the water level and the roof – had me spooked long before Rupe noticed signs that the water level was rising, presumably because of rain on the surface. Only then did he reveal that the weather forecast had mentioned the 'possibility' of heavy showers. We turned back, though Rupe said it would probably be safer to go on and up to some refuge where we could sit out the flood. Naturally, that didn't appeal to me, whereas the open air did, mighty powerfully. So, back we went, in my case in a tearing hurry.

That was my undoing. Rupe had all the gear – ropes, harnesses, lamps, karabiners – and knew how to use it. If I'd followed his instructions, there wouldn't have been a problem. But I was cold, wet and frightened – especially frightened. I wanted out. And out involved climbing a more or less vertical slope, using a flexible ladder. Rupe went first, but hadn't finished lifelining the rope for my ascent when I started after him. Halfway up, I slipped.

'What happened?' Les's prompts had become repetitious by this stage of the story.

'I fell.'

'How far?'

'Far enough. There was plenty of slack in the rope thanks to me not waiting. I hit the floor.' Les winced. 'Broke an ankle. And several ribs. Can't recommend it.'

'Painful?'

'Worse than a hangover from your house red.'

Les ignored the jibe, apparently too caught up in the tale to notice. 'Rupe went to fetch help?'

I smiled. 'Not straight away.'

'Why the hell not?'

'The floodwater. He realized I'd drown if he left me where I was long before a rescue party arrived.'

'So what *did* he do?'

'Hauled me back to a higher level.'

'That can't have been easy.'

'No. But he did it. Most of the time, I was no better than a dead weight. But we made it. He put me in a survival bag, waited till the water had stopped rising, waited some more till it had gone back down again, then went for help. The ducks were still flooded by then, of course, right up to the roof, and for longer stretches. Diving through them must have been pretty scary. The rescue party had oxygen when they came to get me, but Rupe just had his own judgement to back. Lucky for me he was a good judge.'

'Could just as easily have been *un*lucky, though.'

'Too right. Which is why I've never been underground since. Not even down the Tube.'

'You're joking.'

'No. When I lived in London, the bus was always good enough for me. I wouldn't even feel at ease in your cellar.'

'No need to worry about that.' Les suddenly put on a straight face. 'There's no bloody way you're going down there.'

Les was all for me using his phone to call Rupe's employer, keener than me as he was by then to find out what was going on. I claimed (which happened to be true) that I didn't have the phone numbers I needed on me. I went back to the flat to dig them out and decided to take a nap that turned into an hour or more of solid zizz. Unexpected visitations and traumatic recollections can really take it out of a guy. Eventually, around four-thirty, I made the calls.

I got what Win had got: the answering machine on Rupe's home number and some politely worded but totally unhelpful spiel from the personnel department of the Eurybia Shipping Company. 'Mr Alder is no longer with us.' How long had he not been with them? 'I'm afraid I can't say.' Who did he work for now? 'I'm afraid I don't have that information.' How could we find him? 'I'm afraid I don't know.' Thanks for nothing. 'Thank *you* for calling.'

But there were resources I had that Win didn't. (Things really would have been desperate otherwise.) Simon Yardley had been at Durham with Rupe and me and was something big – or at least well paid – in merchant banking. The three of us had met for a drink occasionally in London when we'd all been working there. And I was pretty sure Rupe and he had gone on meeting after I'd dropped out of the picture. I still had Simon's number, so I rang it. It was way too early to find a merchant banker at home, but the message on his answering machine suggested trying his mobile. Unlike Rupe, Simon didn't want to be hard to contact. And he wasn't.

'Hi.'

'Simon, it's Lance Bradley.'

'Who?'

'*Lance Bradley.*'

'Oh, Lance. Well, this is . . . How are you?'

'Fine. You?'

'Never better. Never busier either. Listen, could we do this some other time? I'm—'

'It's about Rupe, Simon. Rupert Alder. Can't seem to get hold of him.'

'Haven't you got his number?'

'He never answers.'

'Try his office. Eurybia Shipping.'

'He's left them.'

'Really?'

'Have you got a mobile number for him?'

'Don't think so. Left Eurybia, you say? He never hinted he was thinking of moving.'

'Have you seen him recently, then?'

'Actually, no. Not now you mention it. Sorry, Lance, but I haven't a clue. And I've got to run – metaphorically, that is. Next time you're in town, give me a bell. *Ciao.*'

Ciao? It was a new addition to Simon's patter and not exactly easy on the ear. Strange how he'd naturally assumed I wasn't in town. He was right, of course, rot him. But maybe not for much longer. Win wasn't going to stop tugging at my conscience until I'd done something more than make a few futile phone calls.

Did they have to be futile, though? I rang Rupe again and left a message, asking him to contact me urgently. I even gave him the Wheatsheaf number to try. My reasoning was that he might be reluctant to speak to his family for some good reason. Perhaps he'd been sacked by Eurybia. That would explain why the money had dried up. But he wouldn't need to worry about speaking to me. He didn't owe me anything. If I was right, he'd probably be in touch.

He wasn't.

CHAPTER TWO

I've never been too sure about chance. It's a slippery commodity at the best of times. That's why I bet on horses, not the Lottery. I like the idea that I can think my way to a fortune. What you win by pure chance you can just as easily lose.

Take my stressless but far from prosperous existence in Glastonbury. After losing a good job, a lovely woman and an over-mortgaged house in London during the recession of the early Nineties, I went to stay with my parents in Street purely as a stopgap. Then I met Ria and, instead of heading back to London, found myself living with her in a flat in Glastonbury High Street, helping to run Secret Valley, her New Age joss-stick and Celtic charms shop. Then Ria chucked in the shop along with me and buggered off to Ireland with a Celtic charmer of the human kind called Dermot, Secret Valley became the Tiffin Café and I went . . . nowhere.

With so much evidence to draw on, it naturally didn't escape my analytical mind that a brief sortie to London in search of a missing friend might extrapolate itself into all manner of complications. I didn't think it likely. But I was aware of the possibility. And I can't deny that it had a certain double-edged attraction. The question was: did I want a change as much as I probably needed one?

The answer was still proving elusive the following afternoon, when I caught the bus down to Street to report my lack of progress to Win. (Car ownership had slipped out of my life even less ceremoniously than Ria some time before.)

Glastonbury is ages deep in history and legend. We all know that, none better than me, thanks to having for a father a man so caught up in Arthurian myth that he insisted on saddling me with Lancelot and Gawain as names to carry to my grave. (My mother was allowed to name my sister, which is how she had the good luck to end up plain Diane Patricia.) The short bus ride took me past Wearyall Hill, where Joseph of Arimathea is supposed to have landed (most of Somerset being under water back then), and over Pomparles Bridge, site of the original *Pons Perilis* from which the dying Arthur is said to have ordered Bedivere to cast Excalibur into the lake. (I was always on Bedivere's side myself. With the Dark Ages looming and smelting technology about to take a nose-dive, throwing away a superior specimen of swordcraft like Excalibur made no sense at all.)

Street, by contrast, is distinctly short on legend. As serious-minded Quakers, the Clarks were concerned with more practical issues. And shoes are about as practical as you can get. At least, Clarks shoes always have been. My father worked for Clarks for close on fifty years. So did most Street males of his generation, along with half the females. All that changed around the time I came back from London, with shoe production transferred to Portugal and the works turned into a shopping centre for 'famous brands at factory prices'. There were jobs to be had there, of course, but not for the likes of Winifred and Mildred Alder *or* their simpleton brother, Howard. I'd assumed they'd been living on the state since then. But now it looked like Rupe had been keeping them afloat, which can't always have been easy for him, however frugally they lived.

Exactly how they *did* live I was about to find out. But first I had to steer a path through various humdrum fragments of my own past. I turned off the High Street opposite the Living Homes furniture store, more familiar to me as Street Junior School, and headed south. Soon I was in Ivythorn Road, off which, at 8 Gaston Close, I entered this life one Friday afternoon in November 1963. At that time, much of the land away to the west was still orchards and fields. Penfrith was in the countryside then. Now the town had crept out to surround it. My parents had moved to a Seventies bungalow in that new stretch of housing. But the Alders hadn't moved. They'd stayed exactly where they'd always been, while the world changed around them.

Hopper Lane still looked stubbornly like a country byway. There were modern houses at the Somerton Road end, but the middle course was all overgrown orchards, weed-choked smallholdings and run-down cottages. The afternoon seemed to grow damper and duller as I pressed on, the air a mix of rotting apples, leaf mush and drifting bonfire smoke. Penfrith itself didn't look quite as bad as I'd thought it might. But that was mainly because the house was almost completely invisible behind a rampant forest of rhododendrons. Logically, they had to be the same plants I remembered as shrubs. But that logic was hard to hold on to.

If Penfrith had been put up for sale in its present state, I'd have suggested advertising it without a photograph. With one, it would have to have been ANY OFFER ACCEPTED. Enough slates were missing from the roof to turn it into a colander in wet weather and the apex had an ominous sag to it. There was more bare wood than paint on the window frames and several of the panes were cracked. Behind them some faded rags that might once have been curtains hung limp and forlorn.

Bending sideways to avoid a swag of rhododendron, I reached the front door and tried the bell. It didn't work – no surprise there – so I gave the knocker several heavy raps instead and found myself with a palmful of rust to wipe away. Several silent seconds passed. I could hardly believe they weren't at home and I was about to try again when I had a distinct, shivery feeling of being watched. I turned to my right – and jumped back in surprise at the sight of Howard Alder staring at me through the front bay window.

'Bloody hell, Howard,' I shouted, 'did you have to give me a shock like that?' He didn't seem to hear and it was pretty obvious his powers of comprehension hadn't improved since I'd last met him. Like Win, Howard wasn't exactly wearing his years lightly (early fifties in his case). He was unshaven, with what hair he had hanging lank and grey to his shoulders. He was wearing some sort of lumpen grey cardigan over a grubby Durham University sweatshirt (a gift from Rupe,

35

presumably), and below that, as far as I could see over the sill, faded pink-and-white-striped pyjama bottoms. This definitely wasn't the new autumn look for men. 'Aren't you going to let me in?'

Howard made a circling motion with his hand that I eventually realized meant something. The door wasn't latched. I turned the knob, paused to give him the thumbs-up and went in.

My first impression was that nothing had changed from how I remembered the place. A narrow hall led towards the stairs. A very large and very old barometer hung on one wall, opposite an ancient piece of furniture combining the roles of mirror, coat-hook and umbrella stand. The carpet and wallpaper were surely the same. Then the musty smell hit me. That was the point: nothing *had* changed. Except that decay is change. And that's what was going on in Penfrith: slowly accelerating decay.

I went into the sitting room and met more of the same. The hearthrug; the three-piece suite; the bureau; the clock on the mantelpiece; the Constable print on the wall, wrinkling in its frame; the vintage television in the corner, tube a lot deeper than its screen was wide: they'd mouldered in their appointed places. And they'd gathered dust. Yes, one hell of a lot of dust. Mrs Alder had kept a clean house if not a modern one, but her children were clearly of a different mind. I couldn't help wondering if Howard's hair was greyer than it needed to be.

He really was wearing pyjama bottoms, over checked slippers through which the toes had worn. He was still standing in the bay window, trying to smile, it seemed, though with Howard you couldn't be sure. Next to him, on the table that had once supported an aspidistra (that *had* gone), was a slew of magazines. Stepping closer, I saw they were his most faithful and just about only reading material: *Railway World.* Not recent issues, of course, but dog-eared copies from Howard's train-spotting days in the Sixties, before Beeching pulled the plug on the Somerset and Dorset line. According to Rupe (who must have had it from his sisters), Howard had never recovered from the closure of the S and D – the ripping out of the tracks, the scrapping of the loco-motives, the physical wrenching of the railway from his life. By the look of it, he was still trying to get back to that lost world of 2-6-2s and 0-6-0s chugging across the heathland from Glastonbury to the sea. Whether he understood a single word now of his childhood reading was a moot point, though. Because Howard hadn't actually said anything as far as I knew – words, I mean, as distinct from vague noises – since August 1977.

That was the summer of his crowning madness. He was still holding down some kind of a job at Clarks then. Rupe and I were thirteen-year-olds, cycling out across the moors on fishing expeditions. But Howard was ranging further afield on his moped. And in his mind ... Well, who knows where from (a letter in *Railway World*, maybe) Howard had got hold of the idea that there was a mysterious hole in the statistics of steam locomotives scrapped in the Sixties and that somewhere the Government was hiding a strategic reserve of them in case of an oil drought or some such emergency. (According to Rupe, there really was a hole in the statistics; but even as a thirteen-year-old he'd had conspiracy theorist tendencies.) Anyway, rumour in the railway world had it that these missing locos were concealed in a vast cavern under Box Hill, in Wiltshire, where the Bristol to London railway line passes deep below an RAF base. Howard took to staging nocturnal expeditions to the area in search of clues. One loco in search of a whole lot of locos, you could say. In fact, I may have said precisely that at the time. But the joke turned sour when Howard fetched up in hospital seriously injured after somehow managing to fall down a ventilation shaft. He was lucky not to be killed, if you can bracket luck with permanent brain damage. How he got into the shaft we'll never know. Even if he could remember, which is unlikely, he couldn't tell anyone. His lips were sealed. (He'd also been bitten by a dog that night, apparently – a nasty enough wound to be distinguishable from his other injuries, which naturally were numerous. A guard dog, Rupe reckoned. But he would reckon that, of course. Personally, I thought Howard was the sort any self-respecting dog would take a lump out of.)

'It's Lance, Howard,' I said, smiling at him. 'Remember me?'

He nodded vigorously and made a sucking noise. I think he remembered.

'Where are your sisters?'

He nodded some more and pointed towards the back of the house, then mimed digging and laughed through a good deal of spittle.

'In the garden? Thanks. I'll try there.'

I left him to *Railway World*, went out into the hall and headed for the kitchen. Not a happy choice of route for anyone with a sensitive nose. Quite a few things seemed to be rotting in unwashed pots and grimy cupboards. Taking care to avoid glancing into the sink, I cut through to the scullery and out by the back door.

The rear garden wasn't as neglected as the front. Although the boundary hedges were running riot and the grass in the orchard away to the side was waist-high, the vegetable plot was well tilled and tended. And there was Mildred Alder, lifting carrots and potatoes with tight-jawed vigour. She was remarkably similar to her sister, though not as erect. And there was a panicky look in her eyes when she caught sight of me and stopped digging that Win would never have been prey to. Mil was wearing a mud-stained navy-blue boiler suit and gumboots. Her breath misted in the air as she leaned on the handle of the fork and stared at me. She said nothing, though I felt sure she recognized me. And my visit could hardly be a complete surprise.

'Hello, Mil,' I said, walking towards her.

'Lance,' she said with a frown, sparing me her sister's preference for Lancelot. 'I didn't think you'd come.'

'Well, here I am.'

'What you got to tell us?'

'Nothing, really. I can't get hold of Rupe.'

'Didn't think you would.'

'No faith in me, Mil?'

'Didn't mean that.' She looked quite flustered. There might even have been a blush on her weathered face. 'Look, here's Win.'

Win had emerged from the orchard, carrying a bucket filled with apples. Like Mil, she was wearing gumboots, below the same skirt and sweater I'd seen her in the day before. (Wardrobes weren't exactly crucial items of furniture at Penfrith.) 'What happened?' she called as she walked round the potato patch to join us.

'Nothing,' I said. 'I've drawn a blank.'

'Only what I expected.'

'I know, I know. You told me.'

Win stopped at her sister's shoulder and plonked down the bucket, then gave me one of her penetrating stares. 'Good of you to come and tell us, Lancelot.'

'Least I could do.'

'And is it all you mean to do?'

'No. I think I'd better go up to London and see what the trouble is – if there is any.'

'There's some.'

'Well, let's find out. I'll go tomorrow.'

'That's good of you. We're grateful, aren't we, Mil?'

'Oh yes,' said Mil. 'It *is* good of you, Lance.'

'He hasn't moved, has he? The address I've got for him is Hardrada Road.' (I'd last visited Rupe in London at a flat in Swiss Cottage. Since then, he'd gone south of the river.)

'Twelve Hardrada Road,' said Win. 'That's right.'

'And when exactly did you last hear from him?'

'Depends what you mean by "hear from him".'

'Well, a letter, I suppose.'

'We don't get letters,' said Mil.

'Not from Rupert,' put in Win. 'He doesn't write. There's just the . . . money.'

'And how does he send that?'

'Straight to the bank. But there hasn't been any . . . since the end of August.'

'Well, when did you last speak to him?'

'Speak to him?'

'Yes, Win. *Speak*.'

'When Mother died,' said Mil. 'Not since.'

A glance passed between the sisters at that moment. But their communications had been finely honed over many years. I hadn't a hope of working out what it meant. Besides, there was plenty else for me to try to work out. Rupe had called in to see me two or three times since his mother's death, on his way to or from a visit to Penfrith. At least, I'd assumed that was why he was in the area. He may even have said so, though I couldn't swear to it. If not, why *had* he come down? Not just to sink a few drinks with me, that was for sure. The thought led to another. When did whatever was going on start going on?

'Rupert's been so busy with his work,' said Win, apparently feeling (correctly) that some kind of explanation was due. But what she offered wasn't much of one. 'We don't expect to see a lot of him.' But they did expect the money he sent them. Was that all this was about? Money to prop up their meagre lifestyle? Some meat to serve with the carrots and potatoes? 'We're worried about him, Lancelot. Truly we are.'

'Let's hope there's no need.'

'Yesterday you seemed sure there wasn't.'

'And tomorrow I'll do my best to find out.' I looked from one to the other of them. 'OK?'

It was only a fifteen-minute walk from Penfrith to my parents' house. But it was more like a hundred years in other ways. The Alders inhabited an overlooked corner of the nineteenth century. They were out of time as well

41

as touch. Mum and Dad, on the other hand, lived in the picture-windowed little-box land of the late twentieth, where lawns were trimmed, cars washed, woodwork painted and appearances maintained. My father liked to read about the past. But he had no wish to live in it.

'Your mother's out,' were his first words when he opened the door to me, somehow implying that I'd only called to see her. 'Scrabble.'

'Still keeping that up, is she?'

'Oh yes. Every Wednesday afternoon.' He plodded off towards the kitchen and I followed. The stoop was getting worse, I noticed. All those years of bending over account books at Clarks had taken their toll. 'I was going to make some tea. Do you want a cup?'

'Why not?'

'Perhaps because you just don't want one.'

'Good to know you still take everything I say literally.'

'How else should I take it?'

'I *would* like a cup of tea, Dad. Thanks.'

'As long as you're sure.' He flicked the switch on the kettle and it came instantly to the boil, as if he'd already boiled it and only turned it off when the doorbell rang. 'Put an extra bag in the pot, would you? The caddy's behind you.'

'Oh, bags, is it?' (I've always had an aversion to the wretched things. More to do with Mum's fondness for packing them around her flower borders as fertilizer than the actual taste of the tea, to be honest.)

'See what I mean?' Dad cocked an eyebrow at me. 'I knew we'd have this carry-on.'

'Forget it. I'll have it as it comes.' I plucked a bag from the caddy and tossed it into the pot. Dad poured in the water and squinted at me through the plume of steam.

'Diane phoned last night.'

'Oh yes?'

'Brian's been promoted.'

'That's good news.' (And horribly predictable into the bargain. Brian was the sort of model son-in-law who came flat-packed by mail order.)

'It is, isn't it?'

'Didn't I just say so?' (God, this sparring we were always reduced to was pitiful.)

'Have you got any? Good news, I mean.'

'Not exactly. I wanted to ask you a favour.'

'What might that be?'

'I need to catch an early train to London.'

'And you're looking for a lift.'

I smiled. 'Yeh.'

'This for a job interview by any chance?'

'No.'

'Thought not. I mean, there'd be no time to have your hair cut, would there?'

'Good point, Dad. Well spotted.'

'How early?'

'Just early. I thought you could look up some times for me on the Net.'

'I suppose I could.' He smiled at some irony he detected in this. 'I'll do that while you pour the tea. I'll have two digestives.'

So off he swanned to his study while I fiddled about with mugs and milk and opened six cupboards in search of the biscuit tin before I found it in the seventh.

I took the tea through to the lounge and found the *Daily Telegraph* lying on the coffee-table, folded to display the crossword. Dad had nearly finished it, but it looked like the last few clues were frustrating him. I'd just begun to give them my attention when he walked in. 'There's a train from Castle Cary at ten to eight. That'll get you to Paddington at half-past nine. Early enough?'

'Sounds fine.'

'I'll pick you up at seven-fifteen.'

'Thanks.'

'Well, the car needs a run. And I tend to wake up even before the crack of dawn these days. So . . .' He sat down and drank some tea. 'This isn't about a job, you say?'

'No.'

'Pity.'

'I'm doing someone a favour myself, as it happens. The Alders. You remember them?'

'How could I forget them?'

'They're worried about Rupe. They can't contact him. He seems to have, well, disappeared.'

'And you're going to find him?'

'That's the idea.'

'Really?' Dad looked distinctly sceptical about my qualifications for the task. 'Have you considered the possibility that Rupert may simply have washed his hands of his family? You could hardly blame him if he had. They're a sorry bunch. Sorrier still when you take their pedigree into account.'

'What *is* their pedigree?'

'Oh, nothing at all noble. But there were Alders farming at Penfrith as early as the seventeenth century.'

'You've been researching the Alders?'

'Of course not.' Dad's expression suggested a more

44

idiotic question would be hard to imagine. 'They merely cropped up in something I was reading recently. There was a skirmish at the start of the Civil War just the other side of Ivythorn Hill. The Affray at Marshall's Elm, it's known as. A Parliamentary force was routed by Royalist dragoons. Among the dead was one Josiah Alder of Penfrith. Historically, the event's something of a curiosity, since the usual date given for the start of the Civil War is the twenty-second of August sixteen forty-two, when the King raised his standard at Nottingham. But the Marshall's Elm Affray took place nearly three weeks earlier, on the—' He broke off and looked sharply at me. 'Are you listening?'

'Yeh, Dad, yeh. I'm all ears. There were Alders at Penfrith in sixteen forty-two. But I'm not sure there'll be any there come twenty forty-two.'

'That'll be because they didn't go on farming the land they were born on. If they had a destiny, that was it. And they abandoned it.'

'Circumstances turned against them.'

'George Alder dying without a son old or sensible enough to take over from him, you mean?'

'Yes. You never knew him, did you?'

'Not at all. We'd never have known any of them but for you befriending Rupert.'

'George Alder drowned, didn't he?'

'So I believe. In the Sedgemoor Drain. It can't have been long after Rupert was born.'

'Before, Rupe's always said.'

'You're right.' Dad chomped thoughtfully on his digestive biscuit. 'It *was* before. Summer or autumn of 'sixty-three. Strange. I'd forgotten all that.'

'All what?'

'Oh, there were some other farming deaths around the same time. Accidents. Suicide. That sort of thing. People started talking about a jinx on the land. The *Gazette* was full of it. For a while, anyway.'

The *Central Somerset Gazette* being full of something hardly made it earth-shattering news. But I was still more than a bit surprised that I'd never heard of the Street farmers' jinx of '63 before. 'How many deaths?'

'I can't remember. Two or three perhaps. Mmm. Maybe I'll check up on that next time I'm in the library. It's an interesting subject.'

'Could you let me know what you find out?'

'Certainly.' Dad frowned at me. 'I thought local history bored you rigid.'

'It does. Usually.'

'But not in this case?'

'That depends what you find out.' I was more curious than I was letting on. Why hadn't Rupe mentioned any of this to me? He loved mysteries, great and small. And this one seemed to involve his own father. Perhaps he didn't even know about it. But, if so, that was surely more mysterious still. I was going to have a lot of questions for Rupe when I tracked him down.

'A jinx on the land,' Dad mused, leaning back in his chair. 'Or a curse.' A faraway look I knew of old blurred his gaze. 'It has Arthurian echoes, don't you think?'

'Since you ask, no.' (Not for me, it didn't. Not Arthurian, that is. But echoes? Yes. I'd have had to admit it had plenty of those.)

'You won't oversleep tomorrow, will you, son?'

'No, Dad. I won't.'

And I didn't.

LONDON

CHAPTER THREE

The train was half an hour late into Paddington, but I'm not sure that's why I felt so down as I wandered out of the station into a London morning that was too warm for autumn but plenty grey enough. The early start from Glastonbury definitely hadn't helped. Plus the fact that I've never been a fan of our not so fair capital. The old nickname of the Somerset and Dorset railway – the Slow and Dirty – suits London down to the ground – and even more below the ground.

Not that I had any intention of descending into the bowels of the Bakerloo. It was the number 36 bus for me: a forty-minute trundle past Hyde Park and Buck Pal, then across the Thames by Vauxhall Bridge to The Oval. Why Rupe, a sworn enemy of all team sports, had moved so close to a major cricket ground was beyond me. The *A to Z* put Hardrada Road within strolling distance of the Hobbs Gates. Maybe he'd just enjoyed ignoring the place.

12 Hardrada Road was one of a terrace of three-storeyed yellow-brick Victorian houses. Smart but

unpretentious, I suppose you'd say. But hell for parking. Number 12 didn't look like its owner had run out on it, though. The top-floor windows were ajar. I rang the bell, feeling I ought to before trying the neighbours. Naturally, there was no answer. Of course, even if Rupe was still living there, refusing to respond to letters and phone calls, he'd likely be out at work at eleven o'clock on a Thursday morning. But since I had no idea where work might be now he'd slipped his anchor at Eurybia Shipping, that thought took me nowhere.

The harassed but helpful mother of two (at least) who opened the door to me at number 10 hadn't seen Rupe in months. 'Not that we ever saw much of him. I thought he was working abroad. Didn't he tell me that? I'm not honestly sure. Ask Echo. She'll know if he's due back.'

'Who?'

'Echo Bateman. His lodger. She normally gets home about midday.'

A lodger! I had the sudden impression getting a fix on Rupe was going to prove easier than I'd anticipated. Little Miss Echo could sort everything out for me. To celebrate this happy thought, I ambled back to a pub I'd passed on my way from The Oval. I had an hour to fill and something was needed to knock out the headache too much coffee and too little breakfast had given me.

The Pole Star was your usual rag-rolled, stripped-pine piece of Nineties chic. A bit bleary and frayed at the edges, maybe, but that's how opening time found the handful of customers as well as the bar, so there were no complaints to be heard. None that weren't drowned out by the roar of a vacuum cleaner in the food area, anyway. Fortunately, hoovering up last night's pizza crumbs turned out to be a token affair. Before I was halfway through my drink, tranquillity was restored. I decided to hedge my bets where the lodger was concerned and tap the barman for information.

'Do you know Rupe Alder? He lives just round the corner.'

'Rupe Alder? Yeh. Not been in for quite a while, though. You a friend of his?'

'From way back. More way back than recently, to be honest. That's my problem. We've lost touch and I don't know where he is at the moment.'

'Can't help you, mate. But there's a bloke who works here in the evening who knows him quite well. Used to, anyway. You could ask Carl about Rupe Alder.'

'And will Carl be here tonight?'

'If he wakes up in time, yeh.'

Things were looking better and better. They always do when my aimless ramble through life assumes the fleeting dignity of a plan. The plan I left the Pole Star with was to buy a packet of extra-strong mints from the newsagent next door, eat one on the way back to Hardrada Road (in case Echo was down on lunchtime drinking), hear what Echo had to say for herself, scout round for a cheap place to spend the night, maybe take in a film somewhere, then gravitate back to the Pole Star to catch Carl in mid-shift.

L.G., as we know, stands in my case for Lancelot Gawain. But sometimes I think it could mean Lucky Guy. Not often, but sometimes. This was one such occasion. A young woman was letting herself in as I hove to at number 12. Tall and broadly built, with short spiky black hair and big bush-baby eyes, she was wearing Post Office uniform and uttered a weary enough sigh in the second before she noticed me to suggest she'd spent several long hours pounding the pavements of south London that morning.

'Echo?'

'Christ, you made me jump.' (Indeed I had. But that's Clarks' finest for you.) 'Do I know you?' The bush-baby eyes contracted as she turned to look at me.

'Your neighbour told me your name. I'm a friend of Rupe's. Lance Bradley.'

'Have we met?'

'No. But—'

'Only you do look . . . familiar.'

'I promise not to be.'

'What?'

'Familiar.' I shaped a grin. 'If you let me in.'

'Is that supposed to be funny?'

'Well, yes. I suppose it is. Look, could we start again? I'm from the sticks. Blame the hokey line on that. I'm looking for Rupe. His family are worried about him.'

'His *what*?'

'Family. Most of us have one whether we like it or not.'

'First I've ever heard of Rupe's. Anyway, you won't find him here. But . . .' She looked me up and down. 'All right. Come on in. I've got you now. You *are* a friend of Rupe's.'

'I did say.'

'People *say* all sorts of things.' She pushed the door wide open and went in, gesturing for me to follow.

The first thing that caught my eye was a large, garishly coloured oil painting, hanging unframed on the wall just inside the door. The second was another similar painting further along the hall past the stairs. They were clearly the work of the same artist. I'd have put money on that. As to what the artist was trying to convey – in slashed lines and violent tones – I couldn't have hazarded a guess.

'They're mine,' said Echo, catching my gaze as she slammed the door behind me. 'Don't feel obliged to give an opinion.'

'Right.'

'Come into the kitchen. Do you want some tea?'

'Why not?' (I really was going to have to think of a better response to offers of refreshment.)

We moved past the Vesuvian canvases and two closed doors to the kitchen. 'That's you, isn't it?' asked Echo, prodding at a picture (framed, this time) on the wall to her left.

It was a photo-montage, like the ones Les produced to commemorate fancy-dress nights at the Wheatsheaf. Only this montage, I saw as I looked at it, was a collection of snapshots from Rupe's life. Some of places – Glastonbury Tor, Durham Cathedral, Big Ben. And some of people – friends I recognized, friends I didn't. Echo's prod had landed on a photograph of me sitting outside a Pennine pub during some weekend jaunt from Durham circa 1983, a bottle of Newcastle Brown clutched firmly in my hand. (OK. What can I say? We all have to make our own mistakes.) 'I'm surprised you recognized me from this,' I muttered.

'Maybe I wouldn't have if you'd had the good sense to

change your hairstyle.' She filled the kettle and lit the gas. 'Bag in a mug OK for you?'

'Fine.' (I could only hope the wince hadn't shown.)

'Now, what's this about Rupe's family? He's never mentioned having relatives.'

'A brother and two sisters. They live at Street, down in Somerset. That's where Rupe was born. Me too. We went to school together. And university.'

'Durham?'

'Right. You're quick, aren't you?'

'No. Rupe *did* mention that. Some time. But the family . . .' She shrugged. 'Not a whisper.'

'How long have you been lodging with him?'

'About a year. Not very much *with* him, though. He's been abroad most of the time. That's really why he suggested me moving in. I needed somewhere bigger for my paintings and he needed someone to look after the place while he was away.'

'Away where?'

'Tokyo. On assignment for the shipping company he works for. There's no mystery. I don't know why his family are worried about him.'

'You aren't?'

'He's in Tokyo.' The kettle began to sing. She took it off the boil and filled our mugs. 'What's there to worry about?'

'Well, they didn't know about Tokyo for starters. You have some way of contacting him there?'

'A phone number. Actually . . .' She frowned at me, almost guiltily. 'I've called him a few times lately. No answer. And he hasn't phoned back. But . . .'

'He's left Eurybia Shipping.'

'He has?'

'Yes.'

'Oh.' The frown deepened. 'I didn't know that.'

'Could I have my tea fairly weak, do you think?'

She seemed puzzled by the request, then suddenly understood. 'Oh, sure.' She hoiked the bag out and handed the mug to me.

'Got any milk?'

'In the fridge.'

I helped myself. 'For you?'

'Yeh.' I poured some into her mug. 'Thanks.'

'Why have you been phoning him lately?'

'Things.' She sipped her tea. 'Odd things.'

'Care to share them?'

She crooked her head at me. 'Can I trust you, Lance?'

'Sure.'

'Rupe said I could.'

'Did he?'

'We were talking once. About people you could really – *really* – trust. He named you. No one else. Just you. Something about a caving accident. Something about . . . going back for a friend you've left behind. Is that what you're doing now?'

'Hope not.' I smiled, trying to lighten the mood. 'What about those odd things?'

'You may as well come through.' She led me back into the hall and opened the door into the front sitting room. 'My room's upstairs. This is Rupe's.'

It was sparsely but comfortably furnished, with minimal decoration. There was a well-filled bookcase in one corner, with a model sailing ship on top. As far as personal touches went, that was about it. But Rupe had never been one for surrounding himself with things. He'd been a minimalist before it came into fashion.

There was a desk beneath the window, on which stood a telephone and answering machine, alongside a neatly stacked pile of letters. Echo walked across to it. 'I've got my own phone. Rupe was adamant I shouldn't bother to deal with any of his calls. Or his post. So, I haven't. But—'

'What?'

'I think someone's been in here and taken some of the letters. Maybe listened to his phone messages as well.'

'Somebody broke in?'

'Not broke, exactly. Slipped a latch on a window at the back, then took a look around. I'm pretty sure there are some letters missing. And the books have been moved. Dust disturbed. You know? Nothing I can swear to absolutely. We're not talking about your average burglary.'

'What about the rest of the house?'

'Nothing. Just down here.'

'Have you reported this to the police?'

'What's there to report? It's not much more than a suspicion.'

I leafed through the letters. Brown window envelopes, for the most part: nothing exciting. The only hand-addressed ones were from Win. The scratchy fountain pen and Street postmark gave her away. Whatever else there'd been . . . had gone. 'You said odd *things*, Echo. Plural. What else has happened?'

'You've turned up.'

'I don't count as odd.'

'If you say so. Anyway, you're not the first. Lately I've had three other blokes round here looking for Rupe.'

'*Three?*'

'Yeh. And liquorice allsorts they were. To start with, there was a bloke from Eurybia Shipping paying what he called a "social call".'

'Didn't he mention Rupe had left the company?'

'Nope. And he didn't seem to know Rupe was supposed to be in Tokyo either. Said he'd been abroad himself.'

'Leave a name?'

'Charlie Hoare. Pretty typical middle-aged London suit. After him came the Japanese businessman. I've written his name down there.' She pointed to a Post-it note stuck to the answering machine: *Mr Hashimoto, Park Lane Hilton.* 'He called towards the end of last week.'

'What did he want?'

'To speak to Rupe. I told him Rupe was in Tokyo, but I'm not sure he believed me.'

'And the third one?'

'A couple of days ago. Some old bloke. He was pretty rough. Said he was looking for Rupe. Didn't leave a name. Didn't say much at all. Shifty. You know?'

'And all this is what prompted you to phone Rupe in Tokyo?'

'Yeh.'

'But no answer. There . . . or here.' I looked round the room, then back at Echo. 'When *did* you last hear from him?'

'When I last saw him. Some time in early September. A flying visit to London, so he said. He only stayed

57

a few nights. Then, back to Tokyo – as far as I knew.'

'Mind if we play back the messages?' I tapped the answering machine.

'Suppose not.'

I rewound the tape and sat down on the black leather sofa to listen to what it contained. Echo joined me. The first message was from a car dealer offering Rupe a wonderful deal, the second from a dentist's receptionist saying his six-monthly check-up was well overdue. We ploughed on through several similar pieces of tele-mush. Then Win's voice, raised and nervous, was in the room with us. *'We haven't received anything, Rupert. Is there something wrong?'* She was on twice more, the anxiety in her tone stepping up each time. Next was a cheesegrater cockney saying, *'You said we were in business. What's with the big silence? Give me a bell. Or I'll come looking.'*

'That's the old bloke who called round,' said Echo.

'Like he said he would.'

'Charlie Hoare here, Rupe. We really do need to talk. So, if you're hearing this, get in touch. Soon.'

And that was it. Apart from one more call from Win. And one from me, of course. 'Where are you?' I murmured as the tape clicked off. 'That seems to be what everyone wants to know.' I stood up, walked over to the telephone and dialled a number.

'Who are you calling?' Echo asked.

'The middle-aged London suit.'

But the suit wasn't in his office. All I could do was join the long list of people leaving messages. 'I'll ask him to call you, sir. What does it concern?'

'Rupert Alder.'

'He's no longer with the company, sir.'

'You'd better explain that to Mr Hoare. Just tell him it's urgent.'

'Is it?' said Echo as I put the phone down. 'Urgent, I mean.'

'Not sure.' I wandered back to the kitchen with my empty mug and she followed. 'Getting that way, though, wouldn't you say?'

I stopped by the photo-montage and looked at a picture of Rupe. It was about the most recent one on display. He was standing on a quayside somewhere, with a Eurybia container vessel unloading behind him. The glaring light and the linen suit he was wearing suggested a tropical location – the Gulf maybe, or the Far East. A breeze was fanning his dark hair and his eyes were narrowed against the sun. His even features and slight build preserved that look of the eternal schoolboy I knew so well. Put him in a Crispin uniform and he could still pass for a teenager mature just beyond his years, not the thirty-six-year-old he really was.

'Seems he was always good-looking,' said Echo as she took the mug from my hand.

'Yeh. Lucky bastard.'

'You're the same age as each other?'

'No need to make it sound so incredible.'

'Is this bloke his brother or something?' She tapped a black-and-white photograph towards the top of the montage. 'I've looked at him a few times and wondered where he fits in. I suppose it's the black-and-white that singles him out.'

I gazed at the picture. It showed a man of thirty or so in jeans and a reefer-jacket, carrying a bag over one shoulder, standing on a railway platform. His hair was short, almost crew-cut, his face pale and raw-boned, the jaw square and jutting. He was holding a cigarette in one hand, in that furtive cup-of-the-palm style between forefinger and thumb. He wasn't looking at the camera and maybe, given that he wasn't in the middle of the picture, the camera wasn't looking at him either. Centre stage was actually taken by the station nameboard, a soulless piece of precast concrete bearing the words ASHCOTT AND MEARE. 'Bugger me,' I murmured.

'What's wrong?'

'Ashcott and Meare was a station on the S and D a couple of miles west of Glastonbury.' Seeing her eyes widen uncomprehendingly, I added, 'The Somerset and Dorset railway.'

'So?'

'It closed in nineteen sixty-six, when Rupe and me were just toddlers. This photograph must have been taken before then.'

'But not by Rupe.'

'Hardly. Howard would be my guess. His brother. Not in the picture, but taking it. A real rail nut, our Howard.'

'Mystery solved, then.'

'Yes. Except . . .' I looked back at the faintly blurred face of the man in the reefer-jacket, then around at all the other more recent – and more colourful – images. 'I never remember Howard with a camera. How did Rupe come across this, I wonder? And why did he want to keep it? Ashcott and Meare was just some peat-diggers' halt out on the moors. Unless it's the bloke waiting there he's interested in. But I don't recognize him. Never seen him before.'

'So I'll just have to go on wondering where he fits in.'

'You and me both.'

I went on peering at the nameless man standing on the bare platform at Ashcott and Meare thirty-five or more years in the past: a phantom passenger waiting for a ghost train. Then, suddenly, Rupe's telephone started to ring.

'Bet you that's the suit,' I said, winking at Echo.

'I never bet,' she responded with the straightest of faces.

'Very wise.' With that, I scooted into the sitting room and picked up the phone.

It *was* the suit. 'Mr Bradley? Charlie Hoare here, Eurybia Shipping. You rang a few minutes ago.'

'They said you were out.'

'Oh, I was. Just walked in.' The chuckling undertone in his voice didn't so much disguise the lie as proclaim it. 'You're on Rupe's phone number, I notice.'

'I'm a friend of his. Trying to track him down on behalf of his family.'

'That'd be the family in Street, would it?'

'Yes. How did—'

'Lucky guess. I dug out his CV. It gives Street as his place of birth. Yours too?'

'Well, yes.'

'So, you're an *old* friend of his.'

'Since schooldays.'

'Excellent. Am I to understand Rupe's family haven't heard from him?'

'Not for a couple of months.'

'Worrying for them. Technically, Rupe's no longer on the strength here. But we like to think of Eurybia as a sort of family too. And you don't forget about a member of the family just because they walk out on you. So, I'd like to help if I can.'

'Do you have any idea where he is?'

'No. But the situation's ... complicated. Isn't it always?' He laughed gruffly. 'Perhaps we could meet while you're in town.'

'How about this afternoon?'

'No time like the present, eh, Mr Bradley? Tell you what, we'll meet at my club. The East India, in St James's Square. It's next door to the London Library. Can you be there at four? It'll be quiet around then. We can chat in peace.'

'All right. I'll be there at four.'

'Excellent. Ah, one thing, though. Jacket and tie. The club does insist on it.'

'I can manage that.'

'See you at four, then.'

'Right. Oh—' But he'd rung off. I'd been about to ask him if he knew a Mr Hashimoto. But it could wait. St James's Square wasn't far from the Park Lane Hilton.

'You're meeting him this afternoon?' asked Echo, as I put the phone down.

'Yeh. At his club.' I rolled my eyes.

'He's keen.'

'He is, isn't he? Suspiciously so, you'd have to say. But—' I shrugged. 'We'll see. Between now and then, I have to find somewhere to stay. So, I'd better be making tracks.'

'You can stay here if you want.'

'Really?' I looked at her in surprise. This was better

than I'd hoped for. The sort of accommodation I could afford wasn't the sort I'd miss.

'I could put some sheets on Rupe's bed. He won't be wanting it, will he?'

'That's kind of you, Echo. Thanks.'

'Well, it's only for a couple of nights at most, isn't it?'

'Absolutely.'

'And if whoever searched Rupe's belongings creeps back for a second go, you'll be on hand to sort them out, won't you?'

'Yeh.' I smiled uneasily. 'There's that too.'

CHAPTER FOUR

Clubland isn't exactly my natural habitat. I'm with Groucho Marx on joining clubs. And I was making Groucho's point pretty amply for him by turning up at the pillared portals of the East India Club in a crumpled jacket and creased shirt. (Well, I was no better at packing than I was at ironing.) At least my tie looked the biz. (Actually, it was Rupe's tie, but let's not quibble.)

Charlie Hoare was waiting for me in the lobby. A mop of grey hair and a fuzz of slightly less grey beard gave him an aptly maritime look. But the uncrumpled navy-blue suit, the discreetly striped tie and the copy of the *Financial Times* wedged under his arm, folded open at the commodities page, declared him to be a man of the City. He fixed me with a no-nonsense stare and shook my hand so firmly that all feeling fled my little finger.

'Lance?'

'Yeh. I—'

'Call me Charlie. After all, this is an informal meeting. Let's keep it that way.' (It wasn't clear to me what other way it could be.) 'We'll go upstairs.' He led the way, chuntering on as we climbed the plush-carpeted treads. 'Handy refuge from the office, this place. And a refuge is what I seem to feel the need of more and more. I offered to put Rupe up for membership, but he wasn't interested. Not very clubbable, our Rupe, but a good sort, even so. Sound, through and through. At least, I always thought so.'

We reached a large second-floor room, where a few members were dozing the afternoon away beneath gilt-framed likenesses of bewigged nabobs. Hoare commandeered a pair of armchairs either side of a low table next to one of the windows, through which I could see the yellowing leaves of the plane trees in the square, hanging limply in the gathering dusk.

'Would you like some tea? Or coffee?'

'Coffee would be nice.'

'Or something a little stronger, perhaps?'

'Too early for me.'

'Really? Oh well. Probably best.' He waved a waitress over and ordered a pot of coffee, then leaned towards me across the table, rubbing his hands together as if settling to business. 'So, you were at school with Rupe.'

'And university.'

'Sounds like you know him very well.'

'I do.'

'What line are you in, Lance?'

'I'm sort of between lines.'

'Can be a dangerous place that – between the lines.'

'How long have you been in shipping, Charlie?' I asked, deciding to ignore the faint hint of a threat in his smiling remark.

'Far too long. But let's waste no time on my inglorious career. Eurybia use me as a kind of ... troubleshooter. Which brings us to Rupe.'

'Is he in trouble?'

'Who knows? But his family must think he might be. You too.'

'We simply can't contact him.'

'Nor me. Nor anyone, as far as I can tell. Characteristic behaviour, would you say, on your old friend's part – dropping out of sight?'

'No.' That wasn't entirely true. He'd never done it before, certainly, but when Hoare had asked me the question I'd been tempted to say it didn't entirely surprise me. There was an unknowable side to Rupe, though whether Rupe himself was aware of it was another matter altogether.

Hoare was about to respond, when the coffee arrived. He paused to sign a chit, then poured for both of us. When the waitress had gone, he said, 'I've known Rupe for seven years, Lance – as long as he's been at Eurybia. But you've known him all your life. How would you sum him up?'

I thought for a moment, then tried. 'Clever, relaxed, adaptable. A bit of a loner, but a good friend to me. Quite serious. Quite hard on himself. But with a wry, detached sense of humour.'

'Capable of playing the game?'

'Yes.'

'But well aware that it *is* a game.'

'I suppose so.'

'Mmm.' Hoare sipped his coffee. 'Well, I'd go along with all of that. It's how he seemed to me. Good at

66

keeping several balls in the air at the same time. And an excellent strategist. He did some good work for Eurybia. Developed some very lucrative business. Circularity's the key to profit in shipping, Lance. It's not just about plying the oceans. Our containers are transcontinental as well. Rupe cracked the Russian connection for us.'

'He did?'

'We have a lot of cargoes finishing in Scandinavia, not many starting. And it's the other way round in the Far East. That means empty ships, which means empty coffers. Rupe handled a lot of negotiations with Russian industrialists to close the circle – send containers on through Russia to the Far East. That's why we posted him to Japan – to smooth out that end of things.'

'And did he smooth it out?'

'Oh yes. At least, he started to. Then, suddenly, back in the summer, he resigned.'

'Why?'

'No idea.' Hoare gave a crumpled grin. 'Not at the time, anyway.'

'But since?'

'Well . . .' He stirred uncomfortably in his seat. 'That's why I agreed to meet you, when it comes down to it. A chap resigns without giving a reason? It's a free country. A free*ish* world. It seemed odd, even a bit curt. All we had was a fax from Tokyo. But Eurybia didn't own him. We had no choice but to let him go. As of the thirty-first of August, he was off our books. And then . . . things started to happen. Weevils started crawling out of the woodwork.'

'What sort of weevils?'

'Do you know what a bill of lading is, Lance?'

67

I shrugged. 'Not exactly.'

'It's a document of legal title, representing ownership of a cargo, issued by the shipper to the customer, who can use it as security against a loan if they wish. But where there's a loan there can also be fraud, if the shipper can somehow be persuaded – or bribed – to issue more than one bill of lading per cargo. Then you might end up with several loans, all secured against the same cargo. Like Rupe did.'

'You're accusing Rupe of fraud?'

'It's pretty hard not to when there's a Eurybia container sitting out at Tilbury with eighteen tons of high-grade Russian aluminium inside it, being wrangled over by lawyers representing half a dozen different Far Eastern banks, all claiming ownership in default of loans to a will-o'-the-wisp outfit called the Pomparles Trading Company.'

'The *what*?'

'Pomparles. Does the name mean something to you?'

'Yeh. It would to any Street boy.' Briefly, I explained the long-ago Arthurian tale of the *Pons Perilis* and its connection with the modern-day Pomparles Bridge. It brought a grin to Hoare's lips.

'Rupe's little joke,' he said when I'd finished. 'He's chairman, managing director, secretary, treasurer and bloody tea-boy of the Pomparles Trading Company. He knows the tricks of the trade as well as anyone. He issued multiple Eurybia bills of lading to his own company for a cargo of aluminium leaving Yokohama, bound for Tilbury. He used those bills of lading to raise loans. Then he resigned from Eurybia, took the money . . . and ran.'

'I don't believe it.'

'I wish you didn't have to. But it's true. And damned embarrassing for Eurybia.'

'Rupe's no con artist.'

'You don't think so?'

'Of course not.' (Rupe had always been honest to a fault in my experience, pathetically obedient to drugs legislation and parking regulations.) 'He just isn't the type.'

'Everyone's the type. If they need to be. And that's what I'm wondering. Did Rupe need to be?'

'Why should he?'

'You tell me, Lance.'

'I can't. Anyway, like I said, I don't believe it. Besides . . .'

'What?' Hoare looked at me enquiringly as my mind tried to make a series of connections. What the bloody hell was Rupe up to? And why, if he was suddenly awash with ill-gotten cash, should he stop subsidizing life at Penfrith?

'How much is this fraud likely to have netted?'

'Well, banks tend to be coy about losses, of course, but eighteen tons of high-grade aluminium at today's prices' – he unfolded his *FT* – 'equates to about . . . twenty thousand pounds. Multiply that by six bills of lading and you have . . . well, you can work it out.'

'How much were Eurybia paying Rupe?'

'You wouldn't expect—'

'Come on. Give me some idea.'

'About sixty thousand. Plus bonuses and expenses.'

'And set to rise – given how well he was doing?'

'In all probability.'

'Then surely it was never worth it.'

'Not in the long run. But something obviously focused Rupe on the short run. That's my point. And I think I can prove it.'

'How?'

'I'm going out to Tilbury tomorrow. Why don't you join me?' He lowered his voice mysteriously. 'There's someone I'd like you to meet.'

'Who?'

'Someone I reckon can convince you that Rupe really has put his straight-dealing days behind him. For good and all.'

I didn't buy Charlie Hoare's version of Rupe as archfraudster for a minute. But I wasn't about to tell him that. Yes, I'd go out to Tilbury if he wanted me to. But I had no intention of letting myself be turned against a friend by whatever I was told when I got there. Bills of lading and the price of aluminium didn't turn Rupe into a villain overnight. Not in my eyes, anyway.

Still, there was no denying that a lot of people were on Rupe's trail, maybe all for the same reason. From St James's Square I walked up to Park Lane and dropped into the Hilton. Mr Hashimoto was still staying there, but he was out. I left a message asking him to call me – 'in connection with Mr Alder' – and caught the bus back to Kennington.

Echo had gone out, leaving me free to search Rupe's sitting room and bedroom for clues to his whereabouts. Naturally, there weren't any. If Rupe was in hiding, he was clever enough to cover his tracks. And if he wasn't

. . . then he was probably in even worse trouble than Hoare seemed to think.

I soon gave up and concentrated on putting together a sardine sandwich instead (hoping Echo wouldn't mind me raiding the cupboard). I called my parents to let them know where I was staying.

After writing down the address and phone number, Mum put Dad on, saying he was keen to speak to me, which had to be some kind of a first.

'I visited the library today, son.'

'Oh yeh?'

'Reminding myself of those farming deaths round here back in 'sixty-three. You said you'd like to know what I found out, so I photocopied some of the *Gazette* articles. Do you want me to send them on to you there?'

'Is there anything interesting in them?'

'Oh yes. I think you could say that.'

'Such as what?'

'Best you read them for yourself. I don't want to be accused of colouring your judgement.'

'Give me a break, Dad.'

'Well, let's just say there's a surprising connection between two of the cases.'

'Meaning what?'

'Meaning Howard Alder. He found his father drowned in the Brue near Cow Bridge, not the Sedgemoor Drain, as I'd always understood.' (Dad and me both. The Brue was the river spanned by Pomparles Bridge. Cow Bridge was the next crossing upstream, a favourite fishing spot for boys like Rupe and me. It was much closer to home than the Sedgemoor Drain. But nobody had ever said that was where Rupe's father had

71

met his end, least of all Howard.) '*And* he was the first to come across a farmer called Dalton after the poor fellow shot himself.'

This really was surprising. There was no denying it. 'Could you send the articles on to me, Dad?'

'I thought you'd want me to. Your mother has the address?'

'Yeh.'

'I'll put them in the post first thing tomorrow.'

'Thanks. One other thing . . .' I hesitated. He wasn't going to like this. 'Could you do me another favour?'

'What is it?'

'Call in at Penfrith and tell the Alders how they can contact me.'

'For God's sake.'

'They don't have a phone, Dad. It's either this or I send them a postcard. And they're anxious for news.'

'Maybe, but . . .' A slowly yielding silence settled on the line. 'All right. I'll, er . . . send your mother.'

Echo still wasn't back by half eight, when I headed round to the Pole Star. The lights were turned down, the music up. The place had slipped into evening mode, with a football match playing on a big-screen telly and lots of drinking straight from the bottle.

One piece of good news was that Carl wasn't the barman sporting a tattooed mass of muscles, but his lanky, pasty-faced, hair-gelled colleague. 'I'm Carl Madron,' he said to me as he prised the bottle-tops off a multiple order of Mexican beer. 'You the guy who was in earlier?'

'Yeh. Lance Bradley. I'm a friend of Rupe Alder's.'

'That a fact?'

'They tell me you know Rupe quite well.'

'A bit.'

'Any idea where he might be these days?'

'No.' He broke off to take some money, then gave me a fraction more of his attention. 'If you're a friend of his, why don't you know where he is?'

'I thought I did. But he seems to have—'

'Disappeared?'

'That's right.'

'Anyway, I'm not a mate of the guy. He used to come in here quite a lot. Early evening, mostly. We'd chat a bit. That's about it.'

'I had the impression it was, well, more than that.'

'Did you?'

'Just an impression.'

'As it happens, I'm getting some grief over your friend. He's let someone down.'

'Oh yeh?'

'Not a nice thing to do.'

'Who is this "someone"?'

'What's it matter to you?'

'I'm trying to find Rupe. His family are worried about him.'

'They probably ought to be.'

'You think so?'

'You let people down, you get into trouble.'

'Look, Carl . . .'

'Tell you what.' He fixed me with a dead-fish stare. 'I could call that someone I mentioned. See if he wants to meet you.'

'That'd be great.'

73

'OK. When I get a chance. You'll hang around?'

'Yeh. 'Course. Thanks.'

'Don't overdo the thanks.' His smile was no livelier than his stare. 'You'll be getting me off a hook.'

And myself onto one? The question hung in the noise and smoke around me. And it didn't go away.

But it did get decidedly blurry. Two idle hours in a pub aren't exactly good for my clarity of thought. By closing time, I was having trouble hanging on, never mind hanging around. That early start was still gouging away at me. Carl, on the other hand, was getting sharper all the time. He'd made the promised phone call, with favourable results.

'Bill' – the someone had half a name now – 'says he'd like to see you.' (Strangely, I'd thought it was *me* expressing a wish to see *him*, but never mind.) 'Wait while we close up and I'll take you round there.'

'Is it far?'

'Far enough. But I've got wheels.'

'Chauffeur service, then?'

'That's right, Lance.' Carl grinned at me. As a chauffeur, he was well short on deference. 'Door to fucking door.'

The car wasn't the sort of thing you saw being lovingly buffed outside a Mayfair casino. It was a cramped rustbucket, with sour-smelling blankets covering the seats. For a barman, though, I suppose it had the advantage that you could always be sure, come closing time, it would still be where you'd parked it.

We headed east, aiming, so Carl told me, for the

Rotherhithe Tunnel. Bill Prettyman – his surname was casually donated somewhere along the way – lived in West Ham. 'An old East End boy,' according to Carl. 'He can tell a few tales, can Bill.'

'Tales about what?'

'Vintage villainy. My dad knows him from way back. Famous as a hard man in his day. And famous as more than that to a few.'

'Are you going to let me in on the secret?'

'I'll let Bill do that. He didn't like me giving Rupe the lowdown on him, so I'd better mind my manners this time.'

'What did Rupe want with him?'

'Different question, same answer. Don't worry.' Carl winked at me, which was about as worrying as it could be. 'He sounded as if he was in a talkative mood.'

I fell asleep before we'd plunged under the Thames and was woken, seemingly no more than a few seconds later, by the car spluttering into silence. We'd arrived at the foot of some shabby stump of high-rise housing called Gauntlet Point. (Actually, the L had dropped off the sign, but even in my far from fully alert condition it seemed obvious what the missing letter was.)

The night air was a shock to the system, I don't mind admitting. A badly needed one, in fact. Carl led me in by a heavily reinforced side-door, pausing to press a button on the bell-panel. 'Just to let him know we're here,' he explained, before starting up the urinal-scented stairs. 'It's only the third floor. And I wouldn't recommend the lifts.'

Bill Prettyman's residence lay at the far end of a

concrete-parapeted landing. Halfway along, Carl paused for a word to the wise. 'Watch what you say to Bill. He can be a bit touchy.'

'But not feely, I hope.'

'That's another thing. Sense of humour. He hasn't got one. Not a fucking trace.'

'I'll try to remember that.'

'You won't have to try very hard. He's not been in the best of moods lately. Thanks to Rupe.'

'What did Rupe do to him?'

But the only answer I got was Carl's sodium-lit grin. Clearly, he just didn't have the heart to spoil the suspense.

'This him, is it?' were Prettyman's welcoming words as the door opened to our knock and his gaze slid past Carl and onto me. He was a short, pigeon-chested little man with a round, frowning face and pale blue eyes that sparkled like two beads of water amidst the arid creases of his skin. His head was shaven as closely as his jaw, doing nothing to soften the mangled jut of his some-time-broken nose. He was wearing a grubby vest and even grubbier tracksuit bottoms. I briefly considered reassuring him that there'd been no need to dress up for my visit.

'I'm Lance Bradley,' was actually my opener. 'Pleased to meet you.'

'Carl said you're a friend of Alder.'

'Rupe, yes.' (Rupe and Bill not on first-name terms, it seemed. Was that good news or bad?) 'I'm trying to find him.'

'Better come in, then.'

We stepped inside and Carl closed the door. A smell hit me as he did so that I'd call a stench if I wanted to be unkind. As to its origins, my suspicions centred on the large, lank-furred dog eyeing me from the kitchen doorway at the end of the passage. I couldn't have named the breed, but I reckoned I knew what it was bred *for*. God help any uninvited visitors to *chez* Prettyman.

It was just as well for my peace of mind that the dog didn't follow us into the lounge. Not that he was missing much. Bill Prettyman lived with bare walls, cheap furniture and a huge wide-screen TV. Homely wasn't the description that sprang to mind. At least the lounge smelled better than the passage, thanks mainly to a haze of cigar smoke. I'd have taken Bill for a roll-up man, but it was a panatella he'd left smouldering in a giant onyx ashtray on top of the TV. He picked it up and took a puff. 'You boys want a drink?'

The choice looked to be Scotch or Scotch. We both chose Scotch. 'Been up to anything exciting, Bill?' Carl enquired as he sat down on the sofa and sipped his whisky.

'I'm too old for excitement. All I want is a bit of comfort. Not too much to ask, is it?'

'No,' I chipped in. 'Not at all.'

'Looks like you've got plenty already.' Bill glared at me. 'The younger generation . . .' He shook his head in despair at us. 'What a fucking washout.'

'Except for me, hey?' said Carl. 'Didn't I say I was your best hope of news of Rupe?'

Bill's expression suggested the point was moot. 'What are you after Alder for?' he fired at me.

'His family are worried about him. I'm trying to track him down.'

'Purely out of the goodness of your heart?'

'Something like that.'

'And where is this . . . family?'

'Street, in Somerset.'

'*Street?*' You'd have thought I'd said Baghdad by his reaction. The frown knotted itself into a scowl. 'He grew up there?'

'Him and me both.'

'That's how he knew, then. Fucking hell. I thought he was too young. He *was*, by rights. But he knew. He knew a sight more than he was telling.'

'I'm not sure I—'

'*Where is he?*' Bill's shout raised a bark from the kitchen. '*Shut up,*' he bellowed. And the dog obeyed. Bill returned his attention to me. 'What did you say your name was?'

'Lance.'

'Well, where is he, Lance? That's what I want to know. Where is he and what's he up to?'

'That's what I'm trying to find out.'

'You've come to the wrong place, then, haven't you?'

'Why don't you let Lance in on what this is about, Bill?' put in Carl.

'To save you the trouble later, you mean? I sometimes wish your dad had taken my advice and drowned you in a sack the day you were born.'

'That's not very nice, is it? I was only trying to do you a favour.'

'Some favour.'

We seemed to be moving in a circle, so I tried to

square it. 'Does this have something to do with aluminium?'

They both turned slowly to look at me. And it was immediately obvious that this had nothing to do with aluminium. 'What are you on, man?' snorted Carl.

'The wrong track, obviously.'

'Yeh, *track*,' said Carl with a smile. 'That's more like it. As in railway track.'

'You may as well go ahead and fill him in, boy,' growled Bill. 'It's an itch you just can't stop scratching, ain't it?'

'Uncle Bill here is a big-time criminal, Lance.' (Carl was all eager garrulousness now – the tale-teller off the leash.) 'He had a hand in the most famous heist of the century. Well, the last century. The Great Train Robbery; August 'sixty-three. You're looking at one of the blokes who laid his hands on the three million quid in used fivers, back when three million quid could buy an Arab oil state outright.'

'It was nearer two and a half million,' Bill grudgingly corrected him. 'And there were a fair few of us to take our whack. I didn't come away with more than a hundred and fifty thou.'

'Which would probably be worth three million today,' Carl went on. 'If you'd stuck it in the building society and led a sensible life.'

'Yeh,' said Bill. 'That's right. *If*. Life's full of fucking ifs. And smartarses to tell you so.'

The Great Train Robbery? I was struggling to catch up, rather like the police back in August 1963. Even those of us still in our mother's womb at the time knew that was when a gang of soon to be famous thieves stopped the

Glasgow to London mail train one night in the middle of the Buckinghamshire countryside and robbed it of a medium-sized fortune in used banknotes that were on their way to the Royal Mint for incineration. Most of the gang had subsequently been caught and clobbered with thirty-year gaol sentences. Some of them had escaped and been caught again. There'd been books and films, rumours of proceeds never recovered and Moriarty types behind it all never identified. It had become part of the nation's folklore. But Bill Prettyman? I'd never heard that name mentioned. And he certainly didn't look like a Mr Big to me. Nor was he living like one. But that, of course, was exactly what he was griping about.

'Bill had the good sense to keep his gloves on during the divvying up at Leatherslade Farm,' said Carl. 'The ones who were caught got careless with their finger-prints. But not our Bill. He got clean away with his share of the loot. Only to have it taken off him by smooth-talking con men over the next . . . well, how long did it take, Bill?' Bill's expression suggested he had no wish to go into details of his systematic fleecing. 'Let's settle for all too soon,' Carl went on with a weak smile. 'Which is why he finds himself passing his declining years in this rat-hole, unable even to strike a lucrative publishing deal in case the police come knocking at his door. The ones who were caught have served their time. The ones who got away . . . can't afford to come clean.'

'Maybe you should do a deal with a publisher,' said Bill. 'Gifted with the gab the way you are.'

'And maybe I would. If I didn't think you'd stick a knife in my gut before I got to spend the money.'

'You're wise to think that, son. Very wise.'

'I don't like to interrupt,' I interrupted, 'but what has this to do with Rupe?'

'Good question,' said Carl. 'See, the thing is Rupe got me talking about the Great Train Robbery one night at the Pole Star and I, well, gave him the idea that I might know someone who was in on it. Nothing specific, mind. Nothing that laid a trail to Uncle Bill's door. But . . . the hint was there. And Rupe was interested. Very interested. He knew a bit himself, apparently. He gave me a name. Asked me to mention it to . . . whoever it was I knew . . . and see if he'd like to meet up and hear more about what had happened to this guy.'

'Who did he name?'

'Fellow called Dalton.' (Dalton? One of the suicidal Street farmers? I was way out of my depth now.) 'Peter Dalton.'

'Know of him, do you?' Bill looked sharply at me.

'No.' (Well, it was almost the truth.) 'Can't say I do.'

'Seems he was a member of the gang as well,' said Carl, at which Bill gave a nod of confirmation. 'Also never caught. In fact, never heard of again. Dropped right out of sight after the robbery.' (Out of this whole vale of tears, in fact, assuming he was the dead farmer.) 'And not just your standard gang member. No, no. Dalton was there on behalf of the gang's prime informant – the mystery man who told them about the train and how much dosh might be aboard. He took an extra cut for his boss. Isn't that right, Bill?' Another nod. 'Then vanished.'

'What did Rupe know about him?'

'That he was fucking dead,' said Bill. 'Dalton was found with his head blown off at some farm he owned, apparently. Near Street. Less than a fortnight after the

81

robbery. Suicide, it was, according to the stuff from the paper Alder showed me. Suicide, my arse. Dead, and no trace of the money? Sounds more like he was rubbed out.'

'Murdered?'

'So Rupe reckoned,' said Carl. 'And he reckoned he knew who'd done it.'

'Who?'

'The mystery man. The source of the info.'

'Why would he kill Dalton?'

'To cover his tracks,' said Bill, with no hint of irony. 'Part of the plan all along, maybe. The cops were on to us that fast, boy. Too fast for fingerprints to be all they had. Somebody grassed us up. And who could have done it better than the bloke who set us up in the first fucking place?'

'Whose identity you never knew?'

'Not me. Not no one. Except Dalton.'

'And Rupe,' put in Carl.

'Alder seemed to think he could flush him out,' Bill continued. 'He didn't say how. Nor how he knew who he was. He said the bloke was called Stephen Townley and that he had . . . ways and means . . . of tracking him down. He reckoned he could force Townley to tell his story and make us all rich by selling it. He had a photo of Dalton, taken from the local rag down in Street. Once I said yeh, that was the same Dalton I'd last seen at Leatherslade back in August 'sixty-three, he seemed sure he could pull it off.'

'He had a photograph of Townley as well,' said Carl.

'*Said* it was Townley,' Bill corrected him.

'Was Townley standing on a railway station in the picture?' I asked.

'Yeh.' Bill gave me another sharp look. 'How'd you know that?'

'It's pinned up in Rupe's kitchen. The station's not far from Street. Well, it wasn't far, when it existed.' (My mind was racing through sand. Rupe had no business knowing about any of this stuff. But he did. *Sure he could pull it off.* I wondered if he was so sure now.) 'When did you meet Rupe, Bill?'

'It's got to be . . . a couple of months.' (That put it during Rupe's last 'flying visit' to London.) 'Which is twice as long as he said he'd need to sort Townley.'

'Maybe Townley proved more elusive than Rupe had anticipated.'

'Or maybe he did a deal with Townley and froze me out. Maybe all he wanted me to do was ID Dalton and tie the fucking string on his blackmail package.'

'You can see Bill's point,' said Carl. 'It does look like that.'

'Rupe's no blackmailer.' (But he was, if Bill was to be believed. That's exactly what he was. Or what he was going to be, if and when he tracked Townley down. Why? He couldn't be in this for the money. Not this and the aluminium too.) 'There has to be some . . . misunderstanding.'

'There's no misunderstanding,' said Bill, with heavy emphasis. 'He promised me a cut of whatever he made out of Townley.'

'Me too,' said Carl, which drew a fleeting glare from Bill.

'And now he's done a runner,' the old man resumed.

(Bill's conclusion was much the same as Charlie Hoare's, it seemed.) 'So, when you find your friend, tell him he owes me. And I want paying.'

'Sure. *If* I find him.'

'Any leads?' Carl enquired.

'One or two. Not very promising, I'm afraid.'

'You'll keep us posted, though, if they come to anything?'

'Certainly. I want to sort this out as much as you do.'

'That a fact?'

'Yeh.'

'But is it a promise?' growled Bill.

'If you like.'

'I do like.'

'Then it's a promise.'

'Good. I'm partial to promises.' He eyed me through a puff of panatella smoke. 'I can hold people to them, see? And I do. Whether they want to be held to them . . . or not.'

'You know, Lance,' Carl said some time later, as we started back towards Kennington in his car, 'for a guy who claims to be Rupe's best mate, you don't seem exactly . . . over-familiar with his character.'

'You're a better judge of it, are you?' I countered, though Carl's point was a valid one, God knows. Good old law-abiding career-ladder Rupe seemed to have turned to skullduggery with all the enthusiasm of a late convert.

'I'm just telling it like it is. My guess is Rupe had a whole load of stuff on friend Townley. Bill didn't give him anything except confirmation of one suspicion.'

'What did he tell you and Bill about Townley? Townley as he is today, I mean.'

'Nothing. Not a fucking thing.'

'Didn't you ask?'

'Bill did. But Rupe clammed up.'

'And you didn't try to prise him open?'

'You've got me all wrong, Lance.' He cast me a leery glance through a wash of amber streetlight. 'I'm not the heavy type.'

'That's reassuring.'

'It's not meant to be. The way I figure it, this Townley has to be a real hard case to have pulled off that stuff in 'sixty-three. Too hard for Rupe to tackle any way he chose to go about it. I don't want to dash Bill's hopes – he's got fuck all else to keep him going – but Rupe isn't coming back with a fat pay-off to share out.'

'What do you reckon's happened to him, then?'

Carl gave the question a moment's thought, then said, 'Not sure, but . . . nothing good.'

CHAPTER FIVE

Going to bed in the small hours with a lot to think about isn't anyone's recipe for a sound dose of slumber. Was Rupe really up to defrauding Far Eastern banks and blackmailing veteran arch-criminals? I doubted it. In fact, I doubted just about everything I'd learned so far. More worryingly, I doubted it was wise to get mixed up in any of it. Cue a hasty retreat to Glastonbury? That at least made sense. And it was a comforting thought that finally lulled me into sleep.

Only to be jolted awake by a noise from the kitchen. Someone was moving about. I checked my watch. It was just gone four. Had the person who'd so carefully searched Rupe's belongings come back for a second look? My heart began to pound.

Then the toaster popped and I remembered: postal workers keep early hours.

'Bloody hell,' said Echo as I staggered into the kitchen to find her munching and slurping. 'Do you normally look this bad in the mornings?'

'This isn't the morning. It's still last night.'

'When did you get back?'

'Too late. Far too late.'

'Did tea with the suit stretch to supper?'

'No, no. I was kept up by someone else. A bloke Rupe knows who works at the Pole Star.'

'Not Carl Madron?'

'You know him too?'

'Difficult for a girl to go into the Pole Star without knowing Carl. He always tries it on. Just as well he's the other side of the bar. Wouldn't have thought he and Rupe had a lot in common.'

'Neither would I.' I looked at the photo-montage and tried to focus on the picture of Stephen Townley. A name and a face and Bill Prettyman's criminal past. What did they really amount to? 'But there are a lot of things I wouldn't have thought about Rupe that it seems I may have to.'

'Such as?'

'I'll tell you later. When I've scraped the fur off my tongue.'

'All right. I've got to dash, anyway. How about you treat me to dinner at a Portuguese place I know?' She grinned, something I felt I'd be unable to manage for quite a while. 'In lieu of rent.'

'It's a deal.' I found myself a mug and poured some tea from the pot Echo had brewed. 'What's the best way to get to Canary Wharf from here, do you think?'

'Tube, via London Bridge.'

'Other than the Tube.' Her eyebrows shot up. 'That's something else I'll explain later.'

* * *

The answer involved a trudge to Elephant and Castle, a bus to Shadwell and another from there to Docklands' nerve centre. I set off in the drizzle-smeared dregs of the rush hour and arrived just as the early starters were taking their mid-morning fag break. The Isle of Dogs had been transformed from a building site into a city unto itself while my back had been turned. A mall about a mile long led me to a phalanx of reception desks at the foot of the Canada Square Tower. A message was phoned up to Eurybia's perch on the umpteenth floor and ten minutes later Charlie Hoare emerged from the lift to greet me.

'Glad you could make it, Lance. I think you'll find the trip worthwhile. Shall we go? Came on the Jubilee Line, did you? Impressive, isn't it?'

Hoare's questions didn't require many answers from me, which suited my less than razor-sharp state of mind. He piloted me to the underground car park, loaded me into his Lexus, weaved his way out onto the A13 and pointed the bonnet towards Essex. He seemed to feel I was in need of a potted biography of Charlie Hoare, man of the shipping world, and that took us well past Dagenham before I needed to do more than nod periodically and throw in the occasional 'uh-huh'.

'I go back to BC in shipping, Lance. Before containerization. Well before, as a matter of fact. Thirty-seven years is a long time. And it amounts to a lot of experience.'

'Must do,' I mumbled. 'That means you started work the year I was born.'

''Sixty-three, yes. The twenty-second of July. I started the same day as the trial of Stephen Ward, you know.

But I've gone on a hell of a sight longer.' He laughed at that and I made an effort to join in. 'I was still living with my folks in Beckenham then. The train used to run into Holborn Viaduct, as was, and I'd walk to work from there. Holborn Viaduct was right next to the Old Bailey, of course. The scrum outside that first morning was unbelievable. The trial of the century, they called it. If I hadn't been so keen to create a good impression in the office, I might have bunked off and tried to get a ticket for the public gallery. As it was, they had to cope without me.' Another laugh.

'Quite a year, nineteen sixty-three.'

'Certainly was. The Profumo affair. The Kennedy assassination. And a damned fine Lord's Test match.'

'Not to mention the Great Train Robbery.'

'That too.' He frowned. 'Funny you should bring it up, actually.'

'Why?'

'Rupe asked me about it quite often: what I remembered, what gossip there was about it at the time. Mind you, we probably discussed Profumo as well. Rupe's always been curious about the period.'

'Has he?' (It was news to me.)

'Oh yes. Well, it *is* interesting, isn't it? The trial of the century and the crime of the century, no more than a few weeks apart. Not that I have any shattering insights into any of it. Politicians caught with their trousers down and East End villains making off with mailbags full of money. Entertaining stuff. Unless you were Harold Macmillan, of course. He had to go after all of that.'

'So, Rupe's curiosity was . . . purely historical?'

'Suppose so.' Hoare thought for a moment as he slowed for a roundabout. 'Frankly, I got the impression Rupe knew more than I did. Especially about the Great Train Robbery.'

'Really?'

'Yes. Odd, when you come to think about it.'

But it didn't seem odd to me. Not at all.

We reached Tilbury and turned in through the dock gates. Hoare seemed to be a familiar face to the gateman who waved us past. Then Hoare put a call through on his mobile to somebody called Colin and arranged to meet him at one of the berths. I gazed around at the ships halfway through loading and unloading, at the cranes and gantries and Lego-like towers of containers. The clouds were low and louring. It had started to rain again. I didn't feel in top form and I certainly wasn't in my element.

'I love ports,' said Hoare, with a lyrical catch in his voice. 'Always have. The foreign flags. The far-flung destinations. The exotic cargoes. "Sandalwood, cedar-wood and sweet white wine".'

'They handle a lot of those here, do they?'

'It's a line of poetry, Lance. Masefield.' He shook his head despairingly. 'Never mind.'

'Isn't this one of yours?' I nodded at the soaring flank of a berthed container ship we were passing. The name EURYBIA slowly disclosed itself, one huge letter at a time. 'What are they unloading?'

Hoare glanced round. 'Frozen meat, at a guess.'

'What would Masefield have rhymed that with, I wonder?'

Hoare frowned, but didn't rise to the bait. 'There's Colin, look.'

A car was parked ahead, next to a container that was standing somewhat forlornly on its own, away from the stacked multitude. A man was leaning against the driver's door of the car, clearly waiting for us. He had one of those round, pliable faces that fold naturally into a smile. A keen wind was blowing in off the river, tugging at his fair hair and at the collar of the yellow safety coat he was wearing over his suit. Behind him, on the side of the rust-red container, the word EURYBIA was painted in white.

We pulled up and got out. 'Colin Dibley, Lance Bradley,' Hoare announced with a grin. Handshakes followed. 'Good to see you, Colin.'

'You too, Charlie. Though it'd be just as good and a sight drier and warmer in my office.'

'I thought we could entice you out for a drink before we get down to business. Lance won't want to stay for that anyway.'

'Suits me,' said Dibley. 'Charlie tells me you're a friend of Rupe's, Lance.'

'That's right.'

'He's given us a bit of a headache with this baby.' Dibley crooked his thumb at the container.

'Is that the famous consignment of aluminium?'

'It is.'

'How long's it been here?'

'More than a month. It arrived a couple of weeks after Rupe paid me a flying visit. After the things he said then . . .' Dibley shrugged. 'I should have known he was letting me in for some kind of trouble.'

'Has it been a lot of trouble?' asked Hoare. 'I mean, for us at Eurybia, yes, but for you, well, there's no shortage of space, is there?'

'Space is money, Charlie. You know that. Besides, there have been the lawyers to deal with. *And* Customs.'

'Suspicious about the contents?'

'You bet. A high-value cargo from Russia always sets them thinking about organized crime. When the owner goes missing . . . naturally they want to take a peek inside.'

'What did they find?'

'Aluminium, so they tell me.'

'Any chance of me taking a peek as well?' I asked, stepping closer to the double doors at the front of the container. There were bolts running from top to bottom, but no sign of a lock.

Hoare gave me a weary look. 'No chance whatsoever.'

'Can't see what harm it would do.'

'None to you, but plenty to me,' said Dibley, reaching past me to finger one of the small pin-and-socket contraptions that prevented the bolts being slipped. 'These are Customs seals. Breaking them's a hanging offence.'

'Just a thought.'

'A pretty pointless one, Lance,' said Hoare. 'Customs have confirmed the contents. Aluminium. That isn't the mystery. The mystery is why Rupe needed to raise so much money on his cargo.'

'And mystery's certainly what he was dealing in when he came here,' said Dibley.

'Time we made for the pub,' put in Hoare, rubbing his hands. 'I need a drink if I'm to listen to this one again.'

* * *

The rain began to get its act together as we left the Docks and drove out through the dismal margins of Tilbury. Dibley asked me some desultory questions about my friendship with Rupe, patently stalling till he could get his palm round a pint and unfold his tale of Rupe's more recent activities. I decided to help him out by throwing in a question of my own. 'Either of you two ever hear of a guy called Hashimoto?'

'Don't think so,' said Dibley.

'Nor me,' said Hoare. 'In our line of business, is he?'

'Not sure. He called at Rupe's house last week, apparently.'

'Did he leave a message?'

'Just that he wanted to speak to Rupe.'

'And Rupe's been based in Tokyo this year,' Hoare mused. 'This Hashimoto must know him from there. Could well be in shipping. I'll ask around. Did he leave a phone number?'

'No,' I found myself saying. 'He didn't.' Some instinct told me to keep a few cards up my sleeve. I was fairly sure Hoare wasn't being completely frank with me. It made sense to return the compliment.

The World's End Inn was aptly named, huddled as it was in the lee of the dyke where the Essex marshes met the Thames, with so much rain falling that it was hard to be sure where one ended and the other began. Inside, though, was the haven that is every decent pub. With drinks bought and lunches ordered, we drew up our chairs at a corner table and Dibley started to tell me what Hoare seemed to think I needed to hear.

'I wouldn't claim to know Rupe as well as you

obviously do, Lance. He's always struck me as a buttoned-up sort of fellow. Even a bit of a cold fish. But straight as a die. No question about that. He used to be out here every few weeks or so and we'd generally have a bite to eat here if we could fit it in. As far as work went, I'd have said he was a real asset to Eurybia.'

'I'd agree,' said Hoare.

'Efficient. That's what he was. Bloody efficient. And that's rarer than you'd think.'

'Rarer than rubies,' intoned Hoare.

'Masefield again?' I asked. But all I got for an answer was a glare.

'Anyway,' said Dibley, 'I'd not seen Rupe for quite a while, thanks to this Tokyo posting, when he turned up here at the end of August. It was the day after the bank holiday. Pretty quiet. Lots of people away. And he hadn't made an appointment. He was lucky to find me in the office.'

'Or unlucky,' said Hoare.

'Charlie reckons he was hoping I wouldn't be in. So he could have a sniff around on the strength of looking for me.'

'What would he be sniffing around *after*?'

'Ah, well, that's the question, isn't it? What was he up to? I didn't know he'd already resigned from Eurybia. In fact, I assumed Eurybia had sent him. It's certainly what he led me to believe. He said the company was worried about a client they'd been dealing with: Pomparles Trading. Had I heard any whispers about them? The answer was no. Of course, it later transpired that Rupe *was* Pomparles Trading. Anyway, we popped down here for lunch. That's when I began to notice a few . . . differences.'

'In Rupe?'

'Yeh. He was drinking more, for a start. I had trouble keeping up. It'd normally be the other way round. And he was . . . well, wilder, I suppose. Talking more loudly than usual. Waving his arms around. Like he was . . . high on something. I asked him about Tokyo, but he didn't seem to want to go into it.'

'What did he want to go into?'

'The past, funnily enough.'

'Nineteen sixty-three,' murmured Hoare.

'Exactly,' Dibley went on. 'Nineteen sixty-three. He asked me what I remembered of it. Well, I was still at primary school then. A few things stuck in my mind, naturally. All the tobogganing me and my brother did. It was a cold winter. We had a lovely summer holiday in Cornwall as well. Then there was the big stuff – Profumo, Kennedy, the Great Train Robbery. I trotted them out, with what little a tacker like me understood at the time. Rupe seemed to be hanging on my every word. When I'd finished, he said, "Ever heard of Stephen Townley, Col?"'

Stephen Townley. So, there he was again. The face in the photograph. The figure from the past. 'Had you?' I asked, to cover my surprise.

'Nope. The name meant nothing to me. I asked Rupe if I should have done, if this Townley had done something notable back in 'sixty-three. Rupe said, "No, you shouldn't have heard of him. But, yes, he did do something notable in nineteen sixty-three. And you will be hearing about it. I'll make sure of that."'

'What did he mean?'

'God knows. He was talking in riddles. Playing some

95

weird game of his own. There's not much that annoys me more than the old "I know something you don't know but I can't tell you what it is" routine. I asked him once what he was getting at and when he dodged the question, I dropped the subject.'

'And Rupe dropped it too?'

'For a while. But he came back to it as we were leaving. At least, I think he did. It was pretty ambiguous. "Wouldn't it be good," he said, "just once, to make a difference?" "A difference to what?" I asked. But all he did was smile at me. Then he muttered something I didn't quite catch – "You'll see," I think – got into his car and drove away. I phoned Charlie when I got back to the office and asked him if Rupe was, well, all right.'

'Not all right, I think we can say now, don't you?' Hoare raised his eyebrows at me. 'I told Colin that Rupe was a couple of days away from serving out his notice to us, that he hadn't gone to Tilbury on Eurybia business, that as far as we knew he was still in Tokyo and that I'd never heard of the Pomparles Trading Company. When I looked into it, though, I found Pomparles on our system as a new client, with a container of aluminium on its way here from Yokohama. I was too busy to do any more about it at the time. If Rupe wanted to play silly buggers, I reckoned that was his affair.' He gave a wry smile. 'Seems I should have taken it more seriously.' Then he looked at me. 'I'm having to now, aren't I?'

Charlie Hoare wasn't the only one being forced to take Rupe's obscure machinations seriously. Everything was getting very complicated. And complications have never agreed with me. Hoare and Dibley returned to the

Docks for their business meeting, dropping me at the station *en route*. On the slow train ride back to London through the unlovely innards of Dagenham and Barking, I tried to kick-start my brain into thinking mode. Rupe had something – something big – on Townley. He needed money – a lot of it – to make it count. 'You'll see,' he'd said to Dibley. But we hadn't seen. Nothing had happened. Rupe had vanished. That was all. Townley was as anonymous as ever. Rupe hadn't made a difference. Not yet, anyway. And he surely should have. Whatever kind of a difference he had in mind.

It had begun in Tokyo. That, at any rate, was a reasonable supposition. Which pointed to the so far elusive Mr Hashimoto. From Fenchurch Street I caught a bus to Trafalgar Square and walked across Green Park through the thinning rain to his hotel.

Mr Hashimoto wasn't in. I was about to ask what the point was of staying at such a swanky hotel if he was never going to swank around the place, when the receptionist said brightly, 'Are you Mr Bradley?'

'Yes. I am.'

'Mr Hashimoto left a message for you in case you called.'

'What's the message?'

'He can meet you here at ten o'clock tomorrow morning.'

'Great. Tell him I'll be here.'

The waiting game didn't seem a bad one to play, given how short of sleep I was. To prove the point, I nodded off on the bus to Kennington and woke up with what felt like a broken neck at New Cross Gate.

I was still in the convalescent phase when I made it back to Hardrada Road. Rupe's phone started ringing as I opened the front door and I was inclined to let the answering machine field the call, but when I heard Win start stumbling out a message for me I picked it up.

'Hi, Win. Lance here.'

'Oh.' Why she should sound so surprised was hard to say.

'Give me your number and I'll call you back.'

This simple suggestion also seemed to throw her, but eventually I got the number of the call-box out of her and we were soon speaking without worrying that the pips were about to interrupt.

'I haven't really got any news for you, Win. I've met a few people up here who know Rupe, but what none of them seems to know is where he is.'

'Oh.'

'I'm sorry, but there it is. I should find out more tomorrow.' (Not least, Royal Mail permitting, what part her brother Howard had played in the discovery of two dead bodies in the Street area, one of them their father's, back in 1963. I was tempted to ask Win about that there and then, but her telephone manner wasn't exactly conducive to delicate discussion.)

'Oh.'

'Why not phone me around this time tomorrow? I might have something to report.'

'All right. I'll do that.' She paused, then said, 'Lancelot?'

'Yes, Win?'

'It was good of your mother . . . to call round.'

'Well, she doesn't live far away, does she?'

'No, but . . .' Another pause. 'It's good of you too, doing all this for us.'

'It's not so much.'

'We're relying on you, you know.' (People doing that had to be either mad or desperate. I suppose the Alders counted as both.)

'I'll see what I can come up with, Win. Let's talk tomorrow. I've got to go now. 'Bye.'

'They're a weird lot, then, are they, Rupe's family?' Echo put the question to me a few hours later, as we toyed with some appetizers in Kennington's foremost Portuguese dining establishment.

'Pretty dysfunctional, yeh.'

'They sound like Stella Gibbons dreamed them up.'

'Who?'

'She wrote *Cold Comfort Farm*.'

'Oh, yeh. Right. Well, cold comfort's about all they're going to get from me, far as I can see.'

'Come on. You haven't done that badly.' She gave me a sparkly smile, though it failed to out-sparkle the spangles on her eye-shimmying orange top. 'You've surprised me with what you've found out already.'

'Have I?'

'Aluminium smuggling. Great Train Robbers. I had no idea I was lodging with such a man of mystery.'

'It's not exactly smuggling.' (I was beginning to wonder if confiding in Echo had been a good idea. But after a couple of drinks I was bound to confide in some-one and Echo had no axe to grind that I knew of.) 'As

99

for Prettyman and this Townley bloke . . .' I shrugged. 'I just don't get it.'

'Perhaps Mr Hashimoto will tie it all together.'

'Maybe. But if he doesn't . . .'

'What?'

'That'll be the end of the road. There's nothing else I can do.'

'You'll just give up?'

'I won't have any choice.'

'Bloody hell.' She looked genuinely disappointed. 'I thought you meant to go on and on until you dug out the truth.'

'You've got me all wrong, Echo. I'm a natural quitter.'

'Oh yeh?' Her gaze narrowed. 'I'm not so sure.'

'Just you wait and see. Meanwhile . . .' I took a big swallow of *vinho verde*. 'Why don't you tell me how you got a name like Echo?'

She shook her head. 'Can't do that, I'm afraid.'

'Why not?'

'A girl has to have a few secrets.' She teased me with a grin. 'But don't worry. I haven't got any that are half as exotic as Rupe's.'

'Now it's my turn not to be sure.'

'Think about something else, then.' Her grin faded away. 'What am I supposed to do if you draw a blank?'

'How d'you mean?'

'Well, should I move out of Hardrada Road? Being lodger to an international commodities crook could be bad for my health.'

'I don't think you're in any danger, Echo.' (Could I honestly say that? Rupe had waded into some pretty murky waters – waters that might one day come lapping at *our* feet.)

'It'd be sensible to move on, though, wouldn't it?'

'Might be, I suppose.'

'I reckon I will. If you pack up and go home to Somerset. Has to be the safest option.' Her face crumpled into a frown. 'And then . . .'

'What?'

'Well . . .' She gazed soulfully into her wine. 'Rupe really will be lost then, won't he?'

CHAPTER SIX

Echo had set off for the sorting office by the time I surfaced the following morning. Over a cobbled-together breakfast, I computed that to be at the Hilton at ten I'd need to be on the bus by half nine. According to Echo, the post was sure to have been delivered to Hardrada Road by then, but her confidence on the point didn't seem to square up to reality. Regular squints out of the window revealed no approaching postie as nine o'clock came and went. Eventually, just as I was about to make a move for the bus stop, along came Echo's tardy colleague, the result being that I had to take Dad's letter with me and start sifting through the contents on the top deck of the number 36 as it lumbered towards Hyde Park Corner.

Dad had done a thorough job with the cuttings, as I might have expected – a clutch of articles reporting sudden farm-related deaths and subsequent inquests along with a couple of feature pieces pondering the meaning of so many fatalities crammed into the summer and autumn of 1963.

The exact number had itself been a cause of dispute. Four or five, according to whether you included Reginald Gorton, owner of a peat-digging business near Shapwick, who'd died of a heart attack early in September. If you were looking for jinxes, I supposed you did. The sequence had started at the end of July, with Albert Crick falling off a barn roof. Then Peter Dalton, none other, had been found dead of gunshot wounds at Wilderness Farm, near Ashcott. The date: Monday 19 August. Within a fortnight of the Great Train Robbery on Thursday 8 August, just as Bill Prettyman had said.

The *Central Somerset Gazette* wasn't to know of a connection – if there really was one – with big-time crime in Buckinghamshire, of course. They said Dalton had inherited Wilderness Farm from his father the year before and was thought by neighbouring farmers to be struggling to make a go of it. Shotgun suicide was lightly implied. The inquest a month later had gone along with that, despite what the coroner had called 'minor inconsistencies in the disposition of the deceased and the weapon'. What did that mean? The *Gazette* wasn't in the business of asking.

As to the discovery of Dalton's body, there was Howard's name in black and white. *Howard Alder, 15, of Penfrith, Street, was cycling along a footpath that passes through the yard of Wilderness Farm when he noticed a figure lying in the doorway of the milking shed.* There was nothing about just how grisly this discovery must have been. Nor any mention of Howard at the inquest. Just as there'd never been a whisper of the event in all the years I'd known Howard through Rupe. Very strange.

And it got stranger. Once you bought into Gorton being part of a sequence, that made three deaths within six weeks. This point only seemed to be seriously seized on after a fourth death, late in October. Andrew Moore, son of the owner of Mereleaze Farm, near Othery, had been knocked off his motorbike by a lorry and killed in an accident at the A39/A361 junction on the afternoon of Monday 28 October. It was the day after the clocks had gone back for winter. The early dusk was held partly to blame. But with Hallowe'en in the offing, some ghoulish theories had started doing the rounds. Dad had copied a few letters to the editor for me. *There may be no basis to the wilder talk of a curse on our farming community, but it is difficult to see so many deaths as coincidental* – that sort of thing.

The fifth and evidently final death was of George Alder himself, on Sunday 17 November. *Mr Alder went out early in the morning,* reported the *Gazette* later in the week. *When he did not return by mid-afternoon, his family grew concerned. His 15-year-old son, Howard, cycled to Cow Bridge and began looking for him along the banks of the Brue, where Mr Alder had taken to walking of late. Howard eventually found his father's body, tangled in reeds, a short distance west of the bridge. Mr Alder is believed to have drowned.*

It was strange stuff to read. The *Gazette* had failed to point out that Howard now figured in two of the clutch of deaths. Perhaps they'd refrained out of sensitivity. Others must have commented on it. And why had George taken to walking by the Brue of late? No suggestions. Not even a hint. What about his wife's pregnancy? There was enough tragedy without dwelling on that, apparently. It wasn't mentioned. The inquest, just before Christmas, brought in a verdict of accidental death. The coroner emphasized that suggestions of a link with other deaths in the area were *as absurd as they are unfeeling*. Bet that put a stop to them.

Cow Bridge, on a November afternoon, Wearyall Hill and the Tor darkening to the north while the poplars along Street Drove stood sentinel to the south, made a spooky setting for a haunting discovery. There'd have been much less traffic on the Glastonbury to Butleigh road back then. It could have been well nigh silent as Howard picked his way along the bank, peering into the cold grey water until he saw . . .

I was born five days later, at Butleigh Cottage Hospital. And Rupe was born the following spring. We began just as all that ended. But what was it that ended? Forget a curse on the land. Howard was the connection the coroner reckoned it was absurd and unfeeling to try to make. Dalton *and* his own father. Plus Townley. Two dead bodies and a photograph. What did it mean? What did it amount to – then *and* now? I hadn't a clue. Or rather I had several. But they were all far too cryptic for me.

Most cryptic of all was Howard himself. He'd never seemed the secretive type. In fact, he'd never struck me as capable of concealing anything. Now I knew better. He'd concealed plenty. OK, that could have been because it was all too traumatic to call to mind. But then nobody had ever mentioned that he'd *been* traumatized. Rupe had always told me Howard was weak-minded from birth. But how would Rupe know? For the first twenty years of Howard's life the only surviving first-hand informants were Win and Mil. They were well aware of how and when his decline set in. Finding his father's dead body floating in the Brue must have speeded him down the slope. But they'd never breathed a word about that. And how had the scene of that death somehow drifted five miles south to the Sedgemoor Drain?

It was a question that bothered Dad as well as me, as he admitted in a note attached to the cuttings.

I could swear we had that story about the Sedgemoor Drain from the Alders themselves. Why would they make something like that up, do you suppose? Howard certainly must have had a bad time of it that summer and autumn. But I checked with your mother and she is fairly certain Mavis Alder never mentioned those experiences as a reason for Howard's feeble-mindedness. I do not recall it cropping up while he was at Clarks either. I suppose no one was likely to remember if no one reminded them. The jinx was a bit of a nine days' wonder. I had forgotten it almost completely. Dalton's death reads oddly to me. Does it to you? 'Inconsistencies in the disposition of the deceased and the weapon'. What was the coroner getting at? Something other than suicide? The police officer mentioned in a couple of the reports – Inspector Forrester – is actually Don Forrester, who worked for Clarks for a few years after he retired from the force. (Howard had left by then.) I see Don quite often, pushing a trolley around Tesco. He must be eighty-odd now, but looks pretty spry. Do you want me to ask him about the deaths – Dalton in particular? It might lead nowhere, of course. Who can say? Let me know. I have nothing better to do. And it is interesting, I have to admit.

My mind was still turning all this over as I hurried through the subway under Hyde Park Corner and up Park Lane to the Hilton. I most certainly did want Dad to put a few questions to Don Forrester. Did he think Dalton had actually been murdered, for instance? If so, who by? The name of Stephen Townley had never made it into the columns of the *Central Somerset Gazette*. But perhaps it should have done. And perhaps it still might.

It was a few minutes to ten as I entered the hotel and headed across the marbled wastes of the lobby towards the reception desk. Technically, I was early. But not too early for Mr Hashimoto. A figure bobbed into my path – short, slimly built and grey-suited. I found myself looking into a calm, sad-eyed Japanese face beneath a schoolboyish mop of silver-shot black hair, gold-rimmed specs glinting in the Hilton spotlights. 'Mr Bradley?' he asked, with that slight but distinctive oriental vagueness around the Rs. 'I am Kiyofumi Hashimoto.'

'Er . . . Pleased to meet you.' We shook hands. There was a hint of a bow on Hashimoto's part. 'How did you know who I was?'

'It was obvious, Mr Bradley. Believe me.'

'Right. Is that good news or bad, I wonder? Being obvious, I mean.'

'It is a fact. That is all.'

'Facts? Well, I could use a few of those.'

'Me too.' (Was he being ironic? I couldn't tell. What's more, with Kiyofumi Hashimoto, it was pretty obvious you'd *never* be able to tell.)

'I'm a friend of Rupe Alder, Mr Hashimoto. If you can help me find him . . .'

'That is what you are trying to do?'

'Yeh. His family are worried about him. He's, er . . .'

'Disappeared.' Hashimoto nodded. 'I am looking for him also. Perhaps we can help each other.'

'Maybe we can.'

'Shall we take a stroll in the park? It will be . . . pleasanter . . . to talk there.'

The morning was too cool and damp by my reckoning for strolling, even if strolling in parks had been a habit of mine, which it wasn't. Hashimoto didn't exactly seem the outdoor type either, hoisting a vast Hilton golfing brolly against the drizzle and stepping carefully through the muddy drifts of leaves in his gleaming lounge-lizard shoes.

'Are you in shipping, Mr Hashimoto?' I asked, as we wandered vaguely west towards the Serpentine.

'No. Microprocessors. My concern to find Rupe has nothing to do with business.'

'It hasn't?'

'Nothing at all. The aluminium is . . . someone else's problem.'

'You know about the aluminium?'

'I have found out about it since coming to London. But it is . . . ancillary . . . to my difficulties.'

'Ancillary?'

'Marginal. Almost irrelevant. You see . . .' He glanced

round at me, squinting slightly through his glasses. 'You are a good friend of Rupe, Mr Bradley?'

'Lifelong.'

'Then we should not be so formal. I shall call you Lance. OK?'

'Fine by me.'

'And you should call me Kiyofumi.'

'Right. Kiyofumi. You, er, met Rupe in Tokyo?'

'Yes.'

'How did that happen?'

'My niece became his girlfriend. I met Rupe at my sister's home two or three times last summer.'

'Your niece . . .'

'Haruko. A good girl.'

'I'm sure she is. So, she and Rupe . . .'

'A typhoon romance.' Hashimoto smiled. 'Her mother was very pleased.'

'Were you?'

'Certainly. Rupe seemed . . .' He shrugged. 'Kind. Charming. Easy to like.' (That description fitted Rupe, all right. Typhoon romancer was a bit harder to get used to, though. Still, if he was going to fall for someone, I supposed it would be headlong.)

'What did Haruko's father think?'

'Her father is not with us, Lance.' (Did that mean dead? I hadn't the nerve to ask.) 'That is why I have to be . . . more than an uncle to her.'

'How serious was this romance?'

'For Haruko, very serious. She hoped to marry Rupe, I think. That is what her mother has told me.'

'And for Rupe?'

Hashimoto sighed. 'I am sorry to say this, Lance. You

are his friend. You must think well of him. But the truth is . . . he strung her along. He did not want to marry her. He wanted something else. Once he had it . . . he was gone.'

'What was it he wanted?' (Somehow, I already knew it wasn't anything obvious.)

'Something that belongs to Haruko's mother – my sister, Mayumi.' Hashimoto stopped and looked at me. 'Rupe stole it.'

'Stole? I don't believe it. Rupe's no—' I broke off. No thief? No con artist? No double dealer? Whatever I'd previously have said you couldn't accuse Rupe of, his own actions seemed to tell a different story.

'Rupe used Haruko to get close to Mayumi. He knew she had this thing that he wanted. Eventually, he persuaded Haruko to show him where it was hidden. Then he stole it. And ran away. Like, as you would say, the thief in the night.'

'What did he steal?'

'A letter. Let us call it . . . the Townley letter.'

'Townley? You know about him?'

'I know. And yet I do not know. Mayumi does not tell me more than she thinks it is safe for me to know. She is fifteen years older than me. Always she has thought she is a better judge of what is good for me than I am. But her judgement is not as acute as she believes. She should not have kept the letter. She should have destroyed it.'

'What's in it?'

'I do not know.' (Was he lying? It was a fifty-fifty guess. His expression gave nothing away.) 'That is one of the things Mayumi does not think it is safe for me to know.'

'But it's a letter from Townley?'

'No. *About* Townley.'

'To Mayumi?'

'Yes.'

'From . . .'

'I do not know.'

'Written when?'

'A long time ago. Many years.'

'Thirty-seven, maybe?'

'Maybe.'

'Did Mayumi know Townley?' (Hashimoto looked to be in his mid to late forties, which put his sister in her early sixties. The arithmetic, such as it was, seemed to stack up.)

'Yes. When she was very young.'

'In Tokyo?'

'Yes.'

'What was he doing there?'

'He was a soldier. American. Based in Japan.'

'And Mayumi was his girlfriend?'

'Not . . . exactly.'

'What then . . . exactly?'

'It does not matter.' (It did, of course. But seeping through Hashimoto's inscrutability was the implication that he was genuinely unsure about quite a lot himself. His sister was holding out on him. But nothing like as much as Rupe had been holding out on all of us.) 'What matters is that the letter is dangerous to Townley. It harms him. It can be used against him. That is why Rupe wanted it. So, can you tell me why Rupe is interested in harming Townley?'

'Not really. Something to do with his brother, I think.'

'Revenge?'

'Sort of.' (But what sort of? Even if Townley *had* murdered Dalton and made off with some of the Train money, why did that matter to Rupe? Why did he care?)

'The letter is not just dangerous to Townley, Lance. It is dangerous to Mayumi. I have to get it back. This is more than honour. This is life and death.'

'It can't be as bad as that.'

'It can. Rupe has strayed into a very dark place.'

'Come off it.' (But the dark was what I was whistling in now.)

'We have to find him.'

'That could be a problem . . . Kiyofumi. I haven't the foggiest where he is. The consensus seems to be . . .' I shrugged. 'Find Townley and you find Rupe.'

'I do not know where Townley is.'

'What about your sister? Does she know?'

'No. She has not seen him – has not heard from him – for more than forty years.'

'I thought we settled on thirty-seven.'

'You settled on thirty-seven.'

'OK. We can agree on a bloody long time?'

'Yes.'

'During which Mayumi has had absolutely no contact with Townley?'

'Correct.'

'Then can you explain to me how Rupe knew they'd ever been acquainted?'

'Ill fortune.'

I waited for him to continue, but he didn't, merely gazing solemnly at me through the shadow cast by the brolly. 'That's supposed to be an explanation, is it? Because I—'

'Excuse me, gentlemen.'

I don't know if Hashimoto was as surprised as me by the interruption. He certainly couldn't have been *more* surprised. A figure had materialized next to us, his approach screened perhaps by the brolly. He was a tall, faintly stooping bloke in a dark, neatly tailored rain-coat. He had short grey hair and a narrow, lugubrious face. His voice was soft and precise, matching his gaze, which moved slowly but studiously from me to Hashimoto and back again.

'My name is Jarvis. You don't know me. But I know you. Mr Hashimoto. Mr Bradley.' He nodded politely at us. 'I also know Rupert Alder. He is, let's say, an interest we have in common.'

'Did you follow us here?' Hashimoto's question had a tetchy edge to it and I can't say I blamed him.

'Not just here. Speaking corporately, that is.'

'*What?*' The guy's oblique style of speech was needling me as well.

'Forgive me. Surprise was inevitable. Antagonism is unnecessary. My card.'

He plucked two business cards out of his pocket and handed us one each. Philip Jarvis evidently represented a company called Myerscough Udal, boasting an address in High Holborn and a clutch of telephone, fax and e-mail numbers. The nature of their business went unspecified.

'We handle confidential enquiries,' Jarvis continued, anticipating the question. 'We're one of the largest operations in the field worldwide. Pre-eminence in such a field is by its nature untrumpeted, of course. We rely very much on personal recommendation.'

'And you have been enquiring into us?' asked Hashimoto.

'Not exactly.'

'Then what . . . *exactly*?' (The guy was definitely getting to me.)

'Mr Rupert Alder is a client of ours. We, like you, are concerned about him.'

'Owes you money, does he?'

'As a matter of fact, yes. But I think he would pay us if he could. Even our fees would not gobble up the proceeds of his aluminium fraud.' (Everyone, apparently, knew all about that.)

'What did he hire you to do?'

'Can't you guess?'

'Find Townley,' said Hashimoto.

'Precisely.'

'And did you?' I pressed.

'No.' Jarvis allowed himself half a smile. 'You could say he found us, though. That indeed is why I'm here.'

'Meaning?'

'Let's step down to the Serpentine. Rippling water calms the mind, I find. I'll explain as we go.'

We started along the straightest path to the lake. And Jarvis, as he'd promised, started to explain. His soft voice forced us to stick close to him if we were to catch every word, as I for one was determined to do. I wondered if it was a deliberate anti-eavesdropping technique on his part. And then I wondered if thinking that was a symptom of paranoia on my part.

'Strictly speaking, gentlemen, I ought not to be telling

you any of this. Myerscough Udal's reputation has not been built on sharing its secrets with third parties. But these are exceptional circumstances. Wholly exceptional in my experience, which is far from inconsiderable. I shall elaborate on that a little later. To begin at the beginning, Mr Alder engaged our services through our Tokyo office four months ago to locate one Stephen Townley, using such limited information as Mr Alder was able to give us.'

'How limited was that?' I asked.

'Very, for our purposes. Mr Alder knew only that Townley was an American, probably in his sixties, who'd served in the US Army and been based at one point in Japan. He also supplied us with the names of two former acquaintances of Townley, one of them deceased.'

'Peter Dalton.'

'You have him. The other was—'

'My sister,' put in Hashimoto.

'Quite so. I do not know how much Mr Hashimoto has told you about his sister, Mr Bradley, so forgive me if I bore you with information already in your possession. In seeking to trace Townley, we went back to his roots and worked forward: standard procedure in our line of work. US Army records and other obvious databases yielded certain simple facts. Stephen Anderson Townley was born in Tulsa, Oklahoma, on May seventeenth, nineteen thirty-two. An only child of a single mother. She is long since dead, by the way. He enrolled in the Army straight from high school in the summer of nineteen forty-nine, aged seventeen, and served thirteen years in all, leaving with the rank of sergeant. He saw a good deal of action in Korea at the start of his military career. After that he was shuttled around like thousands of other soldiers. Particularly significant for our purposes, however, was the year and a bit he spent in West Berlin in the mid Fifties.'

'Why's that?' I asked, as Jarvis paused, either for breath or effect.

'Because Peter Dalton, a farmer's son from Somerset, was serving with the British Army in West Berlin at the same time. We must assume the two men became acquainted during that period. Also because Townley married a German girl while based there. Rosa Kleinfurst. Rosa went back to the United States with him when he was transferred home early in nineteen fifty-five. Later that year, their first child, Eric, was born. A daughter followed eighteen months later. By then, the marriage seems to have been on the rocks. The couple separated, Rosa keeping the children. Townley transferred to Military Intelligence, which means there's very limited information on his activities from that point on. We believe he was based in Japan for the next two or three years, during which period he patronized a bar in Tokyo called the Golden Rickshaw, the proprietress of which was—'

'My mother,' said Hashimoto.

'Indeed.' Jarvis nodded. 'Who knows, Mr Hashimoto? You may have glimpsed Townley sipping his beer at the counter on your way home from school some days.'

'It is possible.' The admission sounded painful.

'Your sister entertained the customers?'

'She was young and pretty. People liked her.'

116

'Quite so. Innocently so, one might say. And her daughter has followed in her footsteps?'

'Yes.'

'I understand the Golden Rickshaw's walls are decorated with photographs of former patrons, taken over the years.'

'It is.'

'I further understand Stephen Townley appears in one of those photographs.'

'He does.'

'Which is how Mr Alder knew your sister had been acquainted with him, possessed as he was of another photograph of Townley, taken a few years later.'

'Yes.'

(So, an earlier question of mine was answered. Rupe had known Townley was an old customer of the Golden Rickshaw and hence likely to be known to Mayumi Hashimoto. There were plenty more questions where that one came from, though. Had Rupe gone to that particular bar by chance? Or had he already suspected a connection with Townley? And did Jarvis know what Rupe had stolen from Mayumi? Did he, in fact, know about the theft at all?)

'We believe Townley left Japan in the spring of nineteen sixty,' Jarvis continued. 'Frankly, we haven't a clue what duties he was assigned to for the remainder of his service. He left the Army two years later. All official trace of him ceases at that point.' (We'd reached the Serpentine by now and begun a slow tramp towards the boathouse. The wind was raising quite a few ripples on the lake, but I was immune to their supposedly calming effect.) 'Mr Alder presented us with a photograph of Townley, apparently taken by his brother at a railway station near Glastonbury in August nineteen sixty-three. The date was of Mr Alder's own computing. He said Townley had been a friend of Peter Dalton and our investigations have certainly shown that to be possible. Dalton committed suicide on August nineteenth, nineteen sixty-three. Mr Alder suspected that Dalton was actually murdered by Townley to cover up his part in the, er . . .'

'Great Train Robbery,' I put in.

'Quite so.' Jarvis stifled a wince. 'Since Mr Alder declined to share with us his reasons for harbouring such an apparently outlandish suspicion, it was difficult to know whether to take it seriously or not. He specifically forbade us to approach his brother, for instance.'

'I doubt you'd have got much out of Howard.'

'Perhaps so, perhaps not. Either way, all that can really be said is that it remains an open question. I know Mr Alder had some contact with a Sixties villain called Prettyman, but I have to tell you Prettyman is a highly unreliable character in his own right. It is unclear whether he was actually a participant in the robbery or not. What those who definitely *were* participants seem to agree on is that the original impetus for the crime came from an anonymous source who fed them vital information.'

'Might that have been Townley?'

'Frankly, Mr Bradley, your guess is as good as mine. The allegation takes us nowhere in the absence of a single hard fact about Townley's life after he left the Army. The 'sixty-three material is fragmentary and uncorroborated. It is also the end as far as Townley goes. When I say that we know nothing from then on, I mean literally that: nothing. Townley is a dead man without a death certificate. A blank. A void. If he's still alive, it's in another man's skin. And we have absolutely no idea who that man might be.'

'What about his wife? His children?'

'Naturally, we pursued that avenue of enquiry, but it yielded nothing. Although the Townleys have never divorced, that appears to be because Mrs Townley has had no way of contacting her husband since he left the Army. He ceased to pay maintenance to her at that point. She has consistently told friends and acquaintances that she believes him to be dead. Their children take the same line. They may be right. They may be wrong.'

'Or they may be lying.'

'That too, of course.' Jarvis smiled faintly. 'There are . . . discrepancies . . . in the banking records of all three.'

'What sort of discrepancies?'

'The sort that imply financial assistance from an unidentified source.'

'Townley,' said Hashimoto.

'It's possible. Mr Alder took the view, indeed, that it was distinctly probable.'

'What did he do about it?' I asked, as Jarvis came to a halt and propped himself against the back of a lakeside bench.

'I'm not sure. That's where this whole matter becomes so confoundedly delicate.'

'You're going to have to tell us what that means.'

'Have to? I think not. But I will tell you, none the less. I met Mr Alder on thirtieth August to review progress on

119

the case.' (Over breakfast, I'd studied Echo's kitchen-wall calendar and worked out that Rupe had visited Tilbury Docks on 29 August. So, it was the very next day that he'd powwowed with Jarvis.) 'Considering the little I had to report, he was surprisingly cheerful. He took it as certain that Mrs Townley and/or her children knew where Townley was and he gave me to understand that he had procured from your sister, Mr Hashimoto, the means to force them to disclose Townley's whereabouts to him.'

'He did not procure,' said Hashimoto. 'He stole.'

'Really? I confess I am not greatly surprised. A letter, he said it was, the nature and contents of which he did not care to reveal.'

'That is right,' said Hashimoto. 'I do not know what is in it myself.'

There was the slightest sceptical twitch of Jarvis's right eyebrow, then he went serenely on. 'Mr Alder left me in no doubt that he intended to use the letter to flush Townley out of his hiding-place. I have neither seen nor heard from Mr Alder since.'

Nobody said anything for a longish moment, so I asked the obvious question. 'What do you think happened?'

'I think he succeeded, either directly or indirectly, in contacting Townley. In fact, I'm sure of it.'

'How can you be?'

'Because, within a matter of weeks of that meeting, our offices were broken into and correspondence and computer disks relating to the Townley inquiry stolen. We invest a great deal of time and money in security, gentlemen. The break-in was highly professional. It had to be. It was also precisely targeted. More or less simultaneously, an anonymous message was passed to us at the very highest level, via a legal practice that often acts for us.'

'What was the message?'

'Drop the case.'

'Simple as that?'

'Not quite. Certain . . . penalties . . . were mentioned in the event of non-compliance. Financial penalties, I mean. It was all very . . . kid-gloved. But it was clear that the sender of the message wielded sufficient influence to ruin us if he needed to.'

'Ruin the company?'

'Quite so.'

'How could he do that?'

'Myerscough Udal is big and successful. But there's always someone bigger and more successful. I believe our directors were firmly persuaded that our most valuable clients would be taken from us if we persisted. We did not persist.'

'You caved in?'

'We had no choice.'

'And you think . . . Townley did this?'

'Who else?'

'But he's just one man, for God's sake.'

'Of whom we know nothing. A state of affairs he's clearly determined to maintain.'

'If you . . . caved in,' said Hashimoto slowly, 'why are you here, talking to us?'

'An astute question, Mr Hashimoto. Why indeed?' Jarvis looked warily to right and left and lowered his voice still further. 'Officially, this meeting is not taking place. If you visit or telephone me at our offices, I will decline to speak to you and deny that we have ever met. Myerscough Udal does not like to be pushed, apparent though it is that we *can* be pushed. We are seriously unhappy about it, gentlemen, yet unable to strike back in any way. We are fearful for the welfare of a client, yet in no position to aid him. We are hamstrung.' He smiled. 'But you are not.'

'What are you getting at?' I asked.

'I tell you things, Mr Bradley. I give you information. What you do with it is up to you. And what I hope you do with it is probably irrelevant. Save to say that I sincerely hope you will . . . do something.'

'Such as?'

'That really must be up to you. What I can say is this. The Townleys had two children – Eric, born nineteen fifty-five; Barbara, born nineteen fifty-seven. Barbara lives in Houston, Texas. She's married to an oil executive, Gordon Ledgister. They have one child – a son, Clyde, born nineteen eighty, currently a student at Stanford University. Eric meanwhile lives with his mother in Berlin. She went back there after the Wall came down. Eric now styles himself Erich. He's gay, by the way. Rosa Townley is sixty-five. She and Erich share an apartment on Yorckstrasse. Number eighty-five. You may be interested to know that airline records show a Mr R. Alder flew from Heathrow to Berlin on third September. There's no record of a return flight. And now' – he pushed himself suddenly upright – 'I must be going. Good morning to you both.'

With that he was off, spring-heeled and striding, back the way we'd come. I wanted to shout after him. But shout what? He'd said everything he had to say. And it was as clear as daylight that he'd say no more. Myerscough Udal had dropped the case. And Jarvis had washed his hands of us. He hurried on. But Hashimoto and I stayed exactly where we were.

It was eleven o'clock by the time we got back to the Hilton – good news for someone as badly in need of a drink as I felt. Hashimoto hadn't said much since Jarvis had dumped us. I reckoned I could see a lot of not very productive thinking going on behind his placid face, though, so I prescribed a drink in his case too and piloted him round the corner to a cosy little boozer in Shepherd Market.

Halfway through my second Carlsberg Special and his first Glenfiddich, Hashimoto seemed to come to some kind of decision. He solemnly lit a Marlboro cigarette, stared into the first plume of its smoke and announced, 'We must go to Berlin.'

'Don't I get a vote on that, Kiyo?'

He looked at me oddly. Maybe my Carlsberg-inspired invention of an abbreviated name for him hadn't gone down well. But, if so, he didn't dwell on it. 'I must find the Townley letter. And you must find your friend.'

'I'm not sure about that. You said yourself he'd strayed into a dark place. Could be a dangerous one too, if Townley's as powerful as Jarvis seems to think.'

'It is true. Mr Jarvis invites us to put our heads into the tiger's mouth. To see if the tiger will bite.'

'I'm sure my mother told me once never to put my head in a tiger's mouth.'

Hashimoto nodded solemnly. 'A mother would.'

'Besides, I have to go home next week. A trip to Berlin's not on.'

'Why must you go home?'

'Oh, this and that.' (A fortnightly date with the dole office was the beginning and end of my commitments, but I wasn't about to admit it.)

'We may not need to be gone for long. And I will pay all your expenses.'

'Would that include a funeral?'

'Calm yourself, Lance. Subtlety is everything in such matters. What do you lose by accompanying me to Berlin?'

'Depends what happens when we get there.'

'Nothing will happen without your consent. You have my word on that. We will judge and agree each step before we take it.'

'What if I don't agree *any* steps?'

'We will take none.'

'I still can't go.'

'Why not?'

'I've left my passport at home.'

'How far is your home?'

'A hundred and fifty miles or so.'

'Then we will go and get it. I have the use of a car. It is in the Hilton garage.'

'When did you plan to set off?'

'For your passport? Now. For Berlin?' He gave the question a moment's thought, then shrugged. 'Tomorrow.'

'So soon?'

'There has been enough delay. Why add to it?'

'Well . . .'

* * *

I never did come up with much of an answer. Which is why, apprehension dulled by several more Carlsberg Specials, I found myself being high-speed chauffeured along the M4 and down the M5 in a courtesy BMW through the midday murk. I didn't doubt Hashimoto's declared motivation: he reckoned he could best protect his sister and niece by retrieving what Rupe had stolen from them. Nor did Hashimoto seem to question my desire to help a friend in distress. There was even some implication that he thought me honour-bound to undo the damage my friend had done. That didn't slice any slush with me, of course. Yet I was, apparently, going to Berlin. The truth was that I was excited by the mystery Rupe had unwittingly dragged me into. And excitement was something my life had been distinctly short of for a long long time. I'd been well and truly suckered by the thrill of the chase.

We made it to Glastonbury in a shade over two hours. Hashimoto wasn't a dawdler behind the wheel. I thought of suggesting a diversion to my parents' so that I could ask Dad to tap Don Forrester for information. But I decided to phone Dad later instead, thereby dodging having to explain to him what I was up to. I even thought of proposing a visit to Penfrith. But I nixed that as well. Too much to tell; too much to ask. With luck, Rosa and Erich Townley would answer all our questions. There might still be an innocent explanation for everything.

(Who *did* I think I was kidding?)

* * *

We stopped at Heathrow on the way back and Hashimoto booked us aboard a Sunday lunchtime flight to Berlin. (Club class, no less.) Then he drove me to Kennington. It was agreed he'd pick me up at ten o'clock the following morning. We were all set.

We were also mad, according to Echo. 'You have absolutely no idea what you're getting into.' (A fair point.) 'I thought you said you were a natural quitter.'

'I am.'

'Then why aren't you quitting?'

'Because that's the thing with quitting, Echo: you have to choose your moment.'

'And this isn't it?'

I had to think about that for several moments. In the end, all I could say was, 'Apparently not.'

BERLIN

CHAPTER SEVEN

Following Rupe to Berlin had its ironical side, since I'd followed him there once before, when we were inter-railing round Europe in the long, hot, sweaty summer of 1984. Berlin had definitely been Rupe's idea. He'd always had more of a sense of history than me. I'd not shared his curiosity about life behind the Iron Curtain and the dismal train journey across East Germany to reach West Berlin had only strengthened my view that we'd have been better off going almost anywhere else. We'd made the standard tourist foray into East Berlin, but I hadn't exactly been in a receptive frame of mind. Tacky commercialism on one side of the Wall and drab uniformity on the other were about the only memories I'd taken away.

Arriving by plane in a smartened-up, unified capital city with too many complimentary drinks inside me was a vastly different experience, of course. So different that I had some doubts about whether it really was the same place. The taxi from Tegel Airport to our hotel sped through an autumnally golden Tiergarten with no

Wall looming ahead, crossed the vanished border and whooshed beneath the Brandenburg Gate into Unter den Linden. Hashimoto had booked us into the Adlon, which he'd been told was the best hotel in Berlin. It looked to me as we were ushered across the vast and sparkling lobby that he'd been well informed. What with club-class travel and *grande luxe* accommodation, I was beginning to think that escort to Kiyofumi Hashimoto was a job I could be persuaded to take on a long-term contract.

High altitude imbibing had left me needing a serious kip. I suggested we meet up in the bar at seven o'clock and Hashimoto seemed happy with that. So, leaving the unpacking (all five minutes of it) till later, I stretched out on the enormous double bed in my lavishly appointed room and let the distant murmur of traffic on Unter den Linden lull me to sleep.

It was dark outside when I woke, woozily identifying the persistent warbling in my ear as the telephone ringing on the bedside table. I couldn't read the time on my watch, but reckoned the caller had to be Hashimoto.

It was. 'Lance. You must come quickly.'

'Start without me, Kiyo. I'll be down in a minute.'

'I am not in the hotel. I am in a call-box on Mehringdamm.'

'Oh yeh?'

'Near the Townleys' apartment.'

'For Christ's sake. Couldn't that have waited?'

'You must come here now. I have an idea.'

'What sort of idea?' (Crazy was my bet.)

'I have no coins left. I will wait for you outside

130

Mehringdamm U-Bahn station. Get here as soon as you can.'

'Yeh, but—' The line went dead. I allowed myself a heartfelt sigh. 'Great.' (It was, of course, anything but.)

As soon as I made it into a vertical position, a dehydration headache announced itself with several mule-kicks inside my skull. And this mule was a powerful critter, unappeased by a pint of Berlin tap water. I left the hotel in something short of tiptop condition.

The taxi drive was a short and fast run south along broad and empty streets. At some point we passed the site of Checkpoint Charlie and returned to what had been West Berlin. Peering at the map I'd cadged from the hotel receptionist, I could see the Mehringdamm U-Bahn station was just round the corner from Yorckstrasse. I found myself wondering if Rosa Townley's family had always lived in the area. Checkpoint Charlie, after all, had been the gateway to the American sector.

Not that I had much time to do a lot of wondering. We were soon at the station. Hashimoto emerged from the shadows round the entrance to greet me as I stumbled out of the taxi. 'Are you OK, Lance?' he asked, squinting at me through the lamplight.

'How do I look?'

'Not particularly good.'

'You amaze me.'

'There is a café at the next corner. We will talk there.'

'We could have talked in the bar at the Adlon.'

'But there is more to do than talk. Come.'

He steered me across the road and down to the next

131

junction. The turning to the right was Yorckstrasse. Hashimoto caught my glance at the sign, but didn't explain until we were huddled round a table in the café, with tea and beer ordered. (The tea wasn't for me.)

'I decided to see where the Townleys live. It is a little way along Yorckstrasse.' He nodded in the general direction. 'An apartment block. Expensive, I would say. The main door opened when I turned the handle, so I—'

'You went in? You mad impulsive devil, you.'

'The Townleys are in flat four. I thought I would . . .' He shrugged. 'I don't know.'

'It might have made more sense for us to plan this together, Kiyo.' (Why I was so calm about it I wasn't sure. Still half-drunk, I supposed.)

'You are right, Lance. I am sorry. I did not think I could do any harm.'

'And did you?'

'No. No harm. Perhaps good. As I was climbing the stairs towards flat four, the door opened and a man came out.'

'Erich Townley?'

'I think it must be. Right age. Right . . . appearance.'

'What is the right appearance?'

'You will see for yourself.'

'How's that?'

'We passed on the stairs, but I doubled back and followed him out into the street. Do not worry. He did not see me.'

'I hope you're right.'

'I am. Trust me, Lance.'

'I'm not sure you're making it easy.'

'Listen.' Hashimoto lowered his voice and leaned

across the table towards me. 'I followed Townley to a bar a little way down Mehringdamm. I think he is still there now. It is a chance to speak to him. To ask him questions when he thinks all you are doing is—'

' *"You"?* '

'It will go better if you approach him, Lance. I am too . . . conspicuous.'

'A second ago you were telling me how he hadn't noticed you.'

'But we *need* him to notice. You. Not me. It will be easier for you.'

'Easier for me to do what?'

'Just talk to him.'

Hashimoto gave me what I think he meant to be an encouraging smile, but it came out as more of an anxious grimace. Though as far as anxiety went I reckoned I might soon be ahead of him. 'Your "plan" is for me to try to chat him up, is it?'

'Chat him up?'

'You know what I mean.'

'Ah yes. I see. Well . . .' Hashimoto spread his arms. 'The thing is, Lance . . .'

'Yeh?'

'I think you might be his type.'

The bar was as close as Hashimoto had promised. Big blank windows somehow failed to reveal as much as a first glance suggested they might. The interior looked dark, half empty and faintly mournful. (It was reassuring, in a way, to realize that Sunday evenings in Germany weren't much jollier than in England.) Hashimoto took himself off to hover at a bus stop on the other side of the street. Leaving me, after some hesitation, to go in.

A bloke matching Hashimoto's description of the man on the stairs was sitting on a bar stool drinking some colourless spirit or other and smoking a fat French cigarette. He was wearing jeans and a white shirt under a three-quarter-length black coat that the sticky warmth of the place hadn't persuaded him to take off. He was tall and thin, knees jutting, back and head bent like an anglepoise lamp. (The bar was clearly built for stockier customers.) His face was lined and drawn, his hair too grey and long for someone so thin on top. I didn't yet know if I was his type, but I was already absolutely certain that he wasn't mine.

The rest of the clientele was scattered around the shadow-cowled tables. Several of them looked pretty stoned. Best way to appreciate the Gothic décor, I supposed, not to mention the New Age funeral-march music seeping out of the cobwebbed loudspeakers. Maybe it got livelier later. And maybe I didn't want to be there when it did.

I plonked myself on the stool next to Townley (he was the only customer sitting at the bar), ordered a Budweiser and ran a few possible chat-up lines past myself. I didn't reckon I was going to be able to force any of them out until I was too drunk to remember Townley's response – if I was lucky enough to get one. The situation had all the makings of a grade-one fiasco. (And whose fault was that?) Then a strange thing happened. Townley spoke to me.

'You American?' (He obviously was, albeit with a clipped vein of *Mitteleuropa* in the gravelly drawl.)

'No,' I tried to reply, but my throat wouldn't co-operate until I'd repeated the word twice. 'No, no.'

'Can't imagine why anybody who wasn't American would order a Bud. Real horse piss.'

'I didn't know there was anything real about it.'

He laughed at that. 'You're English, right?'

'Yeh.' The Budweiser arrived, glassless and gleaming. I took a swig. 'And you're American.'

'I'd have to own to that, yuh. *Half* American, anyways.'

'And the other half?'

'Local.'

'You live here?'

'Yuh. But you're just visiting, right? Vacation?'

'Business.'

'What kind?'

That was a tricky one. 'Does it matter?' (I had to hope it didn't.) 'This is still the weekend.'

'Not that you'd know it, huh?' He glanced around. 'Deader than the Third Reich.'

'How long have you lived in Berlin?'

'Quite a while.'

'My name's Lance, by the way.'

'Pleased to meet you, Lance. I'm Erich.' He shrugged. 'Born Eric. Straddling two nations makes you kinda schizo.'

'I suppose it must.'

'Smoke?' He offered me one of his cigarettes.

'No thanks. I, er . . .'

'Believe the Surgeon-General's warning.'

'Yeh, but . . .' I caught his gaze and tried to hold it. 'Do I look like I lead a clean and pure life?'

'Not exactly. No one could in here, though.'

135

'I've got nothing against vice, Erich.' I unveiled a less than heartfelt smile. 'Nothing at all.'

'You've come to the right city, then. Berlin's got it all, if you don't mind delving into dark corners.'

'Depends what I'm likely to find there.'

'Whatever you're looking for.'

'Sometimes I'm not sure.'

'Maybe you need a helping hand.'

'Maybe I do.' (This was all going too fast for my liking. What had Hashimoto got me into?) 'There are lots of things a guidebook doesn't tell you.'

'Doesn't *dare* to tell you.'

'Worried about scaring people off, I suppose.'

'Tough on those who like to be scared.' He paused for effect. And the effect was quite something. 'Just a little.'

'Yeh.'

'So, is this a walk on the wild side for you, Lance? A nibble at forbidden fruit away from the wife and kids?'

'I don't have any family.'

'That's smart of you. Neither do I. Apart from my mother. Everyone has to have one of those.'

'Plus a father.'

'Technically, I guess.'

'Is your mother German?'

'Yuh. She lives here in Berlin.'

'And Dad?'

'He doesn't live in Berlin.' Townley was still smiling, but there was a hardening edge to that smile. I was edging close to dangerous territory.

'But this is where they met?'

'Where people meet isn't important. It's what they do after they meet that matters.'

'True enough.' (Too true, as far as I was concerned.)

'What shall we do? Now *we've* met.'

'What do you recommend?'

'I'd have to know your tastes.'

'They tend to the exotic.'

'Right.' Townley took a long, thoughtful draw on his cigarette, then said, 'There's a place I know. Several places. I reckon you might enjoy them. Interested?'

'Sure.' (Horrified was nearer the mark.)

'Let's go, then.'

'OK.'

'We'll call in on my mother on the way. She lives just round the corner.' (They both did, of course, but I wasn't supposed to know that. Maybe Townley didn't think admitting to living with his mother was likely to impress me. But we *were* going to see her, apparently. It was a puzzle how he meant to deal with that, a puzzle I couldn't help being drawn by.) 'She's expecting me.' (But not me. No, she definitely wasn't expecting me.) 'Don't worry. We won't stay long.'

We turned left as we exited the bar and headed south – *away* from Yorckstrasse. Not that I could share my concern on the point with Townley. Nor could I risk looking back to see if Hashimoto was following us. I felt stone-cold sober and more than a little perturbed. Which meant, given how far from sober I really was, that I was actually very frightened indeed.

'I had it with the States a long time ago,' said Townley. 'Sooner or later, you have to decide where your soul belongs.'

'And yours belongs here?'

'Absolutely. What about you?'

'Still trying to decide, I suppose.'

'Well, you're younger than me, aren't you? How much younger, I wonder?'

'Er, that would depend on how old you are, Erich.'

'So it would.' Townley chuckled. 'That's what I love about strangers. There's a whole . . . back-story . . . waiting to be told.'

We turned right at the next junction, which was a relief. Maybe, I thought, this was the quickest route to the part of Yorckstrasse the Townleys lived in. Then again, maybe not, because Townley immediately crossed to the other side of the street and started along a path that led straight into the ill-lit heart of a public park.

'We'll cut through here,' my companion said, as if it explained everything. I had an impression of a wooded slope ahead of us. Dim, widely spaced lamps shone thinly on ponds and rockeries. The way was dark and winding. Soon, we'd begun to climb. I dragged my feet, to little effect. What I wanted to do was the one thing I couldn't afford to do: turn back. 'Keep up, Lance. It'd be easy to get lost in here.'

'Are you sure we aren't already?'

'Oh yuh. I know my way.'

'Glad to hear it.'

'What line of work did you say you were in?'

'I . . . didn't, did I?'

'Maybe you didn't at that. So, let me guess. Could it be . . . shipping?'

'Shipping? No. What—'

I'm not sure what I saw or sensed first. A blur of

night-shrouded movement. A scuff of shoe on asphalt. Something, anyway, brought almost instantly into focus by a sharp pain as my right arm was jerked up behind me. I was pulled backwards, struggling to stay on my feet. A hand closed around my throat – tight and choking. Try as I might to prise it away, I couldn't. Townley was strong – far stronger than me. I felt the heat of his breath close to my ear and the steely hardness of his grasp. I tried to wrench myself free, but he held me fast, with a sort of practised ease that told me no amount of struggling would shake him off.

I tried to cry out for help. But all I managed was a hoarse splutter. We stopped moving.

'You are one dumb shit, Lance. You know that? You sidle up to me, all dewy-eyed and simpering, thinking I'm about to fall for your hollow-chested English charm. Do me a favour. Do yourself one. You're looking for your friend Rupe, right?'

His grip relaxed just enough to let me speak. 'All right . . . Yes, I am.'

'Well, you're all out of luck. Because Rupe isn't here. And you're never going to find him.' There was a noise behind me, thin and metallic – a blade being flicked from a handle. 'Your search is over, lover boy.' He released my right arm and in the same instant grasped my left shoulder and yanked me round to face him.

All I had time to do was crouch forward to protect myself. It was nothing more than an instinct. I expected Townley to come at me with the knife. Into my mind flashed the acute but unhelpful awareness that I was about to be stabbed. But I never was.

Something struck Townley under his right arm –

something powerful, moving horizontally. He grunted and fell sideways, hitting the ground hard. As he did so, I straightened up and saw Hashimoto slowly lowering his left leg. He'd dealt Townley some sort of judo kick – the sort that felt like a battering ram, to judge by the effect on its victim. Townley rolled onto his side, shaking his head as he propped himself up on one elbow.

'Stay where you are,' Hashimoto shouted. (I couldn't work out for the moment which of us he meant, so I played safe by standing stock-still.) 'Are you all right, my friend?'

'Yes. I . . .'

'Who the fuck are you?' rasped Townley.

'Someone capable of breaking your arm or dislocating your shoulder – or both – should you force me to do so.' (Hashimoto sounded hellish convincing to me, as I reckoned he probably did to Townley.) 'You have an opportunity to walk away. I suggest you take it.'

Warily and unsteadily, Townley scrambled to his feet, breathing hard. 'Interfering bastard,' he muttered.

'Go on along the path. Leave the park on the far side. We will leave the way you came in. Do not attempt to follow us.'

'You're a Jap,' said Townley. 'A fucking Jap.'

'And you are a violent and foul-mouthed man. It would be no hardship to knock a few of your teeth out. Why do you seem intent on giving me the excuse to do so?'

Townley looked at me, then at Hashimoto, then back to me. 'Do you know each other?'

'Go now,' said Hashimoto, quietly but firmly.

Townley hesitated, taking the measure of himself and

his opponent. There was bluff on both sides. But who was the bigger bluffer? I wouldn't have wanted to bet on it. And nor, apparently, would Townley. 'Fuckers,' he said, almost as a protest. Then he pocketed the knife, turned on his heel and strode away, with a parting toss of his head.

It wasn't until we were back in the café at the corner of Mehringdamm and Yorckstrasse that I stopped shaking like a fever case and became capable – thanks to two large brandies – of something approximating to coherent speech.

'He was going to kill me, Kiyo. Do you realize that?'

'It certainly seemed probable.'

'How can you be so bloody calm about it?'

'It is my nature.'

'Thank Christ you turn out to be some kind of black-belt judoist.'

'In truth, I never progressed beyond the pupil classes. I was a great disappointment to my instructor. But I remember how to kick. For the rest, it is as well that Townley did not put my technique to the test.'

'Now he tells me.'

'Would you have preferred me to mention it in Townley's presence?'

I released a long, sincerely felt sigh. 'I'd have *preferred* not to be in his presence at all.'

'But, Lance, think how much we have gained.'

I did think – for a moment. 'I can't see that we've gained a single bloody thing. We've learned nothing. And now he's on to us. Plus my shoulder may never work properly again.' I flexed the joint painfully.

'You are forgetting this.' Hashimoto slipped something from his pocket and jiggled it in his palm. It was a silver cigarette lighter. 'See the engraving?' He held it up to the light and I made out three intertwined and curlicued initials on the back: *E.S.T.* 'Eric Stephen Townley, I believe.'

'Where did you get that?'

'It must have fallen out of his coat while he was on the ground. He did not notice it. But I did.'

'I don't remember you picking anything up.'

'You were not at your most observant, Lance. Understandably. Fortunately . . .'

'Your night vision's on a par with your kick-boxing.'

'It is Townley's lighter. That is what matters. It is evidence against him. And I can swear that I intervened to prevent him stabbing you.'

'Swear? What are you talking about?'

'I am talking about how it would look for Townley if we reported this incident to the police.'

'Are you crazy? How would it look for *me*? And how the bloody hell would it get us what we want – the whereabouts of Townley senior?'

'You are not listening, Lance. *If* we reported it to the police. Obviously we do not wish to do so. But it is a question of . . . pressure.'

'Well, I've had enough pressure for one night.'

'Likewise Townley, I would think. Where do you suppose he is now?'

I shrugged. 'Soothing his bruised pride in some bar or other, trying not to worry about who we are and what we're up to – and what's become of his precious cigarette lighter.'

'Not home with Mother?'

'I doubt it. He was just leading me on with that story of going round to see her.'

'I doubt it also. Which means we have an opportunity to apply some pressure to Mrs Townley, before her son can warn her against us.'

'You don't mean—'

'Yes, Lance.' He had the temerity to smile at me. 'We have a call to make.'

Hashimoto's strategy, so he explained to me, was based on the reality of our situation. Rupe had been here before us, enabling Erich Townley to guess at once what I was up to. How much Erich knew wasn't clear, but his crack about Hashimoto being a 'Jap' hadn't just been a racist jibe. It meant something to him. It was significant. And it blew our cover, such as it was. Softly, softly consequently wasn't going to catch our monkey. Which left what Hashimoto called 'the frontal approach'.

Number 85 Yorckstrasse was a classy-looking neo-Gothic apartment block, heavy on balconies, porticoes and reclining caryatids. The door – a sumptuously carved affair – was firmly closed. (Maybe Hashimoto had just got lucky earlier, or maybe the time had come for the securing of entrances; it was gone nine o'clock, after all.) Hashimoto pressed the Townleys' buzzer, got no prompt reply, then left his finger on it for just as long as it took – half a minute or so – for the entry-phone to splutter into life.

'Ja?'

'Frau Townley?'

'*Ja.*' (The admission came slowly and cautiously.)

'Is Erich in?'

'He is not here.' (The mixture of German and American in her accent made her tone hard to interpret.)

'We need to speak to you about Erich.'

'Who are you?'

'He is in serious trouble, Frau Townley. It will become more serious if you do not speak to us.'

'I do not understand.'

'Then let us in. And we will explain.'

'Go away.'

'If we do, we will go to the police.'

'*Polizei?*' (Now she sounded worried.)

'They will arrest Erich.'

'What for?'

'Let us in.'

'Why should I?'

'Because you must. For Erich's sake.'

There was a lengthy silence.

'Frau Townley?'

Then the door-release buzzed.

We climbed the broad, marble-treaded stairs past stained-glass landing windows to a tall, double-doored apartment entrance on the second floor. One of the doors stood ajar and peering at us through the gap as we approached was Rosa Townley.

She was no querulous, quavering old biddy, that was for sure. She wasn't as tall as her son, but I'd have bet she towered over most German women of her generation. She held herself well too, shoulders back, jaw square, eyes glaring above high cheekbones and a broad nose. Hers was the kind of face that actually improved with age. Her hair was thick, grey streaked with black, where once it must have been black streaked with grey and before that a pure raven black. Her clothes were black too – a polo-necked sweater and trousers (cashmere and silk, I'd have guessed); simple but far from casual.

'Who are you?' she demanded, grasping the door handle firmly.

'My name is Miyamoto,' said Hashimoto. (It was as much as I could do not to flinch with surprise. Had I missed the announcement that we'd be operating under aliases?) 'This is Mr Bradley.' (Ah, so I apparently *wasn't* operating under one.)

'You are not friends of my son.'

'Do you know all his friends, Frau Townley?'

'I know the type.' (I silently thanked her for the back-handed compliment.)

'May we come in?'

'You have not stated your business.'

'A cigarette lighter.' Hashimoto held it up for her inspection. 'Dropped by your son as he fled after I had intervened to prevent him stabbing Mr Bradley.'

'You are lying.'

'No.'

'What do you want?'

'We want to offer you a way to resolve this matter without reference to the police.'

'Money?'

'No.'

'What, then?'

'It is complicated.' Hashimoto smiled at her. 'Let us in and we will explain.'

The drawing room was as elegant and uncluttered as I'd have expected of Rosa Townley's living space. Polished wood, soft leather and two gleaming chandeliers. You'd have had to call in Forensics to find a speck of dust. Even the King Charles spaniel who eyed us from a cushioned berth on the sofa looked as if he'd been recently shampooed. I didn't doubt this was Rosa's exclusive domain (shared with the dog, of course). Erich probably kept to his own contrastingly styled quarters. (I'd been worrying about what might happen if he returned while we were there, but, oddly, now I'd met his mother, I didn't feel worried at all.)

There was no invitation to sit. To do her justice, Rosa didn't show any inclination to sit down herself. She stationed herself by the fireplace and waited to hear what we had to say. I scanned the mantelpiece behind her for family photographs. Not a one. But the mirror above it looked expensive. So did just about everything else in the room. Whatever the Townleys were short of, it wasn't money.

'Earlier this evening, Frau Townley,' said Hashimoto, 'your son assaulted Mr Bradley in Viktoriapark.' (My God, the man even knew the name of the park. You couldn't fault him for thoroughness.) 'He had his reasons, though he would find them difficult to explain to the police. They would probably infer . . . a sexual motive. We could encourage them to do so if we wished. But we do not wish to do that. Unless you force us to.'

146

'Tell me what you want.' Her voice was hard and unwavering, her logic impeccable.

'We want to know where your husband is.'

She should have looked taken aback. But there was no reaction. Maybe she'd seen it coming. 'My husband is dead.'

'We do not think so.'

'He is dead.'

'How do you finance your life here, Mrs Townley?' I chipped in. 'Not to mention Erich's?'

'What business is that of yours?'

'You don't work, I assume. And Erich certainly doesn't seem the industrious type. So, where's the money coming from? Oil-rich son-in-law? Maybe. Or maybe a not-so-dead husband.'

'Rupert Alder came looking for your husband,' said Hashimoto. 'We know this. What did you tell him?'

'I have never heard of Rupert Alder.'

'Your son has.'

'Eloquent on the subject, he was,' I helped out.

'It is simple, Frau Townley,' said Hashimoto. 'If your husband is dead, or if you continue to insist that he is, we will go to the police. But if he is alive, as we believe, and you are willing to tell us where we can find him . . .'

Without taking her eyes off us, Rosa stretched out a hand behind her to a silver box on the mantelpiece. She raised the lid on a neatly columned stack of cigarettes, took one out, put it to her lips and cocked her eyebrows at Hashimoto. He hesitated, then stepped forward, struck Erich's lighter at the second attempt and lit the cigarette.

We waited. Rosa inhaled deeply and exhaled with

studied slowness. There was one more, shallower, draw on the cigarette before she said, 'You do not understand.'

'Make us,' I challenged her.

'Mr Alder came here, as you say, wanting to know how he could find Stephen.'

'I thought you'd never heard of Rupe.'

'That was untrue. I apologize. But your threats . . . confused me.' (She had a funny way of seeming confused.) 'He came. Without threats.'

'Really?'

'Without threats to Erich and me. As for Stephen, how can you threaten a dead man? I told Mr Alder what I have told you. Stephen is dead.'

'Did he believe you?'

'No. No more than you.'

'Can't say I'm surprised.'

'He wanted me to pass on a message to Stephen.'

'What message?'

'He said he had a letter containing damaging information about Stephen's activities in the summer and fall of nineteen sixty-three. He refused to say what the information was. If Stephen wanted to prevent the contents of the letter becoming public, he was to contact Mr Alder.' She shrugged. 'I told him there was nothing I could do. I told him Stephen was dead. He asked for proof. He expressed the same doubts as you.'

'And you could prove it?'

'No. I have had no contact with my husband of any kind for the past thirty-eight years.'

'Then you can't know he's dead, can you?'

148

'*I* know, Mr Bradley.' She did her considerable best to stare me down. 'To *my* satisfaction.'

'Based on what?'

She devoted a lengthy moment to her cigarette, then treated us to a heavy sigh. 'Very well. I told Mr Alder. I will tell you. I have a friend from childhood – Hilde Voss. She came to my wedding. She knew Stephen well. She knew him before he . . . lost himself.' (I wanted to ask what she meant by that, but it seemed best to let her continue.) 'Hilde still lives in Berlin. I see her often. She is a good friend. But there is something you must understand about her. She has . . . second sight.'

'Oh for God's—'

'It is true. It has many times been demonstrated. Whether you believe it or not is unimportant. It *is* true. Hilde wrote to me a long time ago, when I was still living in the United States, to tell me that she had . . . seen Stephen's death.'

'Where?' asked Hashimoto. 'When?'

Rosa looked at him witheringly. 'I did not mean *seen* literally. Hilde has . . . astral vision.'

'Well,' I prompted, 'what did she see . . . astrally?'

'Stephen died. Violently, nearly thirty years ago.'

'Care to be more precise?'

'I cannot be. Hilde wrote to me . . . some time in nineteen seventy-two. That is all.'

'And that's all you told Rupe?'

'There was nothing more I could tell him. He still did not believe me, of course.'

'Of course.'

'So, he went to see Hilde. She told me later of his visit. I did not hear from him again.'

'Come off it.'

'I did not hear from him again, Mr Bradley.'

'What did Hilde say about his visit?'

'She said she thought she had convinced him.'

'Convinced him? Come on. You surely don't expect me to swallow that.'

'I have no expectation either way.'

'*We* will see Frau Voss,' said Hashimoto.

'Please do. I can give you her address and telephone number. As I gave them to Mr Alder.'

'Hold on.' It was all too pat. And in one important respect it just didn't fit. 'Why was Erich so hostile if Rupe's visit turned out as innocently as you say?'

'Perhaps you annoyed him. Erich is . . . easily annoyed.'

'He tried to kill me.'

'No, no. He must have meant merely to frighten you. That is all.'

'You weren't there.'

'No. But you *are* here, alive and well.'

'Only because—'

'Excuse me,' Hashimoto interrupted. 'This is pointless. We will speak to Frau Voss. After that . . . I do not know. We still have Erich's cigarette lighter. Do not forget that, Frau Townley. If you leave us no alternative, we will go to the police with it.'

'I understand.'

'I doubt Frau Voss will be able to convince *us*.'

'And *I* doubt she convinced Rupe,' I put in.

'You doubt,' said Rosa, giving me a contemptuous glare through a plume of cigarette smoke. 'Yes. That is certainly clear.'

CHAPTER EIGHT

I made it to the bar of the Adlon in the end. So did Hashimoto. As it happened, he might have been better off leaving me to it, because I was soon in the mood to tell him how badly I thought he'd managed the evening. And he, fair-minded fellow that he was, felt compelled to agree.

'Rosa Townley is a cunning woman, Lance. I wanted above all to avoid giving her time to think. But that is exactly what she has achieved by referring us to her friend the clairvoyant. It is not how I had expected it to be.'

'Nothing's been how *I* expected since we arrived,' I complained. 'I could have died tonight.'

'I would never have allowed Erich Townley to harm you.'

'What if you'd lost us in the dark?'

'I did not lose you.'

'You promised, before we left London, that we'd do nothing without discussing it first.'

'There is such a thing . . . as seizing the initiative.'

'In that case, I suggest we go to the police without

151

waiting to hear what Madame Blavatsky has to say. How'd that be for seizing the initiative?'

'It would not be wise.'

'He held a knife to my throat, Kiyo. That's the sort of thing you're *supposed* to report to the police.'

'He never actually—'

'Well, he would have done, believe me.'

'But will *they* believe you?'

'Of course, with you to back—' I stopped and stared at him. 'You would back me up, wouldn't you, Kiyo?'

Hashimoto gave me a helpless look that left me feeling more helpless still. 'We will speak to Frau Voss tomorrow and decide what to do after that.'

'I see.'

'I am sorry, Lance.'

'Of course.'

'I do not believe what Rosa Townley told us.'

'I should hope not.'

'But even so . . .'

'Yes?'

'It *is* . . . remotely possible.'

'What is?'

'That she may be' – he winced as he spoke – 'telling the truth.'

Things look better in daylight, so they say. There was certainly plenty of daylight around when I surfaced late the following morning. The Berlin sky was cloudless, the air crisp and clear. I stumbled down to breakfast, reflecting that maybe the literal dead end Rosa Townley had offered us was the truth after all – and that maybe it was best it should be. Where that left

Rupe was a moot point, of course. But knife-wielding nutters definitely weren't my company of choice, so it was tempting to think that moment to quit I'd told Echo hadn't yet arrived . . . was just about to.

It was a surprise to find Hashimoto in the restaurant, sipping tea and leafing through the European edition of the *Wall Street Journal*. I had him down as a dawn break-faster. To be honest, I'd been looking forward to forking my way through some bacon and eggs with only my thoughts – such as they were – for company. I did my best not to look disappointed.

'How are you feeling, Lance?' Hashimoto enquired.

'Not sure. How do I look?'

'In the circumstances, quite good.' He smiled weakly. 'I have been busy.'

'You surprise me.'

'I have spoken to Frau Voss.'

'Have you now?'

'Frau Townley had already done so, of course.'

'Preparing the ground, no doubt.'

'No doubt. But . . . we shall see. We are to meet Frau Voss for tea this afternoon.'

'I'm sure it'll be a charming occasion.'

'Are you being . . . sarcastic, Lance?'

'Can't imagine why you should think that.'

'Mmm.' He eyed me thoughtfully. 'I know the perfect antidote to sarcasm.'

'You do?'

'Yes. And between now and tea with Frau Voss . . . I think I will administer it to you.'

An hour and a half later, we were clambering out of a

153

taxi in front of two stone elephants flanking the entrance to Berlin Zoo. 'Animals, Lance,' Hashimoto announced, as we queued at the ticket office. 'They clear our minds of all the nonsense we fill them with.'

'If you say so, Kiyo.'

'Did you not have a pet when you were a child?'

'No.'

'Why not?'

'We just weren't that kind of family.' (I dimly recalled a dog being debated at some point. My father vetoed the idea on the grounds that I was nuisance enough around the house without some pooch to feed and walk.) 'You?'

'No.' Hashimoto shook his head sadly. 'There was no room.'

'Domestic quarters at the Golden Rickshaw a bit of a squash, were they?'

'Oh yes. But . . .' He puffed out his cheeks. 'I still miss those days, even so.'

The tone was set. Hashimoto veered between nostalgic yearnings for a lost childhood and rapt gapings at the animals as we trailed around the zoo. The thought that flitted across my mind – seen one manically depressed tiger aching for a chance to rip your throat out, seen them all – went unexpressed. As a way to kill time, I supposed it wasn't too bad, though I could have thought of better. But there was no magical mind-clearing of the kind Hashimoto had promised. I was immune.

But Hashimoto wasn't. And that, I belatedly realized, was the point. We were there more for his benefit than mine. He was particularly drawn to the orang-utans.

Gazing at them as they lolloped around their enclosure, sometimes hiding under pieces of sacking, sometimes casting us soulful glances, he suddenly said to me, 'What really matters in life, Lance?'

'Happiness, I guess.'

'And what makes us happy?'

'Oh, the usual stuff.'

'What would be usual . . . for an orang-utan?'

'Oh, I don't know. Money's out. Travel too, for this lot. Drink and drugs aren't on the agenda either. There's sex, I suppose . . . in the season. And feeding time. At all seasons.'

Hashimoto frowned solemnly at me. 'You are confusing happiness with pleasure, Lance.'

'Am I?'

'Do you think they trust each other?'

'Orang-utanishly . . . yeh.'

'They do not tell lies?'

'Well, they can't, can they?'

'But we can.'

'Yeh.'

'It is our choice.'

'Yeh.'

'So, I choose not to.'

'Well, that's good.'

'I know what is in the Townley letter.'

For a moment, I thought I had to have misheard. 'What?'

'I know what is in the Townley letter,' he repeated.

'But . . . you said . . .'

'I lied.'

'Bloody hell.' I stared at him, genuinely aggrieved.

155

'I am sorry.'

I waited for him to continue, but he showed no sign of doing so, returning his placid gaze to the orangutans. 'Kiyo,' I prompted.

'Yes, Lance?'

'Apology accepted, OK?'

'Thank you.'

'What's in the letter?'

'Ah.' He nodded slowly. 'Of course. That is the trouble with telling the truth.' Then he smiled. 'It does not always make you happy.'

We went to the snack-bar, bought a couple of hot drinks and sat outside by an ornamental lake. It was too cold in the milky sunlight for the other customers. We had the lakeside seats to ourselves. Hashimoto lit a cigarette and huddled down into his coat. I waited as patiently as I could for him to tell me what I obviously wanted to hear.

Eventually, he said, 'This is the truth, Lance.'

'Good.' There was a long pause. 'Well?'

'I cannot tell you.'

'*What?*'

'My sister told me. Because she had to. She never would have done if Rupe had not stolen the letter. She would have kept it secret . . . for ever.'

'Since Rupe *did* steal it, don't you think *I* ought to be told?'

'No. For everyone who knows, there is the danger that they will tell. I promised Mayumi I would keep her secret. And I was taught to keep my promises. But I do not have to lie to you to do that.'

'I'm really glad you're off the hook, Kiyo. No lie, no tell. That's just great.'

'Now you are being sarcastic again.'

'That surprises you, does it?'

'No. It disappoints me.'

'So, we're both disappointed.'

'You should not be. When Mayumi told me what the letter contained, I was angry. I did not welcome the knowledge. It is a burden I would prefer not to bear. I do not want to inflict it on you. You are better off – you are *safer* – not knowing.'

'I'll just have to take your word for that.'

'You must trust me, Lance. We must trust each other. If we find Stephen Townley . . .' He sighed. 'Then I will tell you what is in the letter.'

'Breaking your promise?'

'Yes. Because then . . .' He looked past me, into some future he seemed to see more clearly than me. 'Then I will have to.'

Pressing Kiyofumi Hashimoto to reveal what he'd decided to keep to himself was likely to be about as rewarding as trying to persuade a captive tiger to look contented. We called a truce on the subject and paid a visit to the aquarium before leaving the zoo.

We emerged into the early-afternoon bustle of the shopping centre of West Berlin. I recognized the ruined tower of the Kaiser-Wilhelm-Gedächtniskirche from my 1984 trip with Rupe and took Hashimoto into the new octagonal church next door to admire the encircling blue glass walls. We sat there in silence, lost in our own

157

thoughts, till our appointment with Hilde Voss drew near and it was time to go.

As we started down Kurfürstendamm towards the Café Kranzler, Hashimoto glanced back at the bomb-blasted relic and its ultra-modern successor. 'My sister remembers the bombing in Tokyo at the end of the war,' he said. 'She thinks I am lucky not to have been born sooner.'

'She's probably right.'

'But only probably. I always tell her: the future will show whether I was lucky to be born when I was.'

'Can't argue with that.'

'No one can argue with the future, Lance.'

'Just as well we don't know what it contains, then.'

'Oh, yes.' He nodded thoughtfully. 'It truly is . . . just as well.'

Our immediate future lay in the hands of Hilde Voss. She was waiting for us when we reached the Kranzler – a small, bright-eyed woman in a long red coat, with a flowing scarf, a purple beret and far too many rings and bangles. Physically, she hadn't aged as well as her old friend Rosa Townley. She looked, in fact, about ten years older, despite the dyed hair visible under the beret. The cigarettes she was coughing her way through at a sapping pace had to be one of the reasons. Mentally, however, she was in good shape.

'I told Rosa you wouldn't believe me,' she announced as soon as our tea had arrived. 'Why should you? I am her friend, not yours.'

'Tell me about Stephen Townley,' said Hashimoto mildly. 'We . . . are open-minded.'

'Open-minded?' She laughed uproariously at that until the cough doubled her up.

'How would you describe him?' I asked.

'Stephen? He was a good-looking boy. And Americans, here in the Fifties, well, they were the boys to go for. But Stephen . . .' She shrugged. 'I never trusted him.'

'Why not?'

'Because there was darkness in his heart. I see these things. I sense them. I always have. Rosa saw only . . . the handsome face, the broad shoulders . . . and the passport to the land of cookies and Cadillacs.'

'You're saying he was an evil man?'

'He had evil in him. And it came out. He did not . . . treat her well. But . . . he took her to America, which is what she wanted.'

'Except that now she's back here.'

'What we want changes as we grow older.'

'When did you last see him?' asked Hashimoto.

'Stephen? When he and Rosa left for America in nineteen fifty-five.'

'Never since?'

'Never.'

'Quite a while,' I said, not bothering to disguise the thought that led to.

'A long time, a short time. For me it makes no difference.'

'Come on. You can't claim to have known him well.'

'*Nein*. But you couldn't forget Stephen once you'd met him. He stayed with you.'

'At least until nineteen seventy-two.'

'I see people in dreams. I see events. It is not my fault.

159

Believe me, *mein Junge*, it is more of a curse than a blessing.'

'What did you *dream* about Townley?'

'His death. May second, nineteen seventy-two.'

'You know the exact date?'

'I looked it up. I keep a record of my dreams. You want to see?' She pulled a dog-eared diary out of her handbag. I could see the year embossed on the cover. A page was marked. She held it open in front of us. We craned forward as her index finger tapped at the place. *Dienstag 2 Mai.* Below that, in tiny handwriting, was the phrase *Todestraum: S.T.* 'Dream of death,' she said slowly. 'Stephen Townley.'

'Well, that clinches it, of course.'

'Believe me or not,' Hilde snapped the diary shut. 'I don't care.'

'How did you see him die?' asked Hashimoto.

'Why do you want to know, if you don't believe I did?'

'You may be able to convince us.'

'I doubt it.' She put the diary back into her handbag and rattled her way through another cough. Oddly, it seemed to calm her down. Her gaze drifted out of focus. 'Somewhere hot. Florida. Mexico. I don't know. There were palm trees. And sweat on the faces of the men who killed him. It was night there too. They had . . . long knives. They cut him deep. There was much blood. He died badly. In much pain. The hot blood drained out of him, into the hot night. I saw it.' She shuddered. 'I felt it.'

Hashimoto glanced at me, looking to see what my instinctive reaction was. I'm not sure I had one. It sounded convincing enough, whether you bought the whole second-sight thing or not. But Hilde was no fool.

And Rosa certainly wasn't. They were capable of cooking this up between them – well capable.

'Is this what you told Mr Alder?' Hashimoto asked.

'*Ja*. That is what I told him.'

'How did he react?'

'He did not say much. He listened. He went away.'

'Did he believe you?'

'I think . . . he did not want to believe me. But later . . . he may have.'

'Did he contact you again?'

'There was only one meeting.'

'When was that?' I chipped in.

'Early September.'

'Can't you be more precise? A lady who keeps such meticulous records as you . . .'

She sighed theatrically and fished her current diary out of her handbag, then propped some half-moon glasses on her nose to consult the entries. 'The sixth,' she announced after a few moments.

'And where did you meet?'

Another sigh. 'Here.'

'This very café?' I glanced around, as if trying to picture the scene.

'*Ja*,' growled Hilde, pitching her voice low enough to set off another cough.

'Where is he now?' I asked when the cough had subsided.

'*Wovon reden Sie?*' She stared at me uncomprehendingly.

'I'm asking you where Rupe Alder is now, Frau Voss. With your powers of clairvoyance, that should be no problem, surely.'

'You think you are funny, *mein Junge*?'

'Perish the thought.'

'I do not order the things I see. I do not control them. Your friend, Herr Alder, he . . .' She swatted at some invisible fly – or at me. 'He has not come to me. Living or dead.'

'Pity. I was hoping you might be able to clear the whole mystery up for us. But I was obviously hoping for too much.'

'*Ja.*' Hilde stubbed out her cigarette violently and eyed me across the butt-choked ashtray. 'Much too much.'

'What do you think?' I asked, as soon as we were out of the café, leaving Hilde to her cakes and cigarettes and astral visions.

'I do not know, Lance,' said Hashimoto. 'The important question is: what would Rupe have thought?'

'Same as me. That she's an old fraud.'

'You do not believe she has . . . second sight?'

'Nope.'

'The diary entry from nineteen seventy-two was . . . impressive.'

'Well, it didn't impress me.'

'Mmm.'

'Kiyo?'

He stopped and looked at me. 'It is less straightforward than you seem to think, Lance.'

'How?'

'Frau Voss may have seen this vision and believed it proved Stephen Townley was dead. Frau Townley may have believed it also. Whether it is true or not – whether he actually died in the way she described, whether he is

162

dead at all – is not really the point. If they genuinely believe it, then obviously Frau Townley does not know where we can find her husband. In that case . . .'

He shook his head, but said no more. He didn't have to, of course. The conclusion was as obvious as it was dismal. In that case . . . we were wasting our time. And had been since boarding the plane to Berlin.

I didn't see it that way. During the taxi ride back to the Adlon, I reminded Hashimoto that Erich Townley had shown every sign of meaning to kill me in Viktoriapark. Why – unless questions about his father posed some kind of threat to him? And what kind of a threat could that be if Erich genuinely believed his father to be dead? Hashimoto did not know any more than I did.

Which left us clean out of bright ideas about what to do next. We probably made a disconsolate pair as we plodded into the Adlon and asked for our keys. And that can only have been an encouraging sight for the visitor who was waiting for us.

Rosa Townley was sitting calm and upright in one of the plush-cushioned armchairs in the centre of the lobby. She was wearing another black outfit and was leafing through a copy of *Vogue*. A Galeries Lafayette carrier-bag was propped beside her chair. She didn't even pretend to be surprised to see us.

'Is your tea party over so soon?' she archly enquired as we perched ourselves on a sofa opposite her.

'How did you know we were staying here?' asked Hashimoto.

'Modern telephones,' she replied with a smile. 'Hilde checked the number from which you rang her. And since I was in the area this afternoon . . .' She nodded faintly towards the carrier-bag, as if to draw our attention to the fact that we were merely an add-on to a shopping expedition. 'I hope Hilde told you what you wanted to know.'

'She told us what *you* wanted us to know,' I said. 'May second, nineteen seventy-two. Men with knives down Mexico way. We got the message.'

'Stephen is dead, Mr Bradley. Long dead. That is the only message.'

'It's the only one being sent, certainly.'

'Do you still not believe it?'

'No.'

'Why not?'

'Because your son wouldn't have been willing to kill me to protect a dead man.'

'Erich has told me exactly what occurred between you and him last night.'

'I'm sure he has.'

'If anyone should be going to the police, it is him, not you. And he may – if you continue to harass us.'

'I can hear the echo.'

She frowned at me. 'What?'

'Inside the hollow threat.'

'Frau Townley,' said Hashimoto with sudden decisiveness, 'you have twenty-four hours to consider your position. If, after that, you still refuse to tell us where we can find your husband . . .' He shrugged, almost apologetically. 'You will leave us no choice.'

'Twenty-four hours will change nothing.'

'I hope it will change your mind.' (Personally, I doubted twenty-four *years* could work that miracle, but

164

I supposed Hashimoto's tactics were sound enough.) 'I am sure none of us wishes to involve the police.'

'Then do not involve them.' Rosa made a strange little tossing movement of the chin, then rose from her chair, prompting us to stand in our turn like obedient nephews seeing off a respected aunt. 'As I have tried to explain to you' – she picked up the carrier-bag, which clearly contained nothing much heavier than a pair of gloves, and slipped her *Vogue* inside – 'it is your decision.'

'An ultimatum, Kiyo,' I murmured to Hashimoto as we watched Rosa's exit from the hotel a few moments later, following the fetching from the cloakroom of her superbly cut cream overcoat. 'Nice move.'

'The only move,' he said expressionlessly.

'Do you reckon it'll work?'

'It might.'

'And if it doesn't?'

He looked round at me and spread his hands helplessly. 'At least we have twenty-four hours to think about it.'

If thinking had to be done, I for one had no intention of starting that evening. Hashimoto had discovered that *The Magic Flute* was on at the Komische Oper and suggested tapping the concierge for tickets. I had to explain that several hours of German opera was the last thing I needed. Leaving Hashimoto to soothe his mind with Mozart, I took myself off to the nearest cinema showing undubbed movies. *American Psycho* didn't turn out to be the kind of entertainment a man in my frazzled state really needed. It took several drinks afterwards in a dire pseudo-Irish pub to restore my equilibrium. Around midnight, mind and body on cruise control, I made it back to the Adlon, confident I wouldn't have to think about anything until morning.

I was wrong.

A letter had been slipped under the door of my room. I picked it up (nearly falling over in the process) and tossed it onto the desk, reckoning it was probably notification of a fire drill or lift repairs or some other managerial nicety I could afford to ignore. Then I noticed a red light glowing on the bedside telephone. *Message waiting.*

I slumped down at the desk and looked at the letter. My name was handwritten in capitals on the envelope – MR BRADLEY – with my room number in the top left corner. I didn't recognize the writing. I tore the flap open. Inside was a leaflet advertising open-top bus tours of Berlin. I'd already seen a couple of the green-and-cream vehicles pictured on the cover cruising round the streets. There was a timetable on a separate sheet of paper that slipped out of the leaflet as I opened it. It listed the fares and departure times from the Europa-Center and the Brandenburg Gate. Someone had circled the 12.15 departure from the Brandenburg Gate in red ink. Strange, I remember thinking; very strange.

I went over to the telephone, picked it up and pressed the MESSAGE button. A computerized voice told me something (in German, of course). There was a brief electronic pause. Then the message kicked in. *'What you've been told is true. I have the letter. I am in Berlin. We must meet. You and me. And Hashimoto. Tomorrow. I will let you know how. Trust me.'*

I sat slowly down on the bed, pressed the receiver until the line was dead, then stabbed at the MESSAGE button and listened to the recording again.

There was no doubt about it. In fact, there hadn't been from the moment I heard the first word. The voice was Rupe's.

CHAPTER NINE

Berlin was locked in perfect weather. The sky was a flawless blue, the air crisp, the sunshine as warm as the shadows were cool. The 12.15 Berlin City Tour bus nudged out from its stand in Pariser Platz and crawled between the scaffolded pillars of the Brandenburg Gate as the hyperactive multilingual guide hopped around at the front of the top deck, microphone in hand, closely attended by a dozen or so tourists of varied nationality. Sitting beside Hashimoto at the back, meanwhile, I gave little thought to the lofty views of historical sites our 25 Deutschmarks had bought.

Where was Rupe? Nowhere to be seen. We were where he'd told us to be. But he wasn't. '*We must meet.*' He was dead right there. '*Tomorrow.*' Well, tomorrow had come. And so had we. But he hadn't. '*Trust me.*' I was trusting him, all right. And Hashimoto was trusting him as well. But not exactly wholeheartedly.

'How can we be sure it is Rupe on the tape?' he'd fired as his first doubting salvo that morning.

'I recognized his voice, Kiyo.'

'Voices can be imitated.'

'I couldn't imitate yours.'

'That is because you are not a trained mimic.'

'For God's sake, it's *him*. I know it is.'

'Let us agree that it probably is. How can we be sure he is not being forced to say these things?'

'Why would anyone want to force us to go on a tourist bus trip round Berlin?'

'I do not know. It does not make sense.'

'Unless it really is Rupe.'

'But he could meet us anywhere, Lance. Why the bus?'

Which was a good question. And the only answer I'd been able to come up with was a disturbing one. The bus was a safe and neutral venue, with witnesses on hand. And Rupe could see who was waiting for him before he got on. In other words, he didn't trust us. Or maybe he couldn't afford to. But if everything the Townleys and their tame tea-leaf reader had told us was true – as Rupe had said it was – why was he as nervous as he obviously was? Why the elaborate precautions?

The message had been recorded at 9.27 p.m. Hashimoto had established that in the process of laying hands on the actual tape. (The concierge had clearly thought we were both mad, but had eventually agreed to extract it from the system for us.) Some time after 9.27 p.m. a letter had been dropped off for me at reception. The receptionist had written my name and room number on the envelope. (She couldn't actually recall doing so, but recognized her own writing.) A bell-boy had then delivered it (presumably). All of which told us . . . very little.

But very little wasn't the same as nothing. Rupe knew

we were in Berlin. How? And he knew which hotel we were staying in. How again? Maybe he was keeping the Townleys under surveillance. Or maybe Hilde Voss was supplying him with information. She was clever enough to be playing a double game. The whys crowded in after that thought, of course; the whys and far too many wherefores. If Rupe had been following us, he'd have known I wouldn't be at the Adlon to take his call. Which implied he hadn't actually wanted to speak to me. The message had been all that mattered.

But he was going to have to speak to me soon. And the bus trip gave him plenty of opportunities. *No need to book*, the timetable declared. *Just jump on*. Well, the route map showed a dozen or more stops on our hour-and-a-half tour. Rupe could be waiting at any one of them. And I had to hope he was. If he let us down . . . If his nerve failed him . . . *'What you've been told is true'*. I'd had that from his own lips. There was nowhere to go after this. My search for Rupe ended here. Even if we didn't find him. Whereas for Hashimoto . . . *'I have the letter'*.

'What's in the letter, Kiyo?' I'd asked him earlier, as we waited for the bus. 'You may as well tell me now. Rupe will, soon enough.'

'As you say. Soon enough.'

'Come on. What's the point in holding out on me?'

'What is the point of a promise?' he'd countered.

'That you keep it, I suppose you mean.'

'No. The *point* is that it is freely given.'

'You're not going to go all Zen on me, are you?'

He'd frowned at me as if genuinely puzzled. 'My friend,' he said with deliberate emphasis, 'I have never been anything else.'

170

Presumably, then, it was some Zen mind-control technique that enabled Hashimoto to remain so much calmer than me as the bus cruised round to the Reichstag, where a giant snake of tourists were queuing to visit the dome, but nobody at all was waiting for the bus. It started to get distinctly chilly as we pressed on through Tiergarten, but our guide was only just warming up, regaling us with tired anecdotes about the places of interest we were passing – in which I took no interest whatsoever, but which Hashimoto apparently greeted with rapt attention.

'We're not out here to see the sights,' I grumbled as the bus slowly circled some draughty triumphal column. 'Keep your eyes peeled for Rupe.'

'He will come to us or not, Lance,' said Hashimoto. 'Looking will not force him into view.'

This was true, of course, but hellishly – if not Zenishly – unhelpful. I kept my eyes peeled. (When they weren't blinking away tears brought on by the cold. Hashimoto, of course, somehow managed to look warm and snug compared with me.) I didn't see Rupe.

Once we were out of Tiergarten and back on city-centre streets, the wind dropped and our pace slowed in the lunchtime traffic. We stopped to take on some people at the Zoo, but Rupe wasn't among them. The guide wittered on about the new church and campanile at Kaiser-Wilhelm-Gedächtniskirche and analysed the revolutionary architecture of the Berlin Stock Exchange. Then we started tracking back east along Kurfürsten-damm, past the Café Kranzler, where we'd met Hilde Voss, the sunlight flashing at us from the large gold letters of its sign. It was pushing towards one o'clock now and the Berliners were out in force, shopping and lunching and bustling about their business. It would be easy, I knew, for one man to lose himself in the crowd, to watch us drift by on the bus, squinting against the sun. This, I supposed, was how Rupe had planned it: for us to show ourselves before he had to decide whether to show *himself*.

We passed Kaiser-Wilhelm-Gedächtniskirche again, this time on the southern side, and drew up at a stop a short distance further along Tauentzienstrasse opposite the Europa-Center, the big shopping complex that was the other timetabled departure point for tours. 'There'll be a break here of twenty minutes,' the guide announced. 'If you want to leave the bus to stretch your legs, be sure to be back by one-fifteen, or you'll have to wait for the next bus, at two-thirty.'

Everybody else on the top deck but Hashimoto and me got off. The guide went down for a fag and a chat with the driver. The tourists wandered off for some window-shopping. 'This could be it,' I said, less convinced than I hoped I sounded. 'Twenty minutes for Rupe to clock us and come aboard.'

'And lots of people to obscure his approach,' said Hashimoto, glancing across at the crowded pavement on the other side of the road. 'You are right. It is the likeliest place. At the moment . . . we have the bus to ourselves.'

There were benches spaced along the grassed and flower-bedded central reservation of Tauentzienstrasse, most of them occupied by workers snatching a takeaway lunch. I craned over the rail and studied each bench in turn. There was no sign of Rupe.

'It would also be a strangely appropriate choice,' Hashimoto went on. 'You see the sculpture?'

'You mean the pipes?' Halfway along the central reservation, four twisted and interwoven metal tubes several feet in diameter reared from the ground in what I took to be an artistic statement. (One I couldn't remember being there in '84 and *of* what I couldn't imagine.)

'The pipes. Yes. Nicknamed "Dancing Spaghetti". Symbols of the divided city, according to my guidebook.'

'How does it make that out?'

'The pipes are intended to represent the severed links of a chain, planted in the earth.'

'Oh yeh?'

'A family is rather like a chain, I think. Something to cling to in times of trouble. But at other times . . . it chafes. Friendship is the same, is it not?'

'I suppose it is.'

'I will treat Rupe leniently, Lance. I will not try to punish him for what he has done.'

'You don't need to be so generous on my account.'

'But he is your friend. And you are *my* friend. Therefore I will help him. I hope you would help Mayumi and Haruko . . . for the same reasons.'

I looked round to find Hashimoto smiling at me. I reckoned this was as gushing as the guy ever got. 'I'd do my best for them, Kiyo. Sure.'

'It is all I ask. Oh—' His smile broadened. 'I nearly forgot the other appropriate thing about "Dancing Spaghetti". The tubes are made of aluminium.'

'Aluminium?'

'According to—'

173

'According to your guidebook, yeh.' I looked back at the sculpture. 'Well, you can be as lenient with my very good friend Rupe Alder as you want, Kiyo, but you'll not have to mind if I tell him exactly what I think of him. Where the bloody hell is he?'

'Close, I suspect. Very—'

Something pierced the air just in front of me and Hashimoto gave a strangled gasp. I swung round towards him. The right lens of his spectacles had shattered. For a fraction of a second, I thought he'd been hit by nothing more sinister than some bizarrely ricocheting pebble. Then I saw the raw red gap where his eye should have been. Before I could reach out to touch him he toppled sideways into the aisle between the seats, falling face down with a thump that merged with a crack of metal on metal as a bullet – I didn't doubt what it was – struck the rail near my elbow and pinged past me. I dived for the deck.

Hashimoto's face drew close to mine as I crawled into the aisle. His glasses were askew, his left eye clear and open and staring, his right lost in a gouge of brain and bone from which blood was seeping onto the floor. His lips sagged apart, as if he was still trying to tell me how close Rupe might be. But he was never going to tell me – or anyone else – anything, ever again. Kiyofumi Hashimoto was dead and the fact that he'd been alive and well and talking to me only a second or two before changed nothing.

Another bullet struck the back of one of the seats beyond and above me. I saw the foam splay out of the hole in the leather. Somebody was trying to kill both of us and they weren't about to stop with the job half done. I had to get off that bus. I had to get away. I squirmed past Hashimoto towards the stairs, catching some object on the floor as I went and dragging it with me. I reached down and pulled it out from under me. It was the tape of Rupe's message. It must have slipped out of Hashimoto's pocket as he fell. Only then did I remember that it was Rupe who had lured us into this trap. 'Trust me,' he'd said. And I had. Suddenly, I wanted to find Rupe more powerfully than I could ever have imagined. I closed my hand round the tape, gritted my teeth and made for the stairs.

Another bullet whined overhead. Then I was in the relative safety of the stairwell. I rolled and scrambled to my feet, leapt down the treads two at a time and lunged for the open door at the bottom.

People were scattering in both directions along the pavement, some of them screaming. I saw the guide and the driver crouched by the front wheel-arch. I heard another shot and saw them flinch. Then the guide spotted me. 'Get down,' he shouted. 'You're safer behind the bus. I've called the police.' He held up his mobile for me to see. 'They'll be here soon.'

Maybe they would. And maybe he was safe where he was. But he wasn't the target. I had no intention of waiting to find out what the marksman's next move might be. Hashimoto was dead. And all I could think about was staying alive. The bus had stopped just past a turning and the body of the vehicle would shield me as far as the corner. At least, I hoped it would. I started running.

There may have been another shot as I rounded the corner, clinging close to the shopfronts. I'm not sure. By then my senses were filtering out everything not strictly essential to my survival. I was heading south, away from Tauentzienstrasse. That was all that mattered. But not for long. As I ran, my mind struggled to assimilate what had happened and put together a response. What was I going to do? Where was I going to go? 'This is life and death,' Hashimoto had told me back in London. I hadn't believed him. I did now.

The route south ended in a T-junction. I turned right, breath failing me, legs aching. I was in no condition to run as fast or as far as I wanted to. But still I had to run. Where to? That was the question. Where the hell to? We'd been set up from the start. That was obvious. Rosa Townley had played for time and we'd given it to her. And in that time she and Erich and Rupe too, it seemed, had plotted our execution. They were in it together. And they were all my enemies. My only ally lay dead on the top deck of the 12.15 tour bus.

I had to get out of Berlin. The realization came to me just as I spotted a taxi approaching with its light on. They knew the city. I didn't. If I stayed, I was lost. The police wouldn't believe me. I hardly believed me myself. If I stayed, they'd get me. I flagged the taxi down, ran across the road and jumped in. '*Flughafen Tegel*,' I shouted to the driver.

'*Flughafen Tegel. Ja.*' He started away.

Then I remembered. My passport was back at the Adlon. Without it, I was going nowhere. 'No. Not the airport. Hotel—' I stopped. They knew I was likely to go there. They could be waiting for me. But I had to get my passport. I had to go to the Adlon. Just not necessarily by a direct route. I pulled out my map.

'Komische Oper,' I said, spotting how close it was to the Adlon; I could cut round from there to the rear entrance of the hotel. That, of course, was where Hashimoto had been to see *The Magic Flute*. Just last night, he'd been humming along to Mozart. And now—

'Komische Oper. OK.' The driver picked up speed. We were on our way.

I can't remember much about the taxi ride, except that it wasn't as fast as I'd have liked. In another sense, though, it was too fast, because I'd no better idea of what to do when it ended than when it had begun. Get the hell away was all my stunned reasoning process could come up with by way of a plan of action. Hashimoto was dead and I was lucky not to be dead as well. I wasn't looking for Rupe any more, or Stephen Townley, or an old letter containing an older secret. I just wanted out.

There didn't look to be anyone hanging around the back entrance of the Adlon. I ran across Wilhelmstrasse without waiting for the lights to change, causing at least one car to brake sharply. Then I rushed into the hotel and hurried through the function suites, suppressing the instinct to break into a trot. I knew I ought to be as inconspicuous as possible, but I felt anything but. My shoulder was aching from the scramble off the bus and there was a stain on my sleeve that was probably Hashimoto's blood. I made it to reception without drawing any looks and tried to make the request for my key sound casual while keeping it *sotto voce*. The lobby and bar were busy without being crowded. If anyone was watching the front door, there was a reasonable chance they wouldn't notice me as I took the key and doubled back to the lifts. And you had to have a room key to access the guest floors (by waggling it in front of a sensor in the lift). I reassured myself I was in the clear. (Well, what else could I do?)

I jogged round the corridor from the lift to my room, opened up and rushed in, swinging the door shut behind me as I made for the safe in the corner, where I'd stored my passport and a wad of spare Deutschmarks Hashimoto had given me.

I was stooping in front of the safe, tapping in the combination, when I heard a rattle from behind me, as if my shove hadn't been enough to close the door. I glanced over my shoulder. And there was Erich Townley, pushing the door gently shut and leaning back against it.

'In a hurry, Lance?' he asked, smiling sourly.

I stood up slowly and turned round to face him.

'Oh, you can go ahead and open the safe. I'd like to see what you have inside. Just in case it includes the letter.'

'What letter's that?'

'Trying to be smart when you're as dumb as you are is just pathetic, Lance. You know that? Why'd you come back here?'

'Too dumb not to, I suppose.'

'I heard there was a shooting near the Europa-Center. Some Japanese tourist's on his way to the morgue.'

'Who did the shooting, Erich?'

'Wouldn't you like to know? Not Rupe. He's no marksman. But he's one hell of a decoy, don't you think?'

'Why did you kill Hashimoto?'

'I haven't killed anyone.' He moved towards me. 'Yet.'

'What's in the letter?'

'Maybe you know better than I do. Open the safe.'

'I'm afraid I can't.'

'Why not?'

'I've forgotten the combination.'

'Not funny, Lance.' He stopped a few feet from me. 'Not funny at all.' He reached into the pocket of his coat and took something out. I'd expected it to be a knife. But it wasn't. It was a gun. I stared with a strange, detached fascination at the barrel as he pointed it at me. 'Open up.'

'As a matter of fact, the combination's just come back to me.'

'Amazing.'

I turned and crouched down in front of the safe. I needed the passport above all else. Once I had it— But I couldn't look more than a few seconds ahead. I tapped in the numbers and opened the door.

'Take out everything that's inside.'

This was crazy. Why the hell should he think I had the letter? It made no sense. I picked up the passport and the rubber-banded bundle of cash, holding the handful up for him to see. 'This is all there is, Erich.'

'Stay where you are.' He moved back and crouched down for a view past me into the safe. There was nothing for him to see. 'I guess it was an outside chance anyway,' he said, standing up again. 'Worse luck for you.'

'Why's that?'

'Work it out for yourself.' (I tried not to.) 'Now, stand up. Slowly.'

I obeyed, turning to face him as I rose.

'Empty your pockets.'

That didn't take long. My wallet; the keys to my flat in Glastonbury; a grubby handkerchief; some coins; and the tape.

'Where's my cigarette lighter?'

'Hashimoto has it. Had it, I should say. It's probably in the safe in his room.'

Erich chewed his lip while he thought about that for a discomforting few seconds. It looked like he believed me, even though he didn't want to. 'Dump that stuff on the desk,' he growled.

'OK.' The desk was to my right. I took one cautious step towards it and dropped the whole lot on the blotter.

Erich stared at the scatter of objects for a moment, then returned his gaze to me. 'What's on the tape?'

'That tape?'

'Yeh. That fucking tape.'

'Oh, I wondered—'

'What's on it?'

'Abba's greatest hits.'

He glared at me (it was certain now, beyond a shadow of a doubt: I wasn't his type), then stepped towards the desk and leaned forward to pick up the tape.

'Don't say you're an Abba fan too, Erich.'

'Shut up.'

He looked away for the fraction of a second it took him to grasp the tape. And that, I knew, was the only fraction of a second luck was likely to hand me. I lunged at him in as good a rugby tackle as I could manage. We both went down hard. I braced myself for the gun to go off, but it didn't. Erich hit the floor, grunting as the

180

breath shot out of him. I heard a clunk somewhere behind us and rolled round to see the gun lying several feet away under the desk. A table lamp wobbled above me as I came to rest against the cabinet it stood on. Erich began to scramble back up, his gaze focusing on the gun. I swivelled and kicked, catching him on the side of the head. He fell against the footboard of the bed, clutching at his ear. Then I was on my feet, grabbing the lamp by its heavy brass base. Erich saw me pick it up as he rose onto his knees. But he was too late to block or dodge the blow. I brought the lamp down fast, the rimmed base hitting him somewhere above his left eye. There was a solid crunch of brass on bone.

And then there was Erich Townley, slumped and motionless on the floor, blood oozing from a triangular wound on his brow. I put the lamp slowly back down on the cabinet. My hands were shaking. My *knees* were shaking. I tried to think, quickly and clearly. Had I killed him? I jammed two fingers under his ear and felt for a pulse. Yes. His heart was still beating. He was unconscious, but he wasn't dead. Thank God. I didn't want to leave Berlin as a murder suspect on the run. But leave it I had to, fast. Someone deadlier by far than Erich had been responsible for shooting Hashimoto. He might be on his way to the Adlon as I stood there, umm-ing and ah-ing.

I rushed to the wardrobe, grabbed my bag and flung in the spare clothes I'd brought. Then I threw in my toothbrush and shaving kit from the bathroom, stuffed the items on the desk into my pocket (tape included, along with the all-important passport and cash), and made for the door.

I stopped halfway. I needed an edge over the enemy; any kind of edge I could get. What did Erich have I could make use of? I stooped over him and checked his coat pockets. Some keys he was welcome to keep – and a wallet. All in all, I reckoned he'd have to live without that. I slung it into my bag, closed the zip and headed for the door again. This time, I didn't stop.

I left the Adlon the way I'd come in, by the back door, and picked up a taxi within a couple of blocks. By then I was more or less certain I wasn't being followed. (What my certainty on the point was worth I didn't ask myself.) Mercifully, the route to Tegel Airport didn't go anywhere near the Europa-Center. I imagined Tauentzien-strasse had already been blocked off by the police, investigating what they probably reckoned was an out-break of anti-tourist terrorism. As the taxi sped through Tiergarten, I seriously wondered if I should divert to Police HQ and tell them everything that had happened. But that would mean questions, questions, questions, *and* a long stay in Berlin. I doubted I could convince them I was telling the truth. I was sure there'd be nothing to link the Townleys with the shooting. And I'd probably end up being charged with assaulting Erich. No, I had to go.

But my run-in with Erich had changed something in my mind. Before, I'd been high on fear and the instinct for self-preservation. Now, I was beginning to feel angry. Hashimoto was my friend. He'd said so himself. Maybe, despite the short time we'd known each other, he was a better friend than Rupe had ever been. He deserved to be avenged. And the people who'd killed him deserved to be punished.

But was I the man to do either? Even I wouldn't have answered that question with a resounding and un-ambiguous yes. Just as well when you came down to it, then, that I didn't have much choice about volunteering for the role. The nameless marksman who'd snuffed out Hashimoto's life would come after me. I was sure of that. I was unfinished business. I could go back to England and try to resume a normal life, but the Townleys wouldn't let me. Sooner or later, they'd track me down.

I fished the tape out of my pocket and stared down at it nestled in my palm. Had Rupe really sold out? Or was his message a fake? *'I have the letter. I am in Berlin. We must meet.'* Short, simple sentences, comprising a message left only when it was certain he couldn't speak to me. A spliced tape, maybe, made up of parts of a previously recorded conversation. It was possible. In the right hands, it was probably even easy. An expert would be able to tell. But I wasn't likely to run into one of those. I'd just have to guess. And wait until I could prove I'd guessed right.

If the tape *was* a fake, then it was also a clue to what Rupe had done in Berlin. *'I have the letter'*. *'We must meet'*. He hadn't been talking to me. He'd been talking to the Townleys. Of course. They'd recycled Rupe's blackmail call. *'Trust me'* meant *'You'd better believe I'm serious'*. And they *had* believed him. What they'd done to neutralize the threat he posed I didn't know. But it hadn't been enough, not quite. They still didn't have the letter. Erich's behaviour proved that. They didn't have it and they were prepared to kill anyone who stood between them and suppression of the secret it held.

But what kind of a secret did that make it? What could it possibly be? Hashimoto could have told me. Maybe he would have done, if I'd pressed him harder. 'You are better off not knowing,' he'd said. 'You are *safer*.' Well, I didn't feel very safe. And I wasn't going to, unless I found some way to expose the Townleys for whatever it was they truly were. 'For everyone who knows,' Hashimoto had said, 'there is the danger that they will tell.' Too right. If I ever found out, I meant to tell anyone who'd listen.

And how could I find out? There was only one way. The realization of what it was seeped slowly into my mind as the taxi headed west out of Tiergarten. I unzipped my bag and took out Erich's wallet. What did we have here? Credit cards that were no use to me, tempting though they were – Erich's credit limit had to be higher than mine (probably by a factor of ten), but plastic leaves a trail and I couldn't afford to do that. What I needed was hard cash. Fortunately, Erich seemed to be a serious fan of folding money. He had about three thousand Deutschmarks on him, plus several hundred US dollars. 'Thanks very much,' I murmured, transferring the cash to my own wallet. It was enough to take me a long way. And I had a long way to go. What else was there? Nothing much that I could see, apart from a clutch of membership cards for various clubs.

But hold on. One of them was more of a business card. Gordon A. Ledgister, Caribtex Oil, with an office address in Houston, Texas. He had to be Erich's brother-in-law – the oil executive Jarvis had said Barbara Townley had married. You never knew when I might want to contact *him*. That went into my wallet as well.

The rest was destined for a rubbish bin at the airport. I had as much of Erich's as I wanted.

Thanks to Erich's fondness for the crinkly stuff, added to Hashimoto's generosity with money, I was able to pay cash for my ticket at the Lufthansa desk. I'd be travelling economy, of course. Only two days before, I'd been downing champagne in club class. But champagne – complimentary or otherwise – was the last thing I wanted now.

Just about the first was speed. But that wasn't easily had. Where I was going meant changing planes in Frankfurt and an arrival some time the following afternoon. Would the police come looking for me before I set off? I reckoned not. They were probably still trying to trace which hotel Hashimoto had been staying at. But that didn't mean the wait for the connecting flight wasn't hard on my nerves.

Sitting in the departure lounge at Tegel, trying to stop my thoughts whirling in on themselves, I suddenly realized that there were other people than myself to consider. And I badly owed a couple of them a telephone call.

The first was my father, who seemed strangely unsurprised by my urgent request for him to call me straight back on a Berlin payphone number.

'I spoke to Miss Bateman yesterday,' he explained when we were talking again. (I had to think for a moment who he meant.) 'She told me you'd gone to Germany. What's this all about, son?'

'Too complicated to go into, Dad. We don't want to overload your phone bill, do we?'

'That's true.' (I'd known the point would appeal to him.)

'Why did you contact Echo?'

'Miss Bateman, you mean?' (So, the crusty old sod was determined to cling to formality.) 'Because you asked me to have a word with Don Forrester and let you know the outcome.'

'And what was the outcome?'

'Well . . .'

'Come on, Dad. Remember: you're paying.'

'All right. But Don was reluctant to go into it at first, I can tell you. It took some doing to talk him round.'

'You managed it, though.'

'I did, yes.'

'And I'm grateful. So . . . ?'

'Well, apparently the police considered the possibility that Peter Dalton had been murdered by a friend who'd been staying with him at Wilderness Farm. If the friend left before the shooting, he was obviously ruled out as a suspect, but it was never determined when he actually left, because he was never traced. And the pathologist narrowly favoured suicide as a cause of death, so—'

'Was the friend called Stephen Townley?'

'Townley? Might have been. Don couldn't remember the name. What he did remember, though, was that after finding the body – upsetting enough, you'd have thought – Howard Alder virtually accused this friend of murdering Dalton. The police might never have known about him otherwise, though neighbours subsequently confirmed his existence. What's more, Howard showed Don a photograph of the fellow, taken at—'

'Ashcott and Meare railway station.'

'How did you know that?'

'I've seen the photograph. On Rupe's kitchen wall. But that doesn't matter. What efforts did Don make to track down Townley?'

'None. Officially, it was never a murder inquiry. And Howard wasn't exactly a reliable witness. Although—'

'What?'

'Oddly enough, he *did* come up with a motive for murder.'

'Really? What was that?'

'Howard had taken to sneaking around Wilderness Farm that summer, apparently. A few days before the shooting, he was in the yard, spying through the kitchen window, and he saw – *claimed* he saw – a holdall full of five-pound notes standing on the kitchen table. Well, there was no holdall full of cash at the farm when the police searched it. Howard suggested it was the proceeds of a crime and that . . . Townley, as you call him . . . had stolen it, after murdering Dalton.'

'What did Don make of that?'

'He reckoned Howard had dreamed it up. This was just after the Great Train Robbery, remember. The papers were full of speculation about where the robbers might have hidden the money. Don's theory was that Howard got the idea about the holdall from such stories and used it to blacken Dalton's reputation.'

'Why would he want to do that?'

'Ah, well, that brings us to the reason why Howard was hanging around Wilderness Farm. In some ways, it's the most surprising part of the whole thing.' Dad lowered his voice, as if afraid we might be overheard. 'It seems Peter Dalton was sweet on Mildred Alder. So

Howard believed, anyway. And he didn't approve of Dalton as a suitor for his sister.' (Never mind approval. I was having difficulty even imagining the possibility.) 'That's why he was spying on Dalton. And why he was out to discredit him.'

'Did Don ask Mil about this . . . relationship?'

'Tried to, apparently. But George told him it was just a fantasy of Howard's and Don left it at that. Although he did say that when he called at Penfrith it was obvious Mildred was upset about something. Very upset. Of course, if Dalton really was courting her, it makes suicide less credible.'

'And murder more credible.'

'True enough. But it's all a very long time ago. That's the only reason Don was willing to tell me about it. He doesn't believe in the jinx, of course. Reckons the deaths were just coincidental.'

'And that George Alder drowned accidentally?'

'He's not sure. He seems to think suicide is a possibility. That might explain why the Alders put the idea about later that George had drowned in Sedgemoor Drain – a more likely place for an accidental drowning than the Brue.'

'Why would George want to kill himself?'

'It hardly seems likely he *would* want to, does it? Not with a child on the way. Don was flummoxed. Still is, come to that.'

'I'll bet he is.' (So was I.)

'That's about all I can tell you, son. You could always try asking Mildred about Peter Dalton, of course. Just don't ask me to.'

'I won't. Maybe I'll do it myself when I get back.'

'When's that likely to be?'

'Not sure.'

'Do you want your mother to take any kind of message to the Alders?'

'No. I don't want you or Mum to contact them. Just . . . drop it.'

'*Drop it?*'

'The whole thing. Do nothing. Say nothing. It's best, believe me.'

'I was just beginning to enjoy myself.'

'Then quit while you're ahead. I wish I could.'

'What's that supposed to mean?'

'Nothing. I've got to go, Dad. Don't worry, OK? I'll be in touch.'

'Yes, but—'

' 'Bye.' I didn't enjoy putting the phone down on him, but cutting him off from what I'd become involved in really was the best way to protect him.

And the same applied to Echo. I found her at home, resting up after a long morning on the post round. She sounded not just pleased to hear from me, but relieved.

'Is there something wrong, Echo?'

'I had creepy Carl round here last night, asking where you were and what you were up to.'

'What did you tell him?'

'That you'd gone away without saying where or why.'

'It's a good line to stick to.'

'Didn't make it any easier to get rid of him.'

'But you succeeded in the end?'

'Just about.'

'Good. Now, you remember what you said to me Friday night about moving out?'

'Yeh.'

'I think you should. As soon as possible.'

'Why? What's happened?'

'It's better you don't know.'

'I hate it when people say that.'

'So do I. But it really is better. Find lodgings some-where else, Echo. Forget Rupe. Forget me too.'

'I can't do that.'

'Try.'

'Are you at the airport, Lance?'

'Yeh. How'd you know?'

'I can hear the flight announcements in the background.'

'Right.'

'You're leaving Berlin?'

'I am, yeh.'

'And not to come home?'

'No.'

'Where *are* you going?'

'I'll have to pass on that.'

'You're not quitting, though, are you?'

'No.'

'Don't you think you should?'

'Definitely.'

'Then why don't you?'

I had to think about that for a moment. When the answer came, it was neither illuminating to Echo nor consoling to me. But it *was* true. 'Because the time for quitting has come and gone.'

TOKYO

CHAPTER TEN

I reached the Land of the Rising Sun just as the sun was setting. My confidence wasn't exactly in the ascendant either. While most of my fellow passengers had slept through our night over Russia, I'd spent the blank hours thinking so hard about the bind I was in that my brain had turned to mush by the time another day dawned. Then, eventually, I *did* sleep, deep and dreamlessly – for all of forty minutes before landing.

Travelling as light as I was at least meant I didn't have to hang around the baggage hall at Narita Airport. I made straight for the *bureau de change*, swapped my Deutschmarks for yen, then hit the information desk. The legendary courtesy of the Japanese is the only possible explanation for me going away with a street map of Tokyo on which neat red crosses marked the locations of the Golden Rickshaw bar and the Far East office of the Eurybia Shipping Company, along with a note of their addresses in Japanese. (There'd turned out to be three Golden Rickshaws in the Tokyo telephone directory, but one in such a remote suburb that I ruled it out as a former haunt of American GIs and another, logically enough, was actually a rickshaw-hire firm.)

I studied the map as the N'Ex train sped me into the city. The Golden Rickshaw was in a side-street a shortish distance east of Tokyo's central station. To that extent, my luck was in. (Though the wiseacre I'd sat next to on the plane had assured me that tracking down addresses in Tokyo was like looking for a haystack in a galaxy.) Eurybia's office was quite a way to the south-west, however, so Rupe wasn't likely to have chanced on the Golden Rickshaw while sampling nearby bars. Since it was bang in the centre of the city, he wasn't likely to have lived just round the corner from it, either. No, he'd sought it out. He'd known what he was looking for all along. Though exactly what that was . . .

The Tokyo rush hour was in full swing when I got off the train. It was the usual big city swirl of bright lights and dim humanity, amped up to an oriental pitch I was in no state to deal with. It was also raining hard enough to soak my map as I battled out of the station through a swarm of brolly-wielding commuters. I immediately set off in the wrong direction, then had to double back and soon lost count of how many blocks I was supposed to cover. A department-store doorman eventually put me right and I found the side-street I was looking for. There were several bars along it, all doing a brisk trade, but no immediate sign of the Golden Rickshaw, so I tried my luck in one of the friendlier-looking establishments. A barman wearing sunglasses was a first in my experience, but the inky lenses didn't stop him studying the piece of paper on which I had the Golden Rickshaw's address written down, while opening a beer for me at the same time.

'Seven doors that way, other side,' he announced. 'But it's closed.'

'Closed?'

'Six weeks now, must be.'

'The Hashimotos?'

'Yeh. They run it. The family, you know, for years. Closed now. Gone.'

'Gone where?'

'Hey, they don't tell me.' He wrinkled his nose enough to raise the sunglasses clear of the bridge. 'They just go.'

'The mother and the daughter?'

'Yeh. That's right. Gone. Like smoke.'

Gone like smoke. And so they were. The Golden Rickshaw still had its gilded emblem hanging over the door, but the bar was unlit, its bamboo blinds drawn. Thanks to the headlights of passing cars and the glow of the nearest street-lamp, I could see something of the interior round the edges of the blinds: a bare counter beyond a jumble of stacked tables, chairs and stools, and a slew of unopened mail. They'd gone. No question about it. And those photographs of former patrons decorating the walls? They'd gone too. I could see the nails they'd hung on. But they hung no more. I'd come a third of the way round the world to find a coop the birds had long since flown – without leaving so much as a stray feather behind them.

It wasn't really surprising, I admitted to myself as I trudged back to the station. They knew they were in danger. They *had* known, ever since Rupe made off with the Townley letter. I knew it now too. If I could track them down, so could others. In the circumstances, business as usual at the Golden Rickshaw would have been verging on the suicidal.

But where did I go from here? That was the point. Where *exactly* did I go? There was only one answer, of course. It was the second address written on my piece of paper.

After queuing in the rain at the exit on the other side of the station for ten minutes, I got myself a cab, waved Eurybia's address under the driver's nose until he gave me the thumbs-up, then sat back and surprised myself by falling straight to sleep.

When the driver jogged me awake, my first thought, based on the fare winking at me from the meter, was that it was the following morning. But no, it was barely twenty minutes later and we were at the foot of some alp of a skyscraper. The driver jabbered something at me that seemed to mean 'We're here' and pointed at the steps leading up to the brightly lit entrance. I filled his hand with yen and clambered out.

The Chayama Building fulfilled the office needs of several dozen corporations, listed on the face of a vast gold monolith that formed a sort of way-station between the door and the distant reception desk. Eurybia was on the ninth floor. But making it to the brushed-steel lift doors meant talking my way past a security man who looked big and grim enough to be a moonlighting sumo wrestler. I had my doubts about whether I looked the part for office visits and it was also – according to a huge clock on the wall behind him, with hands as long as javelins and a pendulum as big as a supertanker piston – suspiciously late. I just had to hope Eurybia's staff were a dedicated bunch.

'Hi. Eurybia Shipping?'

The *sumotori* smiled with surprising warmth. 'Who you seeing?'

'Not sure. It concerns . . .' I shrugged. 'Well, Mr Charles Hoare of their London office said I was to call round. Could you ask them if I could go up?'

'What your name?'

'Bradley. Lance Bradley.'

'If they ask . . . what about?'

'Say . . .' An inspired notion came to me. 'Say it's about the Pomparles Trading Company.'

'Pomplees?'

'Pom-par-lees.'

'Pomparlees. OK.'

He picked up the phone, pressed a button and had a brief conversation with somebody in Japanese. I caught my name, and Charlie Hoare's and the agonizingly enunciated *Pomparlees*. My name was repeated – twice. Then he waited, phone cradled under his massive chin, grinning at me like this was one big game – as it was, I suppose. After a minute or so, conversation resumed. But not for long.

'OK.' He put the phone down. 'They say you go up.' He flapped a hand the size of a baseball mitt towards the lift. 'Floor nine.'

There was a bloke waiting for me when I exited the lift. Middle-aged, sober-tied and dark-suited, stocky going on flabby, he had slicked-back greying hair and a large, lugubrious, flat-nosed face rather like a bulldog's, with a long diagonal crease across his forehead so prominent it could have been a scar. 'Mr Bradley?' he ventured, bowing slightly.

'Yeh. Thanks for—'

'I am Toshishige Yamazawa.' We shook hands. 'Pleased to meet you.'

'Me too, Mr Yamazawa.' I glanced along the corridor and spotted a Eurybia Shipping sign above a set of double doors at the end. It looked like I still wasn't actually on the premises and Yamazawa didn't seem to be in a tearing hurry to change that. 'Shall we, er . . .'

'Can I see some identification, please?'

'Passport do?'

'Surely.'

I handed it over and he looked studiously at my photograph, then handed it back.

'Rupe spoke about you.'

'He did?' (That was a surprise, I'd have had to admit.) 'So, you, er, worked with him?'

'Yes. And now I work with Mr' – he nodded towards the Eurybia doors – 'Penberthy.'

'Right.'

'Mr Penberthy is not a happy man. He wanted me to send you away.'

'How did you talk him round?'

'No need. He talks himself round if you let him. But he will soon leave us to it and then . . .' Yamazawa winked at me with so little change of expression that I thought for a moment it was some kind of muscular tic. But no. He was trying to tell me something. 'Then we talk.' (Ah. So that's what he was trying to tell me.)

'Mr Penberthy is Rupe's successor?'

'Successor, yes. But not exactly a replacement.' (I couldn't make up my mind whether his candour was to my advantage or not. Either way, it was the last thing I'd have expected of the nose-to-the-grindstone salaryman I took him to be.) 'I take you to meet him.'

Yamazawa led the way to the doors, where he tapped out a code on a number-pad to gain access. Inside, we walked down a short corridor into a large, stark, grey-furnished office. A block of desks, about half of which were still occupied despite the fact that seven o'clock had come and gone, filled the centre of the room, where assorted Eurybians nursed telephones and squinted at computer screens. None of them paid me the slightest heed.

We pressed on towards a trio of larger, partitioned-off desks, behind one of which sat a thin, blue-suited European. He was leaning back in his chair, conducting a telephone conversation that his frowns and grimaces suggested wasn't pleasing him. He had fair, receding hair and dark shadows round his eyes. His skin had an unhealthy, yellowish tinge to it. All in all, I'd have said his nearest and dearest had good reason to be worried about him.

'Penberthy-san, this is our visitor,' Yamazawa announced as we approached. 'Mr Bradley.'

Penberthy slammed the phone down and frowned at it rather than me. 'Bloody Charlie Hoare,' he said. 'Not in yet. Can you believe it?'

'It's only ten-fifteen in London,' said Yamazawa (sounding deliberately provocative to me).

Penberthy glared at him, then turned his attention to me. 'Mr Bradley, is it?'

'Yes. I—'

'We've had nothing from Charlie Hoare about a visit from you. And this is a pretty odd bloody hour to come calling.'

'Mr Bradley gave Charlie Hoare some information about the Pomparles Trading Company,' said Yamazawa.

'Only the origin of the name,' I explained, grinning to cover my surprise. How did he know I'd done that?

'Very considerate of you,' snapped Penberthy. 'God, if I ever hear the end of this bloody Pomparles business I think I'll be dreaming.'

'It *is* a complicated affair,' said Yamazawa.

'Don't I know it? Complicated enough to get me targeted by burglars in this supposedly crime-free city.'

'You've been burgled?' I asked.

'Oh yes. And not just once. But—' He broke off and eyed me doubtfully. 'Without the say-so from Hoare Who Must Be Obeyed, I'm not sure we should be discussing Eurybia business with you, Mr Bradley.'

'I'm an old friend of Rupe Alder's. I'm trying to find out what's happened to him, on behalf of his family.'

'It's still no can do as far as I'm concerned.'

'I would be willing to help Bradley-san as much as I can,' said Yamazawa.

'Why?' asked Penberthy.

'Why not?'

'Because Charlie mightn't like you to, old man.'

'In that event it would be my problem, not yours, Penberthy-san.'

'Bloody right it would. I'd make sure of that.'

'Of course.' Yamazawa smiled. 'So would I.' (Penberthy looked as puzzled as I felt. What *was* Yamazawa up to?) 'Bradley-san and I can have little talk at the Nezumi. Off the record.'

'It'll be *on* the record if this goes pear-shaped. *Your* record.'

'But if I learn something of importance . . .'

'You'll be in Charlie Hoare's good books. Fine. Go on. I don't care. Do what you like. It's not worth the risk for a few brownie points in my opinion, but, then' – he waved one hand expansively across his desk – 'when did my opinion ever count for anything around here?'

The Nezumi was a small bar a few blocks from the Chayama Building. Yamazawa seemed to be well known there, exchanging a strange Japanese version of high-fives with the barman and several of the customers. Most of them looked to be salary slaves in his own age bracket. They were drinking and smoking at a stiffish pace, inebriation a certain destination – unless asphyxiation got them first.

Yamazawa lit up and ordered a couple of beers. '*Kampai,*' he announced, polishing off half of his in three swallows. 'We drink to health and happiness for Penberthy.'

'We do?'

'A pompous hope, of course.'

'Don't you mean pious?'

'Not sure.' He flicked his tie back over his shoulder, out of harm's way, finished his beer and ordered another. 'But I have done my duty.'

'I get the impression you won't be seeking the presidency of Penberthy's fan club.'

'I couldn't afford to refuse it. But there are different kinds of duty. The office kind. And our kind.'

'You mean friendship?'

'Rupe is my friend *and* yours, Bradley-san. He did me . . . a great kindness.'

'Oh yes?'

'You could say he saved my life.'

'How?'

'A private matter. We leave it there. OK?'

'OK. Though, as it happens, you could say he saved my life too.'

'Strange.' Yamazawa peered at me through his cigarette smoke. 'Rupe is more careful with his friends' lives than his own.'

'You think his life's in danger?'

'For sure. Unless . . . it is already over.'

'Pessimistic bugger, aren't you?'

'It is in my nature. Not in Rupe's, though. He always sees a bright dawn. Which is good . . . unless you are dazzled by the brightness.'

'Do you know anything about the Golden Rickshaw bar?'

'You have been there?'

'It's closed.'

'I know. My fault, you could say.'

'How's that?'

'I introduced Rupe to it. He used to ask me about Tokyo in the old days. Fifties and Sixties. The American bases interested him. One weekend, he got me to drive him round them – Yokosuka, Zama, Atsugi, Yokota. The whole lot. A long day of gates and fences and Jeeps and helicopters. And Rupe looking . . . for something.'

'What was he looking for?'

'He didn't say. But when I mentioned a bar I'd heard about in Ginza with a . . . strange kind of reputation . . .'

'The Golden Rickshaw?'

'Yes. The Rickshaw.'

'And the reputation?'

'My uncle used to mention it. He was a fish merchant. Quite a successful one. The American bases were good customers of his. He got to know some of the men. He talked with them. That's how he heard about the Rickshaw.'

'And what did he hear?'

'Normally the officers used certain bars and clubs, the lower ranks certain other bars and clubs. They didn't mix. Except at the Rickshaw. That made it very unusual. Unique, I should think. It was a long way from the bases, of course. You wouldn't go there without a reason. Or an invitation.'

'Who issued the invitations?'

'Who knows? Uncle Sato didn't, for sure. But he did supply fish to the American Embassy as well as the bases. And he heard the Rickshaw mentioned there also. Or, to be correct, he was asked about it there.'

'*Asked?*'

'Yes. Was the Golden Rickshaw a customer of his? It seemed important, so he said. It seemed like it would make a difference to whether they went on using him. He said no, which was the truth. And they did go on using him. But it was strange, he said, being asked, and being asked at that particular time. You remember Gary Powers?'

'The American pilot shot down over Russia in a spy plane?'

'May, nineteen sixty. That is right. Powers flew his mission from Atsugi Naval Air Station. Uncle Sato was asked about the Golden Rickshaw just a few days after the news broke.'

'What's the connection?'

'Who is saying there is one?'

'You are, good as.'

'No, no, Bradley-san. I am just warming up Uncle Sato's stale old stories, like a loyal nephew should.'

'Did Uncle Sato know the Hashimotos?'

'No. But he knew people who did. Tokyo was a smaller city then. There was nothing said against them. They were a respectable family. They still are.'

'So, you took Rupe along to the Golden Rickshaw?'

'Yes. We went there.'

'What was it like?'

Yamazawa shrugged. 'Like a lot of other places. Quieter than most, maybe. Mayumi Hashimoto was the *mama*. She ran it well. Helped by her daughter. There were no Americans. That time was gone.'

'But there were photographs of that time on display, weren't there?'

Yamazawa looked surprised. 'How did you know about those, Bradley-san?'

'I met Kiyofumi Hashimoto, Mayumi's brother.'

'Ah. He also is looking for Rupe.' Yamazawa nodded. 'Of course.' (I wondered if I ought to tell him then that poor old Kiyo was looking no more, but some instinct held me back.) 'He came to see me shortly after Rupe left Tokyo.'

'Accusing him of theft?'

'Yes. And of deceiving Hashimoto's niece, Haruko. That was a surprise to me.'

'Didn't you know about their engagement?'

'No. I did not. I never even knew Rupe had gone on visiting the Golden Rickshaw after that one time I took him there. He said nothing to me about any of it. He kept his resignation secret too. I only found out he was leaving when London faxed us with news of his replacement.'

'That wasn't very friendly of him.'

'He apologized to me. He said there were . . . reasons . . . why he had to be so secretive.'

'But he didn't say what those reasons were?'

Yamazawa smiled thinly. 'No.'

'Why don't we have another beer?' I asked, glancing at our suddenly empty glasses.

'Good idea.' Yamazawa arranged that with little more than a twitch of the eyebrows. 'You like Sapporo beer?'

'It hits the spot.'

'For sure. Not for Rupe, though.'

'No?'

'He was always careful not to drink too much. I thought it was just . . . self-control. Now I wonder if he couldn't risk it. You know? In case he got really drunk and . . . gave something away.'

'Some of those secrets?'

'Some. Or all. I don't know.'

'He stole a letter from Mayumi Hashimoto.'

'So her brother said.'

'I need to find that letter.'

'But you are not the only one looking, I think. Hashimoto said his sister and niece were in danger because of it. That is why they went away. To hide. And since then . . . there have been the break-ins.'

'You mean the burglaries Penberthy complained of?'

'He lives in the flat Rupe used to live in. It is leased by Eurybia. It has been broken into twice. Nothing has been stolen. But everything has been searched. Thoroughly. Of course, Rupe left nothing there.'

'He took all his possessions with him?'

'Not difficult, Bradley-san. I saw how he lived. One suitcase would have been enough. But you are his friend, so I must be honest with you. He did not take everything with him.'

'Are you holding something for him?' I asked, reckoning I'd caught his drift.

Yamazawa nodded solemnly in confirmation. 'A briefcase. He asked me to keep it safe and secret. I did not tell Hashimoto about it. But that was before the break-ins and the Pomparles scandal. Something is wrong, I think. Very wrong. I have been thinking that maybe the time has come to open the briefcase and see what it contains.'

'I think maybe you're right.'

'Yes.' He took a deep swallow of beer. 'We do it tonight.'

'Where is it?'

'At my flat.'

'How far?'

'An hour on the subway.'

'That could be a problem for me.'

'Why?'

'Claustrophobia.'

'We are all claustrophobics on the Tokyo subway.'

'No, no. I mean it. Really.'

'In that case, I have bad news for you, Bradley-san.' He gave me another glimpse of his thin-lipped smile. 'You will have to pay for the taxi.'

'This is real luxury,' he was enthusing twenty minutes later, as our taxi cruised westwards through the wet Tokyo night, its tyres hissing on the rain-slicked streets, the raindrops on its windscreen blurring the passing ranks of neon-lit signs. 'To tell you the truth, Bradley-san, I don't like the subway either.'

'You suffer from claustrophobia as well?'

'Not exactly. But you've heard of the Tokyo gas attack?'

'Yeh. A few years ago. Some doomsday cult released nerve gas on the subway, didn't they? Were you caught up in that?'

'Yes.' He smiled, which seemed an odd way to remember such an experience. 'I did not get a serious dose. Not of the sarin, I mean. But I trusted life before that day. Then I saw how easily it could all fall apart. I haven't really fitted in since then. Maybe that is why my wife left me. Maybe that is why I have done a lot of things I should not have done. It comes down to chance in the end. My wife wanted me to take the day off. It was a Monday, March twentieth, and Tuesday was a public holiday for the start of spring, so we could have had a long weekend. I was working for one of the bigger shipping companies then. Working hard. I was a dedicated man.

I said I had to go in. And that was the day I stopped' – his smile broadened – 'being a dedicated man.'

I tried to prise out some more details of Yamazawa's brush with death on the subway, but he artfully diverted me into an account of how Rupe had led me into danger – then got me out of it – the very last time I'd ventured any distance underground. I had the impression Yamazawa had already revealed more of himself than he thought wise. But I also had the impression he couldn't really stop himself.

His flat was on the third floor of a drab, mid-rise block in a remote western suburb: one small living room and three windowless cupboards that the fittings suggested were bedroom, kitchen and bathroom. (The modesty of the accommodation didn't stop me being required on entering to swap my shoes for a pair of mules I could barely squeeze my toes into.) A couple of large bean-bags and a low table were about it on the lounge furniture front. Supplementary decoration was confined to a framed wood-block print showing snow falling across warehouse roofs on a moonlit night. It was beautifully coloured and looked far too good for its surroundings.

'My proudest possession,' said Yamazawa, noticing my gaze linger on it. 'You know the artist? Kawase Hasui.'

'I don't know any artists. Especially not Japanese ones.'

'Ah, but Hasui was a genius. You can see that, can't you?'

'I suppose so.'

'My best investment as well as my proudest possession. It would probably bring a bigger price than this flat.'

'Tempted to sell?'

'Often. But I have not yet been desperate enough. Now, to business. Sit down, please. I fetch the case.'

I lowered myself onto one of the bean-bags while Yamazawa hurried away into the bedroom. I heard a cupboard door open and close. Then he was back, carrying the briefcase Rupe had entrusted to his care. It was a slim, black leather briefcase, with combination locks – a standard-issue executive sandwich carrier. 'I do not think we will find the stolen letter inside,' said Yamazawa, laying it flat on the table and kneeling down opposite me.

'No. He'll have taken that with him.'

'But something important, for sure. Something he did not want them to find if they came looking.'

'*When* they came looking. I guess it was always a certainty.'

'It is not going to be easy to break open.'

'Maybe we don't need to break it open.'

'You know the combination?'

'No. But I know Rupe. He chose the name Pomparles for a reason. It'll be the same with the combination. A four-figure number . . . with some secret significance.' I tried 1963. But no joy. 'Too obvious, perhaps. How about a Wilderness Farm connection? Peter Dalton died on the nineteenth of August.' But 1908 didn't work either. Nor did 0863.

'His birthday, maybe?'

I tried it. 'No.'

'His father's birthday?'

'I wouldn't know when that was. But hold on.' (A thought had suddenly struck me.) 'I do know the date of his father's death. The seventeenth of November.' And 1711 did the trick. The case opened.

To reveal a sheaf of papers and a wallet of photographs. 'What is there?' asked Yamazawa, craning over the lid.

'Not sure. Take a look at these pics.' I handed him the wallet, then took out the papers and began leafing through them. They were all photocopies. A lot were of the very same *Central Somerset Gazette* stories Dad had dug out for me, plus several he hadn't, though all on the same theme – the crop of deaths around Street during the summer and autumn of 1963. There were articles from the national press as well, about the Great Train Robbery and the search for the gang and their loot – TRAIN ROBBERS' HIDE-OUT DISCOVERED, blared an August 1963 headline. Others were parts of large-scale Ordnance Survey maps of the Street area, which looked as if they dated from the same period. Wilderness Farm was picked out in yellow highlighter. And so was Cow Bridge. There was also a copy of a page from an old British Railways Western Region timetable showing services on the Somerset and Dorset line, with stopping times at Ashcott and Meare highlighted. Rupe had been plotting the past to prepare for the future. But what sort of future had it been?

'Does it tell you anything?' asked Yamazawa.

'Nothing I didn't already know.' I looked up at him. 'What about the photographs?'

'See for yourself.' He spread them out on the table. They were apparently unremarkable snapshots,

mostly of an attractive young Japanese woman, sometimes posing as solemn-faced as a priestess, sometimes
smiling radiantly. Whichever the expression, there was a
trusting intensity in her gaze that convinced me at once
that she loved the person taking her picture to the point
of adoration. 'Haruko Hashimoto?'

'Yes,' said Yamazawa. 'A most charming fiancée.'

'And this must be Mayumi.' I pointed to a picture of
Haruko standing next to an older woman. They'd been
snapped in front of some kind of temple with other
people wandering past in the background. Both were
lightly and casually dressed. It looked like high summer.
There was a strong family resemblance between the two
women and it was pretty obvious where Haruko had got
her looks from.

'Mother and daughter taking a stroll in Ueno Park,'
said Yamazawa, recognizing the spot. 'Also charming.'

'Until you know Rupe's just stringing them along.'

'He stays out of the picture.'

'So he does.' I looked for Rupe in vain, then noticed
one photograph that appeared to be black and white,
which it obviously couldn't be if it was from the same
film. 'What's this?'

I picked it up to examine, holding it between us so
that Yamazawa could see as well. The picture *was* in
black and white. Three men in lightweight US military
uniforms were sitting at a table in a bar. There were
drifts of smoke and blurred figures in the background at
other tables. One of the three had his back to the
camera and was half in shadow. He was young and slim,
his dark hair cropped just shy of a crew-cut. He was
looking across the table to his left, the light catching his

chin and cheekbone. The man he was looking at was facing the camera, though apparently unaware of its existence. He was stockier and slightly older, with a hint of flab around his jaw and waist and a smile creasing his wide face as he raised a beer bottle in his hand. 'It is a photograph of a photograph,' said Yamazawa. 'One of the pictures from the wall of the Golden Rickshaw.' He was right. There were odd patches of sheen on the print that could only be reflections from the glass in the frame.

'Yeh,' I said. 'And I know why he chose this particular picture.' The third man at the table, also facing the camera, was thinner and grimmer-faced than his beaming companion. He was also slightly younger than in the only other photograph of him I'd seen. Or maybe that was just the effect of his trim, pressed uniform. Whatever the case, there was no mistaking the way he was holding his cigarette behind his palm, between forefinger and thumb, just as he had the day he'd been waiting for a train at Ashcott and Meare station. 'It's Stephen Townley,' I said.

'Who is Stephen Townley?'

'The subject of the letter Rupe stole.'

'An important man?'

'Maybe. Dangerous, for certain.'

'Who are the other two?'

'Haven't a clue.'

'I think we have.'

'I don't see one.'

'The smile.' Yamazawa pointed at the grinning bloke with the beer bottle. Then he picked up another photograph and held it in front of me. 'The smile is the same.'

And so it was. Worn by a forty-or-so years older man.

His hair was still short, but had turned white with age. The surplus flesh under his jaw had become a wodge of fat, the sagging stomach a substantial paunch. But the smile hadn't altered. He was standing next to Haruko Hashimoto, dwarfing her almost, given how much taller and broader he was, grinning amiably at the camera – and hence at Rupe. 'Bloody hell,' I murmured. 'It's the same man.'

'For sure.'

'He's still here.'

'Not here, actually.'

'You can see for yourself.'

'Yes, Bradley-san, I can. But that is not Tokyo.'

I looked more closely. Smiler and Haruko were standing on what was probably a balcony, its railings visible behind them. On the other side of the street below was a neatly clipped hedge and, beyond it, a moat, a stone-block wall and part of what looked like a castle or palace, high-roofed and ornately eaved.

'That is Nijo-jo,' said Yamazawa. 'In Kyoto.'

'Kyoto?'

'Yes. The ancient capital.'

'Are you sure this photograph was taken there?'

'I took my son to Kyoto for a holiday two years ago. We saw many temples. But Koichi preferred the castle of Nijo-jo, because of its so-called nightingale floors. They squeak, however softly you walk on them – an old trick of the shoguns, to warn them of intruders. Koichi loved that. He made me take him several times. So, I remember Nijo-jo. This photograph was taken in somebody's flat, I would guess, overlooking the castle. Rupe must be standing in shadow for the light to be right. So, he is in the room. They are on the balcony.'

'Whose flat?'

'Not Haruko's or Rupe's, obviously.'

'But Smiler's.'

'Probably.'

'An American in his sixties who was based here as a soldier and stayed on – or came back.'

'Could be.'

'And he *could* be sheltering Haruko and her mother. Now.'

'It is as likely as anything else.'

'A flat near . . . what was it?'

'Nijo-jo. Quite a landmark.'

'And Smiler's probably a landmark in his own right round there. Which means it should be possible to trace him.'

'I think you would have a good chance.'

'And I haven't got a lot of chances to choose from, have I? How far's Kyoto?'

'By one of our famous bullet trains, less than three hours.'

I sat back and gazed vacantly at the photographs in front of us. Chances and choices? I never seemed to have enough of either. 'It's the bullet train for me, then.'

With my next move decided, we both relaxed. Yamazawa (Toshi, as I was calling him by now, even though I couldn't shift him from Bradley-san) invited me to stay the night, which was more or less inevitable, given how late it was. He then opened a bottle of some potent spirit called *shochu*, into which we made alarmingly mind-mangling inroads as the night deepened.

Yamazawa had identified another of Rupe's photographs as having been taken in Kyoto – Haruko strolling along a picturesque tree-lined canal; the Philosopher's Walk, he'd called it. This and all the other snapshots of the winsome maiden Rupe had heartlessly strung along led us into gloomy reflections on the human capacity for deceit, which in turn plunged Yamazawa into a morbid analysis of the failure of his marriage, something he admitted to being so ashamed of that he could only discuss it with a foreigner.

But that was only a detour. All conversational roads – if you could call our slurred ramblings a conversation – led back to Rupe, our loyal friend who was clearly capable of big-time *dis*loyalty where others were concerned. That thought got to me in the end and I decided that Yamazawa deserved to be told the truth. So, some time around midnight, I broke the news of Hashimoto's death.

'These are serious people you are mixing it with, Bradley-san,' he said after a lengthy pause.

'Believe me, Toshi, if I'd known *how* serious . . .'

'You never would have got involved.'

'Too right.'

'Then be glad you did not know.'

'*Glad?*'

'Yes. Because you would have done nothing. You would have turned your back on your friend. And that shame – that dishonour – would have stayed with you for the rest of your life.'

'I could have lived with it.'

'For sure. But living like that' – he nodded solemnly to himself – 'is a kind of death.'

'It's the other kind I'm worried about.'

'No need.' Yamazawa grinned at me. 'Our trains are very safe.'

I woke next morning on Yamazawa's lumpy guest futon to a stream of sunlight through the window and a headache for which the word 'ache' was pitifully inappropriate. I felt as if I'd had brain surgery and a scalpel had been left carelessly embedded in my cerebellum. Yamazawa would probably have told me this was what *shochu* hangovers were always like, but a tottering exploration of the flat revealed he was in no position to, since he'd already gone to work – long since, for all I knew – leaving a farewell note Blu-Tacked to the inside of the front door.

Bradley-san,

I cannot give Penberthy more to complain about by being late, so I leave you sleeping like a baby. (I would not let a baby drink shochu, of course.) The easiest way to get to Tokyo station for your train to Kyoto is by subway, but I expect you prefer another way. So, walk down the hill to the local station and take a taxi. To save some yen, take it to Shin-Kawasaki station. That is on the main line. You can travel into Tokyo *above* ground from there. Call me on my mobile (*not* at Eurybia) and let me know what happens in Kyoto. The number is 90-5378-2447. Good luck and stay well.

Toshishige

PS There is nothing for breakfast.

KANSAI

CHAPTER ELEVEN

The *Shinkansen* super-express lived up to Yamazawa's billing and delivered me to Kyoto on the button of the timetable just after one o'clock. The dawn sunshine in Tokyo had flattered to deceive. It was a cold, grey, autumn day in the former capital.

There was nothing in the least venerable about its futuristic railway station, but the taxi ride to Nijo-jo took me past a couple of ancient temples and it was pretty obvious the city beat to a less frenetic drum than its brash young cousin.

There were a couple of tour buses parked at the front of the castle and a steady stream of visitors filing past the ticket barrier, across the moat and in through the high-porched gate. Those nightingale floors were still pulling in the punters. But relics of the shogunate weren't what had brought me. Clutching Rupe's photograph in my hand, I started off round the perimeter, following Yamazawa's directions.

It didn't take long to find what I was looking for. A double-roofed structure – some sort of guardhouse, I supposed – soared above the wall at its south-eastern corner. I'd only to cross the road to the south and look up to match it to the photograph. And I'd only to turn round to see several modern blocks of flats with balconies commanding a good view of it. I was there.

At any rate, I was close. But which block *exactly* did Smiler live in? I covered fifty yards of the pavement three times before I reckoned I had the right angle on the guardhouse. It led me to a six-storey, ochre-coloured block with railinged balconies. Among the bicycles propped near the entrance stood a big old Harley-Davidson motorbike. As transport favoured by the locals it didn't convince. But as an exiled American's token of his easy-riding youth it was a different matter. I took a look at the names next to the bells beside the combination-locked front door. And standing out like a butte in an Arizona of Japanese script was LOUDON, M. I pressed the bell.

No answer. And repetition didn't change that. Loudon, M., was evidently out. *Sans* motorbike, but out. I tried the next bell down, but only got a Japanese woman who didn't speak any English. She had the good sense to cut me off. I tried another bell, with pretty similar results. It looked like I was just going to have to wait for Loudon to return, as he was bound to, sooner or later. At least I'd recognize him when he did.

Half an hour slowly (very slowly) passed. Traffic trundled by. Nobody came or went. I started to feel hungry and was giving some serious thought to shoving off in search of food (and drink) when a young woman cycled to a halt at the roadside and wheeled her bike in towards me.

'Excuse me,' I ventured. 'Do you speak English?'

'A little,' she said, bowing and beaming at me.

'You live here?'

'Yes. I live here.'

'Do you know Mr Loudon?' I flourished the photograph. 'American guy. Here he is. Loudon?'

'Ah, Miller.' It seemed they were on first-name terms, which had to be good, even if she didn't pronounce *Miller* the way they would in Arkansas. 'You friend of Miller?'

'More friend *of* a friend.' She gaped at me uncomprehendingly. 'Do you know where I can find him?'

She frowned. 'He live here.'

'But he's not in.'

'Not in?'

'*Not at home.*'

'Ah. *Sumimasen*. Sorry.'

'Any idea where he might be?'

She thought for a moment, then said, 'Probably . . . he is teaching.'

'He teaches?'

'Yes. How do you say? Some of the time? Part of the time?'

'Part-time.'

'*Hai*. Part-time. Yes.'

'Where?'

'Doshisha most, I think.'

'Doshisha?'

'University. Doshisha University.'

'Where's that?'

'Ah, two kilometres.' She gestured vaguely behind her. 'This way. But you can take the subway. It is near Imadegawa station.'

'Right. Thanks a lot.'

It wasn't the subway for me, of course. I picked up a cab that had just unloaded a few more visitors to Nijo-jo and took the overland route.

I tracked our progress on a map I'd bought at the railway station. We headed east, then north along a wide, straight road past the old Imperial Park. The Doshisha University campus was clearly marked, dead ahead at the northern end of the park.

The taxi dropped me in a leafy driveway that filtered off into a maze of red-brick courtyards across which students were hurrying, on foot or cycle, to their next uplifting class. I stopped a couple of them long enough to try the name Miller Loudon and see if it rang any bells. They talked it over and finally decided that, yes, there was a Loudon on the staff.

'Faculty of Letters,' one of them concluded, pointing towards a triple-arched entrance to one of the buildings on the other side of the courtyard. 'Ask inside.'

I did. Happily, the receptionist turned out to speak excellent English. 'Mr Loudon is one of our part-time teachers,' she agreed. 'That is right. American literature.' She studied a timetable, then the clock. 'He has a class now. Until four.'

'I must see him. Urgently.'

'You can see him. At four. I will give you the room number.' She smiled. 'And you can meet him when he leaves.'

She was right, of course. Bursting in on him in the midst of his students wasn't a smart idea. Four o'clock it would have to be.

And four o'clock it was, or a few minutes after, with the first shadows of dusk gathering in the corridor, when the relevant door opened on the second floor of the Faculty of Letters and a dozen eager-eyed students spring-heeled their way out and past me.

I stepped into the doorway as the last of them left. Miller Loudon, white-haired and paunchy likeness of his photographed self, was shovelling papers into an old canvas knapsack. He was wearing jeans and a tweed jacket over a checked shirt – part academic, part cowboy.

'Miller Loudon?'

'Yuh.' He looked up at me. 'What can I do for you?'

'Not sure. But I believe you know the Hashimotos. Mayumi and Haruko.'

'You *believe*?' He walked over to me with a stiff-hipped limp. 'Who are you?'

'Lance Bradley. A friend of—'

'Rupe Alder's.' He nodded grimly. 'That's whose friend you are, isn't it?'

'Yes. How did you—'

'Never mind. What in God's name are you doing in Kyoto?'

'We need to talk, Mr Loudon.'

'I was hoping we'd never need to. But you're right. We do now. Not here, though.'

'Where, then?'

'Follow me.'

*　*　*

We took the lift down. 'My hip doesn't care for stairs,' said Loudon as we descended. 'I keep asking them to schedule my classes for the first floor, but at my age you don't have a lot of bargaining power. I should be retired by rights, but where else would they find someone who can see inside Hemingway's soul?'

The patter seemed genial enough, but I had the impression it was just a holding operation and that something far less genial was simmering beneath the surface of his remarks. He led the way out of the building, across the courtyard and down the drive towards the road that ran along the northern side of the Imperial Park.

'Mind telling me how you found me, Lance?' he asked as we went.

In answer, I held up the photograph for him to see.

'Holy shit. Where's that come from?'

'It was among some things Rupe left with a colleague at Eurybia in Tokyo for safekeeping.'

'What colleague might that be?'

'Name of Yamazawa.'

'Never heard of him. And let's hope no one else has either.'

'What do you mean?'

'If you can follow the trail, so can others.'

'And that might lead those "others" to Mayumi and Haruko?'

'Shut up until we're off the grounds, can't you? At least *try* to be careful.'

'All right.'

So, chastened into silence, I said nothing as we crossed the road and entered the park. The outer wall

224

was separated from the inner wall surrounding the old Imperial Palace by a vast expanse of gravel, where a few dog-walkers and strollers were dotted about – blurred figures in the encroaching twilight. Loudon took a scarf from his knapsack and draped it round his neck as a concession to the deepening chill, his breath misting as he crunched along.

'There's something I have to tell you . . . Miller,' I began. 'About Mayumi's brother.'

'Oh, there's plenty, yeh, Lance. But if you're honing your breaking-bad-news technique, I ought to let you know that we do get TV and newspapers in this city.'

'You've heard?'

'Take a look at this.' He opened his knapsack and pulled out an English newspaper. At least, it looked to be English, but then I saw the title: *The Japan Times*. And a fraction of a second later I saw Kiyofumi Hashimoto's photograph low down on the front page. *Japanese businessman slain in Berlin* ran the headline. 'The *Yomiuri Shimbun* made a bigger splash of it,' Loudon went on, reading the surprise on my face. 'When you're on the run, you really should pay more attention to the news-stands.'

'On the run?'

'Well, what would you call it?'

'Something that doesn't sound so guilty, I suppose.'

'But you are guilty, Lance, aren't you? The German police obviously think so, even though they haven't come out and said it.'

'Guilty of what?'

'What do you think?'

'Look, OK, strictly speaking I should have stayed and

225

helped the police with their inquiries, but I reckoned Berlin wasn't a safe place to hang around. And would you really have wanted me to anyway? There was nothing I could do to help Kiyo.'

'I'm not talking about Kiyofumi.' He stopped and stared at me. 'Hold on. Are you saying . . . you didn't do it?'

'Didn't do *what*?'

'Kill Eric Townley.'

'He's dead?'

'Oh yeh. Well and truly. Found battered about the head—'

'In my hotel room. Oh my God.'

'So you do know.'

'No. He wasn't dead. Not when I left. I mean, I hit him, yes. With a lamp. But—'

'That's the trouble with German furniture. Heavy.'

'He wasn't dead, I'm telling you. Unconscious, but breathing. And it was self-defence, for God's sake. He had a gun.'

'No mention of that in the papers.'

'What *do* they say?'

'See for yourself.' He handed me *The Japan Times* and I held up the article to read in the dwindling light.

JAPANESE BUSINESSMAN SLAIN IN BERLIN
Kiyofumi Hashimoto, 47, a senior manager with the Fujisaka Microprocessor Corporation, was shot dead on Tuesday while aboard an open-top tour bus in the center of Berlin. German Police say the killing appears to have been the work of a professional assassin.

They believe it is connected with another death in the city on Tuesday, the apparent murder of Erich Townley, 45, a dual German–American citizen found dead from head injuries in a room at the Hotel Adlon. They are trying to trace the person who had been staying in the room, Lancelot Bradley, 37, a British citizen believed to have been with Hashimoto at the time of the shooting.

They are also seeking witnesses to both deaths, especially those who may have seen a man behaving suspiciously in or near the Hotel Botschafter, opposite the bus stop in Tauentzien-strasse where Hashimoto was shot. The hotel has been undergoing refurbishment and its rooms facing Tauentzienstrasse have been empty during the work. It is thought the assassin fired from one of these rooms during the builders' lunch break.

In Tokyo yesterday, Ryozo Moriguchi, Executive Director of the Fujisaka Corporation, paid tribute to Hashimoto, saying—

'Bloody hell,' I mumbled, handing the paper back to Loudon. 'On the run is right.'

' 'Fraid so, Lance.'

'None of this was my fault.'

'Reckon not.'

'It could just as easily have been me as Kiyo who died on that bus.'

'Kiyofumi was a good man. A loyal brother to Mayumi. A loving uncle to Haruko. I knew him. I don't

227

know you. So, you'll understand if I personally regret that it wasn't you.'

'I was trying to help.'

'So Kiyofumi said.'

'He told you about me?'

'He told Mayumi.'

'Where is she?'

'I'm not sure you need to know that.'

'But you *are* sheltering her – and Haruko?'

'I'm doing my best to protect them, yuh. The question is: do I need to protect them from you?'

'I'm no threat to anyone.'

'No? What happened to Kiyofumi doesn't exactly confirm that, now does it?'

'It wasn't my fault. Kiyo was calling the shots.'

'Unfortunate choice of metaphor, Lance.'

'Look, what I mean is—'

'Why are you here?'

'*Why?* Because the Townleys have to be stopped. Can't you see that? Hiding won't cut it.'

'Brave words.'

'Desperate ones, actually.'

'Yuh. Well, I can see how you might be desperate. But not bereaved. And not betrayed. Mayumi and Haruko are two up on you there.'

'I can't change what Rupe did. And I can't bring Kiyo back to life.'

'True enough.'

'But I can do something to stop the Townleys.' (Though God alone knew what.) 'And you can help me.'

'How – exactly?'

'By telling me what this is really all about. Beginning with what's in the Townley letter.'

'Didn't Kiyofumi let you in on that?'

'He did not.'

'Because Mayumi swore him to secrecy.'

'So I gathered.'

'Well, it's the same here, Lance.'

'For God's sake. We're in this together. Whether any of us like it or not. I think I'm entitled to know what it *is* that I'm in.'

'You have a point.'

'Well?'

'It's not my decision.'

'Take me to Mayumi, then.'

'No can do.'

'Why not?'

'Because that might be just what they want me to do.' Loudon sighed and cast a glance behind and in front of us. 'Has it occurred to you that the "professional assassin" who shot Kiyofumi was almost certainly professional enough to account for you as well?'

'What are you getting at?'

'I'm getting at the disturbing possibility that you were *allowed* to escape. For the specific purpose of doing exactly what you have done.'

'You think I've been followed?'

'Maybe.'

'That's crazy. On the plane? Everywhere I've been? No way.'

'A professional assassin is a stalker as well as a shooter, Lance. The whole point of the operation is that you don't know it's happening.'

229

'I'd know.' (But that was whistling in the wind. Would I really have known?) 'Besides, if you're right, why did Erich try to stop me?'

'Disobeying orders, maybe. You and Kiyofumi *were* putting the squeeze on him.'

'All right.' I shrugged theatrically, more annoyed by the thought that I could well have been followed than I was prepared to admit. 'In that case, what do we do?'

'We go to a little bar I know a few blocks from here and talk it through over a drink.' Loudon grinned disarmingly. 'There are some things I *am* allowed to tell you.'

The bar was a cavernous basement under a dry-cleaner's shop. Custom was thin at just gone five on an autumn afternoon and, apart from us, entirely Japanese. 'They don't speak much English here,' Loudon told me as we entered, before exchanging greetings with the *mama* and her few customers in their own tongue. 'And any strangers following us in are going to stand out like Mount Fuji on a clear day. This is as confidential as it gets.'

Nobody did follow us in. We took a pair of stools at one end of the curving bar next to a papier-mâché badger and ordered some drinks. Sapporo and a *shochu* chaser for me, Coca-Cola for Loudon. A surprise, given that I had him down as a hard-liquor man.

'I'll need to keep a clear head,' he explained, without going on to explain why. 'So, you're Rupe's boyhood friend come to find him *and* atone for his misdeeds, right?'

'Something like that.'

'Tough assignment.'

I smiled – less ruefully than I might have done. 'Apparently so.'

'Kiyofumi did tell you exactly how your boyhood friend deceived Haruko, didn't he? How – and why?'

'He made it very clear. So clear I'd have been tempted to give up – but for the fact that by then it was too late.'

'Yuh. Too late. A bitchy little point in time, that. You never see it coming. I surely didn't.'

'When was it for you?'

'When I got too buddy-buddy with Rupe and let him top me up with bourbon till I was ready to spill the beans on the Townley letter. Once bitten, twice shy, Lance. I'll do right by Mayumi this time round if I do nothing else.'

'How long have you known her?'

'More than forty years. From my first visit to the Golden Rickshaw, though I can't exactly recall the occasion. I can't recall her taking my picture for the wall either. But she did. That's how Rupe traced me.'

'This picture?' I took out the wallet of photographs and showed him the one of him with Townley and some other guy as young military men.

'Yuh. That's the one.'

'What *was* the Golden Rickshaw?'

'Just a bar. A popular one, thanks to Mayumi. She was ... radiant ... back then. We came like moths to a lantern. And, like moths, one or two of us got burned.' He chewed over the past for a silent moment before continuing. 'Then again, of course, it wasn't just a bar. Townley and his outfit made sure of that.'

'What was his outfit?'

'Something called a DetMIG – Detached Military Intelligence Group. Linked with the CIA. Their role was to identify soldiers, airmen and sailors who had the skills and aptitude to perform special duties – during *and* after their military service. They used the Rickshaw as a place to size people up. Evaluate them when they were at their most relaxed, with a view to possible recruitment.'

'Did they recruit you?'

'Only as a scout. I was done a few favours and handed a few greenbacks in return for acting as a talent-spotter. I wasn't on the payroll. Not officially. But I was in the loop. You could say I was Townley's snitch if you weren't in the business of sparing my feelings.'

'What sort of talent were you looking for?'

'Oh, the grim, dedicated, intensely anti-communist, faintly manic kind, of course. What other kind?'

'To do . . .'

'Dirty work, Lance. Very dirty work. I never asked for the specifics, but I didn't need to. I understood what the object of the exercise was.'

'I'm not sure I understand. *Exactly.*'

'Well, you can take it – I surely took it – that killing people was going to be on the agenda. As part of any undercover work the recruit was deemed fit for. All in the general and noble cause of defending the United States of America against its enemies.'

'Is this one of those recruits?' I pointed to the third man in the photograph.

'Yuh.' Loudon gave a rubbery grimace. 'Reckon he'd have to be counted as such.'

'Spotted by you?'

'Ah, actually, no. He came by a different route. But Townley certainly had his eye on him. No question about that.' Loudon squirmed in his seat, as if this particular subject made him uncomfortable. 'Leastways, I think so. With only the back of his head to go by, I may have the wrong guy.' Then he relaxed again. 'Look, Lance, it pans out like this. I get drafted in the ranks because I'm too bloody-minded to join the officer cadet corps while I'm at college. I soon realize what a frigging idiot I've been, but by then it's too late. Like we were saying earlier. Anyhow, I wind up here in Japan and Townley and his sinister band of brothers make me feel . . . important, I guess. So, I do a few things for them. I mark a few cards. I oil some wheels. Then I move on. Out of the Army. Back to that privileged existence I should never have left behind as heir to my uncle's furniture business. I forget Townley and his DetMIG. I even *try* to forget Mayumi. I put it all behind me. I walk away. End of story. Or should be. But . . .'

'Not the end.'

'No. Nothing like. Thanks to Rupe.'

'He didn't force you to come back here.'

'I can't deny that.'

'Why did you?'

'Because the country had got its claws into me. Well, the people had. They're a beguiling nation. So gentle, so . . . private. I guess the American way of life just wasn't for me. I sure wasn't cut out for the furniture trade. When my uncle died, I cashed in my share of the business and came here to settle. It's more than a little ironic, let me tell you, me living in the old Imperial capital and revering Japanese culture and all, since this gentle race, as I just described them, were responsible for my father's death when I was only six years old. He was killed in the attack on Pearl Harbor, December seventh, nineteen forty-one. But . . . well, I've made my peace with them on his behalf, so to speak. This isn't my home. But it is where I belong.'

'Townley obviously didn't feel the same way.'

'No. He left as soon as he could and never came back.'

'Leaving behind only his face in this photograph, which Rupe spotted on the wall of the Golden Rickshaw,' I began reasoning. 'He recognized Townley, who he was already interested in because of his connection with Rupe's own family, then—'

'I know nothing about that.'

'It doesn't matter. The point is that Rupe saw his chance to find Townley by romancing Haruko. And she no doubt pretty soon let slip that one of the other people in the photograph was living here, in Kyoto.'

'I got back in touch with Mayumi after leaving the States. And I've stayed in touch since. So, yuh, Haruko mentioned me when Rupe showed an apparently innocent interest in the picture and the history of the bar. Then Rupe suggested a visit. Well, Kyoto's an attractive destination in its own right. Looking me up just seemed to her like a natural add-on to a tour of the temples. It seemed that way to me too. I was pleased to see them.'

'Certainly looks like it.' I held out another photograph for him to see – the snapshot of him with Haruko on the balcony of his flat.

'Yuh. There I am, grinning like the sap he played me for.'

'At some point, you told him about the Townley letter.'

'I was boasting. That's the truth of it. Making myself feel important – and look important to Haruko's future husband, which is what I thought he was – by shooting my mouth off about the old days. I can't say more than that without breaking my word to Mayumi a second time. And that I will not do. But, thanks to me – and Haruko's blindly adoring trust in him – Rupe was able to steal the letter and make his move on Townley. Which put Mayumi and Haruko – and me, for that paltry matter – in more danger than you can possibly imagine.'

'Me too now, I assume.'

'Yuh. That's right, Lance. You too. His friends and his lovers and the friends of his lovers. Rupe's done a thorough job of shafting anyone who ever trusted him.'

'Not intentionally.' (Was I sure about that? I certainly didn't feel it.)

'OK. Inadvertently, then. I'm not sure that doesn't make it worse. He just didn't care what the consequences were. Oh, he put himself in danger too, I grant you. But that was his choice. We didn't get a choice.'

'What sort of man is Townley?'

'Hard, calculating, ruthless.'

'Why does he need to be?'

'Because he isn't in control of this. It's beyond him. Beyond all of us.'

'But you're not going to tell me what it is.'

Loudon gave a weary sigh. 'That's Mayumi's decision, not mine.'

'When can I meet her?'

235

'Not sure. I have to weigh up the risks, Lance. If you've been followed, taking you to her would be the stupidest thing I've ever done. And I've done enough stupid things already. Besides, what sort of help can you offer that would make the risks worth running?'

'Townley is tied in with a murder in England in August nineteen sixty-three. I don't know how exactly. Or why. But if I knew what was in the letter, maybe it would all make sense. Then we might have something on him. The same something Rupe put together.'

'And what would we do with it?'

'Go to the authorities. Make a case. Strike back at him any way we can.'

'That'd never work.'

'Why not?'

'Because—' Loudon made a swatting gesture with his hand and sipped his Coke. 'God, I wish there was vodka in this.'

'Don't they sell vodka here?'

'Oh yuh. They sell it. Sometimes to me. But not this evening.' He leaned back on his stool and stretched, then relaxed again. 'OK. Let's lay it on the line. Everything we do from here on in is risky. Even doing nothing is risky. And a damn sight harder on the nerves than . . . striking back, as you call it. Temperamentally, I'm a retaliatory kind of guy. Not a skulker in corners. I'll speak to Mayumi. She'll decide.'

'When?'

'Tonight. That's why I'm off the sauce. It's a long ride.'

'You're going to see her?'

'Yuh. And if I'm followed, well, on that road I'll surely know it.'

236

'And if not?'

'Then I'll come back for you in the morning. You can bed down at my apartment. I'll phone Mayumi from there and set it up.'

'When did you decide all this?' (It certainly seemed sudden to me.)

'Oh, around the time you walked through the door of my class at Doshisha and introduced yourself.'

'Then why have you been giving me such a hard time about risk assessment?'

'Because there *are* risks. And because I wanted to see what you had to offer in the way of a game plan before I committed myself.'

'So, I've persuaded you, have I?'

'No, Lance, you haven't. Not remotely.' He gave me the same grin he'd worn in Mayumi's photograph – and in Rupe's. 'But I'll do it anyway.'

CHAPTER TWELVE

Miller Loudon's flat reflected the divided loyalties of its owner. One of the living rooms was a tatami-matted oasis of uncluttered calm, the other a Mexican-rugged chaos of sagging armchairs, bulging bookcases and discarded coffee mugs. Maybe each was a refuge for one half of his soul.

The biggest and saggiest armchair unfolded into a bed. (Manufactured, so a badge on the frame informed me, by the Loudon Furniture Works of Williamsport, Pennsylvania – circa 1950, I'd have guessed.) Loudon showed me how to lock it into place, then phoned Mayumi. He conversed with her in fluent Japanese, thereby freeing himself (whether deliberately or not) to say whatever he liked about me; certainly my name *was* mentioned several times. All I actually gleaned was the affection in his tone. It seemed probable to me that he loved Mayumi, though perhaps in a way that had never been openly declared.

He certainly wasn't about to declare it to me. Pausing only to show me where I could find the coffee and the bourbon, he shucked himself into his Harley-Davidson leathers and made ready to leave. 'If I don't phone at eight tomorrow morning, it'll be because I'm on my way back, in which case I'll be here by nine. Got it?'

'Got it.'

'You'll know it's me on the phone because I'll give it three rings and hang up, then call again within a minute. Don't answer it otherwise. OK?'

'OK.'

'Don't meddle with my papers. I know the exact location of every crumpled note.'

'There'll be no meddling.'

'Good. If you want some bedtime reading, I have about half a dozen copies of *For Whom the Bell Tolls*. A dip into that could be kind of appropriate.'

'I'll think about it.'

'Do that. Anything else you need?'

'The phone number of Mayumi and Haruko's hideaway – in case of emergencies.'

'Nice try, but no. I don't want you to have any clues to their whereabouts that you could pass on to a third party.'

'Am I likely to do that?'

'Not voluntarily, no. But we have to consider the possibility that circumstances could arise where it's forced out of you.'

'A consoling thought.'

'I'm not into consolation, Lance. It's a pragmatic judgement. Simple as that.'

'Risk assessment.'

'Exactly right. And now I have to get rolling. While I'm gone . . .'

'Yeh?'

'Try to relax.'

I watched through the chink in the blinds as he roared away into the night. He headed west, which as clues went was pretty meagre. And that, by his reckoning, was just as well.

I kept watching for several minutes. There was no sign of a car going off in pursuit. But then, as Loudon would have been sure to tell me, the only pursuit we were likely to be dealing with was the invisible kind.

I gave *For Whom the Bell Tolls* a miss, but I don't think that's why I failed to nod straight off into dreamland. I was bone weary and not far short of brain dead, but sleep just wouldn't seem to come, even with the help of my absent host's Jack Daniel's.

Solitude by night in a stranger's home isn't a restful experience. In this case, it bred the weirdest illusion in my mind: that I was back in Glastonbury, safe and as sound as I'd ever been, and that none of this had happened – none of it at all. Win hadn't walked into the Wheatsheaf and persuaded me to look for Rupe. Hashimoto hadn't inveigled me into going to Berlin with him. There'd been no rifleman lurking in a half-rebuilt room at the Hotel Botschafter, no fatal struggle with Erich Townley. The bullet hadn't smashed into Hashimoto's brain. The base of the lamp hadn't thumped into Erich's skull.

Illusion it wasn't, I realized as I came to myself to see daylight seeping between the slats of the blinds. Just a dream – albeit one cruelly inverting the normal rules of dreaming. I didn't wake to the reassuring knowledge

240

that the horrors were imaginary. I woke to bleak re-acquaintance with the awareness that they were all real – every one of them.

There was more than an hour to go to the time Loudon had said he'd call. I took a shower and forced myself to eat some toast to soak up the black coffee. (Feeling faintly sick, as I'd been doing for most of the previous two days, hadn't done a lot for my appetite.)

I looked again at the article in *The Japan Times*, which Loudon had left behind. *German Police . . . are trying to trace . . . Lancelot Bradley, 37, a British citizen believed to have been with Hashimoto at the time of the shooting.* How had they worked that out? How had they known who I was? *Lancelot*, for God's sake. It had to be airline records, based on my passport. But they'd moved fast, no doubt about it, mangling my age in the process. My thirty-seventh birthday was still a few weeks off. Not that a few weeks were a small matter to me just then. They sounded like a lifetime. Maybe more than the span of the rest of mine.

That thought led to final abandonment of the toast. If they knew who I was, they knew where I came from. The German Police had probably asked their British opposite numbers to check my home address by now. It could only be a matter of time before they ended up at my parents' door. Maybe I ought to warn Mum and Dad before that happened. But that would be difficult without explaining what I was doing and why. It was around half-past ten the previous evening in England. Mum would just be making the cocoa, blithely unaware – since Martin's in the High Street didn't stock *The Japan Times* – of the trouble her son was in. If I didn't

241

phone now, I mightn't get the chance for quite a while.

But that chance slipped through my fingers sooner than I'd expected. Suddenly, the doorbell rang. I rushed to the window and looked out – a pointless thing to do, since the entrance to the flats was out of sight two floors below me. But that wasn't necessarily the case from the balcony. I unlatched the sliding door and stepped outside, craning over the railings for a view. But the entrance was still obscured by the porch. I heard the doorbell ring again, lengthily. Who the hell could it be? Loudon had said nothing about visitors.

I'd just decided to go back in and wait for them to go away when a figure emerged from the overhang of the porch and looked straight up at me. He was a tall, rangy, middle-aged guy, with fair, thinning hair and a darker-hued moustache, dressed in a short leather jacket, black T-shirt and jeans. He smiled, revealing a set of dazzling white teeth, and held up a hand in greeting. 'Hi.' The accent was American, more drawly than Loudon's. 'You must be Lance.'

'Who are you?' I responded, trying not to show the shock I felt that he knew who I was.

'Steve Bryce. A colleague of Miller's from Doshisha. He asked me to pick you up.'

'He did?'

'Yuh. Trouble with his bike. But what can you expect? More rust in the tank than gas. So, I had my arm twisted. Your taxi awaits.'

'Miller hasn't phoned me about this.'

'He'll still be wheeling that behemoth of a bike back to the farmhouse.'

'The farmhouse?'

242

'Yuh. Where we're going. It's OK. I know where it is. Miller called me from a payphone. Out in the sticks, they only take coins. He did say he wouldn't have enough to call you as well. Since he harbours some antediluvian prejudice against mobiles, we're kind of lucky he made any contact at all.'

'I . . . suppose so. But—'

'Now I don't want to hurry you, Lance, but I have to be back at Doshisha by ten and it must be an hour's drive to the farmhouse, so could we move this along? I mean, hell, I am doing you guys a favour.'

So he certainly appeared to be. But appearances could be deceptive. I looked down at his blandly smiling face and asked myself the obvious question: could I trust him? Loudon hadn't mentioned any friends at Doshisha to me and this was the sort of change of plan he'd have been likely to condemn as too risky if I'd proposed it. But, if his motorbike had let him down and time was of the essence (as it was), he might have felt forced to go for it. In which case I wouldn't be helping anyone by sitting tight. The farmhouse was presumably where Mayumi and Haruko were hiding. And I wanted to speak to them – badly.

'Is there a problem, Lance?'

'No.' I'd made my choice. 'I'll be right down.'

Bryce's small white saloon didn't have any of the glamour of Loudon's Harley-Davidson. But, as Bryce pointed out, it had just chalked up a points victory for reliability. We drove north-west out of Kyoto, sunlight dappling the wooded mountains ahead as the cloud thinned. Bryce asked a stream of questions about my connection with Loudon and the urgent need for me to be ferried out to the back of beyond. It seemed he was pretty much in the dark and he was understandably curious. But he got no change out of me and had given up probing for information by the time we left the city limits.

From then on he was happy to talk about himself – a favourite topic of his, I guessed. The twists and turns of his academic career didn't interest me, of course, but I was content to let him sustain a monologue on the subject while we zigzagged up the ever steeper road between thick stands of conifers. Habitations were few and far between. We'd left the bustling urban world behind with surprising speed and were heading deeper and deeper into the backwoods.

Shortly after we'd passed through the second of two long tunnels, Bryce turned off onto a rough, unmetalled side-road that soon deteriorated into little more than a forest track. He assured me it was a viable short-cut to another main road that would lead us to the farmhouse, but after nearly breaking the axle of the car in a rut that was deep enough to have been left by a rocket trans-porter, he seemed to lose confidence.

'I guess I'd better check the map,' he said, pulling over under the trees. 'Hold on while I fetch it from the trunk.'

He clambered out, walked round to the back and opened the boot. I heard him shifting things around, then it went quiet, but the boot didn't close and he didn't come back. I wound down the window and leaned out. 'You OK?'

'Not exactly,' he replied. 'You better come and look at this.'

'What is it?'

'Just come see.'

'All right.' I sighed and climbed out, imagining, I think, that our encounter with the giant wheel-rut had done some serious damage to the underside of the car, though what Bryce thought I could do about it was beyond me. 'So, what's the—'

The words died in my mouth as I rounded the rear wing of the car and glanced into the boot. Miller Loudon was lying there on his back, trussed with ropes, his face fixed and staring, with a dark, blood-clotted bullet hole in the middle of his forehead.

'I thought she wasn't pulling uphill quite right,' said Bryce. 'Here's the reason: two hundred and seventy pounds of dead weight.'

I stared at him, still too horrified to speak or act. That's when I saw the gun in his right hand, trained on me, and the coil of rope looped over his shoulder.

'Journey's end, Lance. Turn round and start walking into the forest. I'll tell you when to stop.'

I didn't move, just looked down at Loudon's body, then back up at Bryce. Still no words came. I felt sick and helpless and shamingly stupid.

'Come on, Lance. One foot in front of the other. You know how it works. Get moving.'

'Who are you?'

'Just move.' He slammed the boot shut and raised his right arm, pointing the gun at my head. I found myself staring at the barrel, a rock-steady metal extension of his hand. 'OK?'

All my choices had been pared away. There was nothing left but to do exactly what I was told. I turned and started walking.

I'd gone about twenty yards when Bryce told me to stop. I was near the foot of a tall, red-leafed maple standing among the pines. A single leaf from one of the branches slowly fluttered down to rest among the pine needles at my feet as I waited. Was he going to kill me here? Was this where it ended? (If so, I reflected, a forest in Japan was going to be the surprise answer to the question *Where did Lance Bradley finish up?* in a future Wheatsheaf quiz.)

Suddenly, something hard and heavy struck me round the back of neck. I don't remember hitting the ground.

Pain and consciousness met up some time later. Speech and coherent thought were late for the party, though. I was sitting at the foot of the maple tree, my back resting against the trunk, unable to move. Bryce was standing a few yards in front of me, flicking through the contents of a wallet. It looked like . . . my wallet. Then I became aware of the ropes holding me tight against the tree. And Bryce noticed me make a futile effort to struggle free of them.

'Hi, Lance,' he said, smiling at me. 'Welcome back.'

'What . . . what the . . .' My words sounded slurred and subdued.

'Now, a few minutes ago you asked who I am. But it turns out you already know.' He tossed the wallet aside and held up a small white card. 'Gordon A. Ledgister, Caribtex Oil. Pleased to meet you.'

'L-Ledgister?'

'That's right. Although, if you asked the agency I hired the car from, they'd say, oddly enough, that my name is

. . . Lance Bradley.' His smile widened. 'With poor old Miller in the trunk, I guess somebody will be asking them that question sooner or later. But, hey, let's not worry about it. Sufficient unto the day, etcetera, etcetera. Let's get back to the needs of this day.'

'You . . . followed me from Berlin?'

'Got it in one. Stifling my grief at the unscheduled demise of my brother-in-law, I tagged along as you Hawkeyed your way here.'

'You shot Hashimoto?'

'Never mind him. It's the living I want to talk to you about, not the dead. Where are they, Lance? Where are Mayumi and Haruko?'

Clumsily, my thoughts grasped the point that Bryce – Ledgister, as I now had to think of him – was making for me. He'd followed Loudon to the farmhouse. But Mayumi and Haruko hadn't been there. It was the hiding-place. It had to be. But they'd deserted it. Why? There could only be one answer. Loudon had told them to clear out in his phone call the previous evening. He must have reckoned it was odds-on I'd been followed, so he'd decided to flush out whoever was doing the following. He'd put Mayumi and Haruko out of harm's way. But not himself.

'I asked Miller, of course. You bet I did. Very . . . forcefully. But he wouldn't tell me, despite all my blandishments. In the end, I lost patience. Well, you can see how I would, can't you? All this way, only to find that the ladies I was so eager to meet . . . weren't at home. It was a real disappointment.'

'I don't know where they are.'

'Don't say that, Lance. I want you to help me. I want

247

you to *want* to help me. Then maybe . . . I could help you. That's how relationships should be. *Quid pro quo.* But if you can't help me . . . or won't . . . then our relationship isn't likely to last very long. Now, let's try again. Where are Mayumi and Haruko?'

'I don't know. I don't even know where they *were*.'

'Come on. You don't expect me to believe that.'

'No. But it's true.'

'This isn't auguring well for your future, Lance. You do realize that, don't you?'

'Yeh, I do.' But there I'd told him my first lie. Because I'd just seen a figure threading its soft-footed way through the trees behind Ledgister – a slim, lithely built Japanese man dressed in a blue tracksuit. His hair was short and flecked with grey, his face raw-boned and pale. His gaze was fixed on Ledgister. And he was carrying a gun, clasped in both hands in front of him as he picked a silent path through the drifts of pine needles and damp, fallen leaves. I considered the idea for a moment that he was a hallucination: that fear and concussion had conjured him up as an imaginary saviour. But he looked very real. And he kept on coming.

'I don't have the leisure to prolong this conversation indefinitely,' said Ledgister. 'So, maybe I ought to lay it on the line for you. Unless—'

'Put your gun down.' The man in the tracksuit had spoken. Ledgister half-turned and saw him – and saw also the gun trained on him from no more than a few yards away.

'Who the—'

'Put it down.'

'OK.' Ledgister held up his free hand in surrender as

he lowered himself onto his haunches and laid his gun on the ground. 'No problem.'

'Stand up.'

Ledgister did so. 'Now, I don't know who you are, friend, but—'

'No kind of friend to you.'

'Hey, don't be so sure. We might get along real fine if we . . . compared interests. How about money, for instance? Are you keen on that? Earning it, I mean. As easily as possible.'

'Untie Mr Bradley.'

'Who is this guy, Lance?' Ledgister glanced round at me. 'Shouldn't you introduce us?'

'Untie him. Now.' Tracksuit moved closer still, his gun pointing straight at Ledgister.

'OK, OK. I'll do it.'

Ledgister walked slowly round to the other side of the tree, Tracksuit circling after him. I felt a tugging at the ropes, then they slackened and fell away. I rolled away from the trunk and scrambled unsteadily to my feet.

'I'll bet there's not a single rope-burn to reproach me for. Isn't that right, Lance?'

'Sit in Mr Bradley's place,' said my anonymous saviour, his voice unwaveringly calm. 'Tie him up, Lance.'

Ledgister sat flouncily down at the foot of the tree and grinned defiantly at me. I gathered up the ropes, settling for the relatively easy course of dumb obedience while struggling to understand this sudden turning of the tables. Ledgister's question had been a good one. Who *was* this guy?

'What goes around comes around, Lance,' Ledgister whispered as I tied his hands behind his back. 'Luck like yours doesn't last for ever,' he added when I looped the second rope around his chest. 'When it runs out, I'll be waiting.'

Waiting was soon about all he was in a position to do. I tightened the ropes until I'd forced a grunt out of him, then tied them off.

'Good,' said Tracksuit as he checked the knots. 'We go now.' Catching my questioning look, he added, 'Not here, Lance. I explain at the car.' Then he stopped in front of Ledgister and checked his pockets, presumably for concealed weapons. He didn't find any. But, as he looked, Ledgister noticed something.

'Hey, you're missing a pinky, friend.' He was right. The little finger on the man's left hand ended at the first joint. 'You're *Yakuza*, aren't you?' He got no reply beyond the briefest glare. 'You've taken out some expensive insurance, Lance. Let's hope you can afford the premiums.'

'Enough.' Tracksuit stood up and looked at me. Nothing in his expression implied that he had heard a single word Ledgister had said. 'We go.'

I hesitated, scanning the ground for my wallet. There it was, not far from where Ledgister had dropped the gun. I moved towards it.

'Don't touch it.' I stopped and looked round. 'Leave the gun where it is.'

'He's thinking of fingerprints,' said Ledgister. 'Cerebral stuff for a *Yakuza*.'

'It's my wallet I want.' I pointed to where it lay.

'OK.' (Ledgister's sarcasm didn't seem to have had

250

the slightest effect.) 'Take it and walk to the road.'

I did as I'd been told, looking straight ahead as I hurried through the trees. I couldn't hear my nameless companion behind me, but I felt sure he was there. '*Sayonara*, guys,' called Ledgister.

I stopped when I reached Ledgister's car and turned round. Tracksuit was within a stride of me, his gun no longer in view. 'My car is back along the road,' he said softly. 'A short walk.'

'Do you know what's in the boot of this car?' I nodded towards it.

'Yes. I saw. I heard. Do you know where the ladies are?'

'Not a clue. They were being sheltered in a farmhouse, apparently. But they're not there now.'

'They may return there.'

'But I don't know where it is. Only Ledgister knows that.'

'He will not tell us. Check the car. There may be something.'

I opened the driver's door and checked the side-pocket and dashboard shelves. Nothing. I leaned across and yanked down the flap of the glove compartment. There, inside, was a map, folded back on itself. I lifted it out and stared helplessly at a jumble of roads and rivers and contour lines, neatly labelled in Japanese. Then I saw it: a cross in red ink, added by hand. 'This could be it.'

'Yes.' He peered over my shoulder. 'Near Kamiyuge. About fifteen kilometres from here. Good. Bring the map with you.'

'What about Loudon?'

251

'He is dead.' The man stared at me blankly. 'We must go.'

'Ledgister hired this car in my name.'

'But the description the agency give to the police will fit him, not you. And a bullet from his gun killed Loudon.'

'Yes, but—'

'I could have killed Ledgister, but that would make the police think you killed both men. You understand? This is the best way. We will call the police and send them here. OK?'

'Are you . . . *Yakuza*?'

'Yes. But I'm not here for them. I'm here for my brother. Toshishige.'

'You're . . . Yamazawa's brother?'

'Yes. Shintaro Yamazawa. That is me. We have to go, Lance. It is dangerous for us here. If we are seen . . .'

'All right. I understand.'

I didn't, of course. Not the half of it. But leaving made sense. That I couldn't fail to grasp. Yamazawa led the way at a trot back down the track. His green Range Rover was parked under the trees beyond the second bend. We climbed in. Then he threw it round in a five-point turn and we drove away.

'How much do you know?' I asked, wondering just what he and his brother were up to.

'Toshishige asked me to watch your back. This is all. So, I stuck with you from the station yesterday. I saw Ledgister. He didn't see me.'

'Couldn't you have stopped him killing Loudon?'

'If I'd been there, maybe. But I was in Kyoto. Watching your back.'

'Did Toshishige tell you what this is about?'

'He told me some. Your friend put the Hashimotos in danger. The American, Loudon, was hiding them. Toshishige was worried about you. But he should have been more worried about them. You brought the danger with you.'

It was true. I'd trailed a line behind me and Ledgister had followed it. He'd killed twice that I knew of. And if it hadn't been for Loudon's self-sacrifice, it would have been more. 'I have to find Mayumi and Haruko.'

'If they've gone back to the farmhouse, we *will* find them. But we cannot wait there long. You must not be seen in places that connect you to this.'

'I can't just walk away.'

'Better than being carried, I think.'

'Look, I'm grateful, but—'

'Thank Toshishige, not me.'

'He didn't risk his life back there.'

'No risk. I was more careful for me than you.'

'Even so—'

'I saved your life. Yes. I think so. And I like to finish things I start. We still have the death penalty in Japan for murder. So—' He glanced at me without the least flicker of a smile. 'We will go on being careful.'

We rejoined the main road and headed north. Within a few miles, we descended into a valley and came to a village, where Yamazawa stopped at a call-box and phoned the police with his anonymous tip-off. Then we carried on, climbing again into the wooded mountains.

'Do you often do Toshishige favours like this?' I asked, when some of the shock had begun to drain out of me.

'Never one like this before. It is a . . . special case. Your friend, Rupert Alder . . .'

'Yeh?'

'Did not Toshishige tell you this?'

'Not sure. What was it?'

'Toshishige and I both had a fine education, Lance. Our father worked himself to death to make sure we did. He was specially keen for us to learn to speak English fluently. He thought it would help us make good careers. You can guess I was a disappointment to him. He forgot there are openings for fluent English speakers in organized crime as well as big business. He was proud of Toshishige, though. A respectful son. A straight, honest guy. And a hard worker. That was my brother. Until he was gassed on the subway. After that, he changed. He . . . got to like the wild side. That is why Yoshiko left him. She did not approve of me. Toshishige started drinking and gambling. Other women too, I think – the expensive kind. He needed money. More than he earned, you understand? So, I . . . set up a few deals for him.'

'What sort of deals?'

'Smuggling, mostly. A brother in shipping can be useful. Then . . . your friend found out.'

'Rupe knew?'

'Yes. He stopped it, of course. But he didn't report Toshishige. He let him off. It was their secret.'

'Toshishige said Rupe had saved his life.'

'Could be true. The sack. Maybe prison. That would have finished him, I reckon. Maybe your friend realized that.'

'And I'm the beneficiary of the debt of gratitude Toshishige owed him?'

'Yes. That is it. We Yamazawas believe in honour. Lucky for you, I think.'

We went through another village, this one smaller and more scattered, then turned off along a side-road where the going wasn't much better than on the route Ledgister had taken. But the woods were thinner, the views more open and extensive of the hills and mountains around us. Yamazawa stopped to check the map, drove on a short way, then stopped again where a track led down off the road. We were in a shallow valley, with overgrown fields to either side.

'The farmhouse must be down this track,' Yamazawa announced after a further squint at the map. 'Hidden by the trees maybe.'

'It certainly looks like the track's been used recently.' My deduction was hardly Sherlockian. There were plenty of tyre tracks and wheel ruts in the mud.

'OK. We go in.' Yamazawa nosed the Range Rover cautiously off the road and we rolled gently through the pot-holes as the track wound in a meandering curve round the long-grassed margin of a wood bordering the fields.

The farmhouse, which had clearly ceased to play host to any active farming for quite a while, appeared ahead of us. The roof was partly thatched, partly tiled, as if the original building had been extended. There was a veranda out front, with weed-choked flower beds beneath it. Away to one side was a rusty-roofed barn of some kind. In its open doorway stood a Harley-Davidson motorbike.

We pulled up in the yard and got out. Yamazawa

spotted at once that the sliding door leading into the house was half-open. We moved towards it, then stopped at the sight of what were obviously bloodstains on the planked floor of the veranda, smudged as if the person doing the bleeding had been dragged across them.

Yamazawa stepped gingerly past the marks and slid the door fully open. There were more of the same inside. 'Loudon died here, I guess,' he said. 'Then Ledgister dragged him to his car.'

'Mayumi and Haruko?'

'Gone. That is certain. But I will check. You stay here.'

Yamazawa went inside, leaving me to stare down at the bloodstains and across at Loudon's abandoned motorbike. I was partly to blame for what had happened to him, no question about it. Not as much to blame as Rupe, though. I wasn't thinking kindly of my old friend in that moment. 'Why didn't you just leave it alone?' I muttered under my breath. 'You bloody fool.'

Yamazawa was back within a couple of minutes. 'There is no one here,' he announced.

'Loudon telephoned them last night,' I explained. 'I don't know what he said. The conversation was in Japanese. But I think I can guess. He told them to clear out. They're hiding somewhere, probably waiting for a call from him to say everything's all right.'

'There will be no call.'

'No,' I agreed, glancing down again at the bloodstains. 'No call.'

'If you are right, they will not return here. They will wait and wait. And then they will learn what has happened – from the TV, the newspapers.'

'We must find them.'

'You may be safer on your own.'

'I can't just leave them to fend for themselves.' (Besides, though I didn't propose to mention it, there was still the question of the Townley letter. More than ever, I needed to know what was in it.)

'You are determined to look for them?' Yamazawa frowned at me, as if weighing me up.

'Yes.'

'Then ask yourself: what did Loudon plan? He must have realized he was in danger. So, he must have thought about what would happen to them without him. Who would he ask to protect them?'

'There's no one that I know of. Except me.'

'But he did not tell you where he was sending them.'

'Of course not. He was afraid that— Hold on.' I stopped and thought. The only way Loudon could have pointed me in the right direction without letting me in on what he was planning to do was to give me a cryptic message that I wouldn't recognize as such until after the event. Then, if he didn't come through, I'd be able to work out what he meant. 'He recommended a book to me. *For Whom the Bell Tolls*.'

'Ernest Hemingway.'

'You know his work?'

'No. But I am an Ingrid Bergman fan. Therefore I have seen the film. It is disappointing, of course, with that terrible haircut she has in it. But the story is OK.'

'Hemingway's not really my cup of tea. Frankly, as a Hemingway specialist, Loudon should have been able to tell that. The chances of me actually opening the book . . .' I stopped. Of course. Loudon had chosen something he'd been sure I'd ignore – until I turned his remarks over in my mind later. That was the whole point. 'We have to look at that book. It's at the flat.'

'Going there is too risky.'

'I have no choice.'

'You have, I think.'

'No.' I looked straight at him. 'Believe me, I haven't.'

In one of the long tunnels on the road back to Kyoto, we were passed by a car moving at close to the speed of a bullet train in the opposite direction, flashing its headlights in warning. 'The murder boys from Police HQ in Kyoto,' said Yamazawa. 'If Loudon has identification on him, it will not take them long to trace his address.'

'I know what you're saying, Shintaro. But I have to do this.'

'Then we do it quickly, OK? And I am in charge. Understood?'

'It's a deal.'

Short of time or not, Yamazawa parked two streets south of the apartment block. We approached it on foot, from the rear, cutting down a back-alley and hopping over a low fence into a small compound used to store rubbish bins. 'We should be doing this at night,' Yamazawa complained, wrenching back the metal door of a service lift. 'I am breaking all my own rules for you, Lance.'

'How did you know this way in?' I asked, as we started our ascent.

'I didn't. But Japan is a crime-free country. There is always a way in.'

We exited the lift into a bare, concrete stairwell, then pushed through a fire door into a carpeted corridor and followed it round to Loudon's flat.

Pop music was playing on a radio somewhere nearby, but there were no other signs of life. Yamazawa glanced cautiously around, then took out of his pocket a small, right-angled metal tool.

'What's that?'

'A door opener.' He slid the blade in round the jamb next to the Yale keyhole and, after no more than a few seconds' manipulation, slipped the latch. (The fact that Loudon hadn't given me a key ironically made it easier to break in, since I hadn't been able to lock the door on the mortice.)

I made straight for Loudon's bedroom, Yamazawa keeping pace behind me. A dog-eared old paperback copy of *For Whom the Bell Tolls* stood on the bedside cabinet. As I picked it up, I noticed one page had been folded down at the top corner. I opened the book at that page. In the rows of print, only one thing stood out. A name, underlined in pencil – *Maria*. I showed it to Yamazawa. 'Mean anything to you?'

'In the film, Gary Cooper is an American fighting in the Spanish Civil War. He falls in love with—' He broke off. 'Ingrid Bergman plays a girl called Maria.'

'Yeh? So?'

'There is a hotel called the Maria, in Arashiyama.'

'That's a big coincidence.' But it was no coincidence at all. It couldn't be.

And Yamazawa didn't think so either. 'We go,' he said, turning towards the door.

*   *   *

Arashiyama lay out to the west of Kyoto, where the hills subsided to the plain on which the city was built. There was a pretty bridge across a river, a scatter of temples and a sprawl of trinket shops and rickshaw pick-up points. As tourist traps went, it was mightily effective, since half the Kansai region and his uncle from Hokkaido seemed to be clogging the pavements.

'Is it always like this here?' I asked as Yamazawa nudged the Range Rover through the mobs.

'No. But the gardens of Tenryu-ji and Okochi-sanso are specially beautiful in the fall. And this is a public holiday.'

'It is?'

'Yes. *Bunka-no-hi.* Culture Day.'

'So there wouldn't be any teaching going on at Doshisha University today?'

'No. The students will be out with their lovers in the bamboo groves. Maybe their professors also. Why?'

'Nothing.' I was thinking of one of the lies Ledgister had told me to lure me out of Loudon's flat. '*I have to be back at Doshisha by ten.*' The irony was that he'd probably been as unaware as me of the glaring flaw in his story. 'It doesn't matter now.'

'Here's the Maria.' Yamazawa pulled into a car park in front of a medium-sized modern building with whitewashed walls, their glaring plainness relieved by a dazzling abundance of chrysanthemums, in borders, rockeries and window boxes. 'Looks like Maria, whoever she is, is a *kiku* lover,' he added, pausing to flick on a pair of Ray-Bans. 'Too bright for me.'

'Why did Loudon send Mayumi and Haruko here – assuming he did?'

'Because, like you see, Arashiyama's crowded. Good choice, I think. A crowd is safe if you don't want to get noticed.'

'Which they don't. But that also means they may well have booked in under false names.'

'Yes. But they are not experts at the running game. They give themselves away.'

'What do you mean?'

'See that Nissan?' He pointed to a small, mud-spattered red hatchback in a corner of the car park. 'Tokyo number plate. And it looks like it's been down more farm tracks than any other car here.'

'It could be theirs, I agree, but—' We'd surged into motion. 'What are you doing?'

Yamazawa didn't answer. He threw the Range Rover round to the left, then reversed straight across the car park towards the Nissan.

'Hold on. You're going to—' We crunched solidly into its rear wing and stopped. 'What the hell are you doing?'

'Wait here.' Yamazawa opened his door. 'I think I need to report this to the owner of the car.' And with what, but for the Ray-Bans, I could have sworn was a wink, he climbed out.

After Yamazawa had vanished into the hotel, I got out too and wandered round the car park, struggling to prepare myself for the encounter that was surely about to happen. I was the best friend of the man who'd betrayed Haruko and I'd played a part Mayumi couldn't be expected to understand in her brother's death; a part also (more culpably) in a second death she didn't yet know about – but soon would. What was I going to say to them? What were *they* going to say to *me*?

Five minutes passed, according to my watch, though it felt more like half an hour. The sun went in behind a cottonwool cloud. The glare from the façade of the Hotel Maria faded. Then the hotel door slid open and Yamazawa came out with a woman I recognized instantly as Mayumi. A small, trim, erect figure in a beige trouser-suit, she had her grey-black hair gathered in a bun, emphasizing a gauntness I didn't remember from Rupe's photograph of her and Haruko. She was frowning too and looked as worried as she had every right to be. But still in her face there was the shadow of her youthful beauty.

They'd reached the cars and were looking at the damage, discussing it in Japanese, when I came up behind them. I hesitated for a moment, then said, 'Mayumi Hashimoto?'

I saw her flinch as she turned. Whatever name she was going under couldn't stop her responding to the sound of her own. There was fear written starkly on her face as she stared at me.

'I'm Lance Bradley,' I said, looking her in the eye. 'I'm here to help you.'

She didn't respond. She just went on staring. Nothing in her expression suggested that she believed me. To be honest, I couldn't blame her. But I meant it. If it was the last thing I did – which it easily could be – I *was* going to help her.

CHAPTER THIRTEEN

According to the women in my life (who've all had a habit of leaving it), I don't understand – at some fundamental level that they do – what a close and loving relationship is really about. Even Ria, whose middle name certainly wasn't commitment, reckoned I was just too easy to be with. By which she meant (I think) that, when the chips were down, I'd always be inclined to walk away from the table. Why put myself through the *angst* of accepting responsibility for the happiness, or, God forbid, the material needs, of another? Why put myself through any of it?

Because, of course, it's supposed to be worth it. But is it? I'd have liked to debate the point with Rupe that Culture Day afternoon in Kansai. I'd have liked to be able to ask some sympathetic listener, 'Do I really need or deserve this anguish?' (Not to mention the considerable personal risk.) But sympathy for me was out of stock and season. I had, finally and illogically, accepted the responsibility I'd always tried to dodge – responsibility, in this case, for the future of two women I'd never even met before. Yamazawa did most of the talking at first, explaining the grievous realities of the situation to Mayumi as swiftly and as sensitively as possible. (I had to take that on trust, of course, since they conversed in Japanese.) Mayumi scarcely said a word, glancing often and cryptically at me as he spoke. I couldn't have judged from her expression the moment at which she realized Loudon was dead. But, after she'd gone to fetch Haruko, Yamazawa told me he'd held nothing back.

'She is a proud woman, I think. But frightened also. More for her daughter than herself. She will not let you see how upset she is.'

'At least they're not in any immediate danger, with Ledgister under arrest.'

'But Ledgister may not be alone. She understands that. That is why she has accepted my offer of shelter.'

'Where are you going to shelter them?'

'At my home.'

'You're taking them in?'

'Yes. You also, Lance. They cannot stay here. Neither can you. And there is nowhere else to go.' He shrugged. 'It is best.'

I didn't have any choice but to trust him, even if I'd not been inclined to. Nor did Mayumi and Haruko. We loaded their belongings into the Range Rover, leaving the dented Nissan where it was, and set off, crossing the river and heading south through the western outskirts of Kyoto.

'We will take the Meishin Expressway to Ashiya,' Yamazawa said, translating for my benefit something he'd already told Mayumi in Japanese. 'That is where I live. On the coast, between Osaka and Kobe.'

Mayumi and Haruko sat in the back, saying nothing

beyond the odd whispered exchange between themselves. I hadn't the nerve to speak to them at that stage. I glanced as often as I dared at their reflections in the mirror on the back of the sun-visor. Mayumi's composure never slipped, though her bloodshot eyes and the dark rings beneath them suggested it was being tested to its limit. Haruko was less self-controlled, clutching her mother's hand and dabbing at her eyes with a handkerchief to staunch the tears of grief and fear. She'd lost weight since the summer. Her face was paler and thinner than in Rupe's photographs. The smile she'd worn for him was just a memory. Her lover had betrayed her and, because of him, her uncle and her protector in Kyoto were both dead. The only people she and her mother had left to rely on were a cold-blooded, steely-nerved *Yakuza* . . . and me.

The coastal strip west of Osaka was an undistinguished urban sprawl of which Ashiya looked to be the most prosperous part. Yamazawa's house was in the foothills of the mountains above the town, where high walls, conspicuous security devices and a total absence of pedestrians suggested twitchy residents with a lot to be twitchy about. I spotted a couple of Rottweilers patrolling the adjacent garden as we waited for the automatic door leading to the garage to slide slowly up.

'You are thinking that crime pays well,' Yamazawa said to me as we drove in. 'And you are wondering how my neighbours feel about living next to a *Yakuza*.'

'It's none of my business.'

'The answer is that they pretend to believe I lost my

finger in a taxi door and, in return, I do not ask where they got their money from.'

'Get-togethers round the barbecue not the norm here, then?'

'The point of living here, Lance, is *not* to get together.' It was a point he pondered for a moment before adding, 'There is nowhere safer.'

I was happy to believe him. The house was vast and bare, white-walled and strangely un-Japanese, the shortage of furniture somehow conjuring up emptiness rather than simplicity.

A housekeeper evidently hired for her inscrutability talked to Yamazawa in an oriental language that sounded more like Chinese than Japanese (it was actually, I later learned, Korean), then took Mayumi and Haruko off to their quarters. I was left alone, padding round a tatami-matted lounge big enough to hold a ball in (which you could have done without needing to move anything), a pair of fluffy cream guest slippers muffling my footsteps.

A soaring triangular window looked out on to a well-tended garden contained by high stone walls. I noticed the late afternoon sunlight glinting on broken glass concreted into their tops. Uninvited visitors were definitely not welcome. There didn't seem to be any Rottweilers on the premises, though – just a four-foot-high bronze panther bestriding the patio.

I'd been alone there for twenty minutes or so, wondering what was to happen next, when Yamazawa came in to join me, frowning ominously.

'I have spoken to my contact in the Kyoto Police. What he has said is not good.'

'What is it?'

'For such a thing to happen . . .'

'*What?*'

'Ledgister has escaped.'

'You're joking.'

'I do not joke.' (Ever, I assumed he meant.) 'It seems two men from the local station – Keihoku – got there first. After they had untied Ledgister . . .' Yamazawa snorted irritably. 'He shot one of them and lost the other in the forest. I should not have relied on the police. They are . . . *shiroto*.'

'Could he have followed us here?'

'Not possible. He has no car. He does not know the mountains. He is free. But he cannot know where we are.'

'That's something.'

'But not enough. The police will probably think he is you. He hired the car in your name. By now the German police will know you flew to Tokyo. It will look bad for you. Very bad.'

'I don't remotely resemble Ledgister.'

'Do you want to contact the police to explain that to them? I should have killed him, Lance. That is the truth. I should have finished him.'

'You said yourself that would only have made things worse for me.'

'Not much worse than this. You should leave the country. As soon as possible.'

'What about Mayumi and Haruko?'

'They are safe here.'

'For the moment. But you can't shelter them for ever. Besides, how can I leave? I'd be stopped at the airport.'

'I could get you out.'

'To go where? I don't even know what I'm really up against. I have to find out, Shintaro. Do you understand?'

He nodded solemnly. 'Yes.'

'I think Mayumi can tell me.'

'Then ask her, Lance. Soon.'

'Now's hardly a good time, is it?'

'No. But it is the only time you have.' He looked out of the window and sighed. 'I will tell her about Ledgister. Then I will ask her to speak to you. She is my guest, so . . . I do not think she will refuse.'

She did not refuse. The housekeeper brought tea and, a few minutes later, Mayumi came into the room, expressionless and outwardly calm. We sat down and she poured tea for both of us.

'Kiyofumi said you are a good man, Bradley-san.'

'Not as good as he was. And, please, call me Lance.'

'You are involved in this only because you are Rupe's friend?'

'Yes. I suppose it comes down to that.'

'Haruko loved him greatly. She thought – *we* thought – he loved her too.'

'I can't undo anything he did.'

'I know. But . . . he broke her heart.'

'Not beyond repair, I hope.'

'I hope not also. She is young. It is harder for those of us who are no longer young.'

'I told your brother I'd do everything in my power to help you.'

'And, unlike your friend, you keep your promises.'

'The question is, Mayumi: how *can* I help you?'

'Save Haruko. That is all I ask now. I have lost so much. I must not lose her.'

'Why is she in danger, Mayumi? Why are we all in danger? What's in the Townley letter?'

She sat forward and sipped some tea, seeming to grow more solemn still. 'The only way to save Haruko is to make Stephen stop hunting us.' (It was quite a shock to hear her refer to Townley by his first name.) 'We must communicate with him.'

'But he won't listen.'

'I do not think he has heard. I think the man Ledgister is doing this without Stephen's knowledge.'

'Why would he?'

'Because it is not only about Stephen. A son-in-law in the oil business would be in danger too. Miller—' She broke off and looked away, taking time to compose herself. 'Miller explained the consequences to me. There seems no end to it. But there must be.'

'No end to what?'

She gazed at me, her calmness restored. 'I know you want me to tell you. I know you think it will be better if you understand. But it will not be. It will destroy you. It has destroyed enough, I think.'

'Mayumi—'

'Please listen.' She held up a hand to silence me. 'You may have guessed – I do not know – but Miller was Haruko's father.' (I suppose I had guessed, though until she'd said it I hadn't been conscious of doing so.)

'When he came back to Japan, twenty-five years ago, we were together for a while. Then . . . we parted. Haruko does not know this. I would not let him tell her. That is why he told Rupe about the letter. To make himself matter to Haruko and the man she would marry. Also to punish me for keeping him out of his daughter's life. He admitted it to me later. I forgave him. He did not know what was in the letter. He did not know how dangerous it was until I told him, *after* Rupe had stolen it. I kept it in a safe-deposit box at my bank. There were things of Haruko's in the box also, inherited from her grand-mother. She had access to it. Rupe persuaded her to let him see the letter. She would have done anything for him. She did not know he meant to steal it. How could she? She loved him. I think she still does, in spite of what he has done. I cannot tell her that Miller was her father. Not now. But I will. When she is safe.'

'But when will that be?'

'Stephen was trained to kill people, Lance. He was a dangerous man when I knew him. But he is old now. He is not evil. He is probably as frightened as I am.'

'Miller didn't seem to think so.'

'He did not know Stephen as I did.' (And how was that exactly? I wondered, knowing I could never ask.) 'I have to trust what my memories and my instincts tell me. Stephen has lost his son. I have lost my brother. Haruko has lost her father. It is enough. I think he will understand that. I cannot give him the letter. I do not have it. But I will never tell anyone what is in it. I ask you to be the proof of that.'

'Me?'

'I want you to take a message to him from me. I want

you to ask him to end this. Before we all lose everything.'

'How can I do that?'

'Kiyofumi said he has a grandson at Stanford University, in California.'

'Clyde Ledgister. What about him?'

'I want you to speak to Clyde. He will know how to contact his grandfather and there is no other member of the family we can ask. You must persuade Clyde to take you to Stephen. And you must see Stephen face to face. Tell him he has to stop. I will never reveal his secret. That is all I can offer him. But he will believe me, I think. Because even my messenger will not know what the secret is.'

I was caught in a velvet vice. I wanted the truth. But I also wanted to help Mayumi and Haruko. I'd heightened the danger they were in by leading Ledgister to their hiding-place. I was, in some ill-defined sense I couldn't refute, Rupe's representative, obliged to do everything I could to repair the damage he'd caused. Mayumi's plan, desperate as it was, was the only plan in town. Keeping me in ignorance just might win Townley over. (And a very big *might* it was.)

'I am sorry to have to ask you to do this, Lance,' Mayumi said. 'There is no one else I can ask. You do not have to do it. I would understand if you refused.'

There was, of course, as we both knew, no way I could refuse. Mayumi genuinely regretted having to ask so much of me. But she knew she had a right to ask it. And so did I.

* * *

Yamazawa didn't see it that way. In fact, though he didn't say so, it was pretty obvious he thought I was mad. We talked in his study. (Well, I suppose that's what you'd call it, though the fact that it contained nothing beyond a desk, chair, computer, phone and fax made it feel more like an office – a paperless one at that.)

'It is the *kanji* for mountain,' he said, seeing me glance at the single item of decoration – a framed piece of calligraphy on the wall. 'Pronounced *yama.*'

'Like the first syllable of your name.'

'A gift from Toshishige, actually. He sends me a mountain. Then he sends me a man who thinks he can climb one. Without rope. And without knowing how high it is. I have much to thank my brother for.'

'I get the impression you don't think what I'm proposing to do is a very smart idea.'

'You have to decide what is best for you to do, Lance. But there will be nobody to watch your back in California. Mayumi's knowledge of Townley is from forty years ago. I would not like to risk my life on such knowledge.'

'I offered to help her. This is the help she's asked for.'

'Then I suppose you must go.'

'Well, you said I should leave the country as soon as possible.'

'I will see what can be done. You will need a new name and passport. Also safe passage. Stanford University is near San Francisco, right?'

'So I believe.'

He thought for a moment. 'I will need to speak to some friends. The airports will be watched, for sure. So, safe may be slow, OK?'

272

'I'm in your hands, Shintaro.'

'But soon you may be in Townley's hands. You should think about that, Lance. You should think hard.'

As it turned out, I had plenty of opportunity for thought over the next twenty-four hours. Yamazawa was absent most of the time, making arrangements with his 'friends' on my behalf. Mayumi and Haruko kept themselves largely to themselves. We didn't even eat together. I couldn't leave the house, of course, and neither could they. We were prisoners by choice *and* necessity.

As to just how extreme that necessity was, the television was our only source of information. Naturally, I had no idea what was being said on the news programmes about Loudon's murder. For that I had to look to my fellow prisoners. My name hadn't been mentioned, they told me. The reports were thinly factual. A man found dead; a policeman in hospital with a bullet wound; a dangerous fugitive at large in the mountains north-west of Kyoto. All we knew for sure then was that Ledgister was still on the loose.

'But we are safe here, I think,' said Haruko, when, for the first time, Mayumi left us alone together.

'Yes. I'm sure you are.'

'How long will we have to stay?'

'I don't know. It depends . . .'

'On what happens when you meet Townley.' She looked searchingly at me. 'You are taking a big risk for us, I think.'

'I'll try not to take any risks at all.'

'Will you find Rupe?'

'Maybe.'

'He talked to me about you once.'

'What did he say?'

She smiled nervously. 'That he sometimes wondered if he should have lived his life like you.'

'Really?' (It was an idle piece of wondering. Rupe never had enough of my sit-down-and-stop.)

'I asked him if I would ever meet you. He said he was sure I would. I thought—' She blushed and looked down, then started again. 'I thought he meant at our wedding. But now . . . I wonder if . . . really . . .' Her words petered into silence.

'He couldn't have foreseen this, Haruko.'

'I think he might have done. You see . . .'

'What?'

'I know what he did was unforgivable. I know he only pretended to love me. But he is not cruel, Lance. He could only have done as he did . . . for a grand reason.' (For grand read noble? This was surely love at its blindest.) 'In business, he told me once, you must always have a fail-safe. And I think' – she gazed at me through her large, dark, guileless eyes – 'that you are *his* fail-safe.'

Yamazawa returned a few hours later and called me into his study. He handed me my passport (which he'd borrowed earlier). As I took it, I noticed it was closed around a second passport. This one was American.

'Your photograph's been scanned onto the details of Gary Charlesworth Young.'

'Who's he?'

'He was born in New York on May twenty-six, nineteen sixty-one.'

274

'That doesn't exactly answer my question.'

'It's all you need to know. Mr Young does not require his passport any more.'

'We're sure about that, are we?'

'Completely.'

'How long has he . . . not required it?'

'I know people who supply such documents, Lance. There is a trade in them. The source of this one is most reliable. Asking questions is not part of the transaction.'

'I'll bet it isn't.'

'Container ship *Taiyo-Maru* leaves Kobe Monday morning, bound for Europe. It calls at Busan, South Korea, Tuesday, to take on cargo. You can get off there and—'

'I'm leaving by ship?'

'Slow but safe, like I told you.'

'How slow?'

'Train from Busan to Seoul and an evening flight to San Francisco. With the time change, it will still be Tuesday when you arrive.'

'But that's three days from now.'

'These arrangements are secure, Lance. If you try to fly direct, I estimate a seventy-five per cent chance you will be picked up.'

'There's been nothing on the news about me.'

'Maybe not. But I have spoken to Toshishige. The police have been to see him.'

'How did they get on to him?'

'His boss at Eurybia—'

'Penberthy?'

'Yes. Penberthy. That is the name. He contacted the

police as soon as he read about you in Thursday's *Japan Times*.'

'Bastard.'

'Toshishige said the same.'

'What did Toshi tell the police?'

'As little as possible. But they will have made the connection with Loudon's murder by now. So, we have to be careful.'

He was right. And I couldn't explain what was really at the root of my impatience without admitting that he was right about something else as well. Going after Townley was crazy. I'd promised Mayumi I'd do it. But it was still crazy. And the longer I had to think about it, the crazier it got. 'Whatever you say,' I meekly conceded.

'Good. Because there is more care we have to take. It is possible – just possible – that the police will suspect Toshishige of helping you. If they do, they might decide to investigate his friends and . . .'

'His family.'

'Exactly. I do not think they would be able to trace me. I do not think they will try. But we cannot take the risk. Mayumi and Haruko can stay. They have nothing to fear from the police. But you must leave. Tonight.'

He was right, of course. Again. 'OK. Where do I go?'

'I have booked Mr Gary Young into the Hotel Umi in Kobe. I will drive you there as soon as it is dark. Tomorrow night, at twenty-two hundred hours, a man called Ohashi will call for you. He will take you to the container terminal and put you aboard the *Taiyo-Maru*. Officially, you are an employee of the ship's owners – the Seinan Shipping Company. There is a crew of twelve – Japanese master, mate and chief engineer, the rest

276

Filipinos. None of them speak English. But the master has his instructions. There will be no problem.' (No problem, that is, until I arrived in San Francisco.) 'From Busan' – he handed me a thickly filled brown envelope – 'there is enough here in US dollars to take you as far as you need to go.'

'I can't accept that.'

'You must.'

And he was right yet again.

There was time for a last, futile attempt to persuade Mayumi that she should trust me with the secret contained in the Townley letter. But her gentle manner veiled the firmest of resolves. 'If I told you, Lance, I could not let you go. This is the only way.' And in her gaze, lingering on me after she'd stopped speaking, there was conveyed a strange form of blessing, which I knew instinctively was all I'd get from her.

Later, after a final exchange of stilted but hopeful farewells with Haruko and her, I set off with Yamazawa in his Range Rover. Cruising along the empty expressway towards Kobe, he revealed the use he clearly thought I'd be wise to put my fistful of dollars to.

'This is a cellphone number which you can reach me on any time,' he said, handing me a slip of paper. 'Mayumi and Haruko will be anxious to hear what happens.'

'Won't you be?'

'You have an American passport, Lance. And money in your pocket. When you get to California, you will have a choice.'

'I don't intend to run out on them.'

'Sometimes, what we intend . . . we cannot do.'

'I'm going through with this.'

'They will be safe even if you don't. I will make sure of that.'

'I'm still going through with it.'

'OK.' He fell silent as the car surged on towards the lights of Kobe, then said, 'It's your choice.'

SAN FRANCISCO

CHAPTER FOURTEEN

Ten years ago, one of those women whose lives I've drifted across and with and then away from persuaded me that Christmas shopping in New York was something I really wanted to do. The trip wasn't a success, unless you count the fact that it reduced by one the number of Christmas presents we each had to buy that year. It certainly didn't leave me with fond memories of the Big Apple. In fact, it didn't leave me with many memories at all, other than a vague mental picture of the interior of Lucky's Bar on the corner of Sixth Avenue and West 57th Street.

Touchdown in San Francisco, with the passport of a native New Yorker wedged in my pocket, was therefore an experience registering fairly high on the scale of surreality. Various exacerbating factors nudged it higher still. I'd left Kobe forty-eight hours before and crammed a cruise across the Sea of Japan, a train ride through South Korea and a flight over the Pacific Ocean into that time. Thanks to crossing the International Date Line, however, forty-eight hours had been magically reduced to twenty-four and I was about to live Tuesday 7 November all over again.

Then there was that choice Shintaro Yamazawa had smartly pointed out I still had to make. Finality of a kind was approaching, though whether fast or slow was pretty much down to me. Total anonymity had enveloped me since stepping off the *Taiyo-Maru* in Busan and there was no doubting how agreeable the experience was. I'd been handed a chance, after all, that many people would give their right arm for: a fresh start in a strange country with a newly minted identity. In Germany and Japan I was a murder suspect, in England a candidate for extradition to either country. In the United States, on the other hand, I was safe – and a citizen to boot. It was tempting. Yes, it was very tempting. And my track record on resisting temptation didn't bear much scrutiny. Yamazawa had assured me Mayumi and Haruko would be safe. My conscience needn't be unduly stricken. I had let-outs available by the bucketload.

But . . . (There were, of course, always buts.)

I could have taken a cab from the airport, except that then I'd have had to specify a destination. Tricky, when you don't have one. I didn't have much in the way of luggage either, which made the SamTrans bus into the centre an attractive option. It was slow, but I was in no hurry, no hurry at all. Living the same day over and over again would have suited me rather well. Then the time to make that choice would never quite tick round.

I'd bought a *San Francisco Chronicle* before boarding

the bus and leafed idly through it as we trundled up the freeway, with autumn sunlight winking off the waters of the bay to the right and the icing-sugar apartment blocks gleaming at me from the hills ahead. I don't know what I was looking for. I didn't turn to the classified ads in serious search of affordable accommodation. But on some level I was certainly playing with the idea of how I'd go about blending into this new world where nothing was known about me. And maybe it would have come to more than playing – *maybe* – if I hadn't noticed, as I searched past the sits vac for living space to let . . .

ALDER, Rupe.

My gaze had already drifted beyond the name when recognition reached my brain. Suddenly, I was alert, jet lag banished, eyes wide as I backtracked up the page. A mistake, surely? A trick of blurred vision and wandering thoughts. But no. It wasn't.

ALDER, Rupe. We met briefly at Kimball Hall, Stanford, September 15. If you're still here, please call me urgently. Mobile 144671789.

I rang the number from a booth at the bus terminal and got a recorded message telling me the phone I was calling was switched off. All I could do was shout down the line that nobody stupid enough to pay to advertise an unavailable phone number should be enrolled at a prestigious university.

* * *

A couple of Ragin' River ales in a nearby bar soothed my temper, but couldn't stop my thoughts racing off into the wilder realms of speculation. So much for walking away from it all. Some promises just wouldn't take being broken for an answer. I was still on Rupe's trail whether I wanted to be or not. He'd been to Stanford to see Clyde Ledgister. There could be no other explanation. But who'd placed the ad? And why? I was close, all right, closer than ever. I tried the number again on the bar payphone.

And this time there was an answer.

'Hi.' The voice was female, soft and husky, almost as if whispering.

'Is that one-four-four-six-seven-one-seven-eight-nine?'

'Yuh.'

'I'm calling about your ad in this morning's *Chronicle*.'

'Who are you?'

'I might ask you the same question.'

'I'm Maris.'

'OK, Maris. I'm Gary.'

'What can I do for you, Gary?'

'I'm a friend of Rupe Alder's . . .'

'You are?'

'Why are you trying to contact him?'

'I can't get into that on the phone.'

'Perhaps we could meet, then.'

'Maybe.'

'I don't think you're going to get any other response to your ad.'

'You don't, huh?'

'You're lucky I saw it.'

There was a brief silence, then she said, 'OK, Gary, point taken. When do you suggest we meet?'

'Right away suits me.'

'I have classes this afternoon.'

'You're a student at Stanford?'

'Yuh.'

'I could come to you.'

'Where are you now?'

'Downtown San Francisco.'

'OK. Do you know how to get here?'

'Not exactly. I just got into town.'

'Then I am lucky, aren't I?'

'I said you were. Now, how do I get to Stanford?'

An hour's ride on the CalTrain to Palo Alto turned out to be the answer, with a courtesy bus laid on at the station to ferry students, staff and visitors to the university campus. Walking was pretty much out of the question, on account of the sheer vastness of the site. Stanford's acreage appeared close to limitless, with architectural statements of patronal munificence plonked spaciously around it.

The bus dropped me outside the main quad and I made my way through an elegant maze of honey-stoned colonnades to the university bookshop, where the mysterious Maris had said she'd meet me in the in-store café prior to a three o'clock seminar. I'd know her by her hair, she'd assured me. 'Red, and lots of it.'

It was true. I had no trouble spotting her, sipping cappuccino and distractedly turning the pages of a fat textbook. She had the porcelain skin that sometimes goes with red hair, apparently untouched by the

Californian sun. The hair itself was long and lustrous and very conspicuous. She was wearing a baggy grey sweater and cropped trousers. A black rucksack, sagging round book-shaped bulges, lay at her feet. She glanced at her wristwatch a fraction of a second before noticing me. And an expensive wristwatch it looked to be.

'Hi. I'm Gary Young. We spoke on the phone.'

'Hi. Maris Nielsen. Do you want a coffee?'

'OK.'

'You have to buy it at the counter.'

I glanced round at a three-long queue, at the head of which a minute girl in a purple beret was agonizing over her choice of Danish. 'Forget it.' I sat down. 'We don't have that much time, do we?'

'Guess not.' Maris put her book away and gave me her attention. 'So . . . Gary . . . how, ah . . .'

'I'm an old friend of Rupe's.'

'From England?'

'Actually, I'm American by birth.' (It seemed a good idea to flag up my cover story early.) 'But I grew up in England. Rupe and I were at school together.'

'What brings you to San Francisco?'

'This is where Rupe was when his family last heard from him.'

'And when was that?'

'Mid-September. Since then, nothing.'

'Mid-September, huh?'

'Yeh. Which is when you met him, according to your ad.'

'Oh, it's when I met him, all right.'

'How did you . . . meet him?'

'Could I just get something straight first? As far as his

286

family and friends are concerned, Rupe Alder's vanished, right? You're here to find him. But you have no way of knowing whether he's still in San Francisco. No hard idea, in actual fact, where he could be.'

'That's the size of it.'

'Seems you can't help me, then.'

'I might be able to. If you told me why it's so . . . urgent . . . that you contact him.'

'Who said it was urgent?'

'You did.' I plucked the half-page I'd torn out of the paper from my pocket. 'In your ad.'

'Oh yeh.' She sat back, then slowly picked up her cappuccino and sipped it, patently playing for time. 'Well, the wording was just to get his attention, of course.'

'It got mine.'

'Yuh. So it did.'

'Look, Maris—'

'Could we go outside?' She glanced around. 'You know, away from . . . people.'

Out we went, into the clean, cooling air. Stifling the observation that the choice of rendezvous had been Maris's, not mine, I followed her through a pillared and pedimented archway into a courtyard in front of a white-faced mission-style building. Benches, most of them unoccupied, were arranged round a central fountain. Sunlight was dancing in the plashing water. Maris made for the bench furthest from anyone else and sat down.

'Sorry about having to get out of there,' she said as I joined her. 'I don't want everyone knowing my business.'

'I can understand that.'

'I especially don't want Clyde hearing about the ad.'

'Clyde?' I raised my eyebrows to strengthen the impression of ignorance it seemed important to convey.

'My boyfriend. Clyde Ledgister. Did Rupe ever mention him to you?'

'I don't think so.'

'Only I got the impression . . . well, that Rupe had come here to see Clyde. Specifically, I mean.'

'Why was that?'

'I don't know. That was the whole point of . . .' She lowered her voice, though the only people within earshot were absorbed in their own conversation. 'The Arabs were the ones who standardized the incorporation of fountains in architectural design, you know. Odd, when you consider how little water they had to spare. But fountains weren't considered luxuries by your average Middle Eastern potentate. The sound of the water made it kind of hard for eavesdroppers. An early anti-bugging device, I suppose you could say.' She glanced at her watch. 'I don't have all that long, I'm afraid.'

'Why not just tell me why you're so keen to speak to Rupe, then?'

'OK. But if Clyde ever finds out . . .'

'Mightn't he see the ad?'

'Not really. He's out of town at the moment. His uncle's died.' (And was no doubt being buried in Berlin. Yes, Clyde was well away.)

'That's why you put it in today?'

'All this week, actually. Clyde won't be back till next week.'

'Right. So, this was a good opportunity to see if Rupe was still around.'

'Yuh. I mean, OK, it was a long shot, but . . . I'm worried about Clyde. What else could I do to find out what in hell's going on?'

'Why are you worried about him?'

'Because he's not been the same since that day – September fifteen. I knew there was something wrong when I walked in on them in Clyde's room. Your friend, Rupe, well, he was pleasant enough. But the . . . atmosphere . . . was all wrong. I had the feeling . . . he was threatening Clyde. After he'd gone, Clyde just tried to brush it under the rug, said there was nothing wrong, nothing I needed to bother about. But he wouldn't say what Rupe had wanted or how they'd met. And anyhow . . . I can read him like a book. He couldn't fool me. He was scared of something. Something Rupe had said to him, or told him about, or asked him to do. He was real scared. And then . . .'

'What?'

'After Rupe's visit, I couldn't get so close to him, you know? There was a part of him sealed off. We'd always told each other everything. So I'd thought, anyhow. But that all changed. He got to be . . . secretive. And often-times absent, without explanation. Most everyone lives on campus here. Stanford's a self-contained community. San Francisco's a long way off and feels even further. Clyde and I never went into the city much. But after your friend's visit, that altered. I wouldn't be able to find Clyde in the usual places at the usual times. Then someone would tell me they'd seen him heading for the train station. When I asked him where he'd been, he'd just get mad and shout at me to stop interrogating him. So, I stopped.'

'But you went on wondering.'

'Yuh. The more I thought about it, the more it led back to the quietly spoken Englishman I'd met in his room that Friday, September fifteen – Rupe Alder. He didn't say much about himself. At the time, I wasn't interested. But I am now. So, what can you tell me about him, Gary?'

'Nothing that'll answer your questions. He's a professional guy, single, thirty-six years old. Lives in London. Works for a shipping company. *Did* work for a shipping company, I should say. Resigned at the end of August. Nobody knows why. Nor why he came here. What he was up to – what he wanted with Clyde – is a total mystery.'

'There must be some clue to his intentions.'

'Not really. Except . . .' I sensed the moment had arrived when, if I volunteered something, however meagre, I might get a little more in return. But what to volunteer? I couldn't mention Townley. If Maris knew that was the surname of Clyde's recently deceased uncle, it could set some unhelpful alarm bells ringing. 'There's a photograph he seems to have been interested in, pinned up in his kitchen, of someone nobody close to Rupe recognizes. It's possible, going on odd remarks he made to his lodger, that he's, well, looking for the person in the photograph.'

'Do you have the photograph with you?'

'Er . . . yeh.' I burrowed in my bag and produced the snap Rupe had taken of the picture of Townley with Loudon and another man at the Golden Rickshaw.

'It's the guy on the right that Rupe was interested in.'

'How do you know that?' (A fair question.)

'Ah, well, there was another photograph. I mean, there were two on the wall. I didn't bring the other one with me. Only this fellow' – I tapped at Townley's face with my finger – 'appears in both.'

'Where was it taken?'

'Not sure. But, er, the other one . . . was taken at a railway station in Somerset, near where Rupe and I grew up. Now, the station closed – the whole line closed, in fact – in nineteen sixty-six, so the pictures obviously predate that.'

'By how much?' (Another fair question.)

'Well, our friend's in civilian clothes in the station shot. The fashion looks to be . . . early to mid-nineteen sixties.'

Maris's expression suggested such reasoning wouldn't pass muster with her tutors. But she didn't seem inclined to make an issue of my failure to bring the other photograph with me. 'So, how old would this guy be now?'

'Oh, sixty-five, seventy.'

'Sixty-five, seventy.' The computation had given her food for thought. 'That's kind of interesting.'

'Why?'

'Because . . .' She looked away, chewing her thumb pensively, the first thing I'd seen her do that was less mature than she evidently wanted to appear. 'God, this is difficult.'

'What is?'

She glanced at her watch again. 'I really should be going soon.'

'Do you know who the guy in the photograph is?'

'No. Not . . . exactly.'

'But you know something about him?'

'Kind of. I mean—' She shook her head irritably in a flame-red flurry, then said, 'OK. No sense starting down this road if we don't go to the end. One day, a couple of weeks after Clyde had started going missing, I . . . followed him. I saw him getting on the Marguerite – that's what we call the shuttle bus. Well, it goes out round by the children's hospital and the shopping mall on its way to the station, so I knew if I cycled straight down Palm Drive I'd get there first. I also knew – because I'd found the used tickets a couple of times in his waste basket – that these trips of his were all the way into San Francisco. I kept out of sight when the Marguerite pulled in and stayed that way till the train arrived. Clyde was on foot, so he got straight on, without paying any attention to me and a few others boarding the bike car. I didn't really know how I was going to keep track of him at the depot, with the bike and all, but I only lost him for a few minutes. He was waiting for a bus. When he got on one, I tagged along behind. I guess you don't know the city well?'

'Not at all.'

'OK. Well, with the number of stops plus the traffic congestion, it's no problem to keep up with a bus on a bike. We crossed Market – that's the main downtown street – and headed north into Chinatown, where Clyde got off and hopped onto a California Street cable car. He rode that all the way to the terminus on Van Ness, then walked up into Pacific Heights. That's a pretty exclusive neighbourhood, with views of the ocean. I had to hang back quite a lot, so as not to be seen. But Clyde obviously didn't think he was being followed, least of all by me. He crossed Lafayette Park and went into an apartment block. A smart-looking place, portered and all. I couldn't follow him in without giving myself away. And I was too far back to see which bell he'd rung.'

'So what did you do?'

'I sat in the park, sheltered by the trees, with a good view of the entrance to the block, waiting to see how long Clyde would stay. After about twenty minutes, he came out. But he wasn't alone. There was this . . . old guy with him.'

'How old?'

'About the age you said this guy here' – she pointed to the photograph – 'would be now.'

'Did he look like him?'

'Maybe.' She peered at Townley's face. 'It's hard to say. People change. My grandfather's in his seventies and I've seen pictures of him as a young man in which he's barely recognizable. So, it's possible. That's about all I can say. They crossed over to enter the park, so I had to hightail it out of there. I never got a close view of the guy. He looked old – white hair and beard, cut short – but he looked good for his age: upright, neither fat nor thin, holding himself together well. That's as much of a description as I can give you.'

'Have you seen him since?'

'No. I went up there a few days ago – after Clyde had gone away – and hung around the park for a couple of hours, hoping I might see him coming or going. But he never showed.' (Maybe, it occurred to me, because he too had gone to a funeral.) 'That's when I decided to place the ad and see if I got an answer.'

'Well, you did.'

'Yuh, but not quite the one I was hoping for.'

'Don't be so despondent, Maris. Seems to me I can do something you're not really in a position to do.'

'What's that?'

'Well, if you started asking questions at the apartment block, word might get back to Clyde, right? Which I gather you're anxious to avoid.'

'I sure am.'

'So, let me ask the questions for you.' I smiled benignly at her. 'All you have to do is give me the address of the block.'

The autumn light was failing by the time I got off the train back in San Francisco. According to Maris, the bus Clyde had caught from the station was the number 30, so I hung around the crowded stops until a 30 showed up, got aboard and stayed on while it traversed the centre and climbed the hill into Chinatown. The rush hour was in spate and nobody was going anywhere fast. When we crossed the cable-car tracks I got off, faithfully retracing the route Clyde had taken the day Maris had followed him.

The California Street cable car, crammed with tourists and home-going commuters, lumbered its up-and-down way west through Chinatown and Nob Hill towards Pacific Heights. It was slow-going all right, but the gradients would have been too much for me to manage on a bike, even at Maris's age. I could only thank God for Californian gym culture. Without it, we'd have had no idea where Clyde had gone.

Why he'd gone there was still something of a mystery, though less of one to me than to his sorely puzzled girl-friend. I got off at the end of the cable-car tracks on Van Ness Avenue and, finding myself at the door of the Holiday Inn, trailed in after a clutch of tourists and booked a room. From there I called Maris to let her know where I was staying. Her number was unavailable *again*, so I had to leave a message. Then I headed back out, armed with a complimentary street map from reception and walked the two blocks to Lafayette Park as night closed over the city.

Egret Apartments stood close to the north-western corner of the park. It was a tall, slender, softly lit Art Deco block, presenting a broad and handsome frontage to Laguna Street and a high, narrow flank to the night-blanked vista of San Francisco Bay.

There was a gleaming brass bank of numbered bell-pushes beside the double-doored entrance, but no list of residents by name. Since I took it as certain that Townley – if he was Townley – would be living there under an alias, such a list wouldn't have told me much anyway. And the porter, who I could see leafing through an evening news-paper behind a lacquer-topped counter in the lobby, wasn't going to volunteer information about the residents to a stranger for no good reason. I wandered on west, turn-ing the problem over in my mind.

Three blocks took me to the neighbourhood shopping street, where the scents of coffee and cinnamon wafting out of a wayside café reminded me that I was more than a little hungry. I sat on a stool near the door, munching a waffle and sipping a super-heated hot chocolate while I formulated a tentative plan. If I was going to strike any kind of terms with Townley, I first had to contact him. The chances were that he, like Clyde, was out of town. When he returned, I had to be ready for him. And finding out what he called himself was the obvious way to start. But how?

An answer came to me as I watched customers coming and going at the bookstore next door. After I'd panted down the last of my chocolate, I went in and bought a glossy tourist guide to Japan. A plastic bag bearing the name of the shop came with it. Then I dug out the Tokyo street map I'd been given at Narita Airport, marked with the names and locations of the Golden Rickshaw and Eurybia Shipping, and slipped it inside the cover of the book. I reckoned that was sure to get Townley's attention.

Back at Egret Apartments, the porter was still absorbed in the sports pages of the *San Francisco Examiner*. He looked up as I entered and laid the paper aside. 'Good evening, sir.'

'Good evening. I wonder if you can help me with a tricky little problem. Last week, I got chatting to a guy in a café down on Fillmore Street who happened to mention that he lives here. We'd both bought books at the bookstore next door and, when we left, well, our books got mixed up. We took the wrong ones. He got mine, I got his.' I flourished the bag. 'Easy mistake to make.'

'You want to do a swap, right?'

'That'd certainly be neat. Unfortunately, I didn't get the gentleman's name.'

'What did he look like?'

'Well, knocking on, but in good nick. Short white hair and beard. Carried himself well. Sixties, seventies – that sort of age.'

'Sounds like our Mr Duthie. He's out of town right now. Back in a few days. If you care to leave his book, with a note of your name and phone number . . .'

'OK. Do you have a piece of paper?' He handed me a sheet and I scribbled on it: *I know who you are. I guess you know who I am. We need to talk. I will phone after your return.* I slipped that in beside the map and passed the bag to the porter. 'I can't be reached on the phone, I'm afraid. Maybe I could call Mr Duthie when he's back. Do you know when that'll be? You said a few days.'

'By Friday, for sure.'

'OK. And the number?'

'Here's the general number.' He gave me a small card. 'There's always someone here.'

'Thanks a lot.' I'd hoped for Mr Duthie's personal number, but perhaps I'd hoped for too much. I'd got a toe-hold in his life and that was enough. Smiling, I made my exit.

Back at the Holiday Inn, I checked the phone book, but found no Duthie listed at Egret Apartments. Somehow, that wasn't really a surprise. Then I called Maris again. This time, her phone was switched on.

'Clyde's friend is called Duthie. He's also away at the moment. I'll speak to him when he gets back, which I'm assured will be by the end of the week.'

'How will you explain tracing him without dragging me into it?'

'I'll say Rupe mentioned his name.'

'And then?'

'I'll see what he says in response.'

'What if he says nothing?'

'I don't plan to give him that option.'

The brave words were partly attributable to my febrile state of mind. Chronic stress and a haywire body clock were playing havoc with my normally acute instinct for self-preservation. I angled round the corner in search of a congenial bar, settled for an uncongenial one instead, and, two-thirds of the way through my second Ragin' River, was hit by a runaway lorryload of accumulated fatigue. A totter back to the hotel was swiftly followed by a descent into sleep several levels deeper than the norm.

Half of Wednesday had vanished when I rejoined the ranks of the conscious. Since my itinerary wasn't exactly clogged, this represented no problem whatever. After a large lunchtime breakfast, I became a tourist for the afternoon, riding the cable cars to Fisherman's Wharf and shelling out for a boat trip round the Bay.

As the boat nosed out through the swell towards the rust-red span of Golden Gate Bridge, I thought some more about the cut-and-run policy Shintaro Yamazawa had tacitly recommended to me. It was still tempting, but now only in principle. I was going to see this thing through – whatever it was, wherever it led.

On my way back to the hotel, I stopped off at the uncongenial bar. All the talk there was of sensational developments in the presidential election that I dimly recalled noticing some mention of in the paper. They might as well have been discussing the presidency of Mars for all I cared. I was engaged in my own brand of politics, but the time for counting votes hadn't yet arrived.

It is, however, as they say, always later than you think. At the Holiday Inn, Maris was waiting for me. And it was pretty obvious from the expression on her face that she didn't want to reassure herself that I'd enjoyed the sights.

'I got another answer to my ad.'

'Who from?'

'Mr Duthie.' There was an accusation detectable in the anxiety that I could hear bubbling in her voice. 'He wants to meet me.'

CHAPTER FIFTEEN

There was less than an hour to go till Maris's eight o'clock appointment with Mr Chester Duthie in the bar of the Fairmont Hotel. I knew her apprehensiveness about the encounter would turn to terror if I told her what really lay behind it. Even so, she seemed grateful to me for volunteering to take her place, though not as grateful as I was to her for rejecting Duthie's suggestion that she call on him at home.

'He's bound to tell Clyde about this, Gary. I absolutely wanted to avoid him finding out.'

'Maybe I can persuade Mr Duthie to keep his mouth shut.'

'How?'

'Not sure. But there may be a way.'

'Yuh? Like there was a way for you to approach him without implicating me? Seems to me you've done a fine job of landing me right in it.' (This was true, if faintly unfair. She'd done a good deal of the landing herself.)

'Hold on. He doesn't know you're Clyde's girlfriend.'

'It won't take him long to work that out.'

'I think it might.'

'Why?'

'Because, when he meets me, your involvement will fall right off the top of his agenda. I promise.'

That was one promise I could feel confident of keeping, although the exact nature of Mr Duthie's agenda was disturbingly unclear. He'd obviously rumbled us – big time. It was idle to suppose he hadn't connected Maris's advert with the anonymous book donor. But he couldn't have made all the connections. There was a chance I'd be able to take him unawares. (And an even bigger one that it would be the other way round.)

At least the venue for our meeting sounded safe. Maris and I took the cable car up to Nob Hill, where the Fairmont and several other swanky hotels competed for panoramic views. We agreed to meet in an hour or so at the Ritz-Carlton, a little further down California Street. Making the appointment, I was aware that the hour or so in question could prove to contain more than the average sixty minutes' worth.

The bar of the Fairmont was quiet – too late for cocktails, too early for after-dinner drinks. Spotting Mr Chester Duthie wasn't difficult. He looked at his ease, if not in his element, dressed in a dark-blue suit and open-neck maroon shirt – an outfit that only emphasized the whiteness of his hair and beard, as well as the robin's-egg blue of his eyes. The set of his shoulders and the tilt of his chin suggested he'd made few compromises to age – or indeed very much else. His face was lined, but frail was the last description that fitted him. Even sitting in a leather armchair, he had an unmistakable physical presence. It would have been easy to feel afraid of him. And that's exactly what I did feel.

For a man expecting to meet a twenty-year-old girl, Chester Duthie met my approach with a noticeable lack of surprise. I had a nasty feeling he'd known exactly who I was – and what I wanted – from the moment I'd entered the bar.

'Mr Duthie?'

'Yuh.' He drew on his cigarette. 'You must be the guy I met in the café on Fillmore Street last week.' His voice was surprisingly soft, as if raising it had long since ceased to be a necessity. 'I believe your name's Lance Bradley.'

A denial would have been pointless, even if my expression hadn't given me away – as I feared it must have done. 'And I believe your name's Stephen Townley,' I said, trying to recover the ground I'd already lost.

'Why don't you sit down?'

'OK.'

'Cigarette?'

'No thanks.'

'How about a drink?'

'Fine.'

He summoned the waiter with a raised forefinger. 'Another large J and B on the rocks for me and the same for the gentleman.'

'I don't take ice in my whisky,' I said after the waiter had bustled away.

'Time you started.'

'If you say so.'

302

'Let's hope you take the same line on some other recommendations I have for you.'

'Can't promise.'

'No? Well, promises are cheap. Look at Miss Nielsen's promise to meet me here.'

'She's just worried about Clyde. Nothing else.'

'I guessed that. Just like I guessed you'd turn up in her place.'

'Glad not to have disappointed you.'

'You should be. I don't take disappointment well. And a death in the family . . .' He paused while the waiter returned with our drinks, but kept looking at me till the bloke had gone again. 'I take that even worse.'

'I'm sorry about your son.'

'I find that hard to believe.'

'I didn't mean to kill him.'

'Ah, now that I do believe. But he *is* dead. And the German police seem to think you're responsible.'

'It was self-defence.'

'No, Lance. It was murder. Plain and simple. But you didn't do it. There's the irony.'

'What do you mean?'

'We'll come back to what I mean later. You wanted to meet me. That's what the farrago with the book was all about. So, you're meeting me even sooner than you'd hoped, thanks to my early flight home. After Gordon screwed up in Japan, it was odds on you coming here. The porter smelled a rat right off, incidentally. He's not likely to see me with a bookstore carrier-bag under my arm if we both live to be a hundred. As for talking to strangers in coffee-shops, that's not my style. Now, what do you want to say to me?'

'I have a message from Mayumi.'

'Deliver it.'

'She'll never reveal the contents of the letter to anyone if you agree to leave Haruko and her in peace.'

'I have to trust her on that, do I?'

'Yes. I think you know you can. The only two people she did tell – Miller Loudon and her brother – are dead.'

'Didn't she tell you, Lance?'

'No.'

'No?'

'That's what I said.'

'And I believe you. You know why? Because, if you knew what was in the letter, you wouldn't have come to San Francisco. You'd have run for your life. And you'd have been well advised to.'

'Why don't *you* tell me?'

'You have a sense of humour, Lance. That must be why Gordon dislikes you so much. He always dislikes people who crack better jokes than he does.'

'Do you accept Mayumi's offer?'

'Is that what you'd call it – an offer? Sounds more like a plea for mercy to me.'

'And are you a merciful man?'

'What do you think?'

'I think . . . not.'

Townley allowed himself half a smile as he stubbed out his cigarette. 'Honest as well as humorous. My, my, you do have a lot going for you. More than your friend Rupe Alder.'

'Where is Rupe?'

'He threatened me, Lance. And then, when I showed him I wasn't prepared to yield to his threats, he threatened my grandson. I don't know what he thought I'd do about that. But ask yourself: what should I have done? What choice did he give me?'

'What did you do?'

Townley dropped his voice to a gravelly whisper. 'I killed him.'

They were the words I'd half-expected to hear. But still they sent a chill through me. 'He's dead?'

Townley nodded. 'Uhuh.'

'You killed him?' My voice too had descended to a murmur.

'Let's be accurate here. I'm retired from that line myself. I had Gordon handle the job. He enjoys the work, just like amateurs tend to. Do you want to know the particulars? I'd opt not to, if I were you.'

'Tell me.'

'OK. Your friend, your choice. Rupe got heavy with us, so we got heavier in return. Gordon lured him to a rendezvous in Buena Vista Park. The official cause of death was a cocaine overdose. The media evidently thought he got that bump on the head falling over in a drugged stupor. Some Japanese tourists found him. Well, they do go out early, don't they? They were there for the views of the city. I guess dead crackheads count as one.'

I couldn't seem to frame a response. All this way and all this struggle, for the bleak reward of Townley's deadpan report on how he and his murderous son-in-law had neutralized the threat Rupe posed to them.

'Gordon removed anything that could have identified Rupe, of course, and checked him out of his hotel room. At that point, your friend dropped off the edge of the world. Well, the edge of the continent, anyhow, on

305

account of the fact that bodies unclaimed after thirty days are cremated and their ashes scattered in the ocean. Sadly, though, he didn't leave my life so neatly. Gordon searched his room and his belongings and the clothes he was wearing. He found the photocopy of the letter, which was all Rupe had shown me. But not the original. And he still hasn't found it. Rupe must have hidden it. The question is: where?'

'You think I'd tell you if I knew?'

'I do. You see, what you said about killing Eric in self-defence, well, that goes for me and Rupe as well. He wanted me to go public with the whole story. But that would have been suicide. Worse, it would have endangered my family. I had to defend them as well as myself. There really was nothing else I could do. I tried talking him out of it. I tried buying him off. I even tried begging, which doesn't come easy to me. None of it did any good. Your friend was a man with a mission. He was determined to blow everything wide open. He had to be stopped. He *was* stopped.'

'So, you murdered Rupe because he was blackmailing you.'

'That's what it amounts to, yuh.'

'And Peter Dalton? What was your justification for murdering him?'

Townley checked there was nobody even close to being able to overhear us before replying in an undertone. 'Money. I needed it pretty badly then. I was preparing for my very early retirement. I could see what was coming up and I knew I'd have to drop conclusively out of sight if I wasn't to finish up just how Hilde Voss told you I did. Rupe would never have traced me if I'd stuck to my soundest principle: solitude is safety. I've invested wisely over the years. I own Egret Apartments, though as far as the lessees are concerned I'm just another one of them. The only unwise thing I've done is the most human. I stayed in touch with my family. But for that, no one would ever have found me. And the letter could never have harmed me.'

'Does Clyde know what happened to Rupe?'

'No. Nor why it had to happen. And I'd like to keep it that way.'

'I won't tell Maris, if that's what you mean.'

'That's considerate of you.'

'I'm considering *her*.'

'Of course. What a gent in disguise you are. Unlike Rupe. The truth is, Lance, that Clyde didn't even know he had a grandfather alive and well and residing up the road until Rupe told him. I was planning the surprise for later in the boy's Stanford career. Actually, I was waiting for his mother to warm to the idea. Anyhow, Rupe forced the issue and made it clear to Clyde that I wasn't exactly your footstool-and-slippers kind of grandpappy. Left me with a lot of ground to make up. I'd appreciate being allowed to tackle the task the best way I can.'

'Am I missing something here?' (I certainly felt as if I was. Townley had mixed candour with implacability to disarming effect. He wasn't what I'd expected, though whether that made him more dangerous or less I couldn't decide.)

'Are you missing something? You mean in addition to the big picture?'

'What's your answer to Mayumi?' (In the end, after all, there had to be one.)

'Let's get out of here.' He turned towards the bar, where the waiter was refilling the ice bucket. '*Check!*'

'I'm not sure I—'

'Don't worry. I'm not taking you to Buena Vista Park.'

We didn't in fact go further than the square separating the Fairmont Hotel from Grace Cathedral. Townley lit another cigarette and smoked it enthusiastically as we walked slowly round the perimeter of the small park occupying the western half of the square. There were plenty of cars and people about. The street-lighting was good, the location as safe as they come. There were no dark corners, no black-windowed vans. One part of my brain assessed the spot as scarcely less secure than the bar we'd just left. Another part of my brain was having none of it.

'I don't doubt Mayumi's sincerity, Lance. The problem is the letter. While it exists, it's a threat to me and mine. If it fell into the wrong hands . . . the consequences are unthinkable. Mayumi would be forced to talk. There's no question about it. When fire swept this city after the nineteen hundred and six earthquake, it was only stopped by dynamiting the grand mansions along Van Ness Avenue to create a fire-break. You see what I'm saying? Without the letter, I've got to have a fire-break.'

'Mayumi doesn't have the letter to give you.'

'No. But in amongst all this aching sympathy for her and her lovesick daughter, you might ask yourself why she was so stupid as to keep the letter in the first place. If she'd burned it the day it was delivered . . . But I know the answer, of course, which you're in no position to. Fortunately, you *are* in a position to resolve the situation.'

'I am?'

'We're both in trouble, Lance. The only difference is that your trouble is here and now, whereas mine's out there in the future. You're a murder suspect in two continents. I'm a nobody who wants to be sure of staying that way. I can prove you didn't murder anyone. And you can guarantee the continued anonymity of Mr Chester Duthie. I see the making of a deal there, don't you?'

'How can you prove anything – or me guarantee anything?'

'OK. Listen. I chose Gordon as a husband for Barbara because I thought she might need his protection if and when I was no longer able to protect her myself. She never knew that, of course. Now, the downside of protection is that sometimes the guard dog can turn on its owner. Gordon contracted the hit in Berlin to a pro called Ventress. There's a protocol in these things Gordon doesn't understand. When I explained to Ventress that I was his contractor-in-chief, he was willing if not exactly happy to tell me everything that occurred. It seems Gordon added a second hit to the list just before taking off after you. He'd followed Eric to the Adlon and therefore knew Eric had disobeyed orders by deciding to take a personal hand against you. Gordon instructed Ventress to make sure Eric didn't survive that act of disobedience.'

'You're saying . . .'

'Ventress finished Eric off, on Gordon's orders. My son-in-law decreed that my son had become a liability. He's thought that for a long time. There, at the Adlon, he had an opportunity to do something about it. And he took the opportunity. The question now is: what am *I* going to do about it?'

'What's the answer?'

'That's where you come in, Lance. You see, I could tip the authorities off in Germany *and* Japan. I could tell them Gordon Ledgister is the man they're really looking for. Forensic evidence would nail him for Miller Loudon's murder, no question. Since he could also be shown to have been on the scene in Berlin, your version of events would be believed over his. Leaving you in the clear and Gordon . . . where he deserves to be. Eric *was* a liability. Gordon was right about that. But he was also my son. The man who killed him must be made to pay for it. And I don't mean Ventress.'

'Aren't you afraid Gordon will implicate you?'

'No. He loves Clyde – and Barbara. He knows what might happen to them if he shot his mouth off. Besides, he wouldn't know I'd fingered him. He'd have to take his punishment like a man. It's death for murder in Japan, they tell me. Don't worry about Gordon. I made him. I can break him. You should be asking yourself what you can do to encourage me to come forward. I mean, I can settle things with Gordon privately if I need to. I don't necessarily have to rescue you into the bargain.'

'What do you want?'

'The letter. What else?'

'I don't have it. I don't know where it is. I can't give it to you.'

'I think you can. You were Rupe's best friend, weren't you? His best and oldest friend. That means you know the way his mind worked. Which also means you have a better chance than anyone else of figuring out where he hid it.'

'*I don't know.*'

'Not yet. But I'm backing you to learn. You just need a little encouragement.' He stopped. Looking round, I realized that we'd completed a circuit of the square and were back where we'd started, outside the Fairmont Hotel. 'Well, I reckon you have all the encouragement you need now. Don't you?'

I stared at him dumbly. How could I answer? Mayumi had sent me to fall on his mercy. I'd known that to be a fool's errand all along. But I hadn't expected to be offered a second one at the end of it. Nor to realize that it, like the first, was an errand I couldn't refuse.

'Find the letter, Lance. And deliver it to me. Then I'll accept Mayumi's offer. And you'll get your life back.'

I was already late for my appointment with Maris when Townley and I parted, but still I took a roundabout route through Chinatown to reach the Ritz-Carlton. I couldn't decide whether I'd just been handed a lifeline or not. Townley's reasoning was sound as far as it went. I probably did stand a better chance than anyone of working out where Rupe had hidden the letter. But better didn't necessarily mean good enough. And not knowing what the letter contained could be a fatal handicap.

But fatality cut two ways. If I found the letter, I'd know at long last what it was all about. Townley's apparent confidence that I'd refrain from reading it was surely a pretence. I knew what had happened to those who'd learned his secret. That could well be the fate he had in mind for me too, even if he did mean to let Ledgister take the rap for the murders. Two for the price of one was a bargain that would appeal to him. I couldn't trust him. I *didn't* trust him.

And yet I had no choice but to act as if I did.

'Chester Duthie is Clyde's grandfather. A bit of a rough diamond, banished from his grandson's life by Clyde's mother. Rupe was trying to squeeze money out of them by threatening to tell her they'd got together. They paid him off and he left town. That's all there is to it. Chester assures me he won't breathe a word to Clyde about your ad.'

Maris looked at me with wide-eyed scepticism. 'How come a total stranger from England found out about this obscure little family difficulty?'

'Business dealings with Chester, apparently. The old boy wouldn't go into details. Probably because they were . . . legally iffy.'

'And it just so happens that, since then, Rupe has disappeared.'

'Coincidental, as far as I can gather. I'll have to look for him elsewhere.'

'It doesn't have anything to do with the death of Clyde's uncle.'

'Nothing whatever.'

'In fact, it's all much less sinister than it appeared to be.'

'Well, appearances *can* be deceptive.'

'They surely can.'

'How are we for time? I don't want you to miss the last train.'

'Don't worry. I'll soon be going.'

'I didn't mean—'

'Yes you did, Gary. So, maybe I should lay it on the line for you . . . and for Chester. I'll go along with this, for Clyde's sake. I'll let it lie. But there's one thing I want you to know.'

'What's that?'

'I don't believe a single word you've said.'

I couldn't blame Maris for doubting me. I couldn't explain why she was actually in my debt, either. I could only hope she did what she'd said she'd do: let it lie.

The uncongenial bar was still open when I got there and the proprietor seemed happy to ply me with drinks at the rapid rate I set. There's a world of difference – in mood and reason – between getting drunk slowly and getting drunk fast. This was definitely a fast occasion. I had a friend to mourn and to curse. I did both, more or less simultaneously, as midnight slurred into the early hours.

I was at the Public Library when it opened the following morning. It took me no more than twenty minutes to find what I was looking for in their back copies of the *San Francisco Chronicle*, on an inner page of the local news section for Saturday, September 23.

DEATH IN BUENA VISTA PARK

The body of an unidentified Caucasian male, approximate age 30–35, was found yesterday morning in Buena Vista Park. A police spokesperson said the death appeared to be drug-related.

The deceased was smartly dressed. Anyone with information regarding his identity is asked to contact the Police Department.

That was it. One paragraph, four sentences. Not much of an obituary. But it looked like it was the only one Rupe was going to get.

I walked out into the plaza filling the square between the Library and City Hall and made my way slowly round the rectangular pond at its centre. Sunlight sparkled in the fountain and a cool breeze sent fallen leaves rushing past me. Rupe and I were a long way from home and only one of us was going back. I had to go. And soon. But I promised Rupe, and myself, as I gazed up at the dome of City Hall, that I'd come back one day and tell the authorities just who that Caucasian male in Buena Vista Park really was. I'd even try to give him a proper funeral. Though as for a eulogy . . .

Where was the letter? Where could it be? A bank vault seemed the obvious bet. But Rupe would have had some sort of receipt in that case, some documentary proof of ownership. Ledgister had found nothing in his pockets or belongings. He'd drawn a blank at Rupe's house in London and his flat in Tokyo as well. Rupe had chosen his hiding-place well. That much was certain.

It was clear to me he wouldn't have left the letter in Tokyo, since he'd not have wanted to go back there. Nor would he have carried it with him during his dealings with the Townleys in Berlin and San Francisco. A photo-copy was all he'd needed to show them.

So, London it had to be, the only other place he'd

been between stealing the letter and keeping his fatal appointment in Buena Vista Park. It was waiting for him there somewhere, waiting patiently. All I had to do – such a little thing – was find it.

Going back to London was risky, of course, even with the protection of my expertly manufactured alternative identity. There was probably a warrant out for the arrest of Lancelot Gawain Bradley. And there were lots of people there who knew who I was, compared with no one but Townley in California. But I already knew that I *was* going back. I just had to hope I found the letter before the police found me.

LONDON

CHAPTER SIXTEEN

It's an invariable rule of life – well, my life, anyway – that, when you're feeling bored and lonely, a chance encounter with an old acquaintance just never happens. Whereas, when you're trying to keep a lower than low profile, it's hideously likely.

At least I didn't see anyone I knew on the plane, which was just as well since they might have thought it odd when I filed into the non-EU passport queue at Heathrow. With that potential catastrophe in mind, you could say I got off lightly, although when the words 'Hey, Lance,' roused me from my reverie aboard the train into London, lucky was the last thing I felt.

Simon Yardley – for it was indeed my old fair-weather drinking pal – sat heavily down in the seat opposite me, grinning as if our paths crossing had really made his day. Which was ironic, since it certainly hadn't made mine, and the last time I'd spoken to him, seeking clues to Rupe's whereabouts, he'd given me an unceremonious brush-off.

He was looking thinner-haired and jowlier than I remembered, with a sizeable stomach straining his Jermyn Street shirt. And though his suit had undoubtedly been made to measure, the measurements were in need of amendment. 'Well, this is a turn-up for the books. I thought you never stirred from deepest Somerset.'

'I break out occasionally, Simon.' (The good news was that he clearly knew nothing of my involvement in several recent violent deaths around the globe. The bad news . . . was what I was bracing myself for.)

'I've just flown back from LA.' (I uttered a silent prayer of thanks that it hadn't been San Francisco.) 'What about you?'

'Oh, I've been, er, seeing someone off.'

'It's a bugger, this travelling, but you've got to go where the money is, haven't you?'

'Absolutely.'

'Anyway, it's great to see you after all this time. How long's it been?'

'I'm not exactly—'

'Too long, that's for sure. Are you staying up in town?'

'Er, no.'

'Well, what say we slide off for a few jars when we reach Paddington? No sense my going into the office this afternoon. It's Friday, after all.'

'Sorry, Simon. I've got to push on.'

'Really?' The idea that I was in a hurry when he wasn't clearly puzzled him. 'That's a shame.'

'Some other time, maybe.'

'Yeh. Let's do that.' He contemplated the possibility for a vacant moment, then said, 'When you're next up, we ought to arrange a threesome with Rupe.'

I may have winced. I certainly felt as if I had. 'Good idea.'

'A boys' night out. Like the old days.'

'Sounds great.'

'Used to see quite a bit of Rupe. I don't know what's happened to the old bugger. I really don't. Have you—' A thought struck him. 'Hold on. You were trying to track him down a few weeks back, weren't you? You called me at the office.'

'So I did.'

'Any luck?'

'No.' (Well, that was certainly true.)

'Pity. Rupe's always good value.' A grey slab of Hayes-cum-Southall glided past the window as Simon reflected on the point. 'I haven't seen him in six months or more. Not to speak to anyway.'

'Have you seen him . . . without speaking?' My curiosity was suddenly aroused.

'Mmm?'

'When I phoned, you said you hadn't seen him for quite a while.'

'That's right. Like I say. Not to speak to.'

'But you have – technically – seen him?'

'Well, more recently than six months, yeh. But—'

'When?'

'*When?*' Simon puffed out his cheeks. 'Not sure. Back in the summer, it must have been. Late summer. Yeh, around then.'

'Where was this?'

'The City somewhere. Does it matter?'

'Just . . . interested,' I said, trying to sound casual. 'It could be a pointer to where he's living these days.'

'Shouldn't think so. It was, er . . . near the Monument. Rush-hour time. I was heading for Liverpool Street. He was on the other side of the road. There was too much traffic to think of getting his attention.'

'Which way was he going?'

'South. Towards London Bridge. I remember . . .' Simon frowned at the recollection. 'He was grinning. You know, a real ear-to-ear job. Not *at* anyone. He was on his own. It was a bit odd, really. The evening commute doesn't normally fill people with glee.'

'But he seemed . . . happy?'

'Looked over the bloody moon. Faintly cracked, to be honest. Maybe he'd just found out he'd won the Lottery. That would explain why he's gone AWOL. Wouldn't want old chums down on their luck trying to touch him for a hand-out. He's probably on Copacabana Beach even as we speak, sipping something long and strong out of half a pineapple and practising his Portuguese chat-up lines.' Simon gave his Latin fantasy ten seconds or so of rumination, then beetled his brow at me. 'Here, is that why you're so keen to contact him?'

I got rid of Simon at Paddington, where I claimed to be catching a train back to the West Country. He vanished into the Underground. That left me free to make a phone call. It was my second attempt of the day to contact Echo and I got the same result as at Heathrow: no answer. Oddly, there was no longer an answerphone cut-in. Not that I'd have left a message if there had been. I didn't want any record of Lance Bradley's return home.

I sat in the station café, drinking my way through a couple of double espressos to ward off jet lag and trying to apply some cool logic (not normally my speciality) to the problem of where Rupe had hidden the letter. Simon's sighting of him in the City shortened the odds on a safe-deposit box in some Lombard Street strong-room. But where was the key – or whatever he needed to access it? 12 Hardrada Road had to be the likeliest answer. Cunningly concealed, obviously, since his furniture and belongings had already been searched to no avail. But there, somewhere, surely.

Unfortunately, 12 Hardrada Road was a risky destination for me. The neighbours might have been asked about me by the police. I couldn't just roll up there unannounced, especially in daylight. I had to speak to Echo first.

But that didn't seem to be an easy thing to do. She still wasn't in – or wasn't answering – when I rang the number for a third time before leaving the station and booking myself into the unprepossessing but suitably anonymous room-for-cash no-questions-asked Hotel Polaris in Craven Road.

From the lobby payphone I drew a fourth blank before heading out into the mid-afternoon murk. My next move wasn't exactly risk-free either and might have been better left until after I'd tried my luck at Hardrada Road, but with the weekend about to close on my window of opportunity I couldn't really opt for delay. Philip Jarvis of Myerscough Udal had made it obvious he wouldn't admit to knowing me officially. I had to hope that, unofficially, it would be a different matter. Because Myerscough Udal struck me as about the likeliest people to know where Rupe might have squirrelled away an important document.

* * *

Their offices were part of a drab Seventies block, out of which early leavers eager for the weekend were already trickling when I took up position in the next doorway along and tried to melt into the masonry behind an *Evening Standard*. Jarvis was neither slack nor obsessive. I had him down as a five-thirty man, maybe five on a Friday, which left me with anything from half an hour to more than double that to wait. If I was really unlucky, he'd taken the day off or was at home in bed with flu or had a meeting elsewhere. On the other hand, I didn't have anything better to do.

It was, in fact, on the dot of five-thirty that I spotted him emerging into the dank autumn evening. With a scowl at the nose-to-tail traffic and a twitch of his rain-coat collar, he turned and strode towards me – and Holborn Tube station.

I fell in behind and let him put a bit of distance between us and Myerscough Udal before quickening my pace to overhaul him. 'Mr Jarvis,' I called, tapping his elbow with my rolled-up *Standard*.

He stopped and looked round, instant recognition lighting his features. Then, suddenly, it changed, like a switch being flicked. He tensed and drew back. 'What?'

'Mr Jarvis, I have to speak to you. I'm sorry, but it's really very important.'

'Who are you?'

'You know who I am. We met in Hyde Park with Mr Hashimoto.'

'Who?'

'Hashimoto. Come on. A couple of weeks ago.'

'I don't know what you're talking about.'

324

'There's no need to play games. I realize you have to be careful, but—'

'I have no idea who you are or what you want.' He'd raised his voice unnecessarily, as if to make a point to some unseen observer. 'Leave me alone.'

He turned on his heel and strode away at a pace little short of a jog. 'Jarvis,' I shouted. 'For God's sake.' I started after him, but stopped within ten yards.

There was no point pursuing him. The certainty hit me that he'd insist he didn't know me however persistent I was. And I couldn't afford to be *too* persistent, as he might well know. It wasn't what I'd expected, but somehow, now that it had happened, I felt strangely unsurprised. Even the fear that had quite clearly gripped him was, in its way, predictable. It was also more than a little familiar. I was beginning to know the look.

I couldn't imagine Echo doing a Simon Peter on me. But if she never answered her telephone, it might amount to much the same thing. My last piece of advice to her had been to move out. If she'd already acted on it, I was euchred. That would explain the answering machine being disconnected, of course, a disturbing thought to nurse along with a couple of Carlsberg Specials in a jam-packed pub in Covent Garden. What was I going to do if she'd gone?

Then another still more disturbing thought struck me. Jarvis had spoken – when he'd been prepared to – of Myerscough Udal being pressurized by some corporate entity far more powerful than they were. But Stephen Townley was a quintessential loner. He couldn't have brought such pressure to bear. So, who or what *were* we talking about? Caribtex Oil? Or some giant corporation of which they were just a minor subsidiary? And why? Why should anyone, other than Townley and his family, care about him being tied into murder and robbery all those years ago?

I left the pub around eight o'clock and walked across to Leicester Square. I'd decided what to do, but the time to do it hadn't yet arrived and drinking until it did was a recipe for disaster. Whether sitting through a film about a guy with short-term memory loss was a much brighter idea turned out to be academic, because I fell asleep during his second fugue and woke to find the end credits rolling. Time hadn't so much been killed as erased.

I managed to get a taxi at Charing Cross. When we reached Kennington, I asked the cabbie to wait for me in the next street east from Hardrada Road and made my final approach on foot. With early starts at the sorting office, Echo was no night-bird. If she was still living at number 12, she'd be home by now.

But she wasn't. The house was in darkness and there was no response to a succession of lengthy stabs at the bell. What was worse – and more conclusive – was that the curtains were open on all the windows. I took a squint through the letter-box and couldn't make out the outlines of any of her paintings among the shadows of the hallway. All I made out, in fact, was emptiness.

Next morning, dull and early, I was on an empty 36 bus as it trundled over Vauxhall Bridge through what still looked and felt like the middle of the night. I wasn't feeling too good and had difficulty focusing on much beyond the bleary perception that I didn't have what it took to be a postman.

From the southern side of the bridge I trudged down Wandsworth Road in thickening drizzle towards the sorting office. It was nearly seven o'clock, but still as dark as the inside of a mailbag. Echo was probably having a second breakfast in the staff canteen before heading out on her round. Unless she was off sick, of course, or on holiday. Those possibilities didn't bear thinking about, so it was just as well, really, that I wasn't up to thinking about much at all.

The enquiry desk didn't open till eight, according to the sign next to the shuttered door, so I cut round to the loading yard at the back, buttonholed a bloke just going into the sorting office and talked him into asking post-person Echo Bateman to step outside for a word.

'I knew it had to be you,' was her opening remark as she emerged into the yard. 'I've been wondering if I'd ever hear from you again.'

'The past ten days have been kind of hectic.'

'More than hectic, Lance. The police contacted me.' She left the rest unsaid, but rolled her large eyes at me.

'You moved out of Hardrada Road.'

'Your idea, as I recall.'

'Yeh. The thing is, Echo, I need to, er, take a look inside. Do you still have the keys?'

'What's going on?'

'I can't get into that.'

'Not now, maybe.' A van started up nearby, followed by a series of loud warning honks as it began to reverse.

'Anyway, I haven't got the keys on me. And I've got to get out on the round. Come to my new place around midday and we can talk then. Actually . . .' She hesitated, staring at me as the van went on honking. 'Maybe it would be better if we met somewhere else.'

'Should I take that personally?'

'What do you think?'

I shaped a smile. 'I think it's probably a sensible precaution.'

The Ferret and Monkey was far enough into Clapham to guarantee Echo and me total anonymity amidst the young and boisterous Saturday lunchtime crowd. It was difficult to hear each other speak above the piped music and general clamour, but at least that reassured me that it would be even more difficult for anyone else to hear.

'The police wouldn't tell me anything, Lance. But they weren't messing around. It was pretty obvious you were in serious bother. That and your phone call from Berlin clinched it for me about moving out. Radway Road's down a notch from Hardrada Road, but at least I know if I'm broken into it'll be by genuine burglars. Now, what do you want the keys for?'

'I need to search the house.'

'Hasn't it been searched enough?'

'Rupe hid something there. I have to find it.'

'What is it?'

'Can't tell you. Honestly, Echo, it's best if you—'

'Don't know. Yeh, I remember the line. It's wearing thin.'

'It's the only one I've got. I'm glad you moved out. I'm glad you're not involved. Stay that way. I wish I could.'

'Too late to quit?'

'Far too late.'

'Your Japanese friend ended up dead, didn't he?'

'How did you know that?'

'The police were a bit more forthcoming with your father. He was up here last weekend, trying to find out what had happened to you.' (My heart sank. Dad blundering around was bad news – for him and for me.) 'Have you been in touch with him?'

'Not yet.'

'But you will be? He's very worried.'

'It's a promise.'

'Have you learned anything about Rupe?'

'He's not coming back, Echo.'

'Never?'

I shook my head and mouthed 'Dead' at her.

'Bloody hell.'

'What about the keys?'

She just stared at me for a moment, apparently still absorbing the meaning of what I'd told her, then took the keys out of her pocket and plonked them on the table. And still she stared at me. 'You'll be careful, won't you?'

'Oh yes.' I grinned. 'Don't worry about me.'

'I will worry.'

'That's nice to know. Look, I'd better be going.'

I picked up the keys and we both stood up, smiling awkwardly. Echo's smile turned to a frown. 'I nearly forgot. You have another Japanese friend, this one alive and well. The neighbours sent him round to me from Hardrada Road. He's anxious to contact you.'

'Name?'

'I wrote it down.' She handed me a crumpled piece of paper, on which was written, in her enormous capitals: TOSHISHIGE YAMAZAWA – ARUNDEL HOTEL, MONTAGUE ST, WC1.

'When did he turn up?' (And what the hell, I wondered, was he doing in London?)

'The day before yesterday.'

'I'll, er, call round later.'

'You do know him, then?'

'Yeh.'

'And he *is* a friend?'

'I think so.'

'Well, seems to me you need every one of them you can get.'

'I certainly do.'

'I'm one too.'

'I know.'

She leaned forward and kissed me on the cheek. 'Good luck, then . . . quitter.'

As far as I could tell, I made it to the door of 12 Hardrada Road unobserved. I let myself in with a sigh of relief and closed the latch carefully behind me.

Minus Echo's possessions, the contents of the house were noticeably sparse. Rupe had never been one for putting down domestic roots. The photo-montage still hung in the kitchen, of course. I took it down and prised off the backing. There was no letter hidden behind the photographs. There weren't any other picture frames to check. Everything else on the walls had belonged to Echo. I'd searched Rupe's sitting room and bedroom before – albeit without knowing what I was looking for

– and turned up nothing. I went over them again, though, more thoroughly. But the result was the same. None of the books in the bookcase had anything slipped between their pages or wedged behind them. There was no roll of paper concealed in the hold of the model ship.

Checking every potential hiding-place as painstakingly as I needed to was a time-consuming business and I was already worried that I wouldn't finish before it got dark. I certainly couldn't afford to start turning lights on. I decided to try the loft next and was halfway out of the cupboard under the stairs with the stepladder when the doorbell rang.

I crouched back into the cupboard out of sight, but caught the top of the ladder on the lintel above my head, lost my grip and winced helplessly as it crashed against the wall on the other side of the hall. 'Shit,' I murmured. (Inaudibly, for what little that was worth.)

The bell rang again. I stayed where I was, hoping the caller had somehow failed to hear the noise. (Being stone deaf was about the only way they could have done.) There was a third, longer ring. Then the letterbox creaked open.

'I know you're in there, Lance.' The voice belonged to Carl Madron. 'Why don't you quit fucking about and let me in?'

It's not nice when somebody has you at a disadvantage. When that somebody has the leery smile, rodent-like gaze and acid-drop manner of Carl Madron, the experience feels like having a healthy tooth drilled without anaesthetic: excruciating and unlikely to be of long-term benefit.

'I somehow thought you'd be back, Lance, you know that? I've got an instinct for these things. You were just waiting for Echo to up sticks, I'll bet, so you'd have a free run of the place.'

'What do you want, Carl?'

'A friendly little chat would be nice. Least you owe me, really, seeing how I put you on to Bill Prettyman. But it can be *un*friendly if you insist. We had a deal. You were supposed to keep me posted. So, how is it I have to rely on a nosy neighbour to tip me off that you've shown up again – after two weeks of resounding fucking silence?'

'There's been nothing to keep you posted *about*.'

'Is that a fact? Not according to the filth, it isn't. They reckon you've been a very busy boy. A trail of murder and mayhem leading halfway round the world is the tale they tell – if you ask them nicely. But I'm sure you'd rather not talk about that, so I'll keep it simple. What's it worth for me to stay shtum about you being back in town?'

'Why don't you tell me? I'm sure you've already decided what the price tag is.'

'That I have.'

'Well?'

'Comes down to this, Lance. You're caught up in something big. Something fucking huge, as a matter of fact. I know one of the dead guys in Berlin was called Townley, so don't bother to deny there's a tie-in with the Townley Rupe was looking for. That means there's also a tie-in with some vintage crime: the Train. What are we talking about? The high rollers behind it crawling out of the woodwork – or being pulled out? There's this guy I know from one of the Sundays. He's talking serious money for an exclusive on the whole can of worms. By serious I mean there's a lot of noughts on the end. You ought to be interested, believe me.'

'Oh, I believe you.'

'But just in case you need something to kick-start your enthusiasm for talking to him, here it is: I'll keep my mouth shut if you'll open yours.'

'To your Fleet Street chum?'

'That's right.'

'And do I get a cut of that . . . serious money?'

'More a sliver than a cut. But enough to buy yourself some distance from the forces of law and order.'

'Which I'll certainly need if my story gets splashed across the press.'

'You said it.'

'When would you want me to meet him?'

'Sooner the better. I'll give him a bell now if you like. *If* you're definitely accepting my generous proposition.'

'How could I resist a sales pitch like yours, Carl?' (Easily was the truth, but it would be like Carl to believe everyone's motives were as base as his and stringing him along was about the only way I could see to buy the time I needed.) 'I reckon bringing the media into this is probably the only smart move left.'

'You bet.'

'But I have to fit one last piece into the jigsaw first. A piece that could multiply those noughts for you. Maybe for me too.'

'What is it?'

'A letter, implicating Stephen Townley in the robbery.'

'Robbery, as in Great Train?'

'Yeh.'

'Rupe hid it here, did he?'

'It's the only place left to look.'

Carl glanced through the open doorway of the kitchen where we were standing, at the step-ladder propped in the hall. 'Attic job, is it?'

'Maybe. I have to check everywhere. Want to give me a hand?' (I was skating on thin ice now. The last thing I wanted was for Carl to take up the invitation. But the only way to get rid of him was to convince him I was willing to go along with his plan. I was betting on him being too arrogant to demean himself by doing any of the work he felt he could rely on me to do.)

'How long's it going to take?'

'How long's a piece of string?'

'Why don't we find out?' (Well, I never was a very successful gambler, as the bookmakers of Glastonbury could attest.) 'You carry on, Lance. I'll watch – just to make sure you don't miss any corners.' (So, I'd judged his character correctly, but *mis*judged how to manipulate it.)

'We could be here a fair while.'

'That's OK.' He grinned. 'I'm in no hurry.'

As it happened we soon found what we were looking for. *I* found it, actually. Carl was as good as his word and confined his contribution to watching and telling me where to try next.

He was standing on the platform of the step-ladder, with his head and shoulders above the level of the loft hatch, disdainfully observing my dusty scramble between the joists, when the beam of the torch, which I was using to supplement the inadequate reach of the single light bulb, fell on something I recognized.

It was a short strip of red-and-white caving tape. Rupe and I encountered taped stretches in the cave system he'd led me into that day in the summer of 1985 that had nearly ended in my death. 'They're to protect vulnerable areas,' he'd explained. 'Keep-out signs, if you like.'

Keep out – or come hither? The strip was nailed to a rafter, low down near the eaves, where headroom was minimal, deep in the shadow cast by the water tank, which handily blocked Carl's view of me as I trained the torch on the area around the tape. I couldn't see anything, just wood and felt and cobwebs. Then it occurred to me that maybe the tape, hanging vertically as it was, might be a pointer to something below. I flashed the torch down to the joist immediately beneath it. Still nothing. But the tape was clean enough to suggest it hadn't been there long. It had to have some significance. I crouched down and stretched forward, exploring with my hand the insulation-filled gulley next to the joist.

And there it was. A small padded envelope, parcel-taped to the side of the joist. I smiled to myself in a small moment of satisfaction as I ran my fingers across it, while the ankle I'd broken in that long ago caving fall twinged sympathetically.

What to do? It was the question I'd been chewing over since Carl had insisted on sticking around. I could pre-tend I'd found nothing and hope to shake him off, then come back later. But I wasn't sure he could be shaken off, or that I could bring myself to leave the house without the envelope. Sharing the contents with him was both repugnant and risky, since they might well fail to amount to what I'd told him they did. That left only one option, in many ways the riskiest of the lot. But it was the one I went for.

I ripped the envelope free of the joist and backed away until I could stand upright. 'I think I've got something,' I said, turning towards Carl.

'You have?'

'Yeh. An envelope. And a letter inside, I'd like to bet. Let's go down and take a look.'

'OK.'

Carl started to descend as I reached the hatchway. Wedging the envelope into the waistband of my jeans, I sat down on the hatch frame and lowered myself towards the platform of the step-ladder. Even as I did so, I saw my chance. Carl glanced down to check how many steps there were to the floor. Bracing my arms, I swung my feet and struck him a solid blow around the jaw. He grunted and fell, hitting the floor with a thump and lying where he'd fallen, shocked and winded. I kicked the step-ladder, which toppled onto him, then jumped down and turned towards the stairs, while Carl moaned and rolled over, struggling under the weight of the step-ladder.

I took the stairs two at a time and had already reached the bottom when Carl bellowed after me, 'You fucking bastard.' I saw the banisters vibrate as he grabbed the landing-rail to haul himself up. But I was way ahead of him. I pulled the keys out of my pocket, yanked the front door open, plunged out into the street, slammed the door behind me and turned the mortice key in the lock to slow Carl down as much as possible.

Glancing round, I saw the woman from number 10, laden with children and shopping, staring at me in bemusement. 'Hi,' I found myself saying. Then I turned and legged it.

Lucky in love, unlucky at cards. Well, I've never had a lot of luck in either department. But buses are a different matter. My faithful stand-by, the 36, was just pulling away from the Harleyford Road stop when I jumped aboard. Looking back from the platform as it accelerated away, I could see no sign of Carl. He was probably still trying to force open a ground-floor window at 12 Hardrada Road to climb out of. I was rid of him – well rid.

I slumped down on the empty bench seat just inside the bus, panting heavily, and paid my fare to the impassive conductor. Then I tugged the envelope free of my jeans and took a look at it. There was nothing written on the outside to give a clue to the contents but I could feel something small and hard inside. I edged a finger under the flap and tore it open.

CHAPTER SEVENTEEN

The small, hard object was a key, with a number stamped on the bow: 4317. Round it was folded a letter. But it wasn't at all the kind of letter I'd been expecting.

12 Hardrada Road
London SE11

29 August 2000

Dear Sirs,
   This is to confirm the authorization I gave you today to afford access to safe-deposit box 4317 to Mr Lancelot Bradley of 18A High Street, Glastonbury, Somerset.
Yours faithfully,

Rupert Alder

International Bank of Honshu
164–165 Cheapside
London EC4

I stared at Rupe's immaculately word-processed, one-sentence letter as the bus trundled up Vauxhall Bridge Road. It made no sense and yet it made perfect sense. Haruko had said I might be his fail-safe and, bizarrely, it seemed I was. If he never came back – as he never would now – there'd be this, waiting to be found by the only friend likely, in the end, to look hard enough. Not the Townley letter itself, but secure means to lay hands upon it – means only I could make use of.

I got off the bus at Victoria station and took a cab to Cheapside. I had no realistic expectation that the International Bank of Honshu would be open for business on a Saturday afternoon, but still I couldn't resist taking a hopeful peek at the place. As far as bank HQs went, it was neither modest nor grandiose, just a corporate slab of matt steel and bronze-tinted glass. The interior was all gleaming marble and clean-lined wood, with what looked like a water feature towards the rear. That was as much as I could glean from the pavement. And the pavement was as far as I was getting until 9.30 on Monday morning. A discreetly displayed statement of banking hours made that very clear.

It was beginning to get dark, not to mention wet. At St Paul's I hopped aboard a bus bound for Oxford Circus and felt positively grateful for the slow going it made in the thickening traffic. I had some thinking to do. I couldn't be absolutely certain the safe-deposit box contained the Townley letter, but I *felt* certain. The way things stood gave me an excellent chance to deliver it to Townley in circumstances where he could be confident

I hadn't read it. It was a chance I ought to grab with both hands. I'd never find out what his secret was, of course, but if I'd learned anything in the past few weeks it was the value of not knowing that particular secret. The decision, in the end, was an easy one to make.

The Hotel Polaris didn't boast in-room telephones and the lobby payphone was no place to be making a confidential international call from, especially since I might have to leave a message and wait for a call back. That was just one of the reasons why I got off the bus before it reached Oxford Circus and walked up into the fringes of Bloomsbury. Thanks to the note Echo had given me, I thought I knew a hotel guest in the vicinity who might let me swell his phone bill.

But Mr Yamazawa was out, the friendly receptionist at the Arundel informed me, and naturally she didn't know when he might be back. Stifling the temptation to ask if they had any spare rooms – the place being so much pleasanter than the Polaris – I wandered off towards the British Museum, reckoning the pub I remembered opposite the main gate would be as good a source as any of the mound of coins I'd need to call the States from a phone-box.

The pub was full, the bar hard to see for backs. As I squeezed through the ruck, I felt my sleeve being tugged and heard a voice I recognized saying, 'Lance. Here, Lance.'

I turned to see Toshishige Yamazawa grinning up at me from a chair at one of the tables along the wall opposite the bar. He was wearing some kind of plastic mac over generously cut chinos and the sort of shirt I'd last seen sported by Elvis Presley in an afternoon TV showing of *Blue Hawaii*. On the other side of the table, also smiling at me, was a stockily built, grizzle-haired black guy of fifty or sixty, dressed smart-casually in powder-blue jeans, maroon turtleneck and tweed jacket.

'What are you doing here, Lance?' piped Yamazawa.

'I could ask the same of you. And what happened to "Bradley-san"?'

'We both have some explaining to do, for sure. As for "Bradley-san" . . .' He shrugged. 'I do not feel so formal out of Tokyo.' (It didn't look as if he felt so sober either.)

'I'm not complaining, Toshi.'

'Sounds like you've got a lot to talk over,' said the other bloke. 'I'll leave you to it.' He drained his glass and stood up. 'I need to get back, anyhow. Phone my daughter and all.'

'Gus and I have just got back from the Tower of London,' Yamazawa explained (as if that explained everything.)

'Yuh. Pleased to meet you, Lance.'

'You too, Gus.' I shook his hand.

'I'll catch you later, Toshi.' With that Gus manoeuvred his large frame with surprising ease through the crowd to the door.

I sat down in the chair Gus had vacated and frowned at Yamazawa. 'Well?'

'I didn't expect to see you, Lance.' He broke off to wave at Gus through the window. 'I contacted Miss Bateman on the half-chance.'

'Yeh? Well, it's only a half-chance I came here after drawing a blank at your hotel.'

'Surely not. How could you be close to this pub and not come in?'

'What have you been drinking?'

'Old Peppered Hen. Excellent.'

'Speckled.'

'What?'

'Oh, never mind. You want another?'

'Good idea.'

'OK. Hold on.'

I got up, struggled to the bar and returned a couple of minutes later clutching two pints of Old Speckled Hen. (Not usually my tipple but, when in Bloomsbury, do as the Japanese do.)

'Shintaro must have told you what happened in Kyoto.'

'Oh yes. He did. But London is a long way from San Francisco. Does this mean you have taken his advice and abandoned the ladies?'

'No, it doesn't. There's good news on that front, as I'll explain in a minute. Why don't we start with you. Who's Gus?'

'Oh, Gus is from New Jersey. He is here for a holiday, staying at the Arundel. We are both alone. He suggested going to the Tower of London together. Most enjoyable. He took a photograph of me with a Beefeater.'

'Are you on holiday as well?'

'In a way of speaking, yes.'

'What's that supposed to mean?'

'Well, like you know, Penberthy told the police you came to see us. I had to answer lots of questions. So did Penberthy. He complained to Charlie Hoare. He said I had embarrassed him *and* Eurybia. Charlie agreed. He

342

summoned me here to explain why I had assisted you. I could not explain, of course. Very difficult. The Board were not happy. It seems I was already marked down for' – he lowered his voice theatrically – 'bad attitude.'

'They didn't sack you, did they?'

'Yes. That is it, Lance. They sacked me. Cheers.' He took a deep swallow of beer.

'How many of those have you had?'

'I don't know. Isn't there a saying – do not count your hens until they have hatched?'

'I'm not sure it—'

'Instant dismissal. I recommend the experience. Very liberating. They did not want me to work my notice, so . . .' He grinned at me again. 'I take a holiday. Now, what is this good news?'

Half an hour later, with Yamazawa snoring gently on his bed at the Arundel, I sat at the small desk on the other side of his room and put a call through to Stephen Townley.

His phone rang six times before the answering machine cut in, but I'd got no further into my message than saying who I was when he picked up.

'Glad to hear from you, Lance. Where are you?'

'London.'

'Uhuh. What have you got for me?'

'The key to a safe-deposit box. And authority to access it. I've little doubt the box contains what you want.'

'What are you proposing – that I join you for the opening ceremony?'

'It's in a bank vault, which means I can't get to it before Monday morning.'

'OK. In that case, I *will* join you. Where's the bank?'

'Cheapside. In the City.'

'Near St Paul's Cathedral?'

'Pretty near, yeh.'

'When does the bank open?'

'Nine-thirty.'

'OK, Lance, I'll meet you outside the west front of St Paul's at nine-fifteen, Monday morning. Does that suit?'

'Yes. I . . . suppose it does.'

'Good.'

'I—' But the line was dead. Townley had hung up. Even at my expense (well, strictly speaking, Yamazawa's), he'd chosen not to waste his words.

Yamazawa woke up for long enough to assure me he'd phone his brother in the morning and let him know what I was planning. I could have phoned him myself there and then, but 3.30 a.m., as it was in Japan, struck me as no time to be calling anyone, even a *Yakuza*. So, leaving the old fox to sleep off his hens, I walked round to an Italian restaurant I remembered at the top of Shaftesbury Avenue and forked down some pasta, then wandered back to the Polaris via a couple of pubs in Marylebone. With each drink, the prospect looked brighter. Townley had promised me my life back and there'd be no reason after Monday morning for him not to keep his promise. Things were definitely looking up.

They didn't look so bright the following morning, but I put that down to a hangover, the squalid ambience of the Polaris and my genetically programmed aversion to Sundays. It was also raining.

Jet lag was still gumming up my body clock into the bargain, so going back to sleep for a few hours seemed like a good idea. It was a lot later than I'd intended when I called Yamazawa from a payphone at Paddington station and I wasn't very surprised to be told he was out. He'd mentioned he was thinking of visiting Hampton Court and had even suggested I go along with him – and Gus, presumably. I'd declined the invitation. Now, though, I almost wished I'd taken him up on it.

Phoning my parents at that point was a spur-of-the-moment decision. I owed them a call all right. In fact, a call was well overdue, if only to reassure them that their less than dutiful son was alive and well. As they knew, he was also in a lot of trouble. But I reckoned I could afford to hint that he might soon be on his way out of it.

The phone rang longer than I'd expected without being answered. But I let it go on ringing, simply because the idea that they might be out on a Sunday morning struck me as so improbable. I knew their routines too well to think otherwise. Sure enough, the phone was eventually picked up.

'Who is it?' My father's voice was even more peremptorily pitched than usual.

'It's Lance, Dad.'

'Lance? My God. After the worry we've been through. You certainly pick your moments.'

'What's wrong with the moment?'

'It's eleven o'clock.'

'So?'

'Remembrance Sunday, Lance. Some of us like to observe the two minutes' silence.'

'Oh, sorry.' (There were times – and this was one – when I doubted if my father had his priorities right.)

'Where are you?'

'London. Look, do you think you could—'

'Phone you back? Yes, all right. What's the number?'

I gave it to him and hung up. Ten seconds or so later, we were speaking again.

'We've had the police on to us, Lance. You do realize that, don't you? We've stuck by you, but it hasn't been easy. Your mother's been sick with worry. What the hell's going on? The police mentioned . . . murder.'

'It's all one big misunderstanding. You don't seriously think I'm capable of murder, do you?'

'Of course not. But—'

'I need a few days to put myself in the clear, Dad. Then I'll go to the police and explain the whole thing.'

'Perhaps you'd like to explain to *us* while you're about it.'

'Of course. Soon, I promise. In the meantime, I thought you'd like to know I'm all right.'

'Well, naturally—'

'You didn't mention the Alders to the police, did you, Dad?'

'The Alders?' He dropped his voice, as if not wanting Mum to hear what he was saying. 'No, son, I didn't. We said we knew nothing about what you might be up to. It seemed . . . best.'

'It was, believe me.'

'Maybe so. But it goes against the grain, let me tell you.'

'I'm grateful, Dad. Honestly.'

'So you should be. We've had Winifred round here

twice, asking if we've heard from you. I don't like having to cover for you. But I do it. So does your mother. And we're not the only ones. What about poor Miss Bateman? Have you spoken to her?'

'Yes. Echo's fine.'

'She didn't *sound* fine.'

'I saw her yesterday.'

'I'm talking about this morning.'

'This morning?'

'Yes. She phoned while we were having breakfast, asking if we'd heard from you and, if so, how she could contact you.' (I hadn't told her where I was staying, of course, reckoning it was safer for her not to know.) 'She made no mention of seeing you yesterday. Just said she needed to speak to you. Urgently.'

'Hello?' It was a woman's voice, but not Echo's.

'Is Echo there?'

'Who's calling?'

I had to take a deep breath before answering that one. 'Lance Bradley.'

'Ah. She said you might call. I'm Karen. She's been lodging with me.'

'Right. Can I speak to her?'

'No. You see . . . Well, when I got back and found the state she was in, I—'

'What *state*?'

'I gather you know the bastard who did this to her.'

A sickening guess sprang into my mind. 'Carl Madron.'

'So she said.'

'What did he do?'

347

'It could have been worse, I suppose, but—'
'*What did he do?*'

The A and E Unit at St Thomas's Hospital was the usual scrum of walking wounded. After a certain amount of wrangling with the receptionist, I got a message passed to Echo and a message came promptly back that I could go through.

She was in a curtained cubicle in an assessment ward, fully dressed but lying on a bed, propped up by several pillows, her face distorted by a black eye and a swollen bruise to the jaw. Whether she could have smiled at me if she'd wanted to I don't know, because she didn't try, although she did look relieved to see me.

'Are you all right, Lance?' she lisped.

'Am *I* all right? What about you?'

'It's just what you can see, plus a loose tooth and some blurred vision. That's what they're most concerned about, actually. Concussion's been mentioned, though I don't remember blacking out. They're keeping me in for observation. I'm just waiting to be admitted.'

'What happened?' I sat down on the chair next to the bed. 'This *was* Carl, right?'

'Oh yeh. It was Carl. But keep your voice down. I'm saying I was mugged by a total stranger. A very nice policeman was here half an hour ago.'

'For God's sake, Echo. Why didn't you tell them who did it?' (Not to mention whose fault it really was, of course – mine.)

'Because if they took Carl in, he'd blow your cover, wouldn't he? He'd be bound to.'

'Let me worry about that.'

348

'You don't understand, Lance. I've made things worse for you.'

'No. It's the other way round. I had a run-in with Carl yesterday and I should have realized he might take it out on you. All this is down to yours truly and I'm sorrier than I can possibly say.' (But sorrow was only half the story. Looking at her bruised face, what I also felt was very, very angry.)

'You still don't understand. There were two of them. They're after you. And I've made it easier for them to find you.'

'Two of them?'

'They must have been waiting for Karen to go out. She jogs every morning. When I answered the door, they burst straight in. Carl . . . and this other guy.'

'What did the other guy look like?'

'American. Thinning fair hair and a 'tache. Middle-aged but muscular.' She must have seen my jaw drop. 'You know him?'

'Yeh. I know him. But . . . he was with *Carl*?'

'He was. And pulling the strings, as far as I could tell.'

'This doesn't make any sense.' (Ledgister, in London, and in cahoots with Carl. What it did make, failing sense, was my flesh creep with fear and disbelief.)

'I thought they were going to kill me, Lance. Seriously, I did. Carl hitting me was one thing. But the American had a knife. And he was deadly serious. He threatened to slit my throat if I didn't tell them where you were. The blade was this far from my neck.' She raised her hand, thumb and forefinger an inch apart.

I noticed for the first time then that her hand was shaking. I reached out and closed mine around it.

Maybe it was the tenderness of the gesture – or the memory of Ledgister's threat – that brought tears suddenly to her eyes.

'Sorry. God, this keeps happening. Could you . . .' She pointed to a box of tissues on the foot of the bed. I passed the box to her and she dried her eyes. 'Delayed shock. To be expected, apparently.' She blew her nose. 'Sorry.'

'Please stop saying that. I'm the one who should be apologizing for landing you in this.'

'Yeh, well, maybe. And maybe we should both be apologizing to Mr Yamazawa.'

'Why?'

'I didn't know where you were. If I *had* known, I'd have told them. That's the truth. But I had to tell them something. Otherwise . . .' She sniffed and took a deep breath. 'I had no choice, Lance. I've never been so frightened in my life.'

'You told them about Yamazawa?'

'Yeh. I said he knew where you were.' She took another deep breath. 'And they went looking for him.'

The nearest phones were outside the A and E waiting room. They were all in use, but one of the callers was just signing off when I arrived. I grabbed the handset while it was still rocking in its cradle.

'Arundel Hotel. Miranda speaking. How may I help you?'

'I need to speak to one of your guests urgently. Mr Yamazawa.'

'Hold on.' There was a pause of several seconds, then

350

she was back. 'I'm afraid Mr Yamazawa's out. Who's calling?'

'My name's Bradley.'

'Mr Lance Bradley?'

'Yes.'

'Ah. Mr Yamazawa phoned earlier, saying you might call. He left a number where you can contact him.'

'That you, Lance?' The voice was Carl's, somehow sounding even more sarcastic on the telephone than he did in the flesh.

'Where's Yamazawa?'

'Right here. Why don't I put him on?'

'Hello, Lance.' It was Yamazawa. 'I never got to Hampton Court.'

'Are you OK?'

'They have not harmed me.'

'Yet,' put in Carl, coming back on the line. 'That's the operative word.'

'You bastard.'

'Shut the fuck up, Lance, and listen. I reckon you know who else is here. He wants the letter. Meet him on Hungerford Bridge one hour from now. Have the letter with you. If you don't hand it over, your chum Yamazawa commits involuntary harry-karry. Get it?'

I got it.

An hour later I was walking north over Hungerford Bridge beneath a gunmetal sky from which the light was already fading. The Thames was a brown, rain-swollen surge, the cityscape grey and dank. To my left, trains rumbled sluggishly into and out of Charing Cross.

Ahead, a figure was leaning against the railings where the footpath widened into a semicircle, smoking a cigarette and gazing downstream as if genuinely interested in the view.

'Hi, Lance,' Ledgister said as I approached, though as far as I could tell he couldn't have seen me coming. (Metaphorically, of course, he undoubtedly had.)

'You must be desperate to go into partnership with someone like Carl,' I said, resting my elbow on the railings a foot or so away from him.

'I'd surely have to be. But I doubt even he thinks of it as a partnership.' Ledgister turned to face me. 'Now, much as I'd like to stand here all afternoon swapping travellers' tales, I suggest we get straight down to business. Toshishige Yamazawa's the brother of that *Yakuza* asshole who got in my way last time we met. It'd be no hardship for me to even the score by despatching him into the Shinto afterlife, so I advise you not to strain my legendary tolerance. To wrap it up for you, Lance, where's the fucking letter?'

'Here.' I took the envelope out of my coat and handed it to him.

'You've read it?'

'Yeh.'

'Unwise, my friend, very unwise. That means you know what my trigger-happy father-in-law was mixed up in.'

'Something a lot bigger than a train robbery.' (I couldn't stop myself pushing the subject as far as it would go, now that Ledgister thought I knew all about it.)

'The biggest, I reckon you could say, don't you?'

'Guess so.'

'It's every man for himself when you stray into this particular serpent-pit. I aim to be one of the few to come out alive.' He slid the letter out of the envelope. 'I'm sure you can appreciate I won't get to do that without—'

Ledgister stopped as his gaze ran down the sheet of paper in front of him. Then, gritting his teeth, he smiled. But the smile hadn't got anywhere near his eyes when he looked at me.

'You'll be the death of me, Lance, you know that? Such a funny guy, aren't you? Such a fucking funny guy.'

'It's not what I expected either.'

'I don't know why not. You and Rupe obviously shared an acute sense of humour.'

'What do you want to do?'

'You mean aside from chucking you off this bridge?'

'I wouldn't recommend it. I'm your open sesame.'

'So you are.' He peered into the envelope. 'I see we have a key as well. Rupe thought of everything, didn't he?'

'Nothing's really changed except the timescale. I can empty the safe-deposit box as soon as the bank opens tomorrow morning and deliver the contents to you in exchange for Yamazawa.'

'That's how you see it working, is it?'

'A straight swap. Yeh.' (Actually, how I saw it working wasn't so much obscure to me as invisible, but there seemed nothing else for it but to string Ledgister along in the faint hope that I'd think of some way to play him and Townley off against each other.)

'Well, I'm sorry to disappoint you, but straight isn't

how I operate. I'll keep this.' He slid the letter back into the envelope. 'We'll reunite you and the authorization at the bank tomorrow morning. But I'll be there to relieve you of the contents of the box just as soon as you open it.'

'What about Yamazawa?'

'When I'm satisfied Rupe has no more posthumous tricks to pull, I'll call Carl and have him set Tokyo Joe loose.'

'How can I be sure you'll do that?'

'You can't. But you *can* be sure what I'll do to him if you don't turn up at the bank. What time do they open up?'

'Nine-thirty.'

'Nine-thirty it is, then. I'll meet you there.'

'One thing, though.'

'What?'

'About Carl. He told me yesterday he has a journalist interested in buying the back-story to all this. I can't imagine you'd want that to hit the front pages.'

'And warning me about it is just a goodwill gesture on your part, right? Nothing to do with sowing distrust between me and my new buddy.' Ledgister chuckled. 'You can't take away what isn't there to start with, Lance. I don't trust the little sonofabitch in any way, shape or form. But then I don't need to. Whereas you *do* need to trust me. And you can. I'll give Yamazawa the same sort of burial Rupe got if you fail to keep our date tomorrow morning. That's a promise.'

'I'll be there.'

'Yuh. I reckon you will.' With that he moved away from the railing and started walking, tossing back a 'See you then' over his shoulder as he went.

I stayed where I was, watching as he strode on along the bridge towards Charing Cross. This was bad. This was very bad. In point of simple fact, it couldn't be worse. Ledgister thought he had me where he wanted me. So did Townley. And they were both right. But they couldn't both win. Tomorrow morning, they were going to find that out. And, whatever happened, I was going to lose.

Which would have been bad enough, but for the fact that several other people stood to lose with me.

I walked up to the Arundel through the leaden afternoon, a ramshackle sort of idea forming in my head. If I could glean some clue to where they were holding Yamazawa, it might give me a slender advantage. It had struck me that Gus just might know something.

The receptionist identified him from my description as Gus Parminter. But Mr Parminter, apparently, had signed up for an all-day coach trip to Salisbury and Stonehenge. He'd left early and would be returning late. He clearly hadn't been planning to accompany Yamazawa to Hampton Court. He wasn't going to be able to tell me anything.

When I got back to St Thomas's, I found Echo installed in a general ward, looking slightly better – and seeing better, apparently.

'There's only one of you now, Lance. Although you're still a bit blurred.'

'I feel blurred.'

'How's Mr Yamazawa?'

'Don't ask. I'm in a bit of a tight spot. And he's in it with me.'

'I take it that's a huge understatement?'

'Yeh.'

'What are you going to do?'

'I don't know. But I know what I'd like you to do. When do you reckon you'll get out of here?'

'Tomorrow. I'd probably be out now if it wasn't Sunday.'

'OK. Could you do me a favour when you've been discharged?'

'What is it?'

I leaned towards her and lowered my voice. 'Go to the police and change your story. Tell them about Carl. In fact . . .'

'What?'

'Tell them everything.'

CHAPTER EIGHTEEN

I left the Polaris at first light and walked all the way to St Paul's through the damp beginnings of the day. Commuters were out in force, heading for their computer screens and office intrigues. Ordinarily, I'd have pitied them. (Although ordinarily, of course, I wouldn't have been up and about early enough to do any such thing.) Today was different, though. Today, I'd have happily swapped places with any one of them.

It had taken me most of a sleepless night to decide what I was going to do. In the end, the decision had reduced itself to a bleak simplicity. I couldn't do the bidding of Townley and Ledgister. I couldn't protect Mayumi and Haruko as well as Yamazawa. All I could do was serve the lesser evil – and hope I was correct about which that was.

'You're on time,' said Townley as I reached the top of the steps in front of St Paul's. 'I like that.' He turned up the collar of his raincoat and pulled down the brim of

357

his hat. 'The weather I don't like, though. I'd forgotten how lousy it can be here in the fall.'

'You'll like something else even less. Your son-in-law's meeting me at the bank. He has the letter of authorization and the key to the safe-deposit box.'

Townley didn't so much as bat an eyelid in surprise. He looked at me expressionlessly for a moment, then said, 'You shouldn't have allowed Gordon to involve himself in this, Lance. It was supposed to be between you and me.'

'I had no choice. He's holding a friend of mine hostage.'

'I've never had any friends. Maybe now you can understand why.'

'But you do have family.'

'Yuh. And I thought I could trust them.'

'I'm not saying you can't. Gordon's probably planning to hand the contents of the box – the letter – over to you, as agreed. He doesn't know about our deal.'

'He was never planning to stand by me, Lance. I can see that now. He has his own side-deal. Sensible, from his point of view. Far-sighted, even. But dangerous. I don't care to be crossed.'

'I'm not crossing you. I've done my best to honour our agreement.'

'Honour? Let's leave that out of it.'

'I'm just trying to—'

'What you're trying to do is have your cake and eat it. Seldom possible, in my experience.'

'There has to be a way out of this.'

'Oh, there is. You meet Gordon at the bank. You open the box for him. You let him carry off the booty.'

Townley fixed me with his cold-eyed gaze. 'And you leave the rest to me.'

Ledgister was relaxing in an armchair next to the water feature, perusing a complimentary copy of the *Financial Times*, when I entered the foyer of the International Bank of Honshu at 9.32 a.m.

'Good morning, Lance.' He discarded the paper and stood up. 'They're still arguing about the presidency, I see.'

'What?'

'You should interest yourself in politics, you really should. It's the key to everything. All the connections. All the conspiracies. Plain to see, if you know what to look for.' He smiled. 'But I have the feeling you'd like to get straight down to business.'

'Wouldn't you?'

'No merit in delay, that's for sure. We've had enough of that already, I reckon. Your friend passed a comfortable night, by the way.'

'Let's get on with it.'

'OK.' He took the letter of authorization out of his pocket and handed it to me. 'Lead on, why don't you?'

I was required to produce my passport and driving licence by way of identification. Rupe's letter of authorization was taken away for comparison with the bank's records. The words 'Pomparles Trading Company' slipped from somebody's lips. Ledgister and I both remained deadpan. The Pomparles affair – and how the International Bank of Honshu might fit into it – was of no interest to us.

When the back office was duly satisfied, we received the OK to go down to the vault. A punctiliously polite gentleman whose lapel badge proclaimed him to be Toru Kusakari escorted us in the lift. We emerged in an ante-room to the vault, the massively thick door to which stood open, with a security guard in attendance. I signed a form. We entered the vault.

It was a gleaming chamber of solid steel, with banks of numbered lockers along the walls. A doorway at the far end led to a small inner chamber furnished with a desk and two chairs. Kusakari located locker 4317, opened it and lifted out the shallow metal box inside.

'Are you removing the contents or merely examining them, Mr Bradley?' he asked.

'Not sure,' I replied.

'No matter. I will leave you to it. Please.' He handed me the box and pointed to the inner chamber, then withdrew.

I carried the box to the desk and plonked it down. Ledgister produced the key, slid it into the lock and turned. The box sprang open.

Inside, resting extravagantly on green baize, was a single white envelope, with my name printed on it. Ledgister snatched it up and ripped open the flap, then stepped back so I wouldn't be able to read the letter inside.

But it was immediately obvious from his expression that what I was missing wasn't good news. 'Fuck,' he muttered, then glared at me. 'Devious, your friend, Rupe, wasn't he?'

'Was he?'

'Take a look.'

The letter was on Pomparles Trading Company stationery, quoting office addresses in Tokyo and London. The London address was in Mulberry Business Park, SE16. The date shown was the same as on the other letter. This one was signed by Rupe in his capacity as managing director of the company. It was addressed to Colin Dibley at Tilbury Freeport.

Dear Colin,

By the time you receive this you will be well aware of my company's ownership of a consignment of aluminium due to be delivered to Tilbury by Eurybia Shipping (whose employment I will by then have left) on 14 September.

Notwithstanding any legal restraints that may be placed on onward movement of the cargo, I should remind you that this company remains owner of first title pending the resolution of any and all counter-claims and must be afforded access to the cargo for inspection purposes.

This letter authorizes my associate, Mr Lancelot Bradley of 18A High Street, Glastonbury, Somerset, to exercise such right of access at any reasonable time.

Thank you for assisting him in this regard.

Yours ever,

Rupe

'It's in the container,' I murmured, my words lagging behind my thoughts. Of course. That's what the whole Pomparles fraud had been about. Not aluminium. Not money at all. But a means of keeping a small item safe

361

and secure, camouflaged by a big cargo that was in turn immobilized by a transnational legal dogfight. Safe, while Rupe carried a mere copy with him on his hazardous tilt at the Townleys. Secure, until he went to fetch it. Or I did, in his place.

'That's certainly how I read it,' said Ledgister. 'Concealed in the impounded cargo of aluminum.'

'It has to be.'

'Yuh. And *you* have to be there to get it. Seems you and I need to take a ride to the coast, Lance. Right now.'

I tried not to look around for Townley when we left the bank and headed east along Cheapside. Ledgister had a car parked nearby. If Townley had come on foot or by Tube, he wouldn't be able to follow us to Tilbury. In fact, he'd have no idea where we were going. What could he do then?

'You seem kind of preoccupied,' said Ledgister, as we turned down a side-street.

'Oh, I was just, er, wondering why Rupe took such . . . elaborate . . . precautions.'

'You'd take some pretty goddam elaborate precautions if you'd been carrying what he was.'

'Would I?'

'Yuh. Believe me. I should have figured he wouldn't want to carry it with him when he left Japan. This way he knew where it was all the time without the risk of being caught with it in his possession. I really should have thought of the container before now.' Ledgister seemed genuinely annoyed with himself. 'Here's the car.'

It was an anonymous white saloon, not unlike the one he'd hired (in my name) in Japan. He walked round to the driver's side and tripped the locks. As I went to get in on the passenger's side, I suddenly saw his face change expression. He froze, the driver's door half open, his eyes fixed on something behind me.

'Stephen,' he said slowly. 'What are you doing here?'

I turned and looked at Townley, feigning surprise as best I could. From the expression on his face the most gifted physiognomist could probably have deduced . . . absolutely nothing.

'Looks like a case of great minds, Gordon. You reckoned Lance was the key to this. So did I. Hasn't he told you about our deal?'

'No,' said Ledgister. 'That he hasn't.'

'I'd heard nothing from you since Kyoto. I didn't have much option but to put together a fall-back position.'

'I'm sorry not to have been in touch, Stephen. There was a lot of heat on me in Japan. I figured it was safer for you if I stayed underground until I could deliver the goods.'

'And can you deliver them?'

'Reckon so. Jump in and I'll explain as we go.'

I couldn't help admiring the way Townley and Ledgister both rewrote their own recent pasts to reflect a perfect if unspoken accord. I knew Townley doubted every word his son-in-law said, but it was impossible to tell that from any inflexion in his voice. As for Ledgister, what he really thought I couldn't judge, but it was apparent that both men were doing their considerable best to convince each other that their alliance was as strong as ever. Which left me like a spectator at a game of stud poker who knows all the cards on the table, not just the ones with their faces showing.

As we drove east through Aldgate and out along the Commercial Road, Ledgister told some twisted tale that might or mightn't have been the truth about how he'd got out of Japan and headed for London because that was where he'd figured I'd end up. He'd strung Carl Madron along with money and a promise of more to come from a story the media would die for and grabbed Yamazawa to force me to co-operate after Carl's cash-oriented blandishments had failed. Townley for his part reported half of our agreement accurately enough – the letter in exchange for an undertaking to let Mayumi and Haruko live in safety. Naturally, he made no mention of the other half – letting good old Gordon take the rap for a trio of murders. And naturally also, neither did I. Where it was all going to end – other than Tilbury – I couldn't seem to summon the mental rigour to imagine. The clearest thought that came into my head was that I badly needed a drink.

A cosy chat at opening time in an East End gin palace wasn't on the agenda, however. Somewhere along the way Ledgister tossed me his mobile phone and told me to call Dibley. 'Negotiate an entrée for us, Lance. A wrangle at the gate we don't need.'

I had to agree with him there. But how Dibley would react to my improbable transformation into Rupe's business partner I didn't like to ask myself. Perhaps it was just as well, therefore, that Dibley was in Felixstowe for the day, leaving his assistant, a mild-sounding bloke called Reynolds, to mind the shop.

'Certainly I know the container you're referring to, Mr, er . . .'

'Bradley.'

'Mr Bradley. Yes. You're a properly accredited company representative?'

'Absolutely.'

'Well then, I suppose there can't, er, really be any . . .'

'Objection?'

'No. Quite. Look, are you sure this can't wait until tomorrow? Mr Dibley will be back then and I'd be happier if—'

'I'm afraid my colleagues and I are on a very tight schedule.'

'I see. Well, in that case . . . I would have to bring in Customs on this, you understand.'

'Fine.'

'All right, then, Mr Bradley. I'll, er . . . see what I can do.'

'We'll be there within the hour.'

'As soon as that?'

'Yes. Thanks a lot, Mr Reynolds. We'll see you shortly.'

I ended the call and handed the phone back to Ledgister. 'That sounded good, Lance. Yuh, very good. But I reckon we need a little insurance.' He flicked the indicator and veered off the dual carriageway up a slip-road.

'Where are we going?'

'There's some kind of hardware store over there,' he said, gesturing with his thumb. 'We need to be able to open the container if Customs try to block us. Heavy-duty bolt-cutters should do the trick. And a high-power torch won't do any harm.'

Ledgister left Townley and me in the car while he went to buy his 'insurance' (with Rupe's letter in his pocket, I noticed). As soon as he was out of sight, Townley leaned forward in the rear seat and said, in little more than a whisper, 'So far so good, Lance. You're doing well. Keep it up.'

'Do you think he believes you?'

'I would, in his position.'

'And what is his position?'

'More fragile than he thinks. The real test will come when we find the letter. If he's done a deal to deliver it to someone else, it'll show.'

'What will you do then?'

'Don't worry about it. That's my problem.'

'And our agreement?'

'Still in effect.'

'It's just that I don't see—'

'You soon will.' He sat back. 'We all will.'

We reached the main gate of Tilbury Docks a little over half an hour later, with a pair of brand-new XL bolt-cutters lodged discreetly in the boot (where I for one fervently hoped they'd stay). Reynolds had booked us in and we were sent on through with directions to the admin block, where he was expecting us.

Townley and Ledgister stayed in the car while I went up to Dibley's office, where Reynolds was presiding for the day. He was as blandly accommodating in the flesh as he'd sounded on the phone. We chewed over some polite nothings and he perused Rupe's letter. Then he telephoned the Customs House and spoke to someone